I0549061

Cupcakes & Kisses

The Magic Cupcake Series

HEIDI GARRETT

AND

BILLIE LIMPIN

Cupcakes & Kisses by Heidi Garrett & Billie Limpin

Half-Faerie Publishing

Copyright © 2014 Heidi Garrett & Billie Limpin

Find out more about Heidi Garrett at

www.heidigwrites.blogspot.com

Find out more about Billie Limpin at

http://www.sparklingpinkpages.blogspot.com

Cover Art by Char Adlesperger, Wicked Cover Designs

Editing by Vince Dickinson

Proofreading by Donna Rich

ISBN: 978-0-9907691-0-1

Other Books by Heidi Garrett

&

Billie Limpin

The Magic Cupcake series on Facebook

CUPCAKES & CHAOS (2015)
CUPCAKES & FOREVER (2016)

For my fiancé, Jamar: "You will always be my favorite cupcake!"

—Billie

Contents

Glynna's Blissful Dawn Cupcake Recipe

Ingredients:

1 cup flour

1 ½ cups sugar

1 ½ teaspoons baking powder

Handful dried Mimosa petals, any color

1 ½ teaspoons vanilla extract

12 egg whites from large eggs

1 teaspoon morning dew collected from leaves of Nana's Acacia (Yellow Mimosa)

Sift and combine dry ingredients.

Close your eyes.

Imagine someone you cherish.

When your heart is bursting with joy, fold in wet ingredients.

1. Escape From the Cupcake Tower

LYNNA

Will they or won't they?

I watch the lanky young man with dark hair edge toward the display case in the back, while his blonde lady friend inches toward the one in front.

"Can I help you?" I ask.

My Aunt Ophelia is busy securing the window to the outside counter. Although Frosting & Beans closes at five o'clock—in two minutes—I don't want to rush these last two customers.

"Everything looks fabulous," the female murmurs.

The man taps the side of the case.

My hope sparks. "A *Blissful Dawn* cupcake?"

He nods, so I reach for a bag.

"Don't bother." He digs in his wallet. "We're going to eat it now."

The blonde returns to his side, her eyes glittering with anticipation.

He peels back the paper cup and lets her take a bite.

A subtle vibration rushes through my chest.

The blonde giggles. "Your turn." She pushes his hand back to his mouth.

3

The young man's gaze never leaves her face as half the cupcake disappears between his lips.

The sensation of his melting heart flutters through the air. It's the infusion of pink petals from Nana's musical mimosas.

When he holds up what's left of the fluffy vanilla treat, her eyes sparkle with pleasure.

I sigh. It doesn't happen every day, but when it does... Zing!

Her eyes. His eyes. They're inside their own universe.

I don't even try to suppress the enormous grin exploding across my face. When the couple leaves the bakery, I follow them to the door. I can't stop watching their backs as they stroll down Perry Street, holding hands. They're glowing.

I scan the sidewalk. Does anyone else notice the shimmering light surrounding them? Everyone rushes by without a second glance. They're missing it.

Disappointing.

"Glynna, we don't have all night," Aunt Ophelia barks, startling me. She's emptying the cash register and counting the bills before stuffing them into a bank bag.

I lock the bakery's front door and avoid making eye contact with her as I make a beeline to the kitchen. The heels of my flats click against the new ceramic tile. I check the oven a final time to make sure it's off. Then I remove my pink, gingham apron and carefully hang it on one of the hooks on the wall, next to my five other pink aprons. I gaze around the large room once more to make sure every cupcake tray, mixing bowl, and spoon has been returned to its proper place.

Snow White won her prince with a little help from that apple; Cinderella and her prince had the glass slipper!

The hopeless romantics in Spokane? They have my cupcakes.

And Me? Frosting & Beans is my happily ever after.

I don't need a handsome prince.

I just need to escape my Ophelia-enforced-Rapunzel-tower for one night.

I race toward Kristeen's burgundy Jeep Cherokee as if I can control the noise level blasting from her vehicle with speed.

4

Oops! Geez. I trip over my shoe laces and sprawl in the middle of the road. The bass booms, vibrating through my body as I pull myself back up. The beam from the Jeep's off-road lights flood the entire block, and I'm in the spotlight.

My excitement from moments before grinds into full-on panic. God of Cupcakes! Maybe I should have stayed home and finished my latest Colleen Hoover novel after all.

Too late for that.

Back on my feet, I duck as much to avoid the glare, as to avoid being spotted. When I jerk open the passenger door, Kristeen is oblivious, rocking away to Nirvana's *Smells like Teen Spirit*. Arms parallel to the dash board, she's head-bobbing in the Jeep's front seat. "Hey, *chica*."

I wave my hand as if it's on fire. "Turn the grunge metal down!"

"Excuse me? Just because Kurt Cobain is anti-pink—"

"Just get me out of here."

She peels out, tires squealing. "What's up?"

"Probably my aunt, thanks to you."

"Gosh, did Glynna whip up some grumpy cupcakes for dessert tonight?"

Although I've never confessed I'm a witch to my BFF, she knows there's a little something extra in my cupcakes, and she likes to tease. I ignore the jibe. "Next time, why don't you just knock on the front door and tell Ophelia I climbed out my bedroom window?"

Kristeen rolls her eyes. "How many times have I spent the night with you, and no matter what we did, or how much noise we made, she never woke up? The woman could sleep through a zombie apocalypse. Besides, that be-home-before-dark curfew is too sad."

"I know."

"And do you also know you're a scaredy cat for not standing up to her?"

What am I supposed to say? Ophelia is formidable, especially when it comes to protecting me from the dangers of going out after dark. A danger she *implies* is connected to my baking magic cupcakes.

"When is your aunt going to realize her sweet *sobrina* is all grown up?" Kristeen presses. "Hell, we graduated high school three months ago! *Uno. Dos. Tres.*"

5

Kristeen counts the minutes, hours, days since we were unleashed onto the world. She was that thrilled to be free of our freaky science teacher, Mr. Neumeyer, and creepy old gym coach, Mrs. Sennett, forever.

"How many times do I have to tell *you*? My age is meaningless to my aunt."

But Kristeen persists. "If you ever wanna get a real life or score a *papi chulo*—" The girl's always throwing Spanish-isms at me. "—you're gonna have to claim your right to stay out after dark."

"I have a real life." I pull the seatbelt across my lap and jam the buckle into place with a satisfying *click*. "And I don't need a *papi chulo*," I mimic her accent.

"Every girl needs a guy who showers her with romantic gifts and is awesome in bed."

My cheeks flush. "Not everyone is boy crazy like you."

"Hanging out at Frosting & Beans all the time is not a real life," my friend insists.

But it is. Frosting & Beans is a slice of Heaven on earth, blessed by the God of Cupcakes. Whenever I step inside, I feel transported to another dimension. "Hey, I love every minute I spend in the bakery. Making cupcakes makes me feel connected; to myself, to everything, to the world."

Kristeen rolls her eyes again. "Over a century of fighting for women's rights and my best friend spends her days in front of an oven wearing an apron."

"I love my aprons."

"Your pink I-wanna-save-the-world-one-cupcake-at-a-time apron? Seriously, Glynna, every single thing you own is pink."

I re-examine my Venus-colored Converse All-Stars and fuchsia skater dress as she continues to blabber.

"Just looking at your sugary sweet self makes my teeth ache!" She playfully tugs on my hair clip.

"Ow!" My auburn waves tumble down around my shoulders.

"See, now you look—" Her eyes glint with mischief. "—more alluring. And honestly, Glyn, would it have killed you to dress like a grown woman? What's with the Keds?" She pinches my thigh.

"That hurt!" I reach out to smack her. She dodges my fist. "They're Converse All-Stars."

"Whateva." Kristeen clicks her fingers in a loud snap. "I'm telling you, there is so much more you could do with that 'to-die-for-flawless skin.' You've got to start experimenting with more than just cupcakes, *chica*!"

My heart dips. When I studied myself in the mirror before I left, I thought I looked great and Kristeen would approve. She's always urging me to ditch the skinny jeans I live in, so here I am, in a flippy dress.

My gaze shifts to the sheer black number beneath her glam rocker jacket. The black bra peeking through leaves little to the imagination. So not me! If we were times of day, Kristeen would be the stroke of midnight, and I'd be the pale light before dawn.

What the hell? I need to stand up for myself. Baby Steps. First Kristeen, then Ophelia. "For your information, the hippest fashion palette today is rose tones. And I love the color of my shoes and the color of my dress. Pink is—" What am I trying to say? "Pink implies innocence."

Kristeen sears me with those espresso-brown eyes. "Innocence, Glynna? Seriously? What are you trying to pull off? You think you're Eve in the Garden of Eden?"

I can't help but grin. "And what have you been reading lately?"

"Don't worry, not the Bible. But you know what I'm talking about. Before The Fall—when everything was still untainted and pure? You know, before Eve offered Adam the forbidden apple?" She laughs. "Or maybe it was a cupcake."

"So now cupcakes are to blame for the fall of humanity? Seriously? You need to re-read the book of Genesis. Or at least listen to Father Fuentespina's Sunday sermons."

"Please. My point is you've been about rose tones every season since you were two."

"Then why wouldn't I embrace them when they're finally cutting edge?"

Kristeen snorts. "Finally, being the key word."

Why am I not winning? Why do I never win these stupid arguments?

I shift my gaze to the road ahead. "We're going to a bonfire on

7

undeveloped property. It's not even wired for electricity yet. No one is going to notice what I'm wearing."

"Firelight and starlight, baby." Kristeen flicks her raven-colored locks over her shoulder. "That's the most romantic light you're ever going to get. And—" She winks. "—if you're lucky, you'll get to snuggle with Ashton tonight."

My life long crush on Spokane's wealthiest young bachelor is my deepest secret—from everyone but my BFF. Embarrassingly, she sussed it out when we were all of five.

One afternoon, Nana followed the cow-patty streets from Perry Street through South Hill to Manito Park. Kristeen and I were stationed in the sandbox. I heard laughter—the sound of seven-year-old exuberance—and a feeling of electricity shot through my body. I looked around to discover Ashton kicking a soccer ball with his friends. I abandoned my girlfriend and started tagging along from the sidelines, parallel to him and his buddies. Nana had to chase me down. I'd screamed, making a spectacle of myself as she'd dragged me back to the sandbox.

I'd been wearing pink that day, too.

But I hate when Kristeen brings him up. Or acts like I'd ever have—or seriously want—a chance with that entitled *papi chulo*.

I don't, do I?

Then why am I sneaking out *tonight* to go to *his* party when I haven't seen him once since he graduated from high school two years ahead of me?

Does he even know I'm alive?

I mean, who am I kidding? He's just a fantasy, and the idea of me being Ashton's girlfriend is insane! How would we even get together when he never comes to the bakery, and I practically live there?

Besides, if he ever did notice me, his adoring herd would trample me with their designer heels.

"You know what I think, *pobre niña*?"

"I just can't wait to hear."

"You need to meet a guy who will swirl a little whip cream on your cupcakes."

"Seriously, Kristeen, not the whip cream comments."

An image of Ophelia waving a can of store-bought pops into my mind.

8

And what is this, Glynna? We only use from-scratch ingredients in the bakery.

"But whip cream is so yummy, delicious, and smooth." Kristeen gives me an oh–so-innocent look. "You just want to run your tongue across it."

"Stop it!" I scream at the top of my lungs.

She wags a manicured index finger at me. "And if you let your imagination run wild—"

"No!"

"You, *Señorita*, have some hot chili tamales in there somewhere." She pokes me. "And they're just dying to sizzle! All they need is the right push."

"Ow! Stop it! Okay, hands on the wheel, or I'll think you want me yourself!"

She laughs out loud. "Believe me, if I ever swing that way, you, my little hot pink tamale, will be my go-to girl."

My cellphone *pings*. I groan. "If this is Ophelia, I'm going to kill you." I gingerly peer at the small, bright screen. Whew. "Just the gate code to access the party."

We've been told to expect wilderness. A perimeter gate and paved road from the highway to a single dock are the sum of Bass Enterprises' capital improvements to the acres surrounding the man-made lake so far.

"It's crazy, isn't it?" Kristeen mused. "They're going to build an entire gated community around it. It's going to be like their own little town."

"They don't own the lake."

"Uhmm, yes, they do. You can't get in without their code—unless you want to fly by in a helicopter and skydive."

I don't want to restart the Ashton Bass conversation. "Do you even know where we're going?"

"I need to know which exit to take. Can you map it?" she prods.

"Sure."

"How much farther?"

My thumbs dance across my screen. "Twenty-five miles, forty or forty-five minutes. Most of it's off freeway." I give her the directions.

Kristeen flashes a wicked smile. "I'll get us there in twenty."

9

She crushes the gas pedal with her size-five platform shoe, and I slam against the back of my seat.

"Great turnout," Kristeen says as we hike down the endless line of parked cars.

"Mmhmm."

The rhythm of my friend clomping down the road in her heavy shoes drowns out most of the other night noises. Kristeen is about five-feet tall, so her shoes are her favorite accessory. Platforms, wedges, pumps, stilettos; anything to add a few more inches so that strangers don't mistake her for a kid. Although since we've hit puberty, that isn't likely. Kristeen is as curvy as they come.

Tall and straight with narrow hips, my breasts aren't much to write home about, but I don't dwell on the lack.

Three guys approach from the direction of the fire, beer bottles in hand. "Hey, girls."

As soon as Kristeen stops walking, we can hear the music in the distance. One of the guys sways in the middle of the road, dancing to DJ Chuckie's *Skydive*. He holds out his hand.

I give him a blank look. What does he want me to do with it?

Kristeen glides in front of me, accepts his offered palm, and he twirls her around. In the presence of male pheromones, she transforms. No more clunking. The two of them dancing in the middle of the road look better than most of the couples on *Dancing With The Stars*.

The other guys and I just watch.

If I'd dared to wear the same pair of platforms, I'd already be one with the pavement.

The song finishes.

"How's the party?" Kristeen asks, breathless.

"Off to a great start," her dancing partner answers.

"Burning bright," one of the other guys chimes in. "We're going to get some more party fuel. Wanna join us?"

"Nah, thanks, we just got here," Kristeen says.

"What about you, Totally Red Hot and Gorgeous?"

My head swivels. Who's he talking to?

Kristeen pinches my arm.

10

"Ouch!"

"He's talking to you," she whispers.

"Are you sure?" I whisper back.

"Yes."

"Oh, no thanks, I'm with her," I say.

"Ooh, that's sexy," one of the guys responds.

Kristeen giggles. "Oh, my hot pink tamale definitely is."

The guys whistle as they move on.

The heat in my chest crawls up my neck. "Do they really think we're...?"

"Yep. Just like Cara Delevingne and Michelle Rodriguez. We can totally kiss if you like." Kristeen impishly puckers up her uber-bright red lips. "That would really give them something to talk about."

"And that's all I need Aunt Ophelia to hear."

Kristeen stops. "You've got to stop letting that witch run your life, girl."

"Don't say," I drop my voice to a whisper, "the word *witch* in public."

"Listen here, *chica*. We're at a party, and we're gonna have a good time." She reaches up and shakes my shoulders. "So loosen up, already."

"You're right, I'm just... "

"Ever since we graduated, that bakery has consumed you, so just for one night: Let. It. Go."

"You're right." She's right. *Breathe, Glynna, breathe.* The cool, pine-filled air infuses my lungs. "I'm going to have fun tonight."

"That's my girl." Kristeen tugs on my hand. "Besides, if you're going to get in trouble with Ophelia for sneaking out, you better damned well make sure it's worth it. Let's go find the beer and some guys worth swooning over."

We reach a semi-circle of five trucks with their tailgates open. Coolers line the beds. Kristeen digs around in some ice and hands me a can. I pop the top, take a swig, and spew the bitter liquid out. "This tastes like piss." I wipe my mouth with the back of my hand.

"Hey, watch it." A dark figure looms in front of me. With the bonfire behind him, his face is all shadows, but the voice sounds vaguely familiar.

"Oh, sorry," I yelp. "I didn't mean—"

"To give me a shower?" The guy offers an amused smile.

11

My throat catches. Ashton Bass is standing in front of me. I'm too embarrassed to meet his gaze, so my eyes travel south. He's wearing a dark, fitted T-shirt with three white buttons at the top.

I can't believe I'm counting the buttons on his shirt. Or that I gave him a beer shower.

I glance around for a stack of napkins, a roll of paper towels, anything to dry him off. I find nothing. Desperate, I try to wipe off the spray with my bare hands.

Huh? I press with one finger. No give. None. When did Ashton get wash-board abs? I slide my finger down. *Uno. Dos. Tres. Ocho?* Not even my cousin, Leif, has an eight-pack, and he's a brick wall. I freeze. I'm actually counting Ashton's abs.

My gaze travels back up, only to be trapped by his startling azure eyes —and that famous panty-dropping boyish grin.

"Oops! So-sorry," I stammer, and take a step backwards. "Not sure what that was all about."

His eyes will not let go of mine as the warm feelings heating my insides build. "Oh, I don't mind at all. Besides, you seemed to be enjoying yourself." His white teeth shine in the moonlight as another blush-fest attacks by face.

Thank God, it's the middle of the night and not the middle of the day.

"You have to forgive my friend, Ashton," Kristeen says. "She doesn't get out much. And, well, her encounters with the male chest have been severely limited."

Kristeen's intervention is no help at all, and I don't miss the lingering look she gives Ashton's well-toned chest. A bitter pinch grips my heart as I imagine strangling her. Oh, God of Cupcakes! My emotions are out of control. "Kristeen!" I half-whisper, half-scream.

"No?" Ashton's one-word question leaves his lopsided grin firmly in place.

This is becoming all shades of awkward. I squeeze my eyes shut. I'd give anything for a cupcake that could make me disappear after just one bite. That would be some recipe.

"No worries," he says.

I open one eye.

Ashton's grin has grown. His perfect white teeth gleam in the

12

firelight.

I open my other eye.

He brushes his hand over his forearms and shirt. "Just glad to see you out, Glynna."

"You can thank me," Kristeen says.

"Thank you, Krissy," he says.

"Please, everyone stopped calling me that in elementary school."

Ashton digs around in one of the ice chests. "Sorry, didn't mean to offend." He hands me a wine cooler. "This might be more to your taste."

"Thanks," I mumble.

He grabs a couple more bottles of beer and gives each of us a half bow. "Enjoy the party, ladies."

He walks away, backwards, smiling, firelight reflecting from those perfect chops. He must have his teeth whitened regularly because no one's teeth are naturally that bright. When his left foot sinks into a low spot, his whole body dips, and he almost falls. Almost, but he doesn't.

"Nice recovery," Kristeen whispers.

I nod. Whenever Ashton Bass is within twenty yards of me, my tongue ties in knots and my heart races pell-mell around my ribcage.

A little while later, I'm perched on the rail of one of the truck beds. Most of the coolers are empty, so there isn't much traffic. Kristeen has slipped away with the guy she came to the party to hook up with.

I'm content to star-gaze. Outside the city limits, countless bright speckles fill the night sky. When two hands grip the rail on either side of my hips, crowding me, I hike back my foot, ready to nail the presumptuous asshole.

"Glynna, baby," Ashton slurs.

Just the sound of those two words together, coming out of his mouth, create a warm rush in my belly that extends downward. I instinctively try to cross my legs and accidentally kick him in the gut. "Oh, sorry!"

He falls forward over my legs, his chest against my thighs.

What is he doing?

Even though every cell in my body aches to lean forward, I hold tight to the side of the truck bed and push myself back. Somehow he manages to fling his arm around my waist and pull me to him. Somehow, I forget

13

to resist. Maybe I'm in shock. He wraps his other arm around my back and finds the back of my head with his hand. He pushes my face to his, and before I know it, he's completely sucking my face.

Except it isn't slobbery and disgusting like when Edwin tried to kiss me in the seventh grade. Ashton smells of sweat and beer and expensive cologne. It's the headiest combination I've ever inhaled. And even though he's obviously drunk off his ass, his lips aren't slobbery and wet. They're warm and soft and demanding.

My entire body molds against his, completely unresisting, until his friends start clapping and jeering. "Yeah, man," and "Woot!" and "Oh, yeah, getting some of that Hot Glynna!"

My body stiffens. I slam my hands against his shoulders and shove.

He stumbles backwards pawing at his mouth.

"You're so disgusting," I yell, as I wipe his kiss away with the heel of my hand. Thank God, they can't see me quivering or the tears flowing like my eyes have sprung a leak. I push myself from the truck railing and land on the ground in a single leap.

An isolated crack of thunder explodes overhead.

I go straight for Ashton and pump back my elbow. Before I even realize what I'm doing, my fist connects with his cheekbone. "Ouch!" I spread my fingers and shake my hand as if waving it around can relieve the smart. It doesn't.

Ashton wobbles and collapses.

Rain drenches us all in a matter of seconds.

"What the fuck?" Ashton's friends stare into the sky before sloshing over to his horizontal body. It's debatable as to what has shocked them more, the from-out-of-nowhere summer storm, or Ashton's inert form.

He's out cold.

"What the hell did you do to him, Glynna?" When they start laughing again, it sounds like a pack of wild dogs barking. "Did you see that? She clocked him. We need to get him up and out of here before he drowns."

I turn and run. Right into Leif's immovable chest. "What are you doing here?" I gasp.

"Looking out for my cuz," he says.

"Does Aunt Ophelia know I'm—you're—we're—here?"

His cellphone buzzes in his back pocket.

14

"Do you have to answer that?" I ask.

He takes out the phone. "Yes, Mom. We're on our way. She's never been out of my sight."

My entire body sags. "What about Kristeen? We can't just leave her here."

"She's already in the car."

"How?"

"Passed out."

"Wait," I say. "If she's already passed out in the car, you just lied to your mother. Not even you can be at two different places at the same time, keeping an eye on both of us at once."

"Nope. Didn't lie. We've got the full crew out tonight."

"Everyone?" I squeak.

"You know how Mom feels about you going out unchaperoned after dark."

My earlier decision to stand up to Ophelia craters. "What about Kristeen's Jeep?"

"It's probably already parked in her driveway."

"Courtesy of the *crew*?" I use two fingers to make air quotes.

"Yep."

For as long as I can remember, Leif has been in charge of rescuing me from the slightest hint of trouble and cleaning up after every mess I've ever made. I almost ask him if he ever gets tired of it, but it wouldn't matter. Ophelia would silence any complaints he made with: *Glynna's bloodline needs protecting.*

No reason to hold it against her son, he just takes orders. "Thanks, Leif."

"Next time, give me a heads up when you're gonna sneak out."

How much more hopeless can it get? Kristeen is right. Aunt Ophelia is never going to let me go out alone after dark—let alone with some hot lover. I imagine Leif tottering after me when we're in our seventies and giggle.

"What's so funny?" he asks.

I doubt he'll see the humor in my picture of our future. Maybe I could weave a spell of oblivion into a cupcake. If Aunt Ophelia could forget I need protection, surely Leif would be thrilled to be relieved of his

15

babysitting duties.

Besides, more and more, I'm itching to handle my life all on my own.

2. What's Worse Than a Cupcake Hangover?

SHTON

"Get up, Lazy-Ass-ish!"

The decibel of my sister's voice mutes as a pillow smashes into my face. She sounds like one of those little crows that dive-bombed our food when we went to the Wooden Boat Festival in Port Townsend last year. *Shriek! Shriek!* It's hard to say which is worse, her sharp, nasal 'good morning' or being suffocated. When she finally lifts the pillow and allows me to breathe, my eyes squint from the sun's painful glare.

"It should be illegal to open my blinds before noon," I mumble.

She slams me hard in the face with that pillow again.

"What the hell, Lorriene?" I yell, still trying to shield my eyes.

My right cheekbone feels like it's broken, and a relentless throb pummels my head. Wicked Tequila. It's always worse when I mix it with beer, but when everyone started taking shots, I wasn't gonna be the wuss.

I touch the side of my face and flinch. I couldn't feel worse if I'd been

17

hit by a truck. Wait, was I? I sift through my hazy memories of last night, and don't remember wrecking the car. Still, the morning light and pain in my body is making me nauseous. I pull the blanket over my face.

Again with the damned pillow.

"What?" I snap.

Lorriene can be such a pain in the ass. She's two years younger than me. My friends are noticing how she's grown up and filled out. Knowing what assholes they can be, I don't want them near her. But does she listen to me? Hell no. One of these days she's going to get herself in a heap of trouble. As much as she annoys me, I hope I'm around to bail her out when it happens. Like me, she's tall, but where I'm cut, she's all lean curves. It's in our genes. Neither of us works too hard for it. And her dark hair and crystal blue eyes are a guy magnet. Sometimes I wish she wore big, thick reading glasses and had a few zits to keep the players away. No such luck. And being the head cheerleader at school, along with being my sister, makes her one of the most popular girls on campus. And the hottest. Maybe I'm biased, but I don't know anyone at Gonzaga Prep who'd argue with me about that. Lorriene has definitely come into her own and claimed the crown. And nobody wants to cross her, because as soon as they do, they'll experience *Lorienne DEFCON*.

Defending her social clout is something my little sister takes seriously. Just like with the military, there are five levels of alert. Rumor and innuendo for the first time offender can escalate to DEFCON 2 in less than twenty-four hours: an accidental-on-purpose physical assault, which always includes a ruined blow out or nail job. If the person still hasn't registered they've committed a social breach, the Lorriene-manufactured-parental-teacher-humiliation soon follows. (Usually something along the lines of a cheating scandal or sexting.) For those still too dense to back off, she'll ruin your relationship with your boyfriend or girlfriend. Even after instituting DEFCON 4 I've seen my sister take pity if the offender grovels enough. But there's no return from DEFCON 5: the complete and irreversible shunning. When Lorriene drop kicks you off her social radar, you might as well not exist. Most kids figure out the score well before she has to invoke the permanent wall of silence, but a couple of girls; let's just say no one remembers their names.

The worse I usually get is whacked in the head with a pillow, and lots of shrieking. Although when she's really pissed, my sister will pull out the "I'm going to tell *Grand-mère*" card. Lorriene likes to pretend we have French roots. Our grandmother, Tatiana, encourages her. She's originally from New Orleans and can whip up a mean jambalaya. Despite Grandma's birthplace, I doubt there's a drop of real French blood in our lineage. It doesn't matter. Every Sunday night, the Bass family sits down for a pot—more like a cauldron—of Grandma's shrimp *étouffée*. Of course, the tradition includes the obligatory telling of how Grandpa proposed to Grandma after two huge helpings of her signature spicy dish.

"Get your sorry ass up and take a shower. You reek!" Finally, Lorriene drops the damned pillow and wrinkles her nose in disgust.

"If you don't like the way I smell, get out of my room!"

She huffs. "Someone has been sitting at the breakfast table for over an hour. She's on her fifth cup of coffee, waiting for the precious Bass heir to grace her with his presence."

I forgot to mention: Lorriene is jealous that I'm *The* Bass heir. Makes her crazy.

"Doesn't she have some civic function of earth shattering proportions to attend?"

Grandma runs this town like Lorriene runs the high school. If you want to be invited to the parties, or attract wealthy clientele to your business, kissing Tatiana Bass' ass is the way to go. And for an old lady, my grandma's got the tightest ass I've ever seen. Lorriene hints that it's all thanks to Spanx and surgery, but at sixty, Grandma holds her own against women half her age.

Lorriene's eyes sparkle. "Don't tell me you forgot she's taking us out to lunch!"

My stomach clenches. The only thing worse than a tequila hangover is a tequila hangover and lunch with Tatiana Bass.

"And she approves of you wearing that scrap in public?"

My sister's eyes flare. I've just insulted her fashion sense.

"It would be nice if it covered your ass."

"This is a DRESS, caveman, and it cost three-hundred-and-sixty-five dollars."

"Someone got ripped off."

"Yeah? I don't think so. It's the latest from the Tibi collection," she answers demurely, and twirls.

I close my eyes to avoid a glimpse of her butt cheeks. "Damn, Lorriene. Please tell me you're not ever going to wear that to school." I can only imagine what they'd be saying in the locker room, now that I'm not there to shut them up. Lorriene doesn't get what horny animals teenage guys are.

"I might, if I feel like it."

I shake my head. "Has Grandma seen it?"

"Who do you think picked it out?"

I'd hoped Tatiana would be on my side. "Great. I guess I can look forward to beating the hell out of more of your overzealous admirers this summer."

Lorriene grins. "Just like old times."

It's my first Saturday back from my sophomore year at Harvard, and this is one of the things I didn't miss about my sister when I'm away. "You're trouble," I grunt.

"The best kind." She's in rare form. Makes me wonder what's got her so all-fired-up-in-a-good-mood this early in the day. "Come on." She grabs my hand and tugs. "Grandma has missed her favorite grandson."

"Yeah, her only grandson." I've been so looking forward to chilling with some of my buddies at the golf course after my head stops pounding. I'm still scrambling for an escape route, but unless I'm dying, Grandma T won't be having any of it.

"She's waiting." Lorriene puckers up to one of the mirror panels on my walk-in closet and winks. She loves to practice being seductive, as if her male-slaying arsenal needs more weapons.

I wish Grandma would wise up to my kid sister's ways, but the truth is, she'd probably let Lorriene get away with murder. Literally. I might be the Bass heir, but Lorriene is Tatiana's protégé. Those two give *blood is thicker than water* a whole new level of meaning. I shudder. Girls, women, I don't think I'll ever understand them.

Lorriene heads to my closet. "Quite a party last night, don't ya think?"

That was smug. I grunt. Does she know why it feels like I rammed the right side of my face into the pavement? I'm not going to give her the

20

satisfaction of asking her. "Where are we going for lunch?"

"The club."

That means dress shoes and a tie. I should have stayed in Boston. All summer long. "What about Mom and Dad?"

"Mom commandeered the Gulfstream for the weekend. She's shopping in Seattle."

"And you didn't go with?"

"I wouldn't dream of bailing on our lunch date with Grandma."

Lorriene loves the jet, Seattle, and shopping. Not so much our mother. Still, little sis is up to something, but my head hurts too much figure out what. "Dad?"

"Golfing at Manito."

Exactly where I'd like to be. "Grandpa?"

"He might join us if he can tear himself away from the office."

That bit of news only aggravates the feeling of my skull being cracked in a vise.

Grandpa's a workaholic. Nicolas Remington Bass built the family fortune from nothing. He's a great guy, but if you want face time with him, you've got to get Joan, his secretary and the office pit bull, to pencil you in. Even if you're the Bass heir. And no one gets penciled in by Joan that Tatiana doesn't approve of. I think Joan owes my grandmother her life or something. But if Grandpa doesn't join us for lunch, there'll be no one to run interference between me and the girls. I need to come up with a plan to make sure Grandpa isn't a no-show, but I won't be able to think with Lorriene hovering over me like a Black Hawk helicopter on a spy-op.

"I need to take a shower."

Lorriene keeps rummaging through my closet. After she picks out a sun-yellow polo shirt, a plaid pastel Polo tie, and pressed khakis for me to wear, she leans over to choose my shoes. I can see her panties. If she wasn't my kid sister, I'd be all over her. But she is, and the sight pushes my nauseated stomach to the brink. I tear to the bathroom.

At least I reach the toilet in time.

Lorriene's laughing on the other side of the door. "I'll tell Grandma you're almost ready."

I slide down into the thick pile of my bathroom rug. Something's

21

lapping over the fault lines of my headache like water lapping over the sides of a pool. It's something important. I get up on my hands and knees and reach for the edge of the sink. I pull myself up slowly. My stomach and head are both in high-tilt mode. One false move and I'll be clinging to the porcelain god again, and the next round is going to be dry heaves.

I pull myself up to inspect my right cheekbone in the mirror. A thin line of discoloration bleeds from a quarter-sized bruise. I brush my hair out of my eyes and decide it gives me swagger, but why can't I remember how I got it?

I hustle into my walk-in shower and turn on the hot water. God, it feels great pouring over my head and down the back of my neck. If I could just stay in here for a few hours, I'd be good for a whole round of golf.

Not gonna happen. When Tatiana says *jump*, even the Bass Heir asks *how high*? I grab some shampoo and work on accepting reality. This lunch is going to happen.

While I'm scrubbing my scalp, memories from last night start piecing themselves together. I can remember just about everything up until the tequila shots. Glynna Balcora was there. And from what I could see in the firelight, all grown up into something luscious. I smile. My mind drifts. There's something about that girl with her miles of thick red hair and creamy skin. She's so innocent, and last night she was so apologetic when she spit that brew on me. I didn't even feel annoyed. Hell, the truth was, I'd have been happy to ditch my buddies and spend the rest of the night with her. Wait. I *did* try to spend the rest of the night with her!

The distinct taste of Glynna's kiss comes back to me. It tasted like the sweetest cupcake.

My hands drop as my senses pull me down memory lane. The trip ends on my birthday in second grade. Glynna's grandmother brought a tray of cupcakes to the school party. I remember how disappointed I was when I saw them. The icing was all blobby, and the cupcakes themselves were misshapen because of the way the batter had been poured into the cups. But when Glynna had told me she baked them, I figured she was just a kid like me. Even if they looked like the worst cupcakes ever, I could take a bite of one, just to be polite.

I can still remember the shock of that one bite. To this day, I've never had a cupcake that tasted as good. And that's what Glynna's kiss tasted

22

like. A surprising bit of deliciousness wrapped in plain brown paper. Not that Glynna isn't hot. She is, but she's not aware of it, which makes her more alluring. And tempting, just like her cupcakes.

Arghh! I need to clear my mind of her cupcakes and kisses.

I turn the shower knob and wince when the cold water pelts me, but when it slams into my cheek bone, I jerk out from beneath the icy stream. Memories flush back in. That impulsive kiss didn't work out too well. The guys followed me like a pack of hyenas and then... Shit! And then Glynna punched me! I turn off the water while I'm trying to remember if Lorriene was there. Damn. Or maybe Tyler told her. He's got a big mouth.

I step out of the shower. Is that why Lorriene is so fired up this morning? She's got the inside scoop on me kissing Glynna, and getting my lights knocked out? I press the flats of my hands against the edge of the sink and stare at myself in the mirror, bracing myself for what I sense is coming. If my sister has let my falling all over Glynna last night slip out over breakfast with Tatiana, I'm facing a helluva lecture over lunch.

I wrap my towel around my waist and stalk into my bedroom. I can already hear my grandmother's voice rolling around my head: *You're being groomed for someone who's being groomed for you. Someone with the right pedigree. That's what's important for a long-lasting, healthy marriage. Glynna's not even going to college. She's chained to that bakery and taking care of her eccentric grandmother. I promise you, that's not the kind of family you want to marry into.*

My stomach tightens. There's bad blood between my grandmother and Glynna's. It must go way back, even before I was born. I've never been able to figure out what started it. Not that I've really tried. But one thing is certain—Tatiana Bass will never approve of the Bass Heir falling in love with The Elusive Red Cupcake Girl. Hell, she'd create a shit storm if she ever got wind of me just walking into Frosting & Beans.

Depressing. Maybe it was a good thing Glynna punched me. Maybe if I was her, I would have punched me too.

At least I've come up with a plan to lure Grandpa out of the office. Entrepreneurial research. I intend to open a fleet of gyms when I graduate. I didn't plan to discuss them with him quite so soon, but like the old man says, it's never too early to start laying the ground-work.

23

Yeah, he'll be all over that. Get him excited about a business venture and not even Tatiana will be able to get a word in.

Feeling victorious, I send Pap Pap a text. That's what I use to call Grandpa when I was a kid, and that's how I list him in my contacts.

3. Cupcake Revelations

CYNNA

"No, ma'am."

Ophelia's voice freezes me. I'm halfway out the back door with one foot mid-air. I've never considered playing deaf, but this morning the thought actually crosses my mind. Even I'm surprised.

"Glynna Balcora, get back in here."

I'm still frozen.

"Right now."

She wasn't up when I came in last night, which means she's super angry. When she's only irritated, I get the lecture as soon as I walk in the door. But when she's livid, she waits until morning. A nighttime of dread is part of the punishment.

I wonder where Leif and Archi are. I haven't seen either of them since my cousin dropped me off in the driveway last night. Usually, Archimedes—Leif's owl—comes by my window and gives me a goodnight hoot before he goes hunting. But not last night. It's like Ophelia means to isolate me. This morning, I didn't even hear Nana puttering around the kitchen, which is why I'm headed out to the greenhouse to find her.

"Glynna, don't make me tell you again."

25

I want to run. I want to lose myself in the herbs and spices that Nana's taught me to grow with dirt-covered fingers and the love in her heart. I want her to tell me a story that makes me believe a witch like me could have a chance with someone like Ashton Bass. My foot finally touches the ground. For the second time this morning, my thoughts surprise me. I make a slow turn while I lightly run the fingers of my left hand across my right knuckles. They're tender. I still can't believe I punched Ashton in the face. What was I thinking? Or maybe, he deserved that punch? I cringe as I remember his friends sneering. Ass-hats!

At least last night's storm passed quickly, the rain stopping well before Leif pulled onto our street.

I step back into the kitchen, and the screened door closes behind me with a loud *thwack*. I jump. It's a small jump, but it brings me back to the moment and Aunt Ophelia. If burning eyes could set hair on fire, hers would be ablaze. As it is, I'm sure there's smoke rolling off her singed eyebrows.

"What were you thinking?" she asks me.

"I was thinking I wanted to go out with my friends, like all the other people my age do." Wow. Where did that come from?

My aunt registers the change in me too. Her hands form into bird claws. If I was five, she'd be swinging me around the kitchen. But I'm not five. I'm nineteen, and half a foot taller than she is. She only claws air.

"How many times have I told you? There are evil, malevolent, dangerous forces in this world who would love to use your magical abilities for nefarious purposes!"

I almost roll my eyes. I catch myself and grin. Kristeen would be so proud. Something has gotten into me. The memory of Ashton's lips—his hot, gentle, insistent lips, covering mine.

"Are you listening to me, Glynna?"

"I'm nineteen years old, Ophelia."

Her eyes pop open. "You think you can take care of yourself? When the Occultos come for you—?"

"The Occultos?" I ask.

All color bleaches from her face, she sags into the chair next to mine. "I was just... it was a name that came to me."

No, this is the information that I've been waiting for: All. Of. My. Life.

26

I'm not going to let her retreat now. I ease into one of the chairs at our kitchen table. A strange calm permeates me as I visualize Ashton's piercing blue eyes, and the way he looked at me when he handed me the wine cooler. In that one moment, there was something electric between us. I felt the spark, and the memory is charging me with some kind of inner strength. I want to keep remembering it. I want to keep remembering him before he came at me like some wasted-off-his-ass Romeo.

"Glynna, your bloodline is strong. Perhaps, the strongest there is. There are many in the world who would harness your powers for their dark purposes." Ophelia sighs. Her shoulders droop in unfamiliar defeat.

"Ophelia," I say her name gently. "You're my aunt. My blood—my ability to do magic—can't be any stronger than yours or Leif's. Definitely not stronger than Nana's."

Her eyes are wet. Is she crying?

I think about Ashton. And the sensation when his hand brushed mine. Immediately, I feel more centered and in control of the haywire emotions Ophelia's strange behavior is producing in me.

Aunt Ophelia drops her head onto her arms. Her shoulders are shaking. She's sobbing. I'm speechless. What is wrong with her? I inch my chair toward hers. I still believe her vulnerability is an illusion, but she doesn't stop making those ghastly crying noises. I reach out and touch her shoulder. She doesn't jerk away or yell, she just continues to heave. My eyes glance around our cozy white-and-yellow kitchen. There are no breakfast dishes on the table and not one in the sink. As far as I can tell, no one's even made coffee this morning. There's no lingering smell of breakfast.

"Auntie, what's wrong?"

"There's no easy way to tell you what needs to be said."

All right. I get up and walk backwards—into the next room—keeping my gaze on her bowed head. I grab a box of tissues. Our old house is quiet. Leif always opens the bakery early on Saturdays, but where is Nana? For that matter, where is Archi? Our feathery guardian likes to jabber first thing in the morning. It's like we're his nestlings. He wants to make sure we all survived the night before he settles down to sleep for

27

the day in the humongous nest Leif helped him build in the tree outside our windows. But the owl's nowhere in sight, either.

I grab the light cardboard box of tissue and tread cautiously toward my aunt. She doesn't acknowledge me, so I nudge the back of her hand with a Kleenex. She doesn't thank me, but she takes it and wipes her eyes. A few seconds later, she wads the soft sheet in her hand and settles her elbows on the table. "Sit down, Glynna." She pats the chair next to hers. Her voice is thick with the remains of her tears.

I wobble over and plant my seat in the chair, as if it's the jaws of death. What is she going to tell me? A black thought crosses my mind. Oh my God! "Did Nana die?" I screech.

Aunt Ophelia's face displays a flash of normalcy. "Glynna, no! Don't even say that." Her tone is harsh, familiar.

For the first time in my life, her abrasiveness gives me some comfort. My worst fear hasn't been realized. Surely, I can handle anything else. My insides relax. "The house is quiet this morning."

"Nana and I had long talk last night."

My heart catches in my throat.

"We agreed it's time to tell you."

My pulse is racing. "Tell me what?"

She closes her eyes, a dramatic pause.

I'm on the edge of my seat.

Ophelia slides one hand up the side of her face. "I'm not your aunt, not by blood. Nana is not your grandmother... not by blood."

I try to fit the new pieces of what Ophelia is saying together with the old ones—that my mother and father died when I was an infant. "There wasn't a tragic accident?"

"There was—"

"I don't understand."

"Glynna, Nana is your legal guardian. She adopted you when your mother died. But your mother wasn't her biological daughter."

"So... Nana adopted her too?" There's a strange squeak to my voice.

"No—"

In my head, the Titanic hits the iceberg. My world collapses into an icy sea of shock.

Ophelia and Leif are bronze-people. Golden-haired and tiger-eyed.

28

Nana's hair. Who knows what the real color is? She dyes it a new one every six months. Currently, it's magenta. Her eyes are blue, like mine, but she's so short. How could I have not known, never even guessed? Fury and emptiness engulf me. I shove myself away from the table.

"Glynna, sit down." Ophelia the drill sergeant has returned

But I'm drowning in the freezing waters of my new reality. I can't obey. "Who am I?" And why did my precious grandmother—who's apparently not really my grandmother—abandon me to Ophelia for this revelation. "Why didn't Nana tell me?"

"Glynna, sit!"

I pace.

"Fine. Don't sit." Ophelia gets up and heads to the coffee machine.

I want to pull all the dishes out of the cupboard and smash them onto the floor. I want to shove the kitchen table onto its side. Pick up each chair and smash it into firewood. I want to pull the rickety screened door off its hinges and scream out into the world, "My entire life is a lie!" But I just keep pacing.

Outside thunder cracks.

Less than five minutes ago, the morning was inland-northwest-blue sunshine.

Ophelia's grinding coffee beans, tamping them down. She's so methodical, as though this were any other Saturday morning. Her head cocks toward the rumbling sky, but she doesn't say anything.

"Does Leif know?" I ask.

"Yes."

Of course. Leif is her son by blood. She doesn't keep secrets from him.

"Nana knew you'd be upset."

Tidal waves of sadness crash over my anger. Hot tears roll down my face. "I would have rather she told me." The words come out all broken up as rain pelts the kitchen window.

Ophelia approaches me with a steaming cup of coffee.

If I take it, it means I'll sit down with her at the kitchen table and listen to what she has to say. If I don't... cool reason pushes its way through my inner tempest. I need information. As much as I can get before I walk out the door and never come back.

29

I wrap my fingers around the warm mug and sit down at the table, this time, across from her.

"Do you want a croissant?" she asks, getting up, as if everything's already back to normal.

"No."

She shrugs and piles two onto her plate before she comes back to the table. She dunks one into her coffee. Ecstasy flashes in her eyes when she takes that first bite.

We each have a specialty: mine is cupcakes, Nana's is pies, Ophelia's is cookies, and Leif's is croissants and roasting coffee beans. People drive from all over Washington State to have one of his croissants with a cup of his special coffee blend on Saturday mornings. His magic touch—a sense of joy so profound you're sure you've arrived at Heaven's door for the next twenty-four hours. Who wouldn't want to start their weekend off like that? You think we'd be wealthy. My mind sifts back through the years... the lines out the door.

I blink.

"We're all witches," she says. "That's why—" She sighs like this is going to be the most difficult thing in the world to explain. "Nana used to be a midwife."

My tongue is a stone in my mouth.

"Your mother—"

My heart cracks like an egg on those two words. The silent tears start rolling down my cheeks again. All my life, I've ached to know more about the ghost who gave birth to me.

"Was a very powerful Lumina." She shoves the tissue box in my direction then continues. "There are two covens in the world. The Luminas are light, and the Occultos are dark." She's taking bites of her croissant and sips of coffee while she talks, but she doesn't look at me. "Your father—" She hesitates. "Was a very powerful Occulto."

Dark. My father was dark.

Thunder rattles the house from its foundation to the top of the roof.

Ophelia tilts her head toward the ceiling. "You've got to learn to control your emotions, Glynna. Do you want to cause a flash flood?"

I want to fling my untouched cup of coffee across the room. Pound on the table. Kick something. Ashton's lazy grin eases into my brain, and for

30

a millisecond, there's a calm in the center of the gale winds tearing up my heart.

Ophelia's laser eyes burn into my chest. "What are you thinking about?"

"Nothing."

"No, it wasn't nothing." She goes to the kitchen window and looks out. "Now, it's only a drizzle." She whirls around. "You calmed yourself. I've never seen you do it so quickly."

I'm not going to answer questions. Not this morning. I shake my head.

She resettles in her chair, pushes away what's left of her breakfast, crosses her arms, and leans across the table. "Nana delivered you. Your mother asked her to watch over you. To raise you and protect you. She had no one else."

More tears roll down my face. I tug another tissue from the box.

"Pearl couldn't do it all alone, Glynna."

Pearl is Nana's given name. No one besides Ophelia ever calls her that, and Ophelia only does it when she's talking about the past.

"Of course, I couldn't turn my sister away. I understood what was at stake. Pearl, Leif, myself, we're all Luminas too. But Alberto had just died, and there was no money, nothing. It was a difficult time for all of us, but Pearl and I, we leaned on each other, and we had Leif and you to give our lives meaning. Your mother bequeathed Pearl her life savings. They were substantial. We decided to invest them in the bakery—"

"That bakery is as much mine as it is yours."

"Actually—" Ophelia gets up from the table. After she takes the step stool from the pantry, she heads over to one of the kitchen cabinets. An ivory jar, with an enormous violet iris painted on it, is perched on the highest shelf. I've never noticed the beautiful piece before, and I'm curious. It would be an easy reach for me, but Ophelia has to stretch her fingers—even with the stool. Not in the mood to be helpful, I stubbornly remain seated. She brings the jar back to the table and pushes it in my direction.

"What's this?" I ask.

"Open it."

I stop with my fingertips on the lid. What if it's something creepy like my mother's ashes?

31

"Go ahead," Ophelia encourages me. Leif's croissant has taken effect. Her face is bursting with joy.

I pull off the top and search the shadowy interior. Papers. I fish them out. They're folded into eighths. I flatten them on the table. "This is a deed to the bakery," I say.

"Yes."

An airy feeling floats through me. A ray of sunlight pouring in through the kitchen window draws my attention. The rain has stopped. "My bakery," I whisper. "But... " I don't understand.

"We may not be blood, but we're family," Ophelia says.

"But... what about you, and Leif, and Nana?"

"We've always drawn salaries."

I shake my head. I've never thought it was fair that Leif gets paid for working in the bakery, and I don't. But now I understand. It's because I'm the owner, and he works for me.

I raise my head and meet my aunt's gaze. Okay, I guess I can still call her my aunt. "I don't know what to say."

"Legally, you're an adult."

A spike of anger charges through me. "I have been for over a year."

"One day, maybe you'll have a daughter. Then you'll understand the need you have to protect her."

I refold the papers and replace them in the jar. "Is my father alive?"

"Your father is not why we're having this conversation this morning."

"I can't believe we didn't have this conversation a long time ago." My voice is a soft but firm marvel to my ears. "And you still haven't answered my question. Is my father still alive?"

"Your father is a powerful Occulto. Before she died, your mother made it clear to Pearl she didn't want you to have a relationship him."

"Do you know his name?"

"Ask Nana," she says.

"Is she in the greenhouse?"

"Yes, but don't ask her about your father today. Absorb what I've just told you first. Find out more about the Luminas and Occultos before you go searching for him with a fantasy of what you'll find because—" She stops.

"Because?"

32

"Once you understand everything, you may not want to find him."

I drag my fingers through my hair. "I guess telling me what to do is a habit that's going to die hard for you." But a smile plays on my lips. Frostings & Beans is mine! It belongs to me. I can't wait to tell Kristeen. "Uhmm,... who knows about these Luminas and Occultos?"

Ophelia sweeps up her breakfast dishes. "Only Luminas and Occultos, no outsiders. So not one word to your friend."

I'll have to edit the version I tell Kristeen. I return the jar to its place on the top shelf.

"Glynna, that thing that happened... "

"What thing, Auntie?"

"When the rain stopped, what were you thinking about?"

I tousle my hair so strands of it cover my face. "I don't know what you're talking about."

Her golden-brown eyes intensify, while an image of Ashton's bright smile illuminates my brain. I impulsively lean in to give my aunt a hug before heading to the greenhouse.

I'm out the door before she can say another word.

4. Brunch with Tati? I Need a Cupcake ASAP!

 SHTON

The staff at the Burgundy greet me with enthusiasm. I've been coming here since before I could walk, so I know all their names. There's a couple of new faces, but by the end of the summer, I'll know them too. Grandpa is big on treating everyone with respect. Not so much Grandma. She barely acknowledges Urs, the Burgundy's chef, when he comes out to greet us and welcome me back to town.

Christianne leads us to our usual table with the panoramic view of Riverfront Park. Every head in the place turns toward Tatiana and Lorriene as we walk by. I have to admit they're a spectacle, Grandma T in her short, tight, sky-blue day suit, and my sister in that swatch of cloth she's calling a dress. The lunch crowd is mostly women. There are only two other males besides the staff, Urs, and me, in the whole place—and they've got to be under ten. I tug at my tie.

From out of nowhere, the sky cracks open with a rumble and pours down rain.

35

Tatiana sniffs. "The weatherman didn't predict this."

As if it's his fault.

Lorriene frowns. "Damn. If this keeps up, Maddie's going to have to cancel her party tonight. Her parents won't let her move it inside."

Madeleine Wardof is Lorriene's BFOTM–Best Friend of the Moment. It's a dicey position, sure to be short lived, but girls still line up for the honor. Being Lorriene's BFOTM is like being a best seller. At least by the time you fall off the charts, everyone knows your name.

Grandma orders a Basil Orange Martini before she sniffs the air again. "Strange," she mutters.

"What?" Lorriene asks.

"For a moment, I thought I smelled sulfur. Did either of you smell anything?"

We shake our heads.

Grandma's painted eyes and mouth droop–as if we've broken her heart–before she forces a strained laugh and scans the room. "I must be imagining things."

The downpour eases into a light drizzle.

"That was quick," I say.

"Too quick," Grandma muses.

Lorreine's phone *pings*. "Looks like the party and my new Jimmy Choos are back on for tonight. Are you coming, Ash?"

"Keggers are for kids," I quip.

My sister rolls her eyes. "It's Daphne's party too."

Daphne is Maddie's older sister. She's my age. "Where's she going to school?" I ask.

"Bryn Mawr."

"Right."

"She's even more gorgeous now," Lorriene gushes.

If you like paper dolls and mannequins. The Wardof sisters are heavily invested in plastic surgery. Their cut-out plasticized perfection turns some of my friends on, but it doesn't do much for me.

"I'd rather be set up with an inflatable doll."

"Ashton, don't be crude," Tatiana says.

I study my menu because I'm not going to the party, and I'm not going to let Lorriene or Grandma T push me into Daphne's over-toned arms.

36

Grandma is fond of Daphne because she volunteered for every single civic activity Grandma chaired, organized, or supported when we were in high school. Lorriene doesn't even do that, and I'm surprised that level of suck-up-ness doesn't rub my little sister the wrong way.

"Sometimes the truth hurts." I soften the comment with a grin.

"Ashton!" Grandma squawks. "If the Wardof girls see fit to enhance their natural beauty, who are you to judge?"

My head is throbbing again. "I'm not judging. Daphne's just not my type."

"I don't think you know what your type is, darling," Tatiana says. "Daphne is an accomplished young woman who has much to offer a partner. It would be a mistake to let someone steal her away."

I can only dream. Last time I was within ten yards of Daphne, she transformed into Octopus Woman. Every time I turned around, she had a hand on some part of my anatomy. I make a mental note to steer clear of her for the entire summer; because if I run into her at the mall or somewhere, Grandma will probably order wedding invitations.

Lorriene offers up the scoop on Daphne's latest procedure. I tune her out while I try to figure out what I'm going to order for lunch. Most everything on the menu is full of carbs. I decide on the Crab Louie and feel amazingly vulnerable when I close my menu and place it in front of me on the table.

"Daphne would make a perfect wife," Tatiana says.

I choke on the ice from my glass of water and check my phone. No reply from Pap Pap yet.

Grandma's Martini hasn't arrived yet. In spite of my hangover, I wish I'd ordered one too. Maybe I will. More alcohol might be the only way to survive this lunch. "I'm too young to get married."

"Nonsense," Grandma says.

I'm appalled. "No one gets married in their twenties these days."

"Humph. They should."

"Daphne is so sweet," Lorriene chirps, as if all of a sudden she believes in swirls of cotton candy and rainbow-colored unicorns.

"It would be so cool to have Maddie as a sister-in-law."

"Until you replace her with your next BFOTM."

"Hey, don't take out your frustrations on me, big brother," Lorriene

37

snarks.

Stupidly, I jump all over that bait. "What are you talking about?"

"After getting your lights punched out by a girl last night, I suspect your sense of masculinity is vulnerable."

Tatiana's eyes flash. "Ashton, is that true?"

I glare at Lorriene. "No, I just drank too much tequila."

My sister grins. She's loving this. "And it kicked in the second her fist connected with your face."

"A girl hit you last night?" Tatiana is appalled.

"Glynna Balcora," Lorriene volunteers.

When Grandma's Martini arrives, she takes a hefty swig. "Were you out on a date?" She takes another gulp of her drink. It's about two-thirds gone. Her head swivels in search of the waiter before her panicked gaze returns to me. "With her?"

"It was nothing. Lorriene's exaggerating, as usual." I find my little sister's foot under the table and smash it with my heel. She lets out a satisfying yelp, but keeps her eyes on the table. She's been warned. Lorriene likes to mess with me, but she can't afford for me to cut her off. My social calendar is going to be prime real estate this summer, and she'll want to tag along. I'll have to find some way to make things even with her though, because even if she shuts up now, the damage has already been done. Glynna and I are on Tatiana's radar.

"That grandmother of hers is such a pathetic, desperate creature; dyeing her hair all those ridiculous shades as if she were still a teenager." Grandma drains her Martini.

"You know her?" I ask, as casually as possible.

Tatiana's face flushes. From the corner of my eye, I can see that Lorriene is watching Grandma as carefully as I am.

The waiter swings by our table. "Yes, Mrs. Bass?"

Grandma doesn't bat an eye, or ask us if we want anything else. "Another Martini."

We haven't even ordered lunch yet.

"That—that woman!" Grandma sputters.

Lorriene is about to crawl out of her seat, and I'm leaning forward as far as I possibly can, dying to hear this revelation.

Tatiana shakes her platinum-dyed coif as if the truth is too bitter to speak, but my sister and I remain silent and still. Prodding will put an end to any chance of secrets being spilled this afternoon. I risk a glance toward the bar. The bartender is working on Grandma's next Martini. I wish he'd hurry up.

"What about that woman?" I ask as gently as possible.

The waiter arrives with Grandma's drink. She takes it from his hand. Lorriene and I are now staring at our grandmother in utter amazement. Are those tears in her eyes?

"She tried to take my Nicolas from me."

"Oh, Grandma, how could she?" Lorriene swoops in with sympathy, rubbing Grandma's shoulder.

"If I hadn't done what I had to do—" Grandma dabs her eye. "—you two wouldn't even exist."

I'm stunned. Glynna's grandmother and my grandpa? I wonder if they ever kissed. I wonder if her kisses tasted like cupcakes, too. My heart reels. It's a weird intergenerational connection. Nicolas possibly being attracted to the grandmother, and now me; hot for Glynna. My mind tries to grapple with the possibility.

Meanwhile, Tatiana has regained her steel. "You can learn a lot about a girl by observing her female relatives. Especially, the older ones. That Pearl, she's a sly one."

Whatever. I wasn't kissing Glynna's grandmother.

"Where is she going to college?" my sister asks.

I glare at Lorriene who probably got up at the crack of dawn and ordered a dossier on Glynna from some elite internet spy agency. "I don't know."

"Doesn't she work in that falling down bakery on Perry Street?"

"It's not falling down."

"How do you know?"

I don't, but really Lorriene, you're already on my shit list, so why don't you shut your mouth?

"Have you been there recently?" Tatiana picks up the interrogation with a discernible note of panic in her voice. "To the bakery?"

"No, I just got back to town."

"Do you intend on seeing this girl? Have you been keeping in touch with her while you've been at Harvard?"

Why does she care? Up until now, Grandma has been all for me playing the field as long as I use protection. I keep my tone quiet and even. "That's a lot of questions for a Saturday brunch; even for you, Grandma."

She sniffs. "You're not a boy anymore. You're a young man. And you need to start behaving like one. It's time to start thinking about your future; one that includes a suitable young wife and heirs. What you do when you're off at school is none of my business, but when you're home, what you do reflects directly on the family."

All of a sudden I wonder if she's dying or something. Maybe she's afraid if I don't get married tomorrow, she won't live to see her grandkids. "Are you feeling all right?" I ask her.

She gives me a quizzical look. "I'm the picture of health."

"Great." I reach across the table and grab her hand. "I just want to know you'll be around a good long time."

She pulls her hand out of mine. "Just stay away from girls like Glynna Balcora," she huffs.

"What do you mean? Girls like what?"

"Girls with no future and no connections."

I stand up so abruptly my napkin falls on the floor. Grandpa is headed straight to our table. The conversation about my future wife and the sermon about the abomination of Glynna's cupcake kisses has ended.

Tatiana and Lorriene accept this fact. They zip their lips.

I raise my eyes to the ceiling in a silent prayer of thanks to whatever gods exist above.

ATIANA

Nico, my husband, looks impeccable as usual. I raise my cheek so he can air kiss it. When he walks right by me, without observing our public ritual, my blood boils. Appearances count for everything, and small gestures build the necessary facade.

He's failing me.

I force a smile for Lorriene because she doesn't miss a thing. It won't do to have her fretting over my relationship with her grandfather. She needs to remain focused on her mission: Create strategic opportunities for Daphne Wardof to work her magic on Ashton.

He must propose to her by the end of the summer.

I pat my granddaughter's hand and nod toward Nico and Ashton deep in discussion, their heads almost touching. "When men have business on their mind, everything else escapes them."

Lorriene nods.

I order a Martini for Nico. He orders the same Crab Louie Ashton is having. My jaw tightens, but I don't criticize. Men eating salads. A most disturbing trend. Almost as disturbing as my husband's distracted coolness. Might there be an all-too-human-explanation? Dementia? Perhaps Alzheimer's?

A cold thought freezes my breath. After all these years, could my spell be fading?

The timing couldn't be worse. Neither of my grandchildren have shown the slightest aptitude for magic, and without the possibility of a direct heir, I'm at risk of losing everything I've built over the years; the young group of maverick Occultos in Seattle is determined to prove I'm irrelevant, and the coven's High Witch, my old friend, Lyrika, seems to care little for reining them in. My best hope is Daphne Wardof's marriage to Ashton, and a great-grandchild who can do dark magic. Time is ticking. I have to do something before it's too late.

I tap my fingers on the table, counting. Onc... the cancer awareness fundraiser. Two... the charity golf tournament. Three... the Catholic Charities dinner. Four... I can't remember why I cancelled Sunday dinner that week, but I hammer the table with my thumb. It has been more than a month of Sundays since Nico has had a bowl of my shrimp étouffée.

After forty years, why do I always feel as though my relationship with him is so fragile?

Nico's eyes sparkle as he listens to our grandson. Perhaps I'd be touched if I possessed a soul. But I don't, so the awareness is merely data.

41

From the day I abandoned my mother in New Orleans to carve a fortune for myself out west, calculation has been my forte.

Tomorrow night will be Ashton's first Sunday night home for the summer. After church I'll whip up an enormous kettle of étouffée. Ashton and Lorriene can invite their friends. No one in the family will be excused, and I'll make sure Nico eats several bowls.

Finally, my husband graces me with a smile.

I take it the Fates approve of my plan.

"What a lovely surprise, you out of the office so early and on a Saturday." Despite my determination to set the foundering vessel of our marriage aright, my voice is strained. I need another Martini.

Nico pats Ashton's shoulder. "Thank your grandson."

"Oh?"

"He's got some excellent ideas for a new business venture. As soon as I found out about them, I was eager to encourage him."

"Wonderful."

"And that thunder storm!"

"It was hardly a storm."

"When it stopped, I felt compelled to step outside."

My fingers squeeze the stem of my glass. Although I've yet to put my finger on it, there was something off about that squall. To hear it was the impetus of Nico leaving his office doesn't sit well with me. "And here you are."

"Have you been out since the rain? I feel twenty years younger."

"How nice." Perhaps my spell isn't fading. Perhaps Nicolas is being targeted.

If someone has set their sights on my husband, they're aiming for me as well.

Who would dare challenge the most powerful dark witch in the northwestern United States?

Someone who knows I'm vulnerable.

Memories of Liam and Natalia intrude. I banish them. Dwelling on the past will only make me weak.

5. Are You My Cupcake?

CYNNA

My hand grips the China handle of the oriental teapot covered with hand-painted coral-colored mimosa flowers and butterflies, which I've used to bring Nana coffee every morning for years. Despite the storm of emotions within, it's a habit I can't break. My flats *clip* along the mosaic pathway. The bright bits of stone are chipped, but the yellow, blue, green, and red colors of the tile are still vivid. They wind around the side of the garage and up a small hill. I've always thought of this walkway as the yellow brick road, leading to my personal emerald city—Nana's greenhouse. The greenhouse actually sits on the lot next door. It's my favorite place in the world, next to the bakery—my bakery! I still haven't absorbed that reality yet.

I've also made a decision: Aunt Ophelia isn't going to tell me what time to come home anymore. If she wants to send Leif trailing after me, that's her business, but I'm not going to spend another Saturday night as a fairy tale character locked away in some tower.

A strong wind blows between the houses and ruffles the long sleeve of my Eros Pink T-shirt. I'm back in my skinny jeans. I pull to a stop, careful not to let a drop of coffee spill from the pot. My blood is still

43

pumping hot in my veins. If I'm not going to let Ophelia dictate my hours anymore, I'm certainly not going to let Kristeen tell me what color to wear. I'm going to live and die in pink. I think I'll order five more pink aprons from my favorite online store this afternoon! After I stop by Roots and get a Blush pedicure. Just the idea makes me giddy.

But how am I going to face Nana?

I try to collect my thoughts. I've always believed she was my grandmother, and now that I know she's not, will it feel strange? Different? Will I be able to talk with her like I did before?

When the breeze shifts, the uplifting, clean, crisp scent of lavender permeates the air. That smell is as much a part of who I am as anything on this planet. And it's Nana who taught me how to raise and nurture these tender herbs. I crouch down next to one of the stone planters, set Nana's coffee down, and pluck a leaf from its stem. I roll it between my fingers and inhale a big whiff, as if it were an illicit drug. I move to the next container and then the next. They line the walk, each herb and flower imbued with memories of me and Nana.

I rock back on my heels with my elbows on my knees.

My mother asked Nana to take care of me, and that's what she's done with all the love in her heart. But it still hurts that she didn't tell me. Or maybe it just hurts that I've never known my mother and father. Logically, I know that's not Nana's fault. I can't even blame that on Ophelia, but it doesn't change the fact that I'm dying for any scrap of information I can gather about my bloodlines.

Your bloodlines are strong. Ophelia's words echo in my mind. Bloodlines: What an archaic term. It makes me feel like there's something ancient hidden inside me. I've always felt older and more mature than my peers. Especially Kristeen, the wild child. I grin. I need to talk to her soon. I sift through the facts. I can tell her that Nana adopted me. Wait a minute! Ophelia never said exactly what happened to my mother. I assumed she's dead. What if she isn't? I bounce to my feet.

Nana will tell me the truth. She's got to.

After I retrieve the pot I left sitting in the middle of the walkway, I push on the multi-colored glass door of the greenhouse and pause to cherish the sensation of crossing a magic threshold. The entire world seems to stop with me as I breathe in the different scents of exotic herbs, crawling vines, sweet smelling flowers, and sprawling shrubs that burst with life from every nook, cranny, hook, and shelf.

Nana's humming floats from the interior. My eyes water when she starts to sing. I've always told her she could have been a star, the oldest contestant to win *American Idol*. She always brushes my compliments off, but her eyes sparkle whenever I shower her with my genuine affection. We're a mutual admiration society, me and Nana. Hopefully, that won't change. Her soothing voice leads me toward the center of the greenhouse. I wipe my eyes with the back of my hand. When I was a child, Nana sang me lullabies and stroked my hair as I dozed off to sleep each night. Her voice has always made me feel safe. Made me feel like I'm home. But now? I'm questioning everything. Who am I? What about my father? If he's alive, is he looking for me? Is he really an Occulto? And why have Ophelia and Nana been trying so hard to hide me from everyone? What does that really mean—Dark? Like an evil warlock? The image of someone wearing a dark cloak crosses my mind. I shiver, and goosebumps break out on my arms.

Or does he work for the mob as a hit man or something?

"Glynna, dear? Are you in here?" Nana's gentle voice interrupts my thoughts.

"Yes, Nana. I brought you some coffee."

"Ahhh. I know that aroma," Nana says, as she closes her eyes and inhales. She's behaving as if this were any other morning, not the one where my secret history has been revealed.

My relentless questions and feelings of despair fade. Her normalcy and our shared ritual take over. I bend over to peck her cheek before placing the porcelain coffee pot on the vintage table I sanded and painted when I was fifteen. Several of Nana's giant, special mimosas arch over the table. Their vivid blooms burst forth in yellow, red, and pink.

The pink flowers are a concession to me.

Two clean cups sit in the flower's shade.

I pour the coffee into the matching cups and hand one to Nana. "This is Leif's latest coffee discovery."

As if on cue, the mimosas sway and burst into an old Louis Armstrong tune.

I see trees of green, red roses too, I see them bloom...

45

Yes, that's our magical singing mimosas. It's a beautiful sound; one I wish the entire world could hear. But that would bring journalists, and government officials, and who knows who else traipsing to our humble doorstep. Ophelia won't have that. I don't want it either.

The song is definitely affecting me because, *Yes!* I think to myself, *what a wonderful world.*

"Oooh, this tastes delicious." Nana takes another sip. "Even better than his last blend. That boy, he's got impeccable taste." She continues gushing over Leif's latest creation until she finally sets her cup down. "Come, my dear, sit with me."

The mimosas are still singing, swaying, and shaking their leaves like jazz hands. I have to bite the inside of my mouth so a huge smile doesn't bust out on my face.

Nana beams. "See how they sing when they sense your presence, Glynna? I remember the first time I brought you here, inside this greenhouse. You were such an adorable baby, with all that red hair, and those enormous blue eyes." Nana holds her hands up to the side of her head and waggles her fingers. She's looking very nostalgic. "You were crying that day. Oh, you threw a tantrum that scared all the bees and little hummingbirds around!" She lets out an amused chuckle. "And the mimosas, as if they sensed your need for comfort, burst into song. That was the first time I'd ever seen a seemingly ordinary flower turn into something magical. I knew in that moment, there is really something extraordinary about you, my dear."

I stare at the lace, trailing from the ceiling to create a frail white canopy over the sofa. My arms are still crossed protectively across my chest and my heart. Nana again pats the empty space on the cushion beside her.

The garden sofa is surrounded with soft, embroidered floral throw pillows trimmed in lace. I remember falling asleep here when I was a child, as Nana read me fairy tales on lazy summer afternoons.

But now my own life is starting to sound like something from a dark fairy tale. And I'm afraid of turning into the powerful witch, or evil sorceress, in the story.

The mimosas wind down as curiosity overtakes my anger. I unfold my rigid arms and sit.

Nana peers at me through her eyeglasses. "I imagine you're here to seek some answers?"

More tears attempt to spill from my eyes. "It's true, then, what Aunt Ophelia told me? I'm not who I think I am?"

"Hush now, my child." Nana leans forward to embrace me. She soothes my hair and kisses my forehead. "What Ophelia told you this morning doesn't change anything. You're very much our own, Glynna. You're part of this family, no matter what. You must always remember that." She pats my chest. "Ophelia, Leif and I: We love you very much." She sniffs.

My throat constricts. I stroke her wrinkled hands as I let myself wilt inside her hug. The ever-present subtle vanilla smell of her makes my heart swell. It brings back a rushing river of memories. Nana has given up everything for me. She built her world around me and treated me as her own. How could I ever be angry with her? How could I run away from her, leaving her with no explanation? It would break my heart as much as it would break hers. I'm going to have to find a different way to cope with this overwhelming news.

"I knew this day would come. Your Aunt Ophelia and I; we should have told you sooner. But we thought; the less you knew about your complicated history—and who you really are—the safer you would be. I gave my word to your mother that I would keep you safe, that I would hide you away from your father, and from the hands of the Occulto."

"Ophelia didn't tell me what happened to my mother."

Nana whispers the awful revelation, "She died in childbirth."

I killed my mother? Sobs shudder through my body.

Nana doesn't let go as I heave into her neck. "I'm so sorry, child."

"Did you know her? I mean, why did she ask you to take care of me?"

Nana strokes my hair. "By the time you were born, I knew her well. You're a lot like her. Fiery and sweet. Passionate and wise."

"But why did she die? Women don't die in childbirth anymore."

"Unfortunately, some still do."

"Did it have something to do with me?" I ask the question that most terrifies me.

"We did what we could to prepare her, but as far as I know, there's never been another child born between a Lumina and an Occulto. We're

47

forbidden to mate, but that's not why we don't. The truth is we're not attracted to each other. We Luminas are drawn to love and beauty, truth and justice, dignity and peace. Occultos crave domination, violence, destruction and hate."

I pull away from Nana's embrace. "Then how could my mother have loved my father?"

Nana's hand cups my cheek. Her eyes hold mine. "I'm not sure that she did."

I want to retch as horrible scenarios flood my mind. "Did he rape her?" God, I already hate him.

"She never told me that. But Glynna, she refused to talk about him or their relationship. By the time she found me, all she cared about was you and your safety."

"By the time she found you?"

"As a midwife, I was often recommended to those who feared a difficult birth for whatever reason. You were the last birth I attended. Your mother was the only one who ever died." Tears fill her eyes.

All my words stick in my throat.

"You have great powers, Glynna." Nana keeps talking as though she's drowning beneath these secrets she's kept from me all my life, and unburdening them will let her breathe air again. "No one knows of another living witch that has both the Lumina's and Occulto's powerful blood. That is something to take seriously." She gazes at me with her loving eyes. "You're capable of powerful magic. A power the Occultos would like to twist and rein to their dark purposes, no matter the cost." Nana grips my hand tightly. "The Occultos are heartless and cruel, Glynna. They're born without souls. Since the beginning of time, they've clamored for power. It's everything to them. They use black magic to manipulate, to deceive, and to take away every single ounce of goodness that's innate in a human heart. They take and take, but sadly, they seem never to get enough. But having the power that resides in you in their hands; I can't imagine it. Our world would become dominated by their evil and darkness." She sighs. "I doubt even the mimosas would continue to sing for you."

My thoughts splinter into a hundred million fragments as angsty moments of my childhood take on new meaning: Cutting things up, ripping things apart, or shredding them when I was younger; slamming doors, hitting things that couldn't hit me back, and kicking a few holes in my bedroom wall when I got older.

The past couple of years, I've contained my anger better.

Except for last night when I decked Ashton.

And this morning when that freak thunderstorm pounded the city.

Until I recalled Ashton's baby-blues gazing into mine. And then the rain stopped.

Another smile erupts on my face as I recall the last customer's at the bakery yesterday.

"Glynna?" Nana asks.

"You've always encouraged my obsession with baking–"

"When you're really upset, nothing else calms you down."

"Is falling in love... *light?*"

"Oh, Glynna, have you met someone, sweetheart?"

"Uhmm. There is a boy... and when I think about him, my insides swirl with the same sweet goodness I experience when I'm baking." Except it's stronger.

Nana squeezes my hands. "Oh, that's wonderful. Tell me all about him. What's his name?"

"Ashton Bass."

Her grip suddenly cuts off the circulation in my fingers. "Nicolas Bass' grandson?"

"Yes." What is wrong with her? "Do you know him?"

She drops my hands and fidgets with her magenta hair. Her lips turn down and her shoulders sink.

"What Nana?"

She's drifted to some place far away.

"Nana?"

Her hand pats my knee, but she studies something I can't see. "He's Tatiana's grandson too."

"Okay."

"She won't let you have him."

A strange heaviness falls shrouding any light inside me.

Nana stands up. "Glynna, forget him." She walks out of the greenhouse without another word.

49

When the mimosa's start singing *When I Fall in Love*–a Nat King Cole song, I don't even know what to think.

 EARL

The stairs seem so steep this morning. My breathing is labored as I climb them. I use the railing to help me, as the other hand rests against my thumping heart. Glynna's news is such a shock to my old heart.

How many years has it been? Not since I've thought of Nicolas; I think of him every day. When I wake up to greet the sun, he's always in my heart. The memories of our love have sustained me over the years, and made it easy to push aside everything in my life as I've cared for Glynna.

I've always believed that my love for Nicolas has kept his heart strong, kept his soul from withering under Tatiana's spell.

But to think that Glynna is falling in love with his grandson, what a shock! And so dangerous.

After everything we've done to protect her from the Occultos, how long would it take before Tatiana discovered the truth?

Not nearly long enough.

Glynna's so strong, but even I can't pretend she's prepared to take on one of the most powerful dark witches in the Americas.

Oh, what have Ophelia and I done? If we'd told her sooner, could we have prevented this disaster?

I settle on my bed, and drop my head into my hands.

Of all the threatening scenarios my sister and I have imagined through the years, this isn't one of them: Glynna falling in love with Tati's grandson. We should have left Spokane years ago. But I couldn't leave Nicolas.

I gaze into the mirror across the room. Loving scenes shared between me and Nicolas play out like a movie. Witnessing the past with clarity is one of my powers, and for the first time in years, I indulge these memories. Each moment is tender. We were so young and sincere and naive.

50

I click off the images.

How foolish I've been, and how selfish! I'm always living with the hope that someday—someday what?

For almost a decade, I baked every kind of pie I could think of to break Tatiana's spell.

A new scene flickers in the mirror.

Tatiana arrives at my front door, pie box in hand. There was no bakery, no Frosting & Beans back then. Just me, practically living in the kitchen of my apartment. She doesn't wait before she unsheathes her claws. "Pearl, stop sending your stupid pies to Nicolas!"

My mask of innocence is hardly convincing.

Tatiana pushes past me and sweeps into my living room. She sets the pie box on the bar. "If I find out one more client has gifted Bass Enterprises with one of your pies, or if another event caterer serves this slop—"

I thought I'd been rather clever. Reading The Spokesman-Review daily, searching for articles of every business deal Nicolas closed, and keeping a list of his clients. The catering service had been Ophelia's idea. Tatiana pulls the pie tin from the box. Melting chocolate and drooping whip cream slosh across the cheap Formica counter.

"—at one of his luncheons or dinners, someone you love is going to suffer. Do you understand me?"

"Is being married to a man that abhors you starting to wear on you, Tati?"

"Nicolas loves me."

"Is that what you tell yourself?"

"He's a devoted father and husband."

I walk around the counter. Tatiana towers over me. "Only because you've bound his heart with black magic."

Tatiana laughs. "And yet, all your pies have been useless in breaking the power of those bonds."

"Because you won't let him eat any of them." I'm guessing, but I hold up my index finger. "Not even a taste." Unfortunately, Tatiana works by Nicolas' side as his administrative assistant, making sure nothing and no one she doesn't approve of approaches him.

"You're right. I won't. So stop sending them."

51

I hardly look persuaded. "Love endures. It's indestructible." Conviction punctuates every word. I touch my lips as I marvel at my passionate declaration. Tatiana's brow furrows. In the mirror, I can actually see the shadow of dark emotion roll off her. But I'm glowing, and my glow repels her darkness. "What are you afraid of, Tati?"

"Don't provoke me, or you'll find out what I'm capable of."

I truly think I have nothing else to lose. "What could be worse than stealing my future with the man I love?"

"Pearl, I vow to you, I will kill him before I let you have him."

I couldn't be responsible for Nicolas' death, and I believed Tati would follow through with her threat. So I stopped sending the pies.

The image recedes as my heart crumples. Ophelia and I have to do something. We can't let Glynna and Ashton do this. But what if she loves him? Am I going to destroy her life? The same way Tatiana destroyed mine?

GLYNNA

When I get back inside, Ophelia is already gone—thank the God of Cupcakes she runs errands every Saturday, and nothing short of the apocalypse could throw off her routine. She's the last person I want to run into right now.

I don't bother searching for Nana on the first floor, I can sense she's not there. I head upstairs. Nana's bedroom is at the end of the hall. The door is closed. I tiptoe toward it and squeeze my eyes shut when I hear her weeping. I can't just leave her here alone when I don't even understand what is wrong with her.

I stretch the sleeve of my T-shirt over my knuckles and rap against the door. The crying stops. "Nana?"

"I'm fine, darling."

Like hell she's fine. I crack open the door. She's rubbing her face with a tissue. Kleenex is making mint off the Balcora family this morning.

52

Nana gives me a weak smile. I go sit beside her. "Do you know Ashton's grandmother?"

She nods. "I really don't want to talk about it this morning." Her nails graze my forehead as she brushes stray strands of hair from my face. "You said this boy calms you down."

"I'm sure it was just my crazy imagination," I say. "I mean, it's a crazy idea isn't it?"

Nana studies me. "Maybe, we should head over to Frostings & Beans. It has been a long time since we've baked together on a Saturday, and I think it would do us both a world of good."

"Sure." I'm not going to argue or press her when she's in this teary condition that I've never seen her in before.

"We've talked about so many sad things this morning. Maybe I can tell you about Nicolas another day."

My heart sparks at the thought of her confiding in me. I can be patient until she's ready to talk. In the meantime, she's right, baking will be our best distraction.

I look down at my scuffed flats. The bakery will be packed on Saturday, especially if Nana and I both start cooking. The smell of her pies and my cupcakes draw in hordes.

"Let me go put on a dress," I say.

6. What's on the Menu? Jitters and Cupcakes!

 SHTON

I slide into the passenger seat of my grandpa's Subaru Forester. Although Grandma gets a new Cadillac every year, Grandpa is against ostentatious displays of wealth, and limits the amount of money he'll spend on his own vehicle. I can't decide if it's a noble or ridiculous stance. Grandma assures me it's ridiculous. At least the Forester has leather seats.

"Where to?" he asks.

He's been acting strange since he showed up at Burgundy's. Grandma and Lorriene noticed it too. Usually, he's absentminded, and you have to ask him a question three times to get an answer. But not this afternoon. At lunch he didn't miss a beat in the conversation. He even joked with the wait staff. I'm trying to remember if I've ever seen him like this, and I can't remember a single time in my entire twenty-one years when I've seen him this chipper or present.

"Where to?" he asks again.

For all I care, he could take me to the dentist. I'm just thrilled to have been rescued from the ladies. "The office?"

"Not today." He taps the steering wheel. "What did you think of that thunderstorm earlier today?"

"Kind of cool, the way it just blew in and blew out."

Grandpa rubs his chest. "It stirred up something inside me."

I'm not sure what to say.

He smiles at me. I have to tell you, my grandpa is a handsome man. Like Grandma, he takes care of himself. He doesn't pack an ounce of extra weight, and even though he's gray, he's got a thick, full head of hair. And when he smiles, all the ladies within a five-mile radius melt. It has been a while since I've seen that smile.

"Let's go down to Perry Street," he says.

He used to take me and Lorriene down there every Saturday for pancakes, but it has been years. "Sure, Grandpa, if that's where you want to go."

"How does a cupcake sound?"

Fate, fortune, and coincidence have just made a strange intersection in my life. "A cupcake?"

"I was at a client's yesterday afternoon for a lunch meeting. After we finished eating, this young gal brings in a tray of cupcakes. Now, I usually never touch that stuff." He pats his flat belly. "But it was the damnedest thing. When she offered me one, I couldn't say no. Since then, all I can think about is having another one." He whips out his iPhone and flashes the screen at me. Maps is up with directions to Frosting & Beans. "Have you ever been there?" he asks.

After what happened between me and Glynna last night, and after what Tatiana told us about Glynna's grandmother earlier, I'm totally freaked out. "Yes, but it's probably been more than ten years."

He starts the Subaru's engine. "That's way too long."

Perry Street is Spokane's answer to an eclectic art district, sans the galleries and museums. It's a windy little stretch with colorful shops and boutiques, trendy restaurants and bars. As my grandpa drives past the buildings, I realize Lorien's—a health food store named after the forest in the *Lord of the Rings* (not my kid sister!) and located in a building which

56

is a replica of a windmill–and Frosting & Beans are the oldest establishments along the several blocks which make up the district.

This afternoon the streets and sidewalk tables are packed. My heart pounds in my chest as Grandpa searches for a parking space. I've started sweating. I never sweat unless I'm engaged in serious physical exertion. I drag my hand across my slick brow. This is disgusting. The AC is on and it's not even 70 degrees outside.

A strange fear crawls up the back of my neck. I feel like I'm facing down an unruly crowd in a sold-out amphitheater that expects me to sing a rock anthem and I've forgotten the lyrics! God! I don't even know how to fucking sing! I start to feel like I'm going to get a second look at my lunch.

"Ashton?"

I'm bent over in half, staring at the WeatherTech floor liner. Grandpa is hunched over too, his hand on my shoulder. "Are you all right?"

"Just–" I hold up a finger. "–give me a sec."

"You sure?" He's already dialing in the blue tooth connection from the steering wheel.

The last thing I need is an ambulance ride. I wave my hand.

He hesitates.

"Indigestion," I manage.

It's Glynna. The mere thought of seeing her is making me freaking nervous. What is she going to do when she sees me? I imagine her jumping over the bakery counter, *Matrix*-style, and kicking me in the face. Or maybe she'll just turn total Ice Queen and freeze me out without a glance or a word. None of the scenarios I come up with have a happy ending. Maybe I can wait outside while Grandpa appeases his cupcake fix.

"Ashton?"

I force myself to straighten and give him the Bass smile.

The panic-stricken expression melts from his face.

"Maybe I had a little too much to drink last night."

He whacks me on the back. "That's what youth is for! You won't be able to get away with that when you're my age, so enjoy it while you can."

Despite his regimented approach to his own life–he didn't even take a sip from the drink Grandma ordered over his protests–Grandpa's never

57

been a disciplinarian when it comes to me or Lorriene. At the moment, I'm grateful I don't have to stretch for more of an explanation to offer him, because the thought of Glynna's milky skin and her luminous blue eyes derails my thoughts. In my mind, my alter ago is an edgy, hip version of a Super Hero who doesn't bother saving anyone, but he always gets his girl. And I always get mine.

But not every girl can throw a punch like Glynna! Now I imagine her sailing through the air, pulling her *Crouching Tiger, Hidden Dragon* moves on me. I rub my cheekbone. I still can't believe she knocked me out. It had to be a coincidence. The tequila must have kicked in the second her fist connected with my face, just like Lorriene said.

But what about that addictive cupcake kiss?

Pull yourself together, Ashton. It's not like you're going to ask her out. Are you? Actually, I freaking want to! I glance sideways at Grandpa as he finishes parking the SUV. Asking a girl out with Pap Pap as my chaperone doesn't make my top ten list of romantic moves.

"Nervous, my boy?" Grandpa cuts off the engine. His blue eyes twinkle with a knowing smirk. Did he sneak in a secret trip to Grandma's on-speed-dial plastic surgeon or is he just looking exceptionally younger without the aid of chemical peels and collagen injections?

"Uhmm. Nope. Why should I be nervous?" My voice sounds more defensive than I intend it to.

Grandpa chuckles. "Is this about Pearl's little girl?"

"Pearl?"

"The woman who owns the bakery. Doesn't she have a granddaughter?"

Does he know Glynna? I can't remember if we were still talking about the Balcoras when he got to the table at Burgundy's. Still, he's making me sound like some kind of pervert getting all twisted up about a toddler. It's unexpected, coming from him. "Glynna is not a little girl anymore. She's nineteen!"

"Oh, that's right. She's all grown up now!"

Then I realize he's teasing me—and doing a great job of it. I encourage him to keep going, because I'm starting to relax. I love seeing Grandpa in this carefree mood.

I grin sheepishly as I unbuckle my seat belt. "Aww. Come on, Pap

58

Pap!"

Grandpa gives a hearty laugh. "So, what are we waiting for? Why don't you show your Pap Pap your winning moves?" He winks as he pats my shoulder. "Let's go meet your conquest, and have one of those famous cupcakes."

"Or do you just wanna see Pearl?" I'm hoping to get a little something from him, because I can't forget how Grandma reacted when the Balcora's name was brought up at lunch.

Grandpa falls silent. He doesn't answer my question, doesn't even acknowledge it. He opens the car door as if I'm not even there and heads toward the bakery.

I have to hurry to catch up with him.

The breeze is gentle and the air fresh. I inhale deeply. You never get this stuff in Boston; only in the Pacific Northwest. It's almost two o'clock, and soft rays from the June sun are filtering through the tallest trees and buildings. When the wind shifts, that mouthwatering, comforting scent of baked goodies hits me, calling out to all my senses.

We're about half-a-block from Frosting & Beans when I spot her through the crowd. She's framed in the wide rectangular window which opens to the bakery's outsider counter. It's like there's a halo of light around that tumble of awesome red hair. It's so glossy and shiny; she could be in a shampoo commercial. She's leaning across the counter, smiling as she hands a beaming young boy a chocolate cupcake. The boy's dad is scrounging in his pocket, but his eyes are locked on my girl.

My girl? Aren't we moving a little fast here, Bass Man?

The dad and young boy have been replaced at the counter by three young punks. Their tattoo sleeves shake me from my daydreams and remind me how un-edgy and un-inked I truly am. The temperature of my blood flashes from simmer to boiling. They're ogling her, leering at her.

I speed up.

The closer I get to her, the more breathtaking she appears. She twists her hair into a bun at the nape of her neck and stabs it with a pen to hold it in place. A few loose strands escape, flying in the gentle wind, and framing her perfect porcelain skin. I just want to touch her. I can't believe where my mind is going. I haven't even apologized for last night.

59

I don't even know if she's going to talk to me. Plus these wanna-be gang members are crowding around the counter. I have to bob and weave to keep her in my sights.

She's laughing with one of them. My teeth grind. I catch snippets of Spanish.

"Que linda."

Blush. Blush. *"Gracias."*

"De nada, Senorita."

I want to pound the guy's head in with my fist, but I hold off, waiting, hoping he'll cross the threshold of legal provocation to justify a full-on physical assault. Unfortunately, he doesn't. But his two friends' eyes dart everywhere, like they're casing the joint, and assessing Glynna as a target.

A bad vibe surrounds them, so I stop moving and glare. At 6'3", my presence alone can be menacing, and these guys are all under six feet. I want them gone.

"I'm going to step inside," Grandpa says.

"I'll wait here," I mumble, never taking my eyes off Tattoo Trio. By now, they're aware of me glowering at them, and attitude is rolling off them in waves. I take a few steps closer.

NICOLAS

My heart sinks when I step inside the shop and see the young man standing behind the counter. Did I think this was going to be a scene from a movie? I'd walk in, Pearl would greet me, and I'd gallantly sweep her off her feet?

Truly, I've lost my mind.

The young man intrudes on my ruminations. "Can I help you?"

The smell of freshly ground coffee wafts across the bakery. Perhaps, I'll have an espresso while I wait for Ashton. "A double, please."

"Anything to go with that?"

The display cases, filled with enticing treats, promise it will be

60

challenging to order just one of anything. "In a bit. I'm waiting for someone."

"Gotcha," the young man says. "If you want to take a seat wherever you'd like, I can bring your drink to your table."

I turn and the bakery's cheery, colorful interior demands my attention. It's as if I've crossed a threshold and entered a special world where happiness is the only thing that's real. There are two couples and a young family scattered at three different tables. Both couples appear transfixed by a golden haze of love. They gaze at the person sitting across from them as if no one else exists in the world. The sight fills me with longing for my youth. For my Pearl?

What has gotten into me today?

I aim for the booth in the corner. Maybe the caffeine will clear my head, because I've been feeling ridiculously dreamy since those rain showers earlier. I pass the cheerful young family on my way to the table. The boy and girl are laughing and it's infectious. Their parents, hands clasped, smile at me when I join their children's joy with a hearty laugh of my own.

It has been far too long since I've come down to Perry Street.

I glimpse Ashton through the windows. He must be waiting to talk to the girl. Young lady, I correct myself. The red-haired beauty at the outside counter was hard to miss. If that's Pearl's granddaughter, my grandson's got impeccable taste.

The young man delivers my espresso. It's the most delicious cup of coffee I've ever had.

ASHTON

"Hey, the end of the line is back there," some lady shouts, presumably at me.

But I'm staring one of the guys down, and I'm not going to be the one to break eye contact. "I'm not in line to get a cupcake," I growl.

61

"What are you looking at?" The guy I'm having a staring contest with challenges me. His voice is soft, but menacing. No one besides me can hear it.

I shake my head, refusing to let him bait me.

He raises his chin and sneers. I jam my hands into my pockets. It's the only way I can keep myself from grabbing him by the ears and slamming his head against the pavement. He jabs his friend with his elbow, and says, *"Mira él,"* while he tips his head in my direction. The second guy fans out to my other side. Not a good situation for me if they decide to pull some crap.

I snap my head back and forth, doing my best to keep an eye on both of them.

They back away in unison, making gang symbols with their hands.

I twist my torso, following them with my eyes. A shoulder slams into my back. The guy who bought the cupcake. He ducks and tears out running before I can grab him. When he catches up with his friends, they bust out laughing.

I weigh my options. There's not many now that they're retreating, but it's hard to shake the bad feelings they leave in their wake.

There's something unusual about that crew.

When I turn back around, Glynna's disappeared. My heart dive-bombs my stomach. Where did she go? Her cousin, Leif, is helping the customers. His shoulder-length, dirty-blond hair is pulled into a pony tail, and he's wearing a pair of glasses that are as thick as the bottom of two old Coke bottles. He's not bulky, but his biceps and forearms are well-defined. I hope he wasn't at the party last night. I don't remember seeing him. He's kind of a computer geek, so parties are probably beneath him.

I scan the street one more time to make sure the hoods haven't returned. I don't see any sign of them. Maybe the guy just wanted a cupcake, and I overreacted, seeing him flirting with my girl.

I'm afraid the Bass Man has it bad. I shrug off my own amazement and head for the bakery's front door, praying Glynna's inside.

62

Nana's French Silk Pie Recipe

Ingredients:

1 of Pearl's Perfect Pie Crusts

$\frac{1}{3}$ cup sugar

2 large eggs

2 ounces unsweetened chocolate, melted

1 teaspoon vanilla extract

$\frac{1}{3}$ cup butter, softened

2 teaspoons confectioners sugar

1 $\frac{2}{3}$ cups fresh homemade whipping cream

14 petals from Nana's mystical red rose garden

2 teaspoons raindrops collected beneath the first full moon in June

Reserve 1 cup whip cream. Gradually combine other ingredients while believing your dreams will come true. Fill the pie crust, and top with reserved whipped cream.

7. Thank You, Klutzy Kupcake!

GLYNNA

It feels good to splash cold water on my cheeks and forehead. I blot the excess with a paper towel, then examine my face in the mirror.

Does Nana have any pictures of my mother? I need to ask her.

One thing's for sure: I haven't had time to absorb everything she and Ophelia told me this morning, although their stories about Luminas and Occultos seem to have fired up my overactive imagination. It's on hyperdrive.

The last customer really shook me up. When his fingers brushed mine as I gave him his change, I received a shadowy premonition of—what?

I toss the paper towel into the trash can.

Leif can handle the rush at the outside counter for a while. I wouldn't mind tidying up the shop. When things are hectic the displays get messy, and I doubt anyone's had time to wipe down the tables in the past couple of hours.

As I pass by the kitchen doors, I get a whiff of heavenly chocolate. Nana must be whipping up something special. I wish I was hiding out in the kitchen with her, baking like we'd planned, but the regular girls who help out on Saturdays are at band camp this weekend.

65

I'm not sure how Leif handled everything before we got here. I'm almost tempted to text Ophelia to come help. I am her boss! A giggle slips out. Probably best not to rub it in. But it's still hard to believe I own Frosting & Beans. My gaze sweeps the sparkling glass display cases, arched built-in shelves, and round booths. The place looks fantastic. We renovated the entire shop last summer, and the results are better than I'd hoped for. Lots of soft, creamy pinks, light lemony yellows, and glistening whites give the whole place a light-filled ambience, cheerful and inviting. Business is up.

My heart swells with pride. I've put everything I have into the bakery since I could spin an oven dial to 350 degrees, and now it's all mine. The soft joy in my heart explodes into tender gratitude and appreciation for Nana, Ophelia, and Leif. They've helped me create this magical place with their blood, sweat, and tears, too. Frosting & Beans belongs to all of us, and I'm going to have to see what I can do about making sure the ownership reflects that.

Before I start straightening things up, I survey the shop to make sure everyone has been served, and notice an older gentleman sitting in the circular booth in the corner, all alone. I go to retrieve his empty espresso cup. "You're much too handsome to be out on a day like today without company. Waiting for someone?"

His blue eyes twinkle. "As a matter of fact—"

Ding! The chime over the shop's front door goes off.

I can't believe what I'm seeing: Ashton Bass, framed in the afternoon sunlight, looking especially stunning!

And I'm the one stunned!

If he wasn't staring at me, I'd pinch myself. My heart races as I'm magnetically drawn across the bakery. I stumble a little and accidentally knock a few of my favorite pink pens off the display counter.

Really? How can I stumble in flats?

This is bad. Just bad.

Ashton to the rescue. He dives to catch the silly pink projectiles flying through the air! They've sprung to life with a mind of their own and are determined to make me look like a klutz in front of the guy of my dreams!

Evil felt tips! I can't let them win.

66

I lunge forward to grab them myself. The awkward moment becomes even more precarious when my hand collides with his, I lose my balance, tilt forward, and Ashton has to grab my forearms to keep me from doing a face plant in his crotch.

"Uh, sorry about that," I say.

Heat creeps up my face when I shift back onto my heels and my butt grazes the floor—I forgot I'm wearing a dress—not my skinny jeans. My knees are about a foot apart. I'm sure he can see my panties. I push myself forward, and my knees smack against the hardwood floor with a bang.

Ashton's perfect features skew with concern. He still looks amazing. "Are you all right?"

I pretend that I'm not going to have black and blue knees for the rest of the year. "Yeah, yeah, I'm fine." I wave my hand.

Ashton corrals my demon-possessed pens and stands up. He extends a hand. I begrudgingly offer mine, and he pulls me up. Then he doesn't let go. I tug. But he just holds onto my hand and flips it over to examine my knuckles. They're still a little swollen. His gaze shifts from my hand to my face. I can only imagine that my cheeks now match the lovely Salmon Pink shade of my dress.

He finally lets go of my hand. "I'm sorry."

My blood begins to boil as I remember the sound of his friends laughing.

The handsome man waiting at the table alone comes up behind Ashton and clamps his hands on his shoulder. "Is this Pearl's granddaughter?"

"Yes."

Who is this man? And why is he calling Nana *Pearl?*

"Grandpa, this is Glynna. Glynna, this is my grandfather, Nicolas Bass."

It feels like one of my pink pens has gotten lodged in my throat. Nicolas Bass? What is he doing—today of all days—at Frosting & Beans. Nana is going to be finished baking any minute.

Nicolas holds out his hand. "Has anyone ever told you that you bake the most delicious cupcakes in the world?"

Actually, they have, but the way he says it is so charming; my fear for Nana melts away like glazed icing. I hold out hope that we can restart this

67

encounter. "Uhhh, good afternoon, Mr. Bass. Ashton." I smooth my pink floral apron. "What can I get you today?"

"I believe Ashton has already found what he'd like," Mr. Bass says.

Is that a teasing tone?

Ashton shifts uncomfortably and runs his fingers through his soft brown hair. An uncontrollable grin curves my lips upwards. I was just imagining running my fingers through that soft brown hair myself!

God of Cupcakes! His smile makes my insides mix like a batter of eggs, sugar, butter, flour, and chocolate!

Zap. Awareness strikes. If Ashton's grandfather adores me and my cupcakes, then maybe it's not too much to hope that his wife can approve of me too! I'm feeling inspired as I move past Ashton. He smells good. I pause to savor the clean, citrusy scent.

Enough daydreaming! I charge the display counter. "This way, Mr. Bass."

"Oh, please call me Nicolas, my dear."

I open my mouth to tell him about our specials for today—when Nana appears with a fresh whipped cream-covered French Silk Pie. I scrub the benefits of that particular topping according to Kristeen from my mind. The energy between Mr. Bass and Nana is so intense I glance out the front window searching for fireworks.

Nothing but Leif and a long line of customers.

Not even a sparkler even though the magic in the air is palpable.

"Nicolas," Nana says in a voice that makes me breathless with anticipation.

"Pearl."

The way he caresses her name leaves no mystery as to where Ashton inherited his charm. Everything in the shop seems to stop as the unspoken silence between Nana and Nicolas stretches and stretches.

Is it longing? Regret? What is it?

I catch Ashton observing them with equal interest. Then he glances at me with a glint of mischievousness in his eyes. "So, your grandmother and my grandfather, huh?" His voice has the same slight teasing sound his grandfather's did a few minutes ago.

"I, uhmm, not sure."

Nana sets the fresh pie down on the counter. She pulls out a cardboard

68

box, folds the sides, and slips the French Silk decadence inside. When she bends over to get the lid, she slides her hand down her slim hip.

The easy back-and-forth banter between her and Nicolas never hits pause.

It's like they know each other! In the Biblical sense! Is Nana having an affair with Nicolas Bass?

She reaches for another cardboard box, and folds it with such care, as if her hands are dancing. She's tipping her chin, her eyelashes flutter. She's flirting with him!

I imagine the hellish fury of his scorned wife! He points at the cupcakes in the case, choosing. Nana fills the box in her hand. When she's finished, she stacks the box of cupcakes on top of the pie and slides everything toward him. She's glowing.

I resist the urge to yank her by her apron strings and drag her right back into the kitchen. Does she realize what a spectacle she's making of herself; with a married man?

He is married, isn't he? I strain to see if he's wearing a wedding band, but his hand is in his pocket.

Nana and Nicolas are so into each other, they don't even notice me, or Ashton, or the rest of the shop patrons staring at them. Some of the customers outside are peering through the glass.

I fear Nicolas' wife won't be as charming as her husband. Maybe she died. Maybe it was tragic, like cancer.

. No, that would have been on the news, and I've heard nothing.

My eyes flick to the corners of the store ceilings. The very corners where the security company insisted that we install cameras. Thank the Cupcake Gods that I refused. The incriminating evidence of Nana's brazen, shameless, wanton flirtation with the powerful, career-building/career-ending CEO of Bass Enterprises would be captured on DVD and buried in some high-tech labyrinth to be used against me until the day I die.

"Now, look at that!" Ashton whistles softly. "I think Grandpa is a little smitten with your Nana." He flashes that lopsided grin.

Isn't he taking the whole thing in stride?

"Or is it just her pie?" He winks.

Nana's pie? Uh, why does that sound like...? Eeeew!

69

Time to interrupt them, make everyone stop watching!

I take a step back and smash Ashton's foot with my heel. He winces as I cover my hands with my mouth. Holy cupcakes! This is going from bad to worse. "I'm so sorry!"

He reaches out his hands to steady me.

We're standing so close, I can smell his inviting masculine scent again. Did I just take a big whiff? Apparently, when I'm near him, there is no end to the ways I can embarrass myself. Thankfully, he seems to have something else on his mind and hasn't noticed my infatuation with his aphrodisiac aroma.

"Glynna, about last night."

Is he talking about the kiss?

The Nana and Nicolas Crisis unfolding three feet from where we're standing slips from my mind. I glance up at those tempting blue eyes and notice the bruise on the side of his face. Forgive me, Cupcake Gods! I really punched him. As if on autopilot, I reach up and touch his cheek. "I'm so sorry. Does it hurt?" I ask him.

He covers my hand, which is still against his face, with his hand. His stubble tickles my fingers as he gently runs my hand over his cheek. A bolt of electricity races down my spine.

"Well, maybe my pride." He flashes his boyish smile. "I should be the one apologizing, Glynna. I was an ass. Must have been the booze. I'm really sorry."

"Uhh, okay, sure." I attempt to pull my sweaty hand from his.

Did the temperature in Frosting & Beans suddenly rise a little? Maybe Nana left the oven on high.

"So, I was thinking of inviting you out." Ashton has 200% of my attention. "Would you like to go to brunch tomorrow?"

I'm trying to get a word out. One. Single. Word.

"I can pick you up at eleven."

I finally manage a breathless, "Okay."

Is that all I can say? Still tongue-tied and breathless, I stare at him with what I'm sure is the same stupid goo-goo-eyed look he's seen on a thousand other girls' faces.

"So, are we done here, Casanova?" Nicolas Bass asks.

How long has he been standing there?

"Or do you need my assistance in convincing this fine young lady to spend an afternoon with you?" Nicolas winks at me.

Did Ashton just blush?

"Nope, we're good. Ready to go, Grandpa?" Ashton looks a little tense. Maybe he finally remembered his grandmother! "I'll see you tomorrow, Glynna." He gives me one last thousand-watt smile before heading out the door.

Ding! They're gone.

My knees weaken and I slump over the nearest booth. I cannot believe he asked me out for brunch. Why does it feel so huge, like he was asking me to marry him? I can't wait to tell Kristeen about this! She's going to flip out.

I make a slow circle. Nana is singing as she rearranges the cupcakes in the case.

"Nana, or should I say Pearl?"

"What, darling?" she asks, oh-so-innocently.

"Mr. Bass is married."

"I know, but it was so nice to see him. It's been so long." She puffs her hair as she gazes into the mirror behind the counter. "Maybe I should make an appointment at Roots next week, freshen up my color."

"Are you going to see him again?"

Nana laughs and rests her hand on my shoulder. "I doubt it. But—" She pauses.

I'm hanging in suspense. "But what, Nana?"

"Seeing him this afternoon made me feel young again."

What a relief! She's not having an affair with Ashton's grandfather. And then I remember: I have a date with Ashton Bass tomorrow! I glance at the clock above the cash register. We had it especially designed for us. It's a pie in a pie tin—the pie between 6 o'clock and 10 o'clock has been eaten. It's 3:30 pm. I've never had a more momentous day in my life. I peek over at Leif, who is still manning the outside counter. He's making a couple of lattes. The espresso machine is hissing as he froths the milk. I still can't see the end of the line.

"I guess it wouldn't be fair to leave Leif alone for the rest of the day, would it?" I ask.

Nana pats my hand. "Run along, Glynna. I'll stay and help Leif close

71

up. Maybe I'll call Ophelia. It's been a long time since we've gone out to eat dinner together."

I'm torn. I want to know more about Nana and Nicolas Bass, but I have a perfect pair of sandals to wear on my date tomorrow, and they'll look so much prettier if I get that Blush pedicure. Roots closes the same time we do on Saturdays.

I squeeze Nana in a tight hug. "I'll be back in half-an-hour. I'd love to go to dinner with you and Ophelia, too." My genuine response surprises me. I take off my apron, stash it beneath the register, and grab my phone. You can bet I'm going to be texting Kristeen while I get my pedicure.

8. Cupcake... Take My Breath Away!

SHTON

"Pap Pap, you've been holding out on me!" I slide the Frosting & Beans boxes into the back of the Subaru. The boxes—the lightest shade of pink—make me think of Glynna. If I had to guess, pink is her favorite color. Today she had on a pink sleeveless dress beneath her pink apron. A real dress. Not a ridiculous look-at-my-cheeks-and-weep scrap of fashion. I'm trying to remember the last time I've seen a girl my age wearing a dress that reached her knees. It made her look like such a lady. Wait a minute. Is she old-fashioned? Maybe that's why she punched me last night. Defending her honor and all. She had a point. I went up and planted one on her, and I'd never even asked her out. I've never even called her! My buddies spectating and hackling like a pack of hyenas probably didn't help.

I rub the back of my neck. The Bass Man definitely needs to work on his smooth moves. Maybe I'll tap Grandpa. He was certainly spry with Pearl this afternoon. A subject about which he's being evasive.

"Not much to tell," Grandpa yells over his shoulder.

I round to the passenger's door, determined to get some actionable information before we get home.

73

"Did you and Grandma double date Pearl and her husband?"

Grandpa shakes his head. "Pearl never got married."

That isn't good news. "But she's Glynna's grandmother." The comment comes out raspy. If Pearl had Glynna's mother—or father—with a baby daddy and not a husband; I do *not* want to have that conversation with Grandma.

"So how do you and Grandma know Pearl?" I need to get to the bottom of this. I've got to find a way to win Grandma over, get her off Daphne and onto Glynna. Otherwise she might disinherit me when things get serious. Whoa! Bass Man! Weren't you, just this morning, fighting for another decade to sow your wild oats? But it's hard to imagine wanting someone else after those luscious cupcake kisses, and who knows what else she's got tucked away in that silky creamy package of scrumptiousness.

"Maybe we shouldn't mention our visit to Frosting & Beans to your grandmother. It might make her upset."

"Why?"

"Tatiana and Pearl have history."

My heart thumps in my ears. This is what I want to hear. "What kind of history?"

Grandpa tilts his head. "Let's just say they were never friends, and it didn't end well."

That doesn't sound good. "Were you and Pearl friends?"

"A long, long time ago."

"Are you still friends?"

"To be honest, I really never think about her anymore."

"Uh-huh."

"But there was something about that cupcake yesterday, and the thunderstorm today. I had to see her." He shakes his head. "It doesn't make sense, not even to me. But I'm glad we went. It was wonderful to see her. And I've decided that I'm going to enjoy her French Silk Pie." His eyes are twinkling again.

The question catches in my throat, but I have to ask it. "Pap Pap, were you ever in love with Pearl?"

He scratches his head. "I don't think so, but to tell you the truth, I honestly can't remember."

74

This conversation is getting stranger by the minute.

"But don't mention any of this to your grandmother," he says. "It's such a small thing. No need upsetting her; it might put her in a temper."

Tatiana's temper is definitely something that is best avoided.

The next morning, I'm trying to decide between Bermuda shorts and a pair of washed-out jeans, when Lorriene flounces into my bedroom wearing less than she had on yesterday. Much less.

"Just take on the world naked, why don't you?" I say.

"Did you see RiRi working the CFDA red carpet in that see-thru number? I might have to make a similar fashion statement at prom."

She's wearing a string bikini and flip flops, and when she twirls, there is no butt coverage.

"Come on, Lorriene, you're not seriously going out in public in that shoestring, are you?"

"No, chivalrous brother. Hanging out by the pool. Maddie and Daphne will be here in a few." She whips her phone out from her bikini bottom and starts texting.

I'm surprised the string can hold up five ounces.

"You missed a great party last night," she says.

"Looks like I survived."

"Hang out with us. We've got Tecate, lime slices, corn chips and your favorite fresh-made salsa from Santee." The snacks sound good, but the company doesn't.

"Not today, sis."

All of a sudden she notices my hands are full. "And where are you going?"

Damn! I haven't come up with a cover yet. "Me and Tyler are gonna hit some links."

Her Cheshire grin makes me nervous. "Really?"

"Uh-huh."

"You're such a bad liar!"

"What?" Do I really need to explain myself to her? Yes, if I don't want to be bombarded with more questions. My little sister makes Sherlock Holmes look like an amateur.

"Tyler's got a massive hangover."

75

"How do you know?"

She flashes her phone.

See my point? Tyler was my best friend in high school and kind of a fuck-up. He's the only one in our group who didn't make it into the Ivy League. Hell, who am I to judge? Tyler's dad is richer than God—and self-made. Tyler's determined to follow in his old man's footsteps, so he stayed in town and went to work for his dad's construction company. He and Lorriene have gotten tight while I've been away at Harvard. Not sure how that one slipped by Grandma. Maybe I should mention it to her. Because it's not working for me.

"So?" she prods.

"I'm going to brunch."

"With who?" She grabs the jeans. "Wear the Bermudas. They show off your calves."

I roll my eyes, even though I know she's right, and I was leaning in that direction.

"It's a date!" She squeals. Then her whole face drops. "What am I going to tell Daphne?"

"Tell Daphne I'm not ever going to date her. Not even if the Seahawks win the Super Bowl again."

"Ass-ish!" That's her pet name for me. "You are so rude! Who are you taking out?"

"You don't know her."

"I know every date-worthy chick in this town."

I wave my hand. "Get out. I need to get dressed."

She crosses her arms over her chest. "Unless you wanna drop your pants in front of me, tell me her name."

It's hopeless. "Glynna."

"Glynna Balcora? You're taking Glynna Balcora out to brunch?"

"Key point: Out To Brunch. We're not eloping."

"Wow. Didn't realize you were into slumming."

"That's enough, Lorriene."

She nods. "I get it. That's why you're not ready to commit to Daphne, still sampling the buffet. Well, enjoy that sweet piece of ass!"

I grab her shoulders and start shoving her out of my room. "Glynna is not a piece of ass!"

"Get your hands off me, Ashton Bass," she screams.

"Then clean up your mouth and put on some clothes!"

"You really piss me off sometimes!" she shouts back.

"I'm not your fucking lap dog, Lorriene!"

She straightens the string on her bikini. "Wait until *Grand-mère* hears about this," she hisses. I slam my bedroom door in her face. "You better not be late to dinner tonight," she yells from the other side.

Damn. It's Sunday. The family dinner completely slipped my mind. Tatiana will be unforgiving if I miss the first one since I've gotten back from Boston.

I open my door. Lorriene is on the other side, waiting. Could she look more smug?

It's not unusual for me and my sister to break out in screaming matches. We have our own wing of the house, and unless we get crazy loud, our parents and grandparents can't hear us.

"What time is dinner?" I ask.

"Seven sharp. Be there, or bear the brunt of Grandma's wrath."

Her butt swings to the rhythmic flap of her flip-flops as she struts down the hall.

I stand in front of our six-car-garage. Grandpa's Subaru is already gone. I'm disappointed, because it would probably have been my best choice. Glynna strikes me as the kind of girl who's not impressed with a flashy ride. My guess is she's more into simple, fuss-free, and practical.

Not that I don't want to impress her. I really do.

Bass Man, what's with the jitters? Pick a car. It's only brunch!

My dilemma makes clear how little I know about my Cupcake Girl. But the Bass Man is going to remedy that, starting today.

Mom's Range Rover is overkill. So is Grandma's new Cadillac. And forget Dad's Aston-Martin. It's between Lorriene's Beamer and my sweet, old school Firebird.

As far as I'm concerned, it's the sexiest car we've got. Grandpa gave it to me for my sixteenth birthday. He bought one of the first Firebirds himself, years ago, when he got his first big real estate commission check, so it's not just a set of wheels. It's a bit of nostalgia, and a connection between me and Pap Pap.

77

The Firebird it is.

The driving beat of Meghan Trainor's *All About the Bass* grows louder behind me. I half-pivot and groan. The Wardof sister's candy-apple Porsche is heading up the driveway. Damn! The last thing I need right now is an encounter with Octopus Woman. I practically sprint toward the security kiosk.

"Ashton!" Daphne's high-pitched squeal soars over the bass-line.

I pretend I don't hear her and keep moving.

"Ashton!"

Could she squawk any louder?

I grab the Firebird's keys, offer Daphne and Maddie a concessionary wave, and make a beeline across the garage, head down. Staring at my Italian leather sandals, I wonder if I should have gone with the Converse All-Stars instead. Whoa. Bass man doesn't second-guess his wardrobe choices. What kind of spell has Cupcake Girl put on me?

The recognizable *tap-tap-tap* of a female navigating the driveway's gravel in spiked heels reaches my ears. I try to be optimistic. Maybe Lorriene changed her shoes before following me out here to make one final Glynna-dig. Or maybe she wants to apologize for being so nasty-catty.

That would be epic.

Sharp nails squeeze into my bicep.

"You're not leaving are you?" Daphne purrs like a starving 110-pound pussy cat. It's that ugly.

I will myself to attempt polite. "Uh-huh." I cough-chuckle as I throw her a side glance. She has not let go of my arm.

"But you'll be back soon? Right?" Somehow she's maneuvered her pint-size frame between me and the Firebird. Now, she's stroking my forearm with the tips of her nails. I'm guessing she's thinking this will turn me on or something. It's just irritating.

My impulse is to chop my hands up in the air, grab her shoulders, and shove her aside. I refrain. Just barely.

The Bass men are gentlemen. How many times has Grandpa drilled that into my head? I guess for moments like these when my Neanderthal impulses threaten civility.

"Nope, I'll probably be gone the rest of the day." God, I hope so. I

78

search for Maddie. She's practically mating with the Firebird's grill while balancing two full paper-bags and a six-pack. Shouldn't Daphne be helping her carry all that shit?

"Need some help, Maddie?" I ask.

Daphne's hands slide up my arms and squeeze. "Oh, you're such a doll, Ashton."

I don't clarify that I meant she should help her sister.

I swear she's pressing her pubic bone against my manhood. Thankfully, my manhood feels the same way about Daphne as I do: *Get this skank off me.*

I laugh out loud. I can't help it. She's being so over-the-top and ridiculous.

"What's so funny?"

She grabs my chin and forces me to look at her face. It's the first time I get a good look at her latest procedure, a Michael Jackson nose job. That thing could drill a hole in a brick wall. She raises and lowers her eyebrows suggestively.

I doubt she'll share my sense of humor. "Nothing's funny."

She presses her bubble gum breasts against my chest. "Don't leave." Then she blows up into my face.

The smell is rank. What has she been eating?

She does it again.

"God! Daphne."

"What?" Her voice is all panicky.

"Your breath."

She cups her hands over her mouth, blows into them, then takes a whiff with her pointy nose. Her eyes grow wide, and she yelps. "I'm so sorry, Ashton." She's sliding out from between me and the car, walking backwards, enormous blobs of water in her eyes. Maddie's eyes follow her sister. Daphne yanks the six-pack from Maddie's hand and tears across our driveway in the direction of the pool house. I'm always impressed in how fast those girls can move in those heels when they need to.

Maddie's head is swiveling between me and Daphne. "You okay?" she asks me.

"I'm good, but your sister seems upset."

"Yeah," Maddie says. "Where are you going?"

"Brunch. Maybe to the lake."

"A date?"

What's with the fucking inquisition? "Just a friend."

"A girlfriend?" Maddie asks.

"Shouldn't you check on your sister?"

"Who's the lucky girl?"

"You probably don't know her."

"Daphne's really into you," Maddie says.

No duh.

"Like if you were to take her out, she'd probably, you know, she'd probably want to make you really happy," she says.

"Maybe she needs to start with brushing her teeth." I can't believe I said that.

"What did you say?"

"Her breath is a little sour."

"Really?"

I shrug. "Maybe she needs to try some mints or some chewing gum."

"I'll tell her. You know she'd do anything for you, Ashton." She walks toward me, her enormous brown eyes growing huger by the second. "Anything. Do you understand what I'm saying? You wouldn't have to be careful with her. Daphne; she'd be very submissive with you."

Okay. I've got nothing to say to that. Time for me to go. "Running late."

Maddie steps away from the car, but I can feel her eyes watching me as I pull out and head down the driveway.

Those Wardof sisters are getting weirder every year.

TATIANA

"I'm so embarrassed, Tatiana," Daphne whines.

We're sitting in my study, with the door closed. I need to leave for

80

church in a few minutes. I hand her a tissue. "Nonsense. We all experience growing pains, darling."

"But if you'd seen the look on his face!"

"Don't worry about Ashton. I'll whip up a forgetfulness tincture this afternoon and place a few drops on his pillowcase before he gets home. By this time tomorrow, he won't remember a thing."

"Are you sure?"

"Yes, Daphne."

"I'm so sorry, Tatiana. I thought I was ready."

"Not to worry. I'm glad you've begun experimenting while we still have plenty of time. Love potions have always been tricky for Occultos to perfect. Now, tell me exactly how you prepared the spell."

She bites her lip.

"Sit down." I pat the chaise next to me. She needs to get this right. If I do it for her, I'll have to keep doing it for her. "It's best if witches learn to brew their own love potions. The first time was hard for me too. Take a deep breath, and walk me through your process step-by-step."

She recites the ingredients and the order in which she added everything to the cauldron. It sounds like she was meticulous. I can't find fault with any of it.

"It came to a boil rather quickly—"

"Oh, no, no, no! Daphne. Never boil an aphrodisiac."

"I thought," she stammers.

"Simmer! How much of it did you drink?"

"All of it?"

My laughter rings out. "No wonder your breath smells like you've been sucking on a dead toad for the past three months!"

Her eyes flash. "Is it really that bad?"

I'm laughing so hard, I have to wipe the tears from my eyes. "Worse."

"Is there an antidote?"

"Patience."

Her perfectly-shaped eyebrows knit.

"Time. You've just got to give it time to wear off."

"Great."

"It's called witchcraft for a reason. Not everyone is capable."

"Has Lorriene shown any signs?"

81

"Not yet." My abdomen tightens. It galls me that my cherished granddaughter hasn't exhibited a scintilla of Occulto power. But she's got a few more years. Ashton, not as many. "Oh, I haven't given up on either of them, yet. There are stories of great witches and warlocks who didn't come into their powers until the very last moment—on the very day of the twenty-fifth birthday." I sigh.

Daphne nods. "What about Ashton?"

"I confess, I still have dreams he'll grow into a powerful warlock."

"Do you like being married to someone who can't do magic?" Daphne asks.

Her question catches me off guard. "Nicolas may not be a warlock, but who can argue with his talent for business."

"So, I shouldn't worry if Ashton can't do magic?"

A small, tight marble of anger catches in my throat. "Are you saying you're unsure of my grandson as a mate?"

"Oh, no, Tatiana, never. I've wanted to be with Ashton ever since I can remember. I just wondered if there are any advantages to being the only witch in the family, or whether it gets lonely."

The anger in my throat expands. "Lonely? Do I seem lonely?"

"No. I mean. I just. I've heard."

"What have you heard?"

She digs through her purse, pulls out a cream-colored envelope, and hands it to me. "It's an invitation to a Fourth of July party from the Seattle coven."

I hand it back to her without opening it. "Will you be going?"

"Uhmm, well."

"If you're not interested in Ashton, Daphne, darling, please don't waste any more of my time."

When she leans toward me, her hands reached out to clasp mine, I jerk back. Her breath is so offensive.

She covers her mouth with her hand. "Oh, no, Tatiana. I didn't mean that at all. I've never wanted anyone more than I've wanted Ashton. It's just that, sometimes I wonder if it would be easier to learn my spells if I had some peers to study with."

"I see."

She casts a glance around my room. "Could I try to brew the love

82

potion here with you, to make sure I don't make any more mistakes?"

"That would be difficult to explain to Lorriene."

Daphne nods, her eyes downcast.

"Practicing independently builds confidence."

"You're right. I'm sorry. It's just, what if I don't get it right in time?"

"Now, remember Pig Out in the Park isn't until the end of August." I've invited Daphne to attend the closing ceremonies of the annual Spokane event with myself and Ashton. The regional coven gathers the following week. If I can go there with news of my grandson's engagement to an Occulto, no one will challenge me. But if I don't...

I pat Daphne's knee. "You've got until then, almost three months. As long as Ashton proposes to you before he returns to Boston."

"Are you sure I can do this?"

"You really don't have a choice, do you?"

She brushes her platinum hair extensions off her shoulder. "Maybe, Ashton will fall in love with me naturally."

Naturally and Daphne Wardof aren't two words that belong together. "It's better to look at it this way. The love potion will enhance whatever innate affection Ashton has for you. But women like ourselves, powerful women, can't risk entrusting our futures to pure emotion. Even the best men stray, Daphne. A witch can't allow for that kind of exposure."

"So you're okay with it. If Ashton doesn't really love me, and we get married?"

"You're an Occulto, dear. Love has nothing to do with it."

"Right, right," she mumbles.

Youth, so full of ridiculous notions, even in our young Occultos, apparently.

9. Giddy, Giddy, Sweet Cupcakes

CYNNA

"Kristeen," I plead for the nth time. "It's just lunch, okay?"

But I hear my voice quiver. What if I do something clumsy? Or worse, what if I... what if I... Even my thoughts are tongue-tied just thinking about that boy.

Wait, am I getting lightheaded? Seriously?

Breathe, Glynna, breathe.

Thank the God of Cupcakes Kristeen's head is buried deep in my closet, because I'm approaching panic mode right now, and if I don't pull myself together, Kristeen is never going to let me forget about how I freaked out, or passed out.

Breathe, Glynna, breathe.

Before my first date with Ashton Bass. Inner squeal. Does this mean I'm expecting a second date and a third?

Kristeen totally cuts off my fantasy of dating Ashton Bass when she cranks her iPod to full volume. "Do you have to play every single one your five hundred favorite songs *extra loud*? I swear you've scared the living bejeezus out of every living creature within hearing range."

She exits the closet without registering my complaint. "Glynna

85

Balcora! For the love of the sweetest cupcakes you've ever baked, why are you just standing there like a wooden spoon? Move your butt!" She snaps her fingers like castanets while AJR's *I'm Ready* throbs through the hands I just slammed over my ears.

How fitting.

"We got—" She eyes her watch. "—twenty minutes? And we still have to do your hair and makeup!"

Now, she's in high panic mode. Better her than me. She digs in her handbag, which is as big as she is, and starts pulling stuff out like Mary Poppins. I catch the piece of cloth she tosses me. It's not pink, and it's not going to match the sandals I planned to wear.

"This isn't mine."

"Of course it's not. I just confirmed that you don't own a single item of clothing that's not pink!"

"Is it yours?"

She ignores me.

"You're five inches shorter than me, it won't fit."

The second I pout, she's all over me.

"No pink today, Glyn!" Kristeen grabs my shoulders and twirls me around. We face the mirror. "Not when we want Ashton to see you as—" She plays with my hair. "I-wanna-make-you-mine! So, are we on the same page?"

I roll my eyes.

"Let me remind you, WE are on a mission, young lady!" Again with the dramatic voice, as if going out to lunch with Ashton is life or death. I catch my eye in the mirror. What if it doesn't go well, and this is our only date? That would qualify as death, wouldn't it?

Breathe, Glynna, breathe!

Maybe, for once, I need to take my friend's advice. I hold up the fashion contraband in my hands. Oh, wait, it's not a dress. It's an excuse for a dress. I bite my tongue as I shimmy into the black and white fabric.

It's a romper. And it shows off my entire legs. I mean my entire legs. I feel nearly naked. Kristeen ignores my protests and signals for me to turn around, so she can assess the results of her project.

"Do you think I'm going to be able to take one step out of the front door once my aunt sees me in this?" But when I face back into the mirror, I'm surprised. I look grown up.

"How many times do I have to tell you? Ophelia's not your Mommy, and you're not sixteen anymore!"

I swallow the lump in my throat. The right moment hasn't come to tell her that I'm adopted. I'm sure she wouldn't have said that about Ophelia if she knew.

She motions me to the vanity. "Sit."

Knowing how bossy she can be, I don't bother arguing. The time for resistance is over. I sit. Ashton is going to be here any minute, and I need to be wearing something. As I watch Kristeen's machinations in the mirror—dabbing shadow, which brightens my blue eyes, brushing bronzer on my pale cheeks, tugging on my hair—everything settles in deeper, and I get this strange feeling.

It takes me a second to register that it's excitement bubbling up inside me. Kristeen is right. Aunt Ophelia is not my mother! We're not even related. I can wear whatever I want. Anticipation mixes with curiosity and rebellion as Kristeen coats my lashes with three layers of mascara. The effect makes me look light and dark. And it makes me want to find out more about this powerful witch I supposedly am.

"Look at me." Kristeen says. "Open your mouth." She smooths on some lipstick. "There we go." She smacks her lips. "Do like this." I follow her instructions. "Now, look."

I turn back to the mirror. Siren red! "Okay, maybe that's going a little overboard." Even for a witch whose father is an Occulto.

"Glyn, if you want those lips of yours to experience some real action, finally!—" She presses her palms together and looks up to the ceiling. "—you've got to hint passion, sensuality, fire!"

I groan.

"Come on and pucker up," she coaxes me.

"Seriously?"

She waggles her finger. "Don't *ever* underestimate the power of the perfect shade of red, my *chica bonita*! And I spent all morning picking this one out for you!"

"Really?" I feel like a bad witch for giving her such a hard time, when she's only trying to help.

She fans her inspired self. "Honey, this lipstick is gonna take you to

87

places you've never dared imagine!"

I grin, vividly remembering Ashton's soft, warm lips the night of the bonfire, before mentally slapping myself. How long am I going to daydream about one drunken kiss? Maybe my girlfriend is right. Maybe I need to create more memories of those Ashton lips.

I playfully pucker my super reds in Kristeen's direction.

"Aww! Look at you, Glyn. That's perfect! Makes me proud." She wipes a fake tear from her eyes. "Now I get to tackle those gorgeous, glorious red locks." She checks the curling iron. "Just a few strategic curls." She combs out a chunk of my hair and twirls the strands over the curling iron.

"What a waste," I say.

"Huh?"

"You're gonna squander all this natural talent for making plain girls like me beautiful in law school."

Kristeen snorts. "Plain, you are not. Besides, I've been watching law dramas since I was this high." She leans over and practically touches the floor. "When those female attorneys strut into the courtroom, they're looking hot." She fans the air again. "That's gonna be me one day: fancy briefcase, five-inch heels, short, tight suit. I'm gonna put the judge and jury under my spell." She grins. "See the lovely curls? Ashton Bass is going to be *die*-ing to run his fingers through this seductive mess of red." She steps back to survey her handiwork. "Or he might get carried away and just grab it like Rrr." She leans in and playfully pulls my hair.

"Aww! Cut it out, K!" But as I pull away from her, vivid visions of Ashton kissing me with his fingers tangled in my hair, his hands running down my neck and my shoulders, then pulling my hips close to his, blaze through my mind. I shiver. When my gaze returns to the mirror, my cheeks are blotched with color. Kristeen's amused expression doesn't escape me.

"Girl, whatever fantasy is playing in your mind, I encourage you to act it out the second you get a chance!"

I chuckle as I smack her. "You're twisted, crazy, and evil! And I don't know what I'd do without you."

"Well, I think we both know that without me, you'd die coated in cupcake batter and icing still a virgin. And they'd bury you in an apron.

88

What a disgrace!" She shakes her head in slow motion for an exaggerated effect. "But, with the help of some of my enchantments... Oh, how could I forget?" She pulls a pair of sexy peep toe pumps from her bag.

"Yellow?"

"Indulge me," she croons.

"Where did you get these? They can't be yours. My feet are as twice as big as yours."

"I've got connections."

I turn one of them over in my hands. The under sole is bright red. "K, they're brand new Louboutin's." I push the shoe back at her. "I can't wear them."

Kristeen folds her arms stubbornly across her chest. "My girl is not going to out with the most eligible bachelor in this town in flats." She unfolds her arms to wag her finger back and forth. "Sorry. Not gonna happen on my watch."

"You're insane."

"Don't I know it?"

She won't take the damned shoe. Her eyebrows become steeples.

"Oh, no, not the Latina eyebrow arch! All right. All right." I jump up to squeeze her before slipping one foot into the soft lemon-yellow leather. It fits perfectly, just like Cinderella.

Kristeen smacks her forehead. "How could I forget?"

"What?"

"You have a few minutes. Slip into your lucky pink panties, just in case."

"Kristeen Amor Sanchez!" I grab a pillow and throw it in her direction. "You are impossible!"

She ducks. "Hey! I'm just trying to cover all the bases! Cause Ashton sure is going to want to when he sees you." She squeals and dodges as I throw another round of pink pillows. I miss her with every single one, but almost hit Leif, who's leaning against the door frame. He catches the last pillow.

How long has he been standing there?

He tries to hide his amused smile. Apparently too long.

"I hate to cut the pillow fight short, ladies. It's so fun to watch." He

89

hands my pillow over to Kristeen, who is looking at him with way too much interest.

"Oh hi, Leif!" she says. "Aren't you looking yummy today?"

Huh? My BFF is batting her eyelashes and purring at my cousin.

Wait a second. He's not my cousin. Does that make a difference?

The three of us ran around in Huggies together. We're family, even if we don't have the same blood. Leif chuckles again. I give him a more thorough inspection. He's wearing the usual white fitted V-neck T-shirt and sweatpants. Nothing special. Nevertheless, Kristeen is checking him out.

I laugh nervously. "Come on, Kristeen! Seriously? Leif?"

"Nothing this fine escapes my discriminating gaze." Her voice is seductive, and her eyes are traveling from Leif's face, to his pecs, to his abs.

I cover my eyes with my hand. Yesterday, Nana's crushing on Ashton's grandfather, and today, Kristeen is drooling over Leif. And she won't shut up!

"So, Leif, if you ever need my help, any help at all. You know, I'm right here for you."

"Enough!" I chuck my last pillow at her. Kristeen runs behind Leif and circles her arms around his waist. I'm not believing what I am seeing. Leif acts like it's no big deal; like sexy, gorgeous women maul him all day long. Do they?

"Glynna," he says. "I believe your date is parked on the street, gathering courage."

"He's here?"

"No one in this neighborhood has that kind of wheels."

Everything else fades away. My jitters come back mega force. I totter out of my bedroom with Kristeen and Leif behind me. I walk down and across the hall, peeking into Ophelia's bedroom before I enter. It's empty.

I edge over to the window that faces the street, grateful for the sheer day curtains. A shiny black car with an enormous bird painted on the hood is parallel parked in front of the Abbott's house. I recognize Ashton's dark hair.

"Those wheels are so hot!" Kristeen screams in my ear.

I whirl around to tell her, "Please, shut up!" and hammer her in the eye with my elbow.

"*¡Ay!*" She doubles over in pain. "I'm going to be blind," she moans.

When I try to assess the damage, she bats her other hand blindly in the air. "Please, Miss Klutzy, stay away."

"Hey, hey, let me take a look," Leif says.

When Kristeen finally straightens up, her entire eye-socket is red and puffy, and the white of her eye is completely bloodshot.

I'm completely mortified. "I'm so sorry, Kristeen!" It's not the first time I've accidentally assaulted her. Sometimes when I move too fast, I seem to lose all control over my long arms and legs.

Leif is hovering all over her. "Let's go get some ice on that." He takes her hand.

"It's okay, Glyn. Leif is gonna take care of me." She winks at me with her good eye.

Unbelievable. Kristeen could be stretched out in the morgue, and if the medical examiner was hot, she'd probably rise from the dead.

10. The Great Cupcake Inquisition

SHTON

I'm parked in front of the Balcora house. There's an enormous greenhouse on the lot next door to them. I wonder if it's theirs. The house is normal size. At over twelve-thousand square feet, the Bass mansion is not. When I was younger, Grandpa used to take me around with him on the weekends. I'm a good guess-timator of square footage. The home I'm staring at is—max—two-thousand square feet, and I'm being generous. I don't care about Glynna's pedigree, but Tatiana will.

I get out of my car and head up to the front door.

Thump-thump-thump. There goes my heartbeat when I press the doorbell.

The woman I remember always frowning at the bakery answers. I flash her the most winning Bass Man smile. Iron Lady doesn't smile back.

"Good morning, Ma'am." I use my humblest tone of voice.

"Are you lost, young man?" Her eyes bore pointedly at the bouquet of pink tulips in my hand. I'm surprised all the petals don't fall off.

"I, I," I stammer. I have never brought a girl flowers before. I must look like a pathetic fool! Beads of sweat form on my forehead. "I'm here to pick up Glynna. I'm Ashton Bass."

93

She's not impressed by my name.

"Mrs?" I extend my right hand.

"Harrumph. Mrs. Fiorillo." She says tersely, not extending her hand.

I let mine drop. Man, this is awkward. "Mrs. Fiorillo, is Glynna here?" Her eyes narrow.

The parents of every other girl I've dated are so thrilled the Bass Man is taking their daughter out, they fall all over me. Apparently not Iron Lady. An unfamiliar and uncomfortable tightness compresses my throat and my chest causing me to grip a little harder on the flowers. Poor tulips.

Now, I'm getting angry. Why won't this lady let me inside, or at least let Glynna know I'm here? And where is my Cupcake Girl? I try to look past Mrs. Fiorillo into the house's interior. Iron Lady shifts, blocking my vision. At this rate, the fucking tulips aren't going to survive my stranglehold. After a couple of seconds—which feel like forever—I'm ready to give up.

Pearl peeks through the gap between Iron Lady's arms and the door frame. "Ashton, is that you?" She pats Iron Lady's arm. "Ophelia, why don't you invite Ashton in?" Now I know Iron Lady's name is Ophelia. "It's almost ninety degrees outside." She's exaggerating but it is much warmer than yesterday, and I appreciate the consideration. "The poor boy must be melting. Now, come, come." Pearl pushes the door wide open and waves me in, past Ophelia's sour inspection of me. When Pearl reaches the center of the living room, she twirls around. "Welcome to our home."

Ophelia ignores both of us and settles on a sofa, her back rigid and her hands clenched in her lap.

Pearl settles on another cozy printed couch across from her. "Please, Ashton, sit." She indicates the space beside her. "I'm sure Glynna's almost ready."

When I cross the room, I notice a shelf with a row of books and several pictures above the couch; pictures of a smiling, giggling little red haired girl. I freeze.

Nana catches me looking at the pictures. "Ah, there's our little Glynna." She gets up and reaches for the photo in the middle. A girl with the hugest, clearest blue eyes stares out of the frame. She's grinning.

Pink frosting is smeared over her mouth, and she's clutching a cupcake in her hands.

That distinct taste, sweetness, decadence, heavenly–Glynna's lips.

Did I just close my eyes for a moment and imagine her lips? Maybe I did, because when I open them a pair of smooth, long legs is descending the stairs.

I hold my breath.

Krissy and the cousin with the glasses are right behind her. Krissy has her hand jammed over one of her eyes, but she waves with the other. "Hi, Ashton!"

"What happened?" Pearl jumps up from the couch and runs toward the trio, her arms reaching out to Krissy. They're both the same height, short. I wonder where Glynna gets her endless legs from? Definitely not her grandmother. It's hard to follow the conversation between Glynna, Krissy, the guy, and Pearl, because they're talking in hushed whispers.

I glance over to the other sofa. Ophelia's a block of granite. The guy leads Krissy and Pearl to another room. Glynna heads in my direction. She looks stunning in a short black and white mini-skirt. Hey! At least it's not as short as the crap Lorriene's been strutting around in this summer. But then again, I wouldn't mind seeing Glynna in a Brazilian Bikini, on a private beach.

"Are those for me?" she asks.

Embarrassed by my wild imagination, my hand jerks. Glynna dodges my tulip-filled fist, saving me from almost punching her in the breasts in front of Aunt Rushmore. "Yes."

When she reaches for the bouquet, I uncurl my fingers.

"Thank you. They're beautiful," she says. "I'll go put them in some water."

God, please don't leave me alone with your aunt. I give her a limp smile.

"What are your plans?" Ophelia barks as soon as Glynna is out of sight.

"I thought we'd eat lunch first."

"First?"

I cough into my fist. If I reveal my real plans, I doubt she'll let Glynna walk out the front door with me. "Maybe a walk down by the riverfront

95

afterwards."

Her eyes narrow into slits. "In this heat?"

She has a point, although the river and downtown are in a natural valley. "It's usually a few degrees cooler down there. It should be nice later this afternoon."

"How much later this afternoon?"

I want to give her a flip response. Military time and romance don't mix, but I refrain. I have no doubt she'll kick me out of the house if I get smart with her. And that would mean no quality time with my Cupcake Girl. Can't risk it. "Does she need to be home by a certain time?" I ask as respectfully as possible, but my throat is tight.

Ophelia crosses her arms. "I don't like the idea of Glynna going on a date with you."

What in the hell am I supposed to say to that? "Ma'am?"

"Everything comes so easy for boys like you. There's no hardship in your life. How will you ever build character if you never know what it's like to struggle?"

"My grandfather," I start to say.

Her eyes flare. Does she hate my grandpa too? No one hates Nicolas.

"What about your grandfather?"

"He built his company from nothing. He's very firm with me and my sister."

"Hmmph."

It's like she's reading my mind and knows what a huge lie that is. She points her finger. "If anything happens to Glynna while she's out with you—"

"Nothing will happen, she'll be safe with me."

"I'll make sure you'll regret it if you do anything to hurt her." Her harsh glare makes her distaste for me clear.

"Yes, ma'am."

The woman is impervious to the Bass charm.

"Are you ready to go?" Glynna's creamy voice saves me from Ophelia Hell.

"You're wearing that?" Iron Lady asks.

Glynna's cheeks turn the sweetest shade of pink. "Kristeen picked it out."

That earns Glynna a harrumph.

"See you later?"

"How much later?" Ophelia barks.

Glynna looks to me.

"Seven o'clock." As long as I show for her shrimp étouffée, Tatiana will forgive me for being late.

Ophelia shakes her finger at both of us. "Have her home before dark."

The days are so long in the summer, that won't be an issue. "I will."

"Or I'll turn into a pumpkin." Glynna winks as she rests her hand on my bicep and pushes me toward the front door with the slightest pressure.

I take her cue.

GLYNNA

Dry heat hits my exposed legs as Ashton and I flee my aunt's interrogation. I'm handling my heels pretty well—is that why Louboutins are so expensive? You can actually walk in them! I can't believe Ophelia let me out of the house wearing this romper. The one-piece swimsuit with a skirt I wore as a kid had more coverage than this. I self-consciously tug the hem. Ooh, a nice breeze flutters by, and cool air whips around my thighs. I'm almost naked. Thankfully, Ashton's deep voice interrupts my panicky thoughts.

"After you." He pushes open our small wooden gate.

As I walk through, I can't help but notice the crawling red roses have created a wonderful arch overhead. It wasn't there yesterday. The flowers bloom as we pass. I turn my head to look back at them, and a few more rose buds are still unfurling. I hope Ashton hasn't noticed, because even though they're gorgeous, it's just not normal for flowers to bloom right before your eyes. All I want is to be like any other normal girl on a normal first date.

Is that too much to ask of the Cupcake Gods?

97

I feel a smile coming on.

"So before dark, huh?" I catch a few of Ashton's words as we cross the street.

"What did you say? I'm sorry. I spaced out." He opens the car door for me. "Uh, thank you," I say as I climb inside. The seats are kind of low, so I have to pay attention to what I'm doing. The subtle scent of leather and Ashton's cologne hits me as soon as he closes the door.

He slips into the driver's seat next to me. He's so close, it's hard to concentrate and understand the point he's trying to make. "Your Aunt wasn't fooling around with that curfew." He stops in the middle of buckling his seatbelt to flash his boyish grin. Are his blue eyes extra sparkly today? Sparkly? Is that even a description? I will myself to stop staring at those baby blues, but it's impossible. I'm completely spellbound. I should be the one casting spells here! I'm the witch, right? I can't help when an even bigger smile spreads over my face.

"Then I've got half a day to get to know you," he says, almost too quietly.

I'm sure he thinks I'm a total ditz as I just sit there beaming at him.

Say something, Glynna! Say anything! "Well..." My blank mind fumbles for a response. "I guess we don't have to waste any time. You could start getting to know me now. Uhmm, right here–" I make a circular motion. "–inside your car."

Ashton chuckles. There's a mischievous glint in his eyes. "Believe me, I would love to."

Then I come out of my Ashton daze. What did I just say? That he could start getting to know me better, inside his car? I was doing better as a silent-love zombie. "I–I–I–didn't mean," I stammer. "Maybe we could go now?" Okay, that sounded a bit like helpless prey, but I can feel my aunt glaring at us through the curtains.

"Relax, Glyn," Ashton says as he leans a little closer. The way he says Glyn turns me into a puddle. He reaches out his hand.

Is he going to kiss me? Now?

I clap my hand over my mouth. I hope he understands body language, because he can't kiss me in front of Aunt Ophelia. She will tear out of our house and rip me out of this bucket seat. I freeze.

Instead of kissing me, he reaches over to secure my seatbelt. "I

98

promised Ophelia to keep you safe, and believe me, I don't want to be the recipient of her wrath. So, buckle up, milady." He gives me a wink.

Again, my mind freezes. *Come on, come on, Glynna!*

Ashton seems aware of my inner paralysis as awkward silence drowns us in nothingness. That awkward, vicious silence that shows up with the punctuality of a Swiss train to ruin my life. Why can't something witty or funny spill from my lips? At this point it doesn't have to be impressive. Any spoken words will do!

"So, uhmm, how about I play some music?" He doesn't wait for my answer. Why would he? I'm mute. He taps his iPod screen. *Talk Dirty to Me* by Jason Derulo pops up. "Uh, wrong playlist." Ashton fumbles hastily to press the next button.

Did he just blush?

Wild Flower by Color Me Badd fills the car. I settle back into my seat, genuinely smiling as the feeling of being a wildflower, opening to the sun calms me. I finally manage to speak up. "So you're into throw back songs?"

Ashton grins sheepishly. "You mean Oldies? Not really, I mean, not really old." He pauses and looks at me. "I'm more of... Okay! I admit it, my favorite song is—" He puts his hand over his heart. "*When I Fall in Love* by Nat King Cole."

Our mimosas sang that yesterday. I open and close my mouth as a shiver dances along my spine.

"You're surprised? Why? Classics never go out of style. That's why they're called classics." He's got that teasing thing going on in his voice. "And don't tell me that song doesn't work magic with the chicks!"

"With the chicks, huh?" All of a sudden I'm loosening up, feeling a little bold, and I want to challenge him. "Well, play the song then."

He takes me on, crooning along with the song's lyrics as if he's one of the King Cole Swingers. Wow. He can sing, and he's into this song about falling in love forever and giving his heart completely. Maybe there's more to Ashton than his chiseled jaws and rock hard abs. His deep, baritone voice is sending shivers up my spine. A crazy desire to grab him and kiss him right here, right now, overwhelms me. I long to feel his lips on mine. If I was a puddle before, now I'm a sweet delicious pool of overheated frosting. My tongue flicks my bottom lip. I can

99

practically taste the decadent blend of melted butter with chocolate and overflowing ripples of hot fudge, slowly dripping down... down.

Oh, My Sweet and Luscious Cupcakes. I shift uncomfortably in my seat, in the direction of the window.

Ashton is staring at me with his mouth hanging open. "So, am I succeeding?"

"Not quite yet, but you can keep singing," I tease.

"Aww, Glynna!" He exudes boyish charm. "You really know how to make it hard on a guy."

"Let me remind you, Mr. Ashton Bass, I'm not one of the chicks!"

This only causes him to grin wider. "Challenge duly noted and accepted, Ms. Balcora," he says wickedly, determination written all over his face.

A rainbow appears right ahead of us, creating a perfect arc in the sky.

"Isn't that something?" He points overhead as we pass underneath it. "I don't think I've ever seen both ends of a rainbow."

A new level of giddy hits me. My chest swells and overflows with colors. I look out the back window of his Firebird at those colors, all those shades. There hasn't been a drop of rain this morning. That rainbow sprang from my heart. I sneak a sideways glance at Ashton. I want to experience so much more of the magic feelings flowing between us.

I glance at Ashton. "What is it they say about a hidden treasure at a rainbow's end?" The reflection from the sun's ray make him look golden, like a god. That chiseled angular face, his aquiline nose, and those lips that I itch to kiss.

Glynna, get a grip.

"I don't think I'll need to travel to the end of a rainbow to find my treasure, Cupcake Girl."

Did he just call me Cupcake Girl? It's sexy and sweet and romantic. We're at a stoplight and his gaze holds mine. My stomach flips like a four-foot-tall Olympic gymnast swinging on uneven parallel bars. *Passenger Seat* by Stephen Speaks pours from his speakers, building a moment that already feels so high, I could break my neck with one false step.

The boy has one romantic playlist.

11. This Cupcake Longs for Thy Sweet Kiss...

SHTON

I'm singing, and it's not just what I'm singing. I'm singing for her. I sang Glynna an entire Nat King Cole song. Maybe next time, she'll ask me to pull over and dance. I'd dance with her on the side of the road any day. Hell, I'll even try *Gangnam Style*, if she wants me to.

Good Lord, what is happening to me? Bass Man, get a hold of yourself!

And now, I'm carrying on a one-sided conversation in my head. This is her fault. She's so quiet, unlike Daphne, who never shuts up. I like it. My soft, sweet, Cupcake Girl. I bet she never gets really mad.

Okay, except when she cold-cocked me.

But she's so different from Grandma T.

I squeeze my eyes shut for a few seconds and see us walking down the aisle!

My eyes pop open. My pulse is racing. Focus on the road, Bass Man, just focus on the road.

"Are you all right?" she asks in her soft, velvety voice.

I sneak a sideways glance at her, and my treacherous eyes move south to those long, luscious legs and her creamy, porcelain skin. I wonder what it would feel like to run my hand up one of those calves. Would she shiver with delight?

Get a hold of yourself, Bass Man! I'm thinking like an overeager, hormonally-challenged teenage boy!

"I'm okay." I return my gaze to those innocent baby blues. I suddenly feel ashamed for my inappropriate thoughts and rambunctious sexual desires. "Here we are." I pull into the gravel driveway of our cabin on Lake Coeur D'Alene. With Glynna for company the thirty-minute drive has flashed by in a blink. She looks surprised I brought her to this primo spot right next to the water. Good. I want this time to be night and day from the last time, at the bonfire, when I made an ass of myself.

Today, I want to make it up to her.

I turn the engine off and watch Glynna unbuckle her seatbelt. My eyes stray again to those endless legs. How can I not stare at them? They're so gorgeous! She reaches for the door handle.

"Wait!"

Her eyes darken. "What?"

"Let me open the door for you." I hurry to exit my car and make a quick turn, but right before I reach Glynna's door... Whoosh! *Thump!* My face is planted in the dirt, my stomach is hugging the driveway, and my lips are kissing the ground!

Right in front of my face is a trail of snails. Those tiny, creeping, shell-carrying creatures that have freaked me out ever since Lorriene covered me with the suckers one afternoon when I fell asleep in the yard out here. Gross. Why are they looking at me like that? Do they even have eyes?

I push myself up and my hand *crunches* and *splats*. I crush one of their shells and get snail goo all over my hand on my first date with Cupcake Girl. I push myself up to my knees. *Crack. Crunch.* There goes its poor brother and sister. Slime is coating my toe, and little flakes of snail shell are embedded in my knees.

"Oh my God, Ashton! Are you all right?" Glynna jumps out of the Firebird and runs toward me.

I want to crawl under my car and hide, but then she kneels in front of

102

me, and all I can think is: Woman, I'd like to see you kneel before me, but not because I fell on my face!

I tilt my head up and see full rosebud lips, so close. She bites the lower one. It takes all my will power to restrain myself and not grab her right now and kiss her senselessly. But we'd just end up rolling around in cracked shells and snail goo.

I groan as I try to get up without crushing any more of our little guests. It looks like they've cleared out. Glynna offers her hand. I feel like a complete loser.

So much for making a good impression.

"I guess the ground likes me." I smile wickedly and grab her hand, causing her to lose her balance and fall on my chest. "Or maybe it likes you more."

She gasps.

Darn, she feels light and perfect in my arms.

Glynna's startling blue eyes meet mine. I run my fingers down her back and sense her shiver. She rests her hands on my chest. Just her slightest touch sends ripples through my skin.

"I'm sure the ground loves you more, Ashton." She brushes dirt from my face.

I close my eyes, relishing the sensation of her fingers. The smell of freshly baked cupcakes lingers on those hands. Did I hear myself growl? Or was it my stomach?

Glynna glances around. The lake is serene pool of glass today, the clouds overhead puffy. I'm so glad Lorriene didn't figure out my destination. Otherwise, she'd be all over us with her crew, and the stereo would be cranked to an excruciating and unromantic volume. This afternoon, the only sound is the wind rustling through the trees, and a couple of birds singing. I take in a deep breath of pine. Everything's quiet and peaceful, just like my Cupcake Girl.

The Bass Man can recover from his snail snafu. The rest of the day is going to be awesome.

GLYNNA

103

I force myself to keep a straight face as Ashton romances the ground. Something about the confident Ashton Bass with a mouth full of dirt makes me want to laugh out loud. Am I evil? I never pegged him as a klutz, but he's not so different from me, after all. He tripped over his own two feet before going into that nosedive. I bite the tip of my tongue so I won't giggle. He's trying hard to recover, but he's also looking quite embarrassed. That vulnerability is definitely cute!

I want to cuddle him like a puppy. But he's not a dog. He might not appreciate being petted. I stare down at my lap until my face isn't red, then get out of the car.

When I kneel by his side and offer help, he flashes his mischievous grin. He pulls me close, and in a matter of seconds, I find myself on top of him. Yes, right on top of his rock solid chest. I feel dizzy. Those dreamy eyes! Dark blue like sapphires. A moment of silence cocoons us, like the world has stopped spinning.

Ashton's eyes wander to my lips as his hands move gently up my back. Even with layers of clothes between us, goosebumps break out on my arms, and my cheeks burn. Did the temperature rise twenty degrees? My body is possessed by a fever. Baking soda, flour, cocoa powder, sugar; I tick off a list of ingredients to distract myself: milk, vanilla. "Eggs! Can't forget the eggs."

"Eggs?" Ashton's amused voice breaks my concentration.

Did I just say that out loud? "Uhmm." I shift uncomfortably. Aston's chest vibrates as he laughs. He rolls me over gently, but holds my gaze with solemn intensity.

His face is so close. I've stopped breathing. He trails his finger across my cheek. Too gentle. I'm mesmerized by the endless blue skies of his eyes, or are they the calmest water in the ocean? I think ocean, because I feel like I'm swimming.

"I think those eggs are our cue to eat lunch." He doesn't stop smiling as he pulls me up with him.

All I seem capable of is returning Ashton's shy smile. When we reach our feet, I wobble a bit. I guess even Louboutins aren't made for gravel.

104

He holds me steady, and I'm relieved not to follow his nosedive with one of my own.

"Ready for lunch?"

I nod like the silent-love zombie I am.

He circles around to the trunk and takes out a picnic basket. He takes my hand. "If you'll just come with me, milady."

We're hiking in the grass along the side of a cabin.

"Is this your family's?" I ask.

"One of our little getaways."

Around the corner, in the middle of the lawn, is a pink cabana. White benches are piled with pink, lavender, and gold cushions, and curtains in shades of pink and white hang from rafters, which look like they've been fashioned from driftwood. A thatched mat covers the rafters, shading everything. It looks like a scene from *Aladdin*, and I'm Princess Jasmine. The only thing missing is the magic carpet.

I turn in a circle. How much effort did it take to create this?

Out of the corner of my eye, I see Ashton watching me. Is it the sunlight, or is he blushing?

I can't wipe the loopy smile off my face. "It's so pink."

Now Ashton's ears are red. He ruffles his hair and gives me a sheepish look. "I guessed pink is your favorite color."

"I love it." I touch his arm.

Relief fills his eyes.

"So you just happened to have pink draperies and lilac throw pillows lying around," I tease.

"If word gets out, it might hurt the Bass reputation." He winks and I swoon. "So keep it between us."

"Don't worry, Mr. Bass, your secret is safe with me." The heel of one of my Louboutins grabs a big clod of earth and I stumble. Ashton catches me before my knees make a crash landing onto the stone path that leads to the cabin.

"I've got you!"

Boy, does he ever. My knight, my adorable, blue-eyed knight, has swept me off my feet. He's cradling me to his chest, but he drops the picnic basket to do so, and it's rolling down the steep lawn straight into the lake. "Ashton, our lunch!"

Red and Golden Delicious apples fly in all directions like missiles.

"First things first." He enters the cabana. "Let me show you how Bass men take care of our damsels in distress."

I giggle. He's being so silly and romantic.

"Because I'm not taking any chances of you getting hurt on these rocks."

"Pebbles," I acknowledge meekly.

"Didn't you know pebbles are rocks in disguise?"

In his strong arms, I make a soft landing on a pile of cushions.

As soon as he's satisfied I'm not going to roll off and break my neck, he chases after our food. Besides bruised apples, I imagine a single mass of unappetizing food drowned in unrecognizable sauce. Not very appetizing. But watching Ashton race downhill to catch up with the apples is. His forearms flex, and when he bends over to pick one up, I gasp as I cover my mouth with my hands. Oh!

Why am I covering my mouth? I should be covering my eyes, because I'm drooling! But *yum* is the most appropriate word. And I'm not talking about those apples.

After he returns to the cabana, we salvage what we can from the picnic basket: cheese, wine, apples and a loaf of bread.

When we're finished eating, he pulls me by the hand and leads me to a willow tree closer to the water's edge. Although the summer air is hot, the tree's curtain-like branches sway above us in the breeze. The wind tosses my hair.

He puts his arm around my shoulder, and I inhale his fresh, clean, masculine, pure Ashton scent. My entire body responds with teeny ripples of pleasure, and I let out a sigh.

"Want to sit down?" he asks. "I can bring a blanket over here." He brushes the hair from my face as he moves a few inches closer.

For the fiftieth time this afternoon I lose myself in the clearest blue eyes I've ever seen. They make everything around me spin and stop at the same time.

He's so close. Is he finally going to kiss me?

I'm aware of the thrill. The anticipation. The longing. Maybe a little fear? All my emotions are suspended in wonder in that few seconds; the prelude to–

106

Ashton kisses the tip of my nose before his lips find mine.

Excitement cracks and pleasure echoes through every cell in my body. The inner explosion makes my heart pump so hard, I'm sure it's going to burst. Suppressed desire, now unleashed, buzzes through my blood like millions of miniature lightning bolts. My heart and head pound. My world swirls. I lose my balance and sag against the tree. Ashton leans in closer. He never stops kissing me. His lips travel down my neck in gentle nibbles. Shudders of delight race up and down my spine. He's back to my lips, but this time his kisses are deeper. I part my lips to welcome more of him. He releases a strangled groan as if he's on the edge of losing control. When his fingers slip between my thighs, my eyes pop open.

Should I squeeze my legs tight and stop his tender exploration?

"Your skin is so soft and smooth," he murmurs.

I don't want to stop him.

His fingers crawl toward the hem of my romper. The heat of his breath against my neck melts any resistance. My nerves and thoughts have gone completely haywire. Lust untwists in my belly and shoots out to meet his curious fingers. My knees weaken. When I wobble, Ashton steadies me while he continues his sweet probing. His touch is teasing, tempting. I want to close the small distance which remains between us.

My hands press against his chest. His heartbeat is as fast as mine. I've become weightless. As if the ground has turned to marshmallows, or I'm floating in cotton candy clouds. Oh, Sweet Caramels, my thoughts are frosted, iced, and sprinkled with golden stars. Oh my! I've never felt like this before. Not even when I'm baking.

"You taste so fucking good, Glynna." Ashton murmurs. He kisses me over and over until I'm so drunk from his lips that I can barely take anymore. I slowly open my eyes. Little baby tornados are swirling a few feet above us. I could reach out and catch one. I hold up my hand. The transparent ice cream cone-shapes swoosh to me. Their ice cold water pelts us.

"What the hell?" Ashton jumps, and his kisses stop. Disoriented from the splashes of water, he looks up. "Is it raining?" He glances side to side, continuing to search for the source of the mini-downpour.

Would Ashton believe me if I told him we were interrupted by baby twisters our passion conceived?

107

"Water must have been caught in some of those branches," I say. Now that the tiny cyclones are gone, I wonder if I imagined them. Although my hair and face and shoulders did get a splash.

Ashton ruffles his hair. "Yeah, maybe we better get out from under this tree." He leads me back to the cabana.

We're just about to revisit all those cushions when his cellphone simultaneously *rings* and vibrates.

12. A Cupcake Remembers

ICOLAS

Out of sorts, I pad along the dark hardwood floors that lead to our state-of-the-art kitchen, which I rarely have need to enter. But the help always take Sundays off, and if I want one of those cupcakes, I'm going to have to fend for myself. No one else has bothered to flip on any of the hall lights—I don't either—so it's a long walk of shadows, which suits my mood.

Most Sundays I rise early to play golf, avoiding Tati before she heads to church, We've slept in separate bedrooms for a long time now, and I'm relieved our routine has protected me from her keen powers of observation this morning. She'd register my strange state with a glance, and the interrogation would begin.

I suspect whatever answers I might offer as to why I'm still in my pajamas and bathrobe at noon would displease her.

I've been restless since I saw Pearl yesterday. I can't remember the details of the dark dreams that kept me tossing and turning all night, but I recall now that I woke up several times gasping for air. Now, all I can think about is the box of cupcakes I brought home from Frosting & Beans. I hope Tati hasn't found them. She'd smash them in the latest-

109

greatest-model trash compactor.

Tati likes new, shiny, and expensive. She also relishes being the first to possess cutting-edge technology. I'm sure the AI robot is coming soon if it's not already on order.

Nothing is too costly for my wife when it comes to furnishing our home, a fact I'm reminded of whenever I peruse our monthly expenses. Sometimes I'd like to dump *her* in the trash compactor.

Perhaps I exaggerate.

I've always admired Tati's ability to manage our household and complicated social relationships. But we've grown distant over the years. Not so unusual, this, from what I observe of my peers.

After a time, one doesn't have any real friends remaining.

Creating parallel lives is a common solution to the rift that grows in long-term marriages. Why would I expect our marriage to be faultless?

But Tati and I were never close.

I stop walking and rub my eyebrows.

A mental dam has burst, and every disturbing insight I've ever silenced about my wife's behavior over the past forty years is spilling into my awareness. I've overlooked my wife's fierce temper, smoothing over her sharp edges whenever possible. Tati takes care of herself, and as a man who is aging well, I appreciate that she hasn't let herself go.

But then, she'd drink the blood of infants if she believed it would make her appear more youthful.

Lorriene and her grandmother are fiercely attached to one another. Troubling, that relationship. What kind of hold does Tati have over the girl?

"Hi, Dad."

I'm standing in the doorway of our cavernous kitchen—blinded by the brushed steel and glistening white appliances. Gregor, our son, sits at the enormous kitchen table with the bakery haul spread before him. The smell of fresh brewed coffee and decadent pastries fills the room. Even though Gregor is something of a disappointment, I'm glad for the distraction of his presence. "Anything left?" I ask as I head to the coffeemaker.

"Plenty."

"No golf this morning?"

"Feeling lazy," Gregor says.

When isn't he feeling lazy? I give my head a firm shake, hoping to clear the negative impressions of my family that insist on intruding.

"You all right, Dad?" Gregor asks.

I join him at the table with my full mug of coffee. "Fine."

Gregor pushes the pale pink boxes in my direction. A couple of pieces of pie and most of the cupcakes are left.

This morning I want to try another one of those cupcakes, and the one with the sweetest shade of pink frosting and glittery sprinkles is calling my name. I hold it to my nose before taking a bite. A heady scent of vanilla and raspberry swirls around me. The best raspberries in the world are grown in the Inland Northwest. An image of Pearl and me, picking raspberries at Green Bluffs, pops into my mind. My hand trembles as my chest constricts.

The image floats away. Why is everything so hazy? A thick wet cloud of fog settles in my mind.

"Dad, are you all right?" Gregor asks again. Across the table, my son's forehead is creased with concern. He is as passive as his mother is domineering, and that weakness has always been a source of bitter disappointment to me.

The admission rips through my chest.

I let my hand drop until my wrist is propped against the edge of the table, the cupcake perched between my thumb and forefinger, untasted. "Do you love Alise?" I blurt out.

Gregor's eyes widen. "Love?"

"Do you love your wife? Do you love Ashton and Lorriene's mother?"

Confusion clouds my son's eyes. He shoves aside the stack of newspaper on the table in front of him. "We make a good team, like you and mom," he says.

"Then I'm sorry."

"For what?"

"For setting such a miserly example of human relationships."

Gregor's mouth drops open.

I stare at the pink icing on the cupcake. "I'd hoped your marriage was more satisfying than mine." I raise the enticing treat to my mouth and take a bite. My eyes close as I savor the springy cake and foamy pink

111

glaze. Longing coats my tongue. As soon as I swallow the first bite, I have to have another one. I peel the paper away from the cake with little effort. My fingers and toes tingle as the invisible band around my chest tightens.

A black anger in my heart wars with the taste of sunshine bursting on my tongue.

I take a third bite and remember Pearl's lips pressing against mine; so soft and tender and delicious. The anguish in my chest intensifies. I shove the last of the cupcake into my mouth, wiping the crumbs from my lips and chin with the back of my hand.

Lightheaded, I sway in my chair. If I was standing up, I'd probably lose my balance and topple to the floor.

Gregor's on his feet, iPhone in hand. "Dad!"

Memories from over forty years ago flood my mind as a devastating fury detonates my heart. A ring of blackness cracks open in my mind before I lose consciousness.

ATIANA

I'm sitting in the third row of pews at Saint Gabriel Parish church. Couples and families surround me. The weekly sermons are tedious, but I suffer them in order to be cast in a desirable light. A pity Nico can't join my charade. Religious artifacts: shrines and altars, crosses and holy water, can do me no harm, but exposure to them can weaken, even undo, a black magic spell.

I'm fortunate my husband isn't a believer.

A lightning bolt of pain rips through my head. I clamp my hands over my ears. A high-pitched ringing threatens to burst my eardrums. I violently twist left and right before I realize I must look like a bad scene from *The Exorcist*.

The sanctuary and the men and women seated around me fade in blinding light. Someone's hand is on my shoulder, but their voice is far away. I squirm in my seat, elbowing the person on my right. I can't make

112

myself be still, and I think I'm muttering gibberish. The splicing feeling advances downward and deepens in my chest. My torso flings forward. I grip the wood railing in front of me as the white light fades and the sanctuary returns. I claw at my throat. It feels like I'm choking on a gallon of sand.

"Harry has called an ambulance," the woman seated next to me assures me. My hat has landed in her lap.

The pain is diminishing, but the sensation of a giant bruise extending from my jaw to my pelvis remains. As my sight and presence of mind returns, I realize I've been spiritually attacked by another witch. Medical attention is the last thing I need.

"No ambulance," I croak.

Hands pull me down as I struggle to stand.

"Please," I gasp. "I need fresh air."

Harry stands beside me. "Are you sure you can walk?"

"Yes."

Father Fuentespina is frozen in the pulpit. I mouth a request for forgiveness and squeeze out of the pew. By the time I get to the end of the row, people are standing to make my passage easier. Harry is still right behind me. When I'm sure I can walk without assistance, I convince him I'm well enough to make it outside. "Just a strange spell, damage done." I indicate the disruption around me, but offer a tepid smile at the root of my honesty. "Nothing more to fear." I hope.

I straighten my shoulders. Here comes my hat, being passed from hand to hand. I reach for it and fan my face. I feel like I'm standing in the blazing inferno of hell itself.

Harry's hand is on my elbow. "Please, let me walk outside with you."

It's going to take another scene that I can't risk to get rid of him, so I relent. Everyone watches us as he escorts me to the doors. Pastor Fuentespina resumes his sermon before they close behind us.

I check my watch as Harry keeps his eyes glued to my every move. Donald, my chauffeur, eats breakfast at the Chow Queen a few blocks down the street. I'll need to call him to pick me up if I don't want to wait for another thirty-five minutes, but other than my hat, my hands are empty.

"Lose something?" Harry asks.

113

"In the commotion, I left my purse inside. Could you be a dear and fetch it for me?"

I'm steadier on my feet, but indicate I'll sit on the steps to wait. Harry helps me settle down before he rushes back inside. As soon as he's gone, I try to figure out what just happened. My mind focuses on the Seattle coven. With Gregor possessing no magical ability, I fear them coming after my power.

Could they have unleashed a psychic attack on me? I glance around as if the culprit might be in physical proximity. The streets are empty.

I mull over whether I should reach out to Lyrika. We used to be allies, but the more financially successful Nicolas and I have become, the more Lyrika and I have drifted apart. It's a strange dynamic, that with all our abilities, we Occultos can't draw raw wealth to us. There has to be innate financial instincts in the first place. I don't think she's ever forgiven me for marrying a normal human and having it pay off so handsomely. I'll have to spend time strengthening my shields. No one needs to tell me I've grown lax. But another possibility pokes at the edge of my awareness.

The sensation of bright light doesn't point to Occultos. Our black magic smothers, suffocates, darkens, shades, and buries wherever it aims. It doesn't illuminate. Indeed, the second possibility is more disturbing than any power depletion by the Seattle coven.

For the past twenty years, we've all been searching for Liam Gallagher's rumored child, the mixed heir, the only Occulto-Lumina believed to exist.

That briefly blinding white light, that only inconvenienced me, really, points in such a direction.

Harry interrupts my thoughts when he hands me my purse.

"Thank you, I'll just call my driver and be on my way."

"My wife will kill me if I don't wait here until you're safely in your car."

I force a smile as I dig for my phone. There are eleven text messages. "No! This can't be happening!"

"What is it?" Harry asks.

"It's Nicolas! He's had a heart attack!" I speed dial Donald. He already knows. "Yes, I'm waiting outside St. Gabriel's." I disconnect the call. "He's on his way," I explain to Harry. "When I didn't answer, they contacted him."

My Cadillac is already at the curb. Harry helps me to my feet.

As Donald drives me to the hospital, I try to understand. Could someone have attacked Nicolas and me simultaneously? It's disturbing to think they'd try to get to me through him. Nico is my anchor. Without him, my world and everything I've worked for will fall apart.

He can't die.

13. Cupcakes: Just What the Doctor Ordered

ASHTON

My heart catches when I see the text from my dad. "Shit."

"What is it?" Glynna asks.

"My grandfather is on the way to the hospital. He's had a heart attack."

Glynna's mouth flies to her rosebud lips. "You have to go. Now."

"I'll drop you off."

"No, don't waste time. You need to get to him as soon as possible. I can call Leif to come pick me up from the hospital."

My thoughts careen as I take Glynna's hand and lead her to the car. "It's such a shock. Pap Pap has always been so healthy, with regular checkups and the best doctors."

"Maybe it's nothing serious. He'll be all right."

For the first time in my life, I consider the future without my grandpa. Life looks grim without Nicolas to reel Tatiana in. "He has to be all right," I say.

Thank God it's Sunday and there isn't any traffic. I break the speed limit all the way back to Spokane. When we reach town, I tear toward Spokane Medical Center. My throat is dry, and I don't have anything to say, so I just drive. I guess Glynna understands the Bass Man is off his game. I sneak a peek at her. She's got her arms crossed over her chest. I can tell she's worried, and it means a lot to me that she cares about my grandfather.

We pull into the parking garage, and I'm running toward the elevator. She's right behind me. I force myself to stop, even though she's doing a pretty good job of keeping up with me in those heels. When I stop, she slips them off and catches up to me barefoot. If my grandpa wasn't on his way to ICU, I'd sweep her up in my arms and plant a huge kiss on those luscious lips, but he is, and I'm feeling nauseous.

The parking garage elevator opens, and we step in together.

When we exit, we have to cross a skywalk to get to the main lobby. I'm looking for my dad, or Lorriene, or Grandma. All I see are strangers. I'm guessing Mom's still in Seattle. I wonder if anyone's called or texted her. Dad must have. Glynna tugs on my arm and points to the information kiosk.

"Mr. Bass is on the 4th floor." The lady peers over her reading glasses at Glynna. "Only family is allowed."

"I'm his grandson."

"That's fine, but—"

I grab Glynna's hand. "She's my fiancé."

The woman closes her mouth as I lead my Cupcake Girl to the next set of elevators. If she was Daphne, she'd be squealing and snaking all over me, but Glynna remains calm. She doesn't even react. "I just said that—"

"I want to go with you," she says.

Everything she says is as perfect as everything else about her.

The *whir* and *beeps* of countless machines beneath a blanket of silence greet us when we exit the elevator at the fourth floor. Again, I search for a familiar face. Glynna nudges me toward the nurse's station. A short, dark-haired lady eyes us with quiet sympathy when I tell her my name. She points down the corridor to Waiting Room A. "Your family is gathering in there."

I thank her and hurry down the hall. I'm still holding Glynna's hand

118

tight.

"Dad!" The old man is crunched over with his elbows on his knees and his head in his hands. Lorriene is draped over him, her eyes red. Daphne and Maddie are sitting on the other side of my sister. Their slight sunburns and baggy beachwear indicate they came straight from the pool.

Daphne jumps up and runs toward me. She throws her arms around my neck in a stranglehold. "I'm so sorry!" she squeals. At least her breath doesn't smell like a sewer. Maybe she gargled a bottle of Listerine.

Glynna tries to release my hand, but I don't let her.

Finally, Octopus Woman lets go of me, although she doesn't go far. Why are she and Maddie even here? I have to bite my tongue not to bark at them to leave.

"Ashton." When my dad eyes Glynna appreciatively, something inside me burns, but I shove it aside.

"What happened?" I ask him.

"We were in the kitchen and he was eating a cupcake," my father says.

I sense Glynna flinch and put my arm around her shoulder. "It's not your fault."

She nods, but doesn't look convinced.

"What's his condition?"

"It's not good." My father releases a long, sad sigh.

My eyes tear up. Pap Pap can't die. I drop Glynna's hands to rub my eyes. I've got to pull myself together.

"They can't find any blockage, so there's nothing to operate on," my father whispers.

"Then what happened?" I ask.

"His heart just stopped."

"I don't understand."

"I don't think the doctors do either.

GLYNNA

119

Ashton's grandfather almost *died* while he was eating one of my cupcakes.

I try to convince myself that it's a coincidence, but I know it's not. I need to talk to Nana, but I can't just jump up and leave Ashton.

God of Cupcakes, what if I *killed* Ashton's grandfather?

The spike of high heels pounding linoleum approaches. Tatiana Bass sweeps into the waiting room. I want to crawl under my plastic chair, but I don't think I'll fit. Tatiana gives me a fleeting glare. "Gregor, what happened?" she screeches.

"We were sitting at the kitchen table and he just—"

"He just what, Gregor?"

"He was asking me these strange questions, and then he just crumpled."

"Crumpled? Where is the doctor? What are they doing?"

"They don't really understand what happened. They can't find anything wrong with his heart, but he's in a coma."

"I need to see him!" Tatiana charges back out into the hall, screaming for a doctor.

"Maybe I should call Leif now," I whisper to Ashton.

He takes my hand. "Would you mind staying with me a little longer? I can't," his voice quivers, "I can't do this alone. Would you stay with me for just a little while?"

I need to talk to Nana, but I can't say no to Ashton's watery blue eyes. He looks vulnerable. My heart is being squeezed. "I'll stay as long as you want."

A man in a white coat enters the room with Tatiana on his heels. She scrutinizes me in another head-to-toe hate-filled sweep. Beneath the fluorescent lights, her eyes look coal-black. Without thinking, I draw on the light inside me for protection. I feel the invisible veil surround me.

Tatiana's eyes narrow, piercing into me. "She needs to leave," she says to Ashton.

"I want her to stay."

Tatiana's lips press together. I can see the struggle in her jaw. Will she

120

escalate her demand, or acquiesce to her grandson, who I wish would allow me to slip away unnoticed? Daphne flits over to Tatiana's side and squeezes her in an embrace. Like me, Maddie stays seated in her plastic chair, observing everyone.

The doctor coughs, and Daphne releases Tatiana.

"We're still running tests, but the cause of Nicolas' collapse isn't yet apparent."

"Is he going to live?"

To everyone present, the answer to Tatiana's question is the only one that matters.

The doctor crosses his arms and gazes beyond the family. "He'll live, but at this point, we can't guarantee what his mental or physical capacity will be when, or if, he wakes up."

Tatiana sways. The doctor and Daphne catch her.

Gregor jumps up and helps her to one of the plastic chairs. "Get her something," he tells the doctor who indicates the nurse hovering behind him before he leaves the waiting room.

"I'll need to contact her primary care physician before he can prescribe something," the nurse says.

Although, Ashton's grandmother turns five shades of purple, she allows her son to provide the nurse with the information she needs. Minutes later the woman returns with a tiny paper cup and flimsy plastic glass filled with water.

Tatiana argues about the sedative.

"There's nothing we can do but wait," her son insists. It will help you to remain calm."

Tatiana eyes the two small blue pills warily. "Let me make a call first."

"Who do you need to call?" Gregor asks.

"Fine. I'll take the damned pills." She shoves them in her mouth and takes a gulp of water.

"How long before they take effect?" Gregor asks the nurse.

"Fifteen minutes or so."

"Lorriene, our phones don't work in here. Go downstairs and text Donald to meet us out front," Gregor says. "Ashton, help me take your grandmother downstairs."

"No," Tatiana says. "I need to be here when Nicolas wakes up."

121

"Go home and get some rest," her son says. "I'll stay here and send for you if there's any change."

Tatiana's eyes are becoming less focused. Surprisingly, she doesn't argue.

Lorriene hurries out into the hall while Ashton goes to help his father.

They're barely out of the room when Daphne says to me, "Maybe it's time for you to go too. This is a private, family matter."

Even though she's not family, I'm not going to argue with her. I grab my shoes.

"Are those real Louboutins?" Maddie asks.

"Yes."

"I didn't realize selling cupcakes was so lucrative."

I plaster a huge smile across my face, because I'm so not going to waste my time with her. Kristeen would be proud.

The Wardof sisters exchange glances.

Maddie makes a ring with her thumb and index finger and pokes her other index finger through it. Apparently, she's just getting started. "So that's what you and Ashton have been doing all day."

My black temper uncoils in my belly. Don't push me, stupid girl. "We went to lunch."

"For four hours?"

If I carried a compact, I'd check to see if black smoke was pouring from my ears. "I wasn't aware we broke one of your dating rules."

Her older sister snorts.

Before I reach the hall, Daphne practically shouts, "Don't get your hopes up."

I turn around slowly. The boom of thunder cracks outside the hospital, and the waiting room window shows dark clouds building. "I didn't realize Ashton was incapable of speaking for himself."

The catty grin slides off Daphne's face as a flash of lightning illuminates the black sky outside the window.

"I'm just trying to be helpful," she says in her most fake-sincere voice. "His grandmother will never accept Ashton having a serious relationship with someone like you, and I don't want you to get hurt."

My entire body pulses with unconfined fury. Big splats of rain hit the window. Hail quickly follows. "I understand. My grandmother would

122

never want me to get involved with anyone who has friends like you."

A large chunk of hail slams the window behind them. The glass turns opaque as a spider web of cracks damages the pane.

Their mouths flop open at the same time as they spin around to see. I march to the elevators, head high, back straight. I've got to get out of here before I do more serious damage. I jam the elevator button several times.

Why is it taking so long?

Of course, when the doors slide open, my prince charming is standing in front of me. He may not be feeling so charming once his friends report our disagreement.

"Thanks for coming," Ashton's father says as he scoots past me.

Ashton blocks the elevator entrance.

I'd have to duck and twist to get inside. When he steps in my direction, I have no place to go but backwards. When my back is against the wall, he puts his arms up on either side of me.

He leans forward so close our foreheads are touching.

My face is flushing.

"Do you really have to go?" he asks in a whisper.

"I don't think your friends want me around as much as you do. And I know what your grandmother thinks."

He pulls his arms back, but reaches up with his hand to caress my cheek.

I momentarily close my eyes so I can focus one-hundred-percent on how his touch feels.

"Did they say something?"

"We exchanged some words. I'm sorry. Everyone's tense and upset."

Ashton's brow furrows.

"It's probably best if I leave you with your family... and close friends."

He presses his hand over his eyes. "The Wardof sisters are not my close friends."

"Really, I should go."

"At least, let me take you downstairs and wait with you until your cousin shows up."

"Okay."

When the elevator opens again, Lorriene steps out. "Where are you

123

two off to?" she asks in a bratty sister voice.

"Glynna's gonna call her cousin to pick her up."

"That guy with the tats?" Her interest is strangely intense.

I just roll my eyes and nod.

"Does he really have a pet owl?" she asks.

"Archi," I bite out the word.

"Cool-sexy," she says. Or did she just purr?

Her curiosity about Leif ticks me off. He's two years older than me—the same age as Ashton—and Lorriene is still in high school. How does she know him? I try to shrug it off. Maybe they met at the bonfire, and she's just fawning over him because he's fresh meat. I better warn my cousin to keep her away from his coffee and croissants! Judging by her level of interest, one whiff of either and he'll never be rid of her.

But I have to admit, Lorriene is as full of surprises as her brother. I'd never have figured she'd fall for a lower-on-the-food-chain computer geek even if he is muscled and inked.

I'm relieved to see her stay put when the elevator finally pings open, despite hoping for a cat fight just a few minutes ago.

Why am I craving violence?

I rub my hand across my heart which is being pulled in two opposite directions. Because that's who I am: Dark and light.

When we step outside, Ashton pulls me over to a bench beneath an awning. The rain is still coming down.

I pull out my phone and call Leif. "He's on his way."

Ashton reaches for my hand. "Don't let my sister and her friends get to you. Lorriene's a little territorial when it comes to her big brother."

"Your grandmother, too?" I ask.

Ashton shrugs. "Grandma requires special handling. But don't worry, I've got twenty-one years of experience with her. There's very little she can deny her favorite grandson."

I smile, but notice he didn't say *nothing*. Why do I think that I'm going to be the one battle that Ashton is going to lose with her? A rumble of thunder accents my depressing thoughts.

When Leif pulls up to the curb, Nana is in the front seat. The window rolls down before I can say goodbye to Ashton and send him back inside.

Nana's all made up and she's wearing one of her nice dresses. "Is he

124

all right?" she asks.

"No, but we need to give his family some time to be alone with him." I break the words apart and carefully emphasize each one.

Leif is already out of the car and coming around to open Nana's door. I bite back a groan. "Nana, he can't have any visitors."

"I've waited over forty years for this moment, I can wait a few more hours."

What is she talking about? I glance at Ashton to see how he's taking this mystifying statement, but he seems unfazed. Maybe he didn't hear her. I can only hope.

"What floor?" Leif asks. He's going to park the car then join us.

"The fourth," Ashton answers. He's already got Nana's elbow and is ushering her inside, the perfect gentleman. I watch Leif pull away from the curb. Either I stand here like an idiot, or I follow Ashton and Nana back inside. Before I turn, a sleek, black Cadillac double-parked a few spaces ahead catches my eye. The windows are black, but the vehicle gives me a chill.

14. Cupcake Commotion

EARL

Ashton is such a gentleman, so much like his grandfather. He leads me through the crowded hospital foyer. Glynna is right behind us. I wish I could explain to her what's going on, but this is between me and Nicolas. If he's going to die, I have to tell him I love him one more time. I have to tell him I've always loved him, and I have to apologize.

It's clear now, I should never have acquiesced to Tatiana's threats. Light is always more powerful than dark, if you believe. But I lost my faith, and I've been paying for it every day for forty years. Now, I fear Nicolas has too.

When we reach the fourth floor, Ashton ushers me toward a room.

"Wait!" Glynna says. "Please," she says to the boy, "I need a moment alone with my grandmother."

"Sure. I'll just wait for you both inside."

"Thank you," I say.

Glynna's gaze follows him as he enters the room. Three young women about her age are hovering around a man who looks so much like Nicolas. I assume it's his son. As soon as Ashton crosses the threshold, the blonde zooms over to him like some killer bee. She throws her arms

127

around him. Glynna looks like she's about to commit murder before she turns to face me. There's something feral in those darkening blue eyes. She appears so unlike my sweet, gentle Glynna. I fear it's her Occulto blood manifesting, and there's nothing I can do to stop its expression, other than continue to love her as much as I can.

"What is going on?" she asks me. Clearly, she's unhappy to see me. "Why are you here, Nana?"

"I need to see Nicolas."

"He's in a coma."

"It doesn't matter. He'll know I'm here."

She releases a sigh of frustration. "Nana, what has gotten into you these past few days? First you flirt with Nicolas at the shop in front of God and everyone, and now you're here! What if Tatiana Bass comes back? Even if she doesn't catch you here, Lorriene is going to tell her! You have to go home."

I stand firm. My granddaughter has no idea what's at stake. I say nothing, and try to speak to her with my eyes. *Please, trust me,* I try to say.

"Not now, Nana!"

"Glynna." I reach for her hand. She needs to understand at least one thing. "I'm not afraid of Tatiana anymore."

The young girl who favors Nicolas' grandson has noticed us standing out in the hall. She's whispering to her friend.

"Well, that's just great," Glynna says. "I'm so glad you've found your courage. Could we please go home? Now!"

"I'm not leaving until I see Nicolas."

"They're not going to let you see him."

My eyes tear up.

Glynna grabs my elbow and pulls me toward a row of chairs a few feet down the hall. "Nana, you don't understand. He was eating one of my cupcakes when he had his heart attack. If Tatiana Bass finds out I killed him—"

"Oh, dear, Glynna, is that what's got you so upset?"

"Yes!"

"Listen to me, sweet girl, if anything, eating one of your cupcakes has saved Nicolas' soul."

"What are you talking about?"

High heels are pounding down the linoleum. I close my eyes as I turn my head. Tatiana Bass is flying toward us. Her arms are waving at her side and her black eyes are lasered on me and my granddaughter.

"Pearl! How dare you try to sneak up here the moment I leave!"

I pull my hand from Glynna's. This is my battle not hers. Although I'm almost a foot shorter than Tatiana, I rise from my seat to stand tall and straight. "Where were you going, Tati? Home to whip up a batch of shrimp étouffée?"

Tatiana's eyes bulge. "What did you do to him?"

"Are you frightened, Tati?"

"Gregor!" Tatiana screams.

Everyone comes running out of the waiting room, not just her son. Several of the nurses are frozen in the hall.

"What mother? What's wrong?" Her son is by her side.

Her son. It should have been my son. I just gave up all those years ago. I just let her win.

"I want these two out of here," Tatiana screeches. She's afraid. "They don't belong here. She—" Tatiana spears her finger at me. "—will not see your father."

I draw strength from her panic. Four decades of lies are at risk, and we both know it.

The three young girls are simultaneously gaping and gloating. Ashton, to his credit, has maneuvered around them. His hand is resting on Glynna's shoulder, but he remains quiet. Perhaps out of respect for his father who speaks in an even tone.

"Mom, I thought you were going home to get some rest."

"I was, until I saw her!" She shoves me.

Glynna jumps up. Ashton's hand falls away from her shoulder. The thick waves of my granddaughter's fury swirls with the force of a centrifuge. She positions herself between me and Tatiana. "Don't ever touch my grandmother again."

"Glynna, calm down," I whisper.

A hospital siren wails. Nurses and doctors spill out of rooms up and down the hall. There's a tornado alert. Glynna snorts.

"Gregor!" Tatiana screams. "Get them out of here."

129

"We're not going anywhere," Glynna says.

Tatiana's narrow eyes are studying my granddaughter too intently. "Doctors," Tatiana moans. "Someone, please help us. These women will not leave my husband alone."

"Yes, please help us," Glynna's voice is steel. "My grandmother wants to press assault charges against this lunatic."

Tatiana's hand drives toward my granddaughter. Her son knocks it down before the slap connects with Glynna's cheek. I gasp.

Two security guards are heading in our direction.

I need to create a distraction.

"Ladies, ladies." They edge between us. One faces Glynna and me, the other faces Tatiana and the army of her family. Somehow Ashton is caught between the two groups.

"Who's the family?" One of the guards asks.

"We are," Tatiana shrieks.

The security guards nod. "Ladies," he says to us, "Only family is allowed in ICU. Will you allow us to escort you out?"

I stumble into one of the chairs lining the hall and grasp at my heart. I hold my breath for as long as I can.

"Oh my God! Help her!" Glynna screams.

Two orderlies come running with a bed. A nurse is right behind them. Once they have me strapped down and are wheeling me away, I wink at my granddaughter. I want her to know I'm all right. She runs after us as they roll me into the elevator.

"Where are you taking her?" Glynna asks.

The attendant pushes button number one. "The emergency room is on the first floor."

Ashton is right behind us. "Glynna." She acts like she doesn't hear him, but I see him grab her arm. "Let me know when your grandmother's all right."

"Sure." Glynna hangs her head. "I'm not sure what's gotten into her..."

I've embarrassed her, but I'm not leaving this hospital until I see Nicolas. Hopefully, one day, my dear Glynna will understand.

"Be safe," Ashton says.

"Huh?"

"The tornado..."

"Right. Yeah, you too."

The elevator doors slide close.

 ATIANA

"I'm going to kill that woman."

"Mother, please. You need to calm down."

"She has no business coming here and badgering your father."

"Mother, please sit down."

"Ashton, I forbid you to see that girl again."

"Grandma—"

"Did you hear her? She threatened to press charges against me!"

"Ashton, it has been a hard day for everyone," Gregor says. "We need to help your grandmother calm down."

"Sure. I'll make a coffee run."

The moment he leaves, he's going to go find her. I can see it in his eyes. "Daphne, go with him."

"I'm fine," he protests.

"Oh, Ashton, I don't mind helping." Daphne runs to catch up with him.

He doesn't make it easy for her. I do wish he had some natural affection for the girl. She's the only person who has an inkling of what's really at stake here. Not one of my descendants has a whit of Occulto ability, and it hits me hard. Not one of them understands why it's so dangerous for Pearl to be here. Not one of them understands why Nico is so vulnerable. For the first time in a very long time, I feel truly alone.

And that redheaded girl of Pearl's; how dare she challenge me? How dare she threaten to have me arrested? I'm going to have to cook up something unpleasant for her. Perhaps I'll start with a Repulsion Spell. Just in case Ashton ever decides to circumvent my orders to see her again.

131

But first I must assure Pearl doesn't see Nico. Especially not in his current weakened state, when I'm not sure what is happening to him.

These are the times I regret not forming stronger alliances with the Seattle coven. They could be so helpful now. And Pearl was right. I must get home and whip up some of my love-inducing étouffée. I need to have it ready as soon as Nico gains consciousness.

I bounce out of my chair and pace. As long as Pearl is in this hospital, I'm on lockdown. For all the Lumina claims of dignity and honor, she's a sneaky little thing.

ASHTON

"What's up with that girl and her grandmother?" Daphne asks as we thread through the hospital cafeteria line.

"I'm not sure."

"Don't you think it's weird?"

"What?"

"That old woman coming up here to visit your grandfather."

"Maybe they've known each other a long time."

"I doubt it," Daphne says.

Why is she meddling? Though, I admit I'm curious about Pearl and Pap Pap's history as well. Gathering from Grandma's reaction, I'm beginning to think there's much more to it. "It looked to me like Grandma and Pearl know each other pretty well, too," I say.

"Well, your grandmother obviously doesn't want her here."

"Can't argue with that."

"So, did you have fun on your date?"

"I don't want to talk about Glynna." Why can't she stop talking?

"Are you mad at her?"

"No." I'm piling muffins and packs of crackers and cheese, and little bowls of fruit onto a tray. I'm hoping food will take everyone's mind off the drama that just unfolded on the fourth floor.

132

"You sound mad."

"Not at her."

"Are you mad at your grandmother?" Daphne squeals right into my ear.

"No." My patience is running thin.

"You sound upset."

"I'm upset that my grandfather is in here. I'm upset that he had a heart attack. And I'm upset that the doctors can't find anything wrong with him."

"Oh," Daphne says.

I order a tray of lattes before digging money out of my wallet to pay the cashier. "Can you carry that?" I ask Daphne when the coffees are ready.

She stands as close to me as possible when we get in the elevator. It's going to be a really long night, and I just want a few minutes alone to slip away and check on Glynna. Lorriene and I are used to Grandma T's temper, but I know firsthand, it can be tough to bear the brunt of it. I'll feel better when I know my Cupcake Girl is all right.

In the meantime, I'm starting to piece together the love triangle which is Pap Pap, my Grandma, and Pearl. It may have been years ago when Pap Pap and Pearl were in love, but they still have feelings for one another. Their big affection showdown yesterday at Frosting & Beans made that pretty obvious.

I probably should have been more surprised when Pearl showed up at the hospital this afternoon. If there's a scintilla of a chance that her presence can help Pap Pap hang onto life, I'm glad she's here. I don't care how much it upsets my grandmother.

I'm angry at Grandma T for causing such a ridiculous scene, shoving Pearl, forbidding me to see Glynna, and sending me out on a leash with Daphne.

Who does she think she is? No matter how often I try to stand up to her, I never do. But this match-making game she's playing between me and Daphne! I can't even stand being near Octopus Woman. And marrying her? I might as well dig my own grave.

Daphne nuzzles her chin against my side. This is the last straw.

I'm done with Grandma running my life. It's time for me to get some balls and kiss the Bass fortune goodbye. If Pap Pap built his financial

133

empire from nothing, then maybe I can too.

By the time we get back to the waiting room, things have calmed down. But when Grandma glares at me, I glare right back at her. She and Lorriene are not going to run me anymore.

Daphne and I hand out the food and coffees.

Dad is still trying to convince his mom to go home and get some rest.

I wish him luck, and if I was in a more cooperative mood, I'd offer to go with her. But I want to see Glynna. I step out into the hall and head to the nurse's station. They tell me that I can get cellphone reception on any floor except this one. I head for the stair well.

When I check my phone, there's a text from Glynna.

Nana's fine. Going 2 keep her overnite for observation.

Thanx for update. Are U OK?

Pearl is very emotional. Sorry about fight w/Tati.

Don't worry. We're OK.

What about your grandpa?

Haven't heard anymore. MayB no news is good news.

MayB. I hope.

Wish I could C U.

May B seeing each other is not such a good idea.

What R U saying?

Your gma doesn't care for me.

I care for you.

How many chicks have u made swoon with that pick up line?

There's only 1 girl I care 2 make swoon.

Ahh U R good!

So she swoons? ;)

Totally melting! ;)

What room is Nana in?

523

Come up later if I can get away?

Sure.

"Where have you been?" Lorriene asks.

"Can't a guy take a piss without getting grilled?"

She doesn't call me on my lie. I guess we've all had enough fireworks for one day.

When I sit back down, Daphne reaches for my hand.

I jerk it away. I'm sick of her forcing herself on me when I don't even want to be around her. "Shouldn't you girls be going home?" I ask.

"I appreciate their support," Tatiana says.

"Well, I'm going downstairs. I need some fresh air."

"What about the tornado?" Maddie looks pointedly out the window.

"Looks like it's clearing off. The sky isn't as dark as it was earlier." I check my watch. It's seven o'clock. I try not to think that we were all supposed to be sitting down to our Sunday night shrimp étouffée tradition right now.

This time Grandma doesn't stop me or send her spy after me. I skip the elevator for the stairwell. I take two steps at a time up to the fifth floor. I stop outside room 523 to dispel the tension in my neck and shoulders. Fending off Octopus Woman has me on edge. I don't want to carry that negative energy into Pearl's room.

Glynna is sitting next to her grandmother, who's propped up with about five pillows. Her cousin is on the other side of the bed. Glynna jumps up when she sees me.

"Ashton," Pearl calls out a greeting with her sweet voice. "Have you heard anything else about your grandfather?"

"No, ma'am."

She pats her bed. "Come, sit here for a minute."

I settle on the bed beside her.

Pearl takes my hand. "I apologize for upsetting your Grandmother earlier."

"She'll be fine."

"You seem like such a kind boy with such a good heart," she says.

I'm not really sure how to respond, so I just say, "Thank you."

"Glynna told me Nicolas was eating a cupcake when he had his heart attack."

"I wasn't there, but that's what my dad told me. But it wasn't Glynna's fault. I don't think that."

"Shh-shh," Nana says. "We know it wasn't Glynna's fault. Ashton, I need to see your grandfather. Just once. Can you help me?"

135

My heart bangs around in my chest. If I help Pearl see my grandfather, Grandma T might kill me. But I can't shake the feeling that having Pearl close by will do Pap Pap a world of good.

Tati's Shrimp Étouffée Recipe

Ingredients:

½ cup oil
½ cup all-purpose flour
1 cup chopped yellow onion
½ cup chopped green bell pepper
1 cup chopped celery
3 cloves garlic finely minced
½ teaspoon black pepper
½ teaspoon white pepper
½ teaspoon Red Devil Chili or more as desired
2 pounds medium shrimps
5 grams ground Venus fly trap

As you add each ingredient, recite incantation:
Flaming passion like darkness bind,
Burning desire obscure and blind,
Make him mine, hold him tight,
Possess what's in my sight.

This spell is best served weekly.

15. When a Cupcake Realization Hits...

GLYNNA

"You shouldn't have asked Ashton to help you, Nana." My words are soft and full of love, but I'm worried how all this is going to play out if Tatiana finds out.

How will she not know? She's like a vulture.

Nana pats my hand. "Did you see the two of them yesterday?"

"Ashton and his grandfather?"

"They're very fond of one another. And he wants to help. Everything is going to be fine."

"I wish I could believe you, but I've got a bad feeling about this."

"Don't worry about Tati. Ophelia's bringing pie."

Whoever eats one of Nana's pies is positively disposed toward the giver. If the giver is Nana, the affect is tenfold.

"Ashton's grandmother is not going to be eating any of your pie!"

"No?" She gives me a sly smile.

"Nana, what are you up to?"

139

My phone *pings* before she can answer. Now that we're off the ICU floor, it's working again. "It's a text from Kristeen."

Nana waves me away. "I need to take a little nap before Ashton returns."

"You sure?"

She nods as she closes her eyes. I step out into the hall to call my friend.

"Hey, girl!" Kristeen's chipper voice is music to my ears. "How did it go with Mr. Hotness?"

"You're not going to believe what happened."

"You didn't? Already?"

I roll my eyes. "No, it was nothing like that."

"You mean you're still Miss Virginia?"

"Oh, yes, very much so."

Her loud sigh broadcasts her disappointment.

"But it wasn't a failure of your sweltering red lipstick. In fact..." My mind returns to this afternoon, when everything was melting.

"What? Don't keep me in suspense!" she screams in my ear.

"The lipstick worked great, but Ashton's grandfather had a heart attack."

"That wasn't very romantic of him."

"I don't think he had a say in the matter."

"No. But still. What craptastic timing."

"Kristeen, we're all, I mean all, up here at the hospital."

"Girl!" she squeals. "Are you up there providing him moral support?"

"Not exactly." I tell her about Lorriene and Daphne and Maddie. Then I tell her about Tatiana and Nana.

"Sizzling hot tamales! When did Nana become so feisty?"

"I know! And you should have seen her yesterday at Frosting & Beans. She had Nicolas eating out of the palm of her hand. People were stopping on the street and staring in the windows watching them!"

"Ai-yi-yi! And to think I missed it all! Maybe I should come join the party tonight. What time are visiting hours over?"

"Actually, Ophelia's on her way here now, and I have a sneaking suspicion visiting hours aren't going to be an issue. Do you think you could meet her down stairs and help her bring up the pie? I'm pretty sure she's bringing enough to feed a small army." I walk over to one of the long hall windows. It's still drizzling, but I think the tornado may have been a false alarm. "The weather's calmed down. It should be safe to drive now."

Ashton kissed me before he went back downstairs. It was a quick, gentle kiss, but that was all it took to quell my inner chaos... and the dangerous wind funnel threatening Spokane.

"Sure thing, *chica bonita*. I'm already half-dressed."

"Great, I'll text my aunt and tell her you'll meet her in the lobby."

When I hang up, I'm grinning ear-to-ear. Kristeen's infectious enthusiasm has woken up my inner rebel. Won't it be awesome to pull something over on Tatiana? In fact, the more I consider Nana's plan, the more I'm convinced of its simple genius. Who wouldn't want a slice of delicious pie on a Sunday night?

PEARL

"Leif?"

"Yes, Nana."

"Can you help me out of bed?"

He hurries over. His arms are solid muscle, but he's gentle with me.

"You've gotten so strong."

"Can't let anything happen to my girls," he says.

I let out a little laugh. When my feet are solid on the ground, I head to the private bathroom. He turns on the light for me. "Can you hand me my dress?" I ask him.

"You can't leave until they discharge you."

My sister should be proud. Her son has grown into such a responsible young man. "Oh, I'm not going anywhere. I just want to look nice when Nicolas wakes up."

He doesn't argue as he hands me the hanger.

"Thank you. I'll be just a few minutes."

I turn on the water and run a damp paper towel beneath my eyes to

141

clear the smudges of makeup. If Nicolas does wake up, I want to look my best. I fluff my hair and change into my dress, smoothing out the wrinkles. Once I'm pleased with the reflection looking back at me from the mirror it wavers:

I'm eighteen years old, and sitting alone in my apartment. It's almost midnight. My eyes are swollen, and there's a mountain of tissue on the table next to me. I don't like to remember this night, but I need to understand exactly what went wrong if I'm going to fix it now. I'm still wearing the dress I made especially for my date with Nicolas. It's made from organdy, with a fitted waist and bodice. The long, gauzy sleeves sweep out like wings every time I move, and whenever I stand up to pace, the soft, full skirt swirls around my slim hips. I've tried to call Nicolas a million times—he doesn't answer his phone—and in the past hour, I've started calling every hospital in Spokane—Nicolas Remington Bass hasn't checked in, or been checked in, to any hospital or emergency room.

He's never stood me up before.

Something dreadful must have happened.

The mirror wavers.

A frantic knocking at the door wakes me up. I'm on the couch, still wearing my organdy dress. Sometime in the wee hours of the morning, I passed out from heartbreak and exhaustion. I run to answer the door.

When I open it, my heart crashes like a thousand China plates.

It's only the paperboy trying to sell me a subscription to The Spokesman-Review.

I mumble something before slamming the door in his face. It's time to call my sister, Ophelia. She has a car.

The mirror wavers once more.

NICOLAS

I'm dreaming. At least, that's what it feels like, because my body feels light, and I'm so young. I'm driving my new cherry-red Firebird Trans Am. I just got it this morning, and I couldn't wait to take Pearl for a spin.

142

She's in the passenger seat beside me. Her long brown hair swirls around her shoulders. She has on a pale yellow sundress, and the sunlight spilling through the windows highlights the golden suntan on her arms and legs. I've never been so happy.

When I sold my first commercial property last month, the commission was enough to buy this car and an impressive engagement ring from Harry Ritchie's. I've made reservations for dinner tomorrow night at the Davenport Hotel. I'm going to propose. If Pearl says yes, I'll be the happiest man in the world.

When I park the car in front of her apartment complex, we linger because I want to remember this moment forever. Even though it's late in the day, the sky is bright blue without a cloud in sight. I caress Pearl's shoulder and her skin feels like velvet. When she blushes, my heart does a little somersault. I've never met a sweeter girl than Pearl. But there's so much more to her than that. She's also patient and industrious. Qualities I admire. She's tiny and has a hard time finding anything that fits her in the stores, so she designs and sews most of her clothes. The girls from the wealthiest families in town don't look as good as she does. And I've never felt more like myself around anyone. When I'm with my girl, all the walls come down. Something about her makes me excited and relaxed at the same time. It's easy for me to imagine the adventures we're going to share as we grow old together.

Right now, her steady, wordless gaze is melting me. I tug on her hair.

She lets her head fall back, and I brush her soft lips.

"I want you. All of you. I want to remember everything about you. I want to remember this," I say as I kiss her soft lips again. "And this—" I plant another kiss on her neck. I feel her shiver and inhale the vanilla scent, which seems to be so much a part of her. "I need to remember every shiver your body makes in response to mine."

She murmurs her delight.

I can't stand to let her go, but if I keep this up, she's never going to make it inside. "It's always hard to say goodbye to you."

"It's not goodbye. It's just I'll see you tomorrow, right?"

"Pick you up at 6 o'clock?" I ask.

"Can't wait." Her cheeks crinkle into an infectious smile.

I force myself to get out of the car and circle around to open her door.

143

She's wearing a pair of those platform shoes that are in fashion now. They're almost as tall as she is, so it's a mystery how she moves with such grace when I take her hand and help her out of the Firebird, but float she does. I keep hold of her as we head toward the lobby of her apartment complex.

"One more kiss to hold me over?"

She leans into me. Her breath is like lavender and lemons. My heart races with desire. I run my fingers through her hair and settle my hands on the smooth skin of her face. A crazy part of me wants me to bend down on my knee right now and ask her to marry me. A strange fear possesses me: If I don't ask her in this moment, I'll never get the chance again. But I argue with my senseless panic. This isn't romantic enough. When we tell our children and grandchildren about the day I proposed to their mother and grandmother, I need Pearl's memory of the day to be perfect, a day she'll cherish forever.

Asking her here and now won't do.

In less than twenty-four hours. Be patient, Nicolas.

When I climb back into my car, dark clouds appear out of nowhere. They tear across the sky, leaving a midnight sky in their wake. I flip on my headlights. There's no moonlight, and not a single star in the sky. What happened?

The next day I stop by Jambalaya's for lunch. Ever since I tasted their wicked shrimp étouffée a few weeks ago, I've been stopping by for a serving almost every day around 11:00 to beat the lines. The cook is a young woman who moved here from Louisiana. She certainly knows her way around a kitchen.

Lately, I've started thinking about lunch as soon as I wake up in the morning. Unusual for me, my mind won't settle down until I've had at least one platter of the delectably spiced shrimp and rice. Today's not any different.

"Nico," Tatiana greets me the second I walk through the door. She's the cook, and she knows what I'm here for. Over the past week, she's taken to serving me herself. Big Frank, Jambalaya's owner, doesn't seem to mind her offering me the VIP treatment, and I have no reason to complain.

"Your usual, Nico?"

"Please, Tati."

Once I'm seated, she waltzes toward me with a generous portion of her specialty. She's got on platforms, tight bell-bottom jeans, and a sheer peasant blouse with bell sleeves. Tati always dresses on the saucy side, and I have to admit she's a beautiful woman. Not beautiful like my Pearl, but beautiful like something dangerous and tempting you need to be wary of. She settles in the booth opposite me and pushes the plate of thick roué, shrimp, and rice in my direction.

The smell of the food in front of me is spicy. I dig in. When I take the first bite, everything and everyone else in my life is forgotten: the rest of my day's appointments and my date tonight with Pearl slip from my mind. A cloak has dropped over my heart, suffocating my feelings. The only thing I'm aware of is the tantalizing creature seated across from me, feeding me the best meal I've ever tasted. I barely remember my own name, because when Tatiana coos "Do you like it, Nico?" I look around to see who she's talking to.

She laughs. It's a sharp, shiny tinkle. Her red painted lips are moist and full of promise. She leans across the table and her ample cleavage draws my attention. That seems to delight her, and she wiggles more provocatively.

The diamond ring in my pocket begins to throb.

"Eat up, Nico," she encourages. "Every last bite. I made this batch especially for you."

I slurp the bowl's contents. "It's delicious."

With every bite, she radiates more and more sexual energy.

"Are you dating someone, Tati?"

She throws back her head and laughs. Every man in the room is staring at her, desiring her. The fact that she's in the booth with me makes me feel puffed up. I can't help but think if Tati Caron were riding next to me in my new cherry red Trans Am, I'd be the envy of every guy in here.

"What time do you get off work?" I ask her after I take the last bite of étouffée.

She takes the bowl from me and squeezes out of the booth. "You enjoyed that so much. Let me get you another bowl, eh?"

Her hips sway all the way to the kitchen.

When she returns, she slides into the booth right next to me and pushes

145

the second loaded plate of shrimp in my direction. It's just as delicious as the first. But before I'm done with this one, she's got her arm draped over my shoulder, I can feel her breast pressed against my arm and she's nibbling at my ear. I've never wanted a woman so badly in life. Blood is rushing in my head and my ears. My heart is pumping red-hot desire.

There's only one thing in the world that makes any sense. I reach into my pocket and slip the engagement ring on my pinky finger. I hold it in front of her and watch her eyes shine.

"You want to be my girl?" I ask her.

She flings her arms around me and something inside me dies. She eases the ring from my finger and slips it onto her own. She gets up on her knees and plasters my head and my face with kisses. Her lips are like ice.

When she jumps up and screams the news of our engagement to the rest of the restaurant's patrons, there are as many puzzled faces as cheers.

I'm so old now. My hair is gray and thinning. I look behind me, and the road is empty. What have I done with my life? The world around me looks like a war zone, everything demolished, destroyed and in ruins. A barren tree clutches at the sky. I step closer. A mass of muscle nested among its colorless branches throbs weakly.

Is that, could that be... my heart? It's barely beating.

Overhead a flock of black birds flutter their wings.

A black egg falls from the sky and cracks at my feet.

A lifetime of sorrow bleeds out.

Oh, God, Pearl, what have I done?

EARL

The mirror ripples.

Tatiana answers Nicolas' door. She's barely dressed in something gauzy. She flaunts the diamond solitaire on her finger. Ophelia has to hold me up to keep me from collapsing. When we reach the car, my sister asks me, "Did you notice anything strange?"

146

"Besides Nicolas being engaged to someone other than me?"

"She's a witch," Ophelia says.

"A Lumina would never break up a love relationship."

"Exactly."

I gaze at my boyfriend's shuttered apartment, sickened by images of naked, twined limbs and guttural cries of lust. "An Occulto?"

"Spokane is so small and inconsequential, we've been fortunate most of them have chosen to live in Seattle. But it was only a matter of time. Occultos are everywhere these days."

"Do you think she knows we're Luminas?"

"Not yet."

"We can't reveal ourselves, Ophelia."

"You can't just let her steal your boyfriend, Pearl!"

"Maybe she'll grow tired of him."

"I don't think that boulder on her finger is about a fling."

"I can't believe this is happening."

"Well, it is, and if you don't do something, you're going to lose Nicolas forever."

The mirror wavers. I don't need to revisit all the useless memories of me baking pies Tatiana wouldn't let Nicolas taste.

The reflection returns me to today.

"It might have taken me forty years and Nicolas landing on his deathbed for me to find the strength to fight, but I've found it, Tatiana."

16. Who Can Resist a Cupcake?

 SHTON

I keep watching the clock on the wall outside the waiting room.

Lorriene plops down in the chair next to me. "Waiting for someone?"

"You and the Wardof sisters should take Dad, Mom, and Grandma home." Mom got to the hospital about forty-five minutes ago. It looks like Grandma T isn't holding it against her that she was in Seattle when everything went down. I'm relieved. All we need is another emotional explosion.

"Like hell, Grandma's not going anywhere."

"They're all exhausted."

Lorriene's eyes brighten, and she pops up from her chair. "Leif?"

Glynna's cousin has come bearing gifts, slices of pie on a tray. Their fresh-baked smell drowns out the pervasive odor of antiseptic.

My head swivels in Grandma's direction. She's puffed up like a spitting cobra. Does she know who this guy is? I hope not. I hope she's just offended that he dared to enter the room. On the other hand, Lorriene is salivating. She's not going to reveal pie guy's true identity.

"For us?"

The giddy in my sister's voice makes me give Glynna's cousin a closer

149

look. He's pulling off a worn tee, chinos, and some ratty sneakers beneath a dingy white apron. Definitely not Lorriene's usual top-shelf dude. Maybe the tat sleeves on his arm, and the long hair tied back in a pony-tail, give him a common man appeal, because if my sister's not careful, she's going to be slobbering in a minute. The truth is he looks like he could work in the hospital cafeteria. I wonder if that's intentional.

A few feet away, Tatiana's interest has pricked along with my mom's. Grandma's transformed from venomous snake into... Is that an expression of appreciation? Mom's getting herself an eyeful too. I turn back to Leif. Maddie has just glued herself to his side.

Lorriene and Maddie each take a slice of pie and tear in. We're all starving. Hospital food sucks.

My grandmother squirms in her seat. "Where did that come from?"

"They just came out of the oven downstairs," Leif says. "We like to offer them as a courtesy to the family members who stay past visiting hours."

He's an impressive liar.

Grandma rubs her tummy and softens her voice. "I've been so worried about my husband, I haven't eaten a bite all day."

Leif hurries over, all smiles. "We've got blueberry, banana cream, and chocolate."

Tatiana gingerly inspects his offerings. "What flavor do you recommend?"

Is she flirting with him?

"For someone with your discriminating palate, I'd definitely go with the blueberry. The berries are fresh and ripe, so we add very little sugar."

"Mmm," Grandma murmurs. "That sounds perfect."

He hands her the pie and a plastic fork. Grandma is religiously against plastic cutlery, but she cuts off a corner of the pie with the white tines. "Oh, dear," she giggles. "This is amazing."

"Glad you like it."

"Oh, I love it." Grandma's lost in a berry haze.

"Do you have another slice of the blueberry?" Mom asks.

Neither Mom nor Grandma miss the flexed ink on Leif's biceps as he delivers a plate to Mom. They're as bad as Lorriene and Maddie, having noisy food orgasms over the gooey mess on their plates.

Dad opts for banana cream.

I don't want to miss out on all the fun. "I'll try the chocolate."

It's outrageously good. Maybe Leif and I can hang out sometime. Especially, if he brings along some more of this awesome pie. Maybe I should get his phone number and add it to my contacts. Then I notice Daphne staring with big, sad eyes. "Come on, have a piece," I say. You can tell she's starving, because she's been staring at the Styrofoam plates since Leif walked in the room.

"It's so worth blowing your diet," Maddie pipes up.

"You can barf it up later," Lorriene giggles.

"I'm not really hungry," Daphne lies.

I almost offer her a bite of mine.

Leif holds out his tray.

She scoots back in her seat.

"You sure you don't want to try the banana cream?"

"Banana's a fruit!" Maddie offers shrill encouragement.

"Oh, all right." Daphne takes the plate Leif is handing her. "I guess a few bites won't kill me." She takes a few bites. Her eyes are glued to his butt as he exits the room. Another reason for me to like the guy. If he could relieve me of Octopus Woman, I'd adopt him as my long-lost brother.

I hear him handing out the rest of the pie to a couple of nurses as he heads toward the elevators.

When everyone's finished eating, I gather up the trash.

Dad pulls me to the side. "I'm gonna take your mom and the girls home, do you mind staying here with Grandma?"

"You sure you can't get Grandma to leave too? She's gonna be miserable if she stays here all night. I can call with any news."

"Do you know if that woman is still in the hospital?" my father asks.

"You know, I think it was just a false alarm, and they sent her home." I should probably feel worse for lying to my old man, but it seems Leif has inspired me with his great acting. A few white lies aren't such a big deal.

"Really?" my dad's eyebrows fly up.

"Yeah, kinda crazy, huh?"

"I'll say." He wags his head. "I thought those two were going to come to blows."

151

"Good thing they didn't."

He nods. "Let me talk to your grandma one more time." He checks his watch. "She really needs to get some rest, and she's not going to get any sleep here."

I cross my fingers. The pie has made everyone agreeable and sleepy, a perfect combination.

It takes thirty-five long minutes before I'm sitting by myself in Waiting Room A.

I give it fifteen more minutes before I head up to the fifth floor. It's a little past 10 o'clock. Visiting hours have been over for more than an hour.

When I reach the fifth floor there are empty pie plates with plastic forks perched on them all over the nurse's station. The one lady behind the desk doesn't even look up as I walk by.

What I don't expect is Krissy. She waves and grins as if she hasn't seen me in twenty years. "Ashton!"

But I'm looking for my Cupcake Girl. "Where's Glynna?"

"Bathroom," Krissy mouths as she points to the closed door to my right. "Sorry about your grandfather."

Pearl's room is getting crowded. Iron Lady is there too. There's a couple uncut pies on a rolling table, along with stacks of paper plates and a pile of plastic forks and knives. Iron Lady doesn't acknowledge me. Pearl is sitting on the edge of her bed, dressed in street clothes. Her hair is combed and she has on some lipstick. She smiles at me and reaches for my hand. I step closer to the bed. She's such a cute old lady. I can see why my grandfather is still attracted to her. I bet she was quite the looker when she was young. My heart is commanding me to make her happy, at least, to make her smile.

"I appreciate your help," she says.

"You're welcome."

Glynna steps out of the bathroom, and trips over a crack in the linoleum. Her hands slam into my chest.

I don't miss Krissy's grin.

My Cupcake Girl blushes, and it's the sweetest thing I've ever seen. Everything she does, even her klutzy-ness, makes me adore her more. Oh, I don't mind if she keeps on stumbling. In fact, if it throws her into my arms a little more often, all the better. I love catching her, and those lips! I internally groan. I can't seem to get enough of those rosebud lips!

God, Pap Pap is in a coma, and I can't stop thinking about her and how she responded to my kisses at the lake.

Glynna thanks me for catching her as she straightens up, then comes around me to stand next to her grandmother. "Ready, Nana?"

"Has everyone been served some of my pie?" Pearl asks.

"*Sí. Sí.* Yes. Yes," Krissy says. "We made sure we didn't miss anyone."

"Did you make all those pies, Pearl?" I ask.

Her eyes twinkle. "Did you have a piece, Ashton?"

"Yes, ma' am. It was the best chocolate pie I've ever tasted."

"I'm so glad you enjoyed it," Pearl says. She's such a lady. "Are you ready, Glynna?"

"Yes."

"If you don't mind, Ashton, Glynna is going to join us."

"That's a great idea." She could probably say, "Let's dump your grandmother in the Spokane River," and I'd probably say, "That's a great idea," too. The little old lady's got me wrapped around her finger.

Everyone scoots out of the way as I take Pearl by the elbow and escort her into the hall. Glynna is right behind us. I can smell her strawberries-and-cream fresh scent. I want to eat her up.

"We'll be here when you get back," Krissy promises.

I get the feeling no one is going anywhere.

The corridor is empty as I lead Pearl and Glynna to the stairwell, so no one stops us or asks any questions. When we get to the fourth floor there's a nurse behind the desk and two hanging over the counter.

"Where are you going?" One of the nurses turns to ask as we walk by.

"I need to see his grandfather," Pearl says.

"Of course," the nurse says. "Do you know where he is?"

"Do you know his room number?" she asks me.

"No, I haven't been in to see him yet."

The nurse behind the counter checks her screen. "It's 472. Take a right and go down to the end of the hall. His room will be on the left."

The nurses should be calling security and tackling us, but they're nodding and waving at Pearl like they've been expecting her. I wonder if

153

she has this kind of effect on everyone. Drawing out the desire to do good and be kind.

Glynna comes up even with me as we head to my grandfather's room, but we don't say much, because the hospital is so quiet. Besides, even though the nurses haven't done anything to stop us from seeing Pap Pap, it doesn't make sense to draw unnecessary attention to ourselves.

 PEARL

"Nicolas, I'm here."

Although he doesn't respond to my voice, I can feel my spirit searching for his.

"I'm so sorry I didn't stop you from marrying that witch." The emotion I've crushed between duty and fear for forty years seeps through my eyes. "I lost faith, Nicolas. There was a part of me that believed you wanted to be with her. I was a fool, I see that now. But I thought, for so long, that if you didn't really love her, if you didn't really want to be with her, if you really loved me, that her spell couldn't hold you. I kept waiting for you to wake up, and when you never did, some part of me believed you didn't love me. But when I saw you yesterday, the last forty years evaporated. It was like you were twenty-one and I was eighteen again. I saw it in your eyes. You still love me, Nicolas, just as I still love you. You've always loved me. And I realize now, I've always had the power to break Tati's spell. I was just too afraid or weak." My tears are coming fast and furious as I admit the truth to myself, as much as to him. "Because I didn't have faith in your feelings for me, look what's happened to both of us. We've spent the best years of our lives apart, separate, and isolated from one another." The loneliness of an endless string of days crushes my tongue. I can't say anything else. I search for Nicolas' hand beneath the covers. It's hot with fever. I hold it as if I were holding on to his life. Maybe I am.

"Nicolas, please don't leave now. Give me a chance to make things right." I let my head fall against his chest. The beat of his heart is so faint.

154

"Nicolas, please, please, don't leave me yet."

I'm not sure how long I stay there with my head resting on his sheets, sobbing out the poisonous doubt that corrupted my supposedly incorruptible Lumina heart. But when I feel Glynna's hand on one shoulder and Ashton's hand on the other, I know they're ready to leave. I just don't know if I'll be able to go with them.

 **ICOLAS**

"Pearl!"

Even though I'm shouting her name at the top of my lungs, no sound is coming out of my mouth. I can feel the feather light touch of her fingers against my hand, the soft weight of her head against my chest. I long to embrace her, but my hands and arms won't move. My body won't obey me, it's as though it's frozen, silent, impenetrable.

After all these years, Pearl is right here, and I can't reach out and touch her.

 **EARL**

"I'm sorry," I whisper to Glynna and Ashton. "I can't leave yet."

"I don't think we should stay much longer," Ashton says. I can hear the concern in the boy's voice, but now I understand. I abandoned Nicolas to Tatiana's black magic before, and I'm not going to make the same mistake again.

"Glynna, dear, would you please let me spend a little time alone with him?"

I hear their worried whispers behind me.

"We're going to step outside for a few minutes, Nana."

155

I turn to face them. "Thank you, Glynna. Thank you, Ashton. I just need a few minutes."

When they're gone, I stand in front of the mirror in Nicolas' bathroom. It wavers, and I bring all my power to bear. This will be the second time in my life I've dabbled with memory, and I tell myself, this time it won't be a disaster.

Ophelia is standing next to me on Nicolas' doorstep. Fear is pressing against my heart, squeezing out the love. My fist trembles when I raise it to knock on the door.

I will change the future now.

I gaze at my clenched fingers and open my hand. I concentrate on all the times I've felt the wonder of Nicolas' fingers wrapped around mine. I recall how regenerating it is when we touch each other, skin-to-skin; how it fills me up in a way that food never can or will. I pour all my energy into my emotions. When they shoot up my arm, I remember what it feels like to have Nicolas' arms pulling me close to him in an embrace.

I imagine my head against his chest and listen. The rhythm of his blood as it pumps through his heart hypnotizes me.

When we're one, I draw a deep breath of his life into my lungs.

Our energy intermingles, my breath with his blood, his breath with my blood. Two gold threads entwine, binding us together. The thread lengthens as it spins for miles and miles through time.

I think "indestructible, indestructible, indestructible."

When the golden thread reaches Nicolas in his hospital bed, I anchor it with faith. Our love was never lost or destroyed. It never died. I simply opened my hand and let it go a long, long time ago. When my heart and my head are clear of doubt, and the truth is all that remains, I travel back to the day I let go.

The gold thread of our love lies in the palm of my hand. This time, I don't let doubt become a strong wind, ripping the kite string from my loose grip. This time, I close my fingers around the shimmering bond and hold tight to it, as I bang on the door of Nicolas' apartment.

"Who are you?" Tatiana eyes me with suspicion.

"I'm Nicolas' girlfriend."

She waves the diamond solitaire in my face. "I'm his fiancé."

"You're a witch."

156

"Ah," she laughs. "Then you must be, too."

"He doesn't love you."

She opens the door wider and waves to him. "Try to tell him that."

I enter the darkened foyer of his apartment. "Nicolas! Nicolas!"

He comes out of his bedroom with wet hair and a towel wrapped around his waist. Outrage threatens the clarity of my intention. I slip and slide between the naive girl who underestimates the power of a black magic spell, and the woman whose corrosive doubt cast an even darker pall. My fingers want to spread like wings, but this time I clench my fist tighter around the golden thread of our love.

"We're going to get another chance, Nicolas." I ignore his puzzled expression as I press my fist against his sternum. "We're going to get another chance."

The mirror sends me back to the present. My clenched fingers luminescent with the afterglow of a successful Lumina spell.

17. The Cupcake Duel

CYNNA

Two nurses shove past me and Ashton into Nicolas' room. When the door is thrown open, it sounds like all his monitors are bleeping at once. Ashton chases the nurses into the darkened room. One of the nurses has flipped on the lights, and the fluorescent bulbs are flickering.

"What happened, Nana?"

Nicolas argues with the nurses. "I'm telling you, I'm fine."

They're trying to keep him from getting out of bed. "Please, wait, Mr. Bass. We need to let a doctor examine you."

His head dodges around them. "Pearl?"

"I'm right here, Nicolas."

"Will you stay with me until the doctor comes?"

"I'm not going anywhere."

"Pap Pap, we were so worried about you," Ashton says.

Nicolas reaches for his grandson's hand and squeezes it. "Where's your grandmother?"

"She went home."

"Good. Good. Where's my phone?"

A nurse points to a chest of drawers. "You might want to check in

159

there for his personal items."

"Do you want to use mine?" Ashton asks.

"You wouldn't happen to have Frank Langton on speed dial would you?"

"It's almost midnight, Pap Pap."

"I need to talk to him right now."

A troubled expression flickers across Ashton's face before he goes to dig through his grandfather's personal effects. He doesn't look at me when he hands Mr. Bass his phone.

As soon as the nurses satisfy themselves that Mr. Bass seems fine, and step away from his bed, Nana goes to sit with him. He's holding her hand.

"Can you please give us some privacy?"

Mr. Bass is talking to everyone but Nana. We file into the hall while she remains seated beside him.

Ashton is visibly shaken, and he won't look at me.

"Who is Frank Langton?" I ask him.

"The best divorce attorney in Spokane."

The blood is draining from my face. "Divorce?"

Ashton doesn't answer me. He crosses his arms and starts pacing. The nurses have returned to their station after marveling over Mr. Bass' miraculous recovery.

But is Mr. Bass going to divorce Tatiana? I can see the headlines splashed across the front page of *The Spokesman-Review*—pictures of Tatiana and Nicolas with Nana inserted between them, the news ticker running across the bottom of the local newscast every single night: Frosting & Beans Love Triangle Update!

I'm not sure what to do, but I can't leave Nana here alone. What if Tatiana shows up? Does the hospital have to contact her and tell her that her husband woke up?

Her husband! Nicolas Bass is her husband. Her husband!

Breathe! Glynna, breathe!

I shoot Ashton one more glance. He's off in his own little world. I turn the other direction and head to the stairwell. As soon as I can, I start texting with Kristeen.

Mr. Bass woke up. He's OK.

Cupcakes & Kisses

Nana's magic? God of Cupcakes, what if she put some spell on him? Is that why she asked us to leave? Oh, I can't even think about the possibility. My cupcakes can only activate real love, but there are love potions.

U still there?

Yes.

Is Ashton overjoyed?

Not exactly.

Huh?

Mr. Bass asked every1 but Nana 2 leave room. He wants 2 talk to a divorce lawyer.

OMG!

You're not kidding.

Need me?

Uh-huh. I can't just leave her here. What if T shows up?

B right there!

I'll B outside room 472

When I return to the corridor outside Mr. Bass' room, Ashton is on the phone. Otherwise, the hall is empty.

Nana, please come out of that room!

It doesn't take long for Kristeen to show up.

Ashton doesn't even acknowledge her.

She throws her arms around me. "Are they still in there?"

"Uh-huh."

She lets go of me and presses her face up against the small square pane of glass in the door.

"Kristeen!"

Ashton glares in our direction.

I tug on Kristeen's shirt. "He is never going to ask me out again."

"He is looking grouchy."

Finally, the door to Nicolas' room opens. It's Nana. I grab her arm, and it takes me a minute to realize she's not moving. "We've got to go!"

"Nicolas wants me to stay here with him."

"I think Nicolas Bass can take care of himself. We, on the other hand, do not need another World War III encounter with his wife!"

Ashton shoves past us, jostling my grandmother.

161

"Hey!"

Nana holds up her hands. "Don't get upset with him."

"He almost knocked you down."

"He's had an emotional day," she says.

"We all have."

"Glynna, there are some things I need to tell you, but it's so late," she says.

"Is Mr. Bass going to divorce Tatiana?" I ask.

Nana wraps her arms around herself and plucks at her sleeves. "Nicolas and I used to be in love."

"Used to be?"

"Glynna, we still are."

"Oh, Nana, you are way too old to be having a mid-life crisis. And so is he, by the way."

"This isn't a mid-life crisis for either of us."

"How do you know?" I drag her down the hall. This time she lets me. "Did you put a spell on him? Nana, please tell me you didn't!"

She shakes her head. "Tatiana put a spell on him. Years ago! And I just let her have him. It was the worst mistake of my life."

"Tatiana Bass is a witch too?"

"Glynna, she's an Occulto. She doesn't have a soul, and she doesn't love him."

I have to think about this. Oh. My. God. "Is Ashton an Occulto too?"

"I don't know."

"But he might be?"

"Maybe. They have until their twenty-fifth birthday to show their powers."

Have I been swooning over a warlock without a soul my entire life? I have got to get over him, right now.

Nana grabs hold of my hands. "Glynna, your cupcake broke Tatiana's spell."

"What?"

"Her spell suffocated his real love, but when he bit into your cupcake, his heart woke up."

Nana must be exaggerating. "Are you sure?"

"He asked me to marry him as soon as his divorce is final."

162

Tatiana is going to destroy my business. My business. It hasn't even been forty-eight hours and it's all over. I shake my head. I have to stop baking cupcakes if they're going to break up marriages and families.

And Ashton and me? God, how can there even be an 'us' now?

"Glynna, aren't you happy for me?" Nana asks.

"Happy for you?" My voice is high-pitched. But her big brown eyes are so full of love and joy. "Yes, Nana. I'm happy for you," I say flatly.

I am so scared for her, and for myself, and for everyone we know.

After Nana slips back into Nicolas' room, I grab Kristeen by the hand and lead her to the stairs. When I say goodnight to Ashton, he doesn't respond. My friend won't stop chattering as we climb the stairs. She can't be around if Tatiana shows up. I've never seen two witches fight, and I don't want to. I try not to dwell on this afternoon when Tatiana's black eyes drilled into me. I had no idea that she and her grandson are soulless.

There's the slightest chance Ashton has a soul, but I'm pretty sure Lorriene doesn't. Occultos. I wonder if they know my father.

When we get back to room 523, Ophelia and Leif are calm.

"Nana won't leave Nicolas," I tell them. "But I'm really worried. Tatiana is probably going to show up any minute and murder her. What should we do?"

"I'm not going anywhere," Kristeen says. "This is history in the making."

Why did I ask her to come up here? I have to make her see reason. "Kristeen, you're the only one here who doesn't have a family member as a patient. You could get in trouble if there's an investigation. You need to leave."

"What are you talking about? This is a hospital, not a military installation. There's not going to be any investigation."

"Maybe Leif could drive you home?"

"Ooh, that is the one thing that might tear me away, but what about my Jeep? I can't just leave it here. Parking is a fortune."

Shrieking. We all fall quiet. It's faint, but someone is shrieking.

I'm the first one out the door. The corridors are dark and empty. My ears strain to locate the source of the wailing. It sounds like it's coming from the floor below.

163

Nana!

Kristeen, Leif, and Ophelia pound down the stairs behind me. As soon as I open the door to the fourth floor, I duck. Streaks of green and red fly through the air. Ophelia elbows past me.

"What's going on?" Kristeen squeals.

About ten feet away, Tatiana and Nana stare each other down. They're both heaving, and while Tatiana's hair is a snarled rat's nest, not a strand of Nana's magenta hair looks out of place. Maybe it's just the dim lighting.

Why don't I have more faith in my grandmother? Why do I assume Tatiana Bass can whip her ass, but not the other way around? A few yards away, Lorriene and Ashton are frozen, their mouths hanging open.

Ophelia stops when Tatiana is equidistant between her and Nana. Neither sister says a word, but they simultaneously raise their hands and begin chanting some obscure language. Tatiana whirls around. Tendrils of black lightening arc from her body. They extend all the way to the tips of Ophelia's and Nana's fingers, as if the pair are drawing out her evil. Lorriene screams. It looks like her grandmother is being electrocuted.

"What are they doing?" Kristeen asks.

"Draining her energy," Leif volunteers.

"Are they witches or something?"

"Or something," Leif pushes his glasses up his nose.

"Wow," Kristeen says.

Tatiana's body folds, and she settles in a heap on the ground.

Nana and Ophelia drop their hands.

Lorriene runs to her grandmother, calling her name. She gets no response.

"Did they kill her?" Kristeen asks.

"No," Leif says. "She's just stunned."

"We have to get Nana out of here," I say.

"We can't leave Nicolas alone with Tatiana," my cousin insists.

"You're kidding, right? He's a grown man," I say.

"No, I'm not kidding. He needs to come with us." Leif is already racing down the hall to Nicolas' room.

"Did you know your aunt and grandmother were so badass?" Kristeen asks me.

"I had no idea."

"This is so loco!"

A flash of light catches the corner of my eye. "What are you doing?"

"Getting it on film! No one is going to believe this unless they see it."

I lunge for my friend's phone. "No!"

"Hey, *chica*, give it back."

I toss the images in the virtual trash can as fast as I can. "Here."

She thumbs through her camera roll. "Hey, why did you delete them all?"

"I don't want anyone to see them."

Kristeen shakes her head. "You're really pissing me off, Glyn."

"You'll forgive me. That's what friends are for, right?"

"Leave my grandfather alone!" Lorriene screeches to Leif, who's leading Nicolas, Nana, and Ophelia in our direction. The effect of Nana's pie has worn off. Probably the adrenaline, it sucks up magic like a sponge.

Nicolas says something to his granddaughter, which I can't hear, but it doesn't calm her down. She lunges at Leif. Ever the gentlemen, he twists and pivots out of her reach.

"You asshole!"

Leif has garnered one-hundred-percent of Lorriene's attention while Nicolas, Nana, and Ophelia continue their advance to the stairwell. Ashton is focused on his grandmother, still a heap of linen and stacked high heels on the ground. I want to apologize for what Nana and Ophelia have done to her, but what would be the point when our relationship is already over?

My heart feels as wrinkled and lifeless as Tatiana's body, and I realize I can't take any more emotion, trauma, meltdowns, tornadoes, or fireworks. I'm done. But Lorriene isn't. She keeps throwing herself at Leif. He's remaining a gentlemen, despite the bloody scratch on his cheek.

I inch toward them. Kristeen is right behind me. My aunt, grandmother, and Nicolas have reached the stairs. I can hear them descending. One less thing to worry about.

"Hey, Lorriene, it's late. Why don't we all call it a night, and let your grandfather and grandmother work this out between themselves?" I ask.

165

She whirls on me. "Are you kidding me? My grandmother is probably dead."

Even from where I stand, I can tell Tatiana's alive. I can't see her chest rising, but her face is flushed with color."

"Your grandmother is going to be fine. She's just stunned."

"What are you, a fucking doctor now?"

"No."

"Then shut up."

"Lorriene, you need to get your grandmother home," Leif says.

"How? Do you have a gurney? Because that's what we're going to need to cart her out of here."

Leif watches Lorriene as he moves closer to Tatiana.

"What are you doing? Leave her alone! Hasn't your crazy family already done enough to her?"

"Yeah, man. Just keep your distance," Ashton warns.

Leif crouches a few feet away from him and slowly edges closer to Tatiana, but Lorriene makes a human missile of herself, and they both go sprawling. Lorriene ends up on her back with Leif crouched over her. They're frozen, gazing into each other's eyes. What's that look? Their chemistry is palpable. Did Leif cast a spell on her? I don't even know if he's capable of something like that.

"Oh my God!" Kristeen squeals. "I'm so jealous."

"Don't be. It's just some lame moment from a dystopian romance, the final moment before Armageddon. It's not real." It can't be.

"I don't know, Glyn." Kristeen's eyes are round. "There's practically sparks flying off of both of them. Can't you feel the heat?"

"It's nothing!"

Now Kristeen's wide eyes are trained on me. "Glyn, you're jealous."

"Of my cousin?"

"No. Because that's not you and Ashton," she whispers.

I hate it when she's right.

Leif slides off Lorriene. She remains immobile, staring at the ceiling.

"She looks vanquished," Kristeen whispers.

"Or petrified?" What is he up to?

Leif's eyes are still fixed on the bratty princess. His soulful eyes are more than just pretty. When his gaze shifts to Tatiana, Ashton shoves

166

him away.

My cousin holds up has hands. "Man, I'm not gonna hurt her."

"Go," Ashton says. "You and your family have done enough damage tonight, just get out of here," he growls.

His angry words rips my heart out of my chest.

Leif searches the hall. When our eyes meet, I nod. Although it will take Tatiana longer to recover without the aid of magic, she's going to be fine.

My cousin stands up and eases toward me and Kristeen.

"I hate you!" Lorriene yells at his back. "Don't you ever bring me pie again!" She spits onto the floor.

I can't forget the look in Ashton's blue eyes. Disappointment. Does he blame me for what's happening between his grandfather and grandmother?

Kristeen laughs and grabs hold of Leif's arm. "You've got the princess all hot and bothered."

He rolls his eyes.

Then we turn and run. When we reach the parking lot, we divide up. I ride back to the house with Kristeen. Someone's going to have to whip up a spell to bend her memories before she goes home.

18. Hocus Pocus... Cupcakes

ASHTON

"Ashton, what the hell was that?" Lorriene asks.

"I don't know."

"Did you see them lobbing those fireballs at one another like something out of a freaking paranormal movie?"

I'm trying not to think about it because my mind can't really accept what my eyes saw. I grunt something noncommittal.

"Do you think she's going to be okay?" Lorriene smooths Grandma T's skirt and settles her hand in Grandma's palm.

"Her breathing is steady, and it's gradually getting stronger. I'm going to try to carry her downstairs. Whose car are you driving?" I ask my sister.

"Hers."

"Is Donald downstairs?"

My sister whips out her phone. "I'll meet you downstairs."

"No, you can text him as soon as we get off this floor. Help me get Grandma to the elevator first."

I balance on the balls of my feet and slide my arms behind my grandmother's back and knees. She's light, but it's a struggle to stand

169

up. Lorriene steadies me when I almost tip over.

The halls are deserted as we head to the elevators.

"It's positively creepy," Lorriene says what I'm thinking. "Where did everyone go?"

When the elevator opens with its familiar loud ping, I squint in the bright lights of the interior. Lorriene pushes me in. "The phones don't work in the elevator, either," she says. "I'll take the stairs."

My sister should join the track team. Donald is pacing when the doors slide open to the lobby. I won't let him take Grandma from me. My mind, not to mention my heart, has been so wrenched around today. I was falling in so deep with my Cupcake Girl. What happened? It was as if her grandmother put a spell on me. And then I helped her destroy my grandparents' marriage. Pap Pap wants a divorce. It has to be a momentary lapse. Any sweet feelings I had for Pearl evaporated the second my grandfather said he needed to call Frank Langton in the middle of the night.

Having a walk down memory lane is one thing, but a divorce? I've seen so many of the parents of my friends divorce, and watched as their family relationships irrevocably alter. It's never for the better. Even though Pap Pap and Tati aren't my parents, it's almost worse. As much as Tatiana irritates me, she's woven deep into the fabric of my life. Pap Pap can't just abandon her after all these years.

Maybe he banged his head when he collapsed at the house.

"Have you ever heard if a head injury can affect your ability to reason?"

"Yeah, I think they had more than one episode about that on House before the series ended."

Lorriene is a walking encyclopedia of pop culture. "He shouldn't have left the hospital without seeing a doctor." We've reached Grandma's car and Donald opens the door. I slide Grandma gently onto the seat. "You go with them. I'll meet you back at the house."

"Sure." Lorriene squeezes in next to Grandma.

On the way home, I'm trying to put the pieces of the puzzle together; my grandparents' history with Pearl, Leif offering everyone in my family pie, while he was disguised as a hospital employee, my betrayal of my grandmother, my grandpa's decision to get a divorce.

I can't believe he left with them.

I can't believe he left us for them.

And what about the explosive light show between my grandmother and Pearl? Weird memories surface at the edge of my mind. My grandmother's study, which I rarely enter anymore. It's more like a chemistry lab, with its shelves of dark, unlabeled bottles, ancient books, and burners.

No, Bass Man, your grandmother and Pearl are not witches. No way.

But...

Since I can remember, Grandma has made me homemade soaps, shampoos, bubble bath when I was a toddler. And in the past few years things like aftershave and cologne. I always believed her homemade presents were her token way of apologizing for being too controlling. I rub my jaw. But her gifts have always made me relent. She'll want me to do something, and I'll get my backbone up. A new bar of soap will appear in my bathroom. I'll use it, and over the next few days, I always come around to her way of seeing things.

Not every time, Bass Man.

I'm trying to remember one time when I stood my ground after one of Grandma T's presents, but I can't. Not a single one. Is that why Pap Pap wants to divorce her? Does he get little homemade presents from her too?

My stomach tightens in knots. I don't like what I'm figuring out.

If my wife was casting hocus-pocus spells on me, I'd be furious. But what about Nana and those pies?

Maybe I need to warn Grandpa that he's running from one witch into the arms of another. I pull into the garage. Outside the moon is full. No tornado, but there's a steady drizzle, like the sky is crying.

I shake my head as I walk over to Grandma's Cadillac. When I reach the car, I'm relieved to see Grandma is regaining consciousness. Now, it's more like she's drowsy, as opposed to passed out.

"Oh, Ashton," she throws her arms around me and buries her head in my neck. "What has that awful woman done? I can't live without Nico." She sobs. My heart is breaking into a million little pieces. "Promise me you won't see her awful granddaughter again. Promise me, Ashton."

"I promise, Grandma. That's over." The words are dust in my mouth,

171

but there's no way me and Cupcake Girl are gonna make it. I've never realized it until tonight, but family is the most important thing in my life. Grandma and Grandpa can't get a divorce. There's a reason we all live together in this house. It keeps us strong and united against the outside world. That's not gonna change.

It can't.

The Bass Man won't let it.

After I slip off her jacket and Lorriene takes her shoes, we tuck Grandma into her bed. Although she's still wearing her blouse and skirt, she looks comfortable. "We should keep an eye on her to make sure there's no lingering damage from whatever it was that happened," I tell Lorriene. "Do you mind sleeping in here on the divan?"

"Sure, big bro."

"Thanks," I give her a peck on the top of the head. It has been a long time since I've done that, but she's had a rough day too.

"Hey, you okay?" she asks.

"Yeah."

"You upset about that girl?"

"It was just one date. Besides, she's not really right for me."

"Too bad it took all this to make you see the light."

Her comment kind of pisses me off. Like she thinks she's so damned smart? "I guess you've already forgotten drooling over the tattooed Pied Piper this afternoon?"

"God, Ashton, why did you have to bring him up?"

"Maybe what happened tonight gave you some clarity too."

She rolls her eyes. "Fine. You've made your point."

"No more bakers!" We say at the same time. It has been a long time since that's happened too.

We break into grins until Lorriene asks, "You think Grandpa is really going to divorce Grandma?"

"No. I think it's just a lapse. I'm not sure what's going on, but he hasn't been himself the past few days."

"What do you mean?"

Do I dare confess our trip to Frosting & Beans to my little sister?

"I just mean he's seemed distracted."

172

"Yeah, by her," Lorriene hisses.

She's talking about Pearl, but I'm too wiped out to go there with her. "It's gonna all work out. He probably just needs a few days to clear his head. Things will be back to normal in no time."

Lorriene suffocates me in another big hug. "I love you."

 ATIANA

"Lorriene, what time is it?"

"3:27 am."

Now that my eyes are open, my mind is wide awake. My body is still drained from my fire fight with Pearl. It was foolish of me to engage. Elemental magic, transforming energy into earth, water, air, or fire, is exhausting. And at my age, what was I thinking?

My grandchildren saw it all, and it will be days before I'll have the strength to whip up a potion to make them forget. I'll need help.

"Where is my phone?" I ask.

"In your purse, on the dresser. Are you going to call Grandpa?"

"Hardly."

"Why not?"

"As long as that witch has him under her spell, he's not going to listen to a word I say."

Lorriene bursts into hysterical laughter.

"Is that funny?"

"What if she really is a witch?"

I ignore her outburst as I sit up and throw my legs over the side of the bed. My toes dig into my plush Persian rug. "I need to get out of these clothes."

My granddaughter brings me a pair of silk pajamas. She can't stop giggling. I search my nightstand with my fingers for my reading glasses. When I find them, I put them on and reach for my purse.

Lorriene's laughter finally dies down. "What are you doing?"

173

"Some research."

"But it's so late."

"And yet I'm afraid I'm going to have a hard time falling back to sleep."

"Are you going to call a lawyer?"

"What? No!"

"You should. You should find the best divorce attorney in the world."

"Darling, let's not get ahead of ourselves."

She punches one of my pillows. "I hate the Balcoras."

"A sentiment I share."

My agreement seems to calm her. She returns to the divan.

After I dig my phone out of my purse and arrange my pillows around me, I glance at my precious girl. She's fallen back to sleep.

I Google Liam Gallagher. He's still posing as a telecom magnate on the East Coast. It's almost 7 am there. He'll be up if he slept at all. I press my phone against my lips. Although Liam is the most powerful and well-connected warlock on the continent, he stepped back from Occulto politics over a decade ago and no longer holds a formal office. If I call him, and ask for his help, it's something I won't be able to undo. He'll want something in return. What will it be?

I slide out of bed and pace.

When I abandoned my mother in New Orleans all those years ago, I never thought I'd regret it. But I can't help but wonder where I'd be standing tonight had I stayed and defended her.

My mother wasn't the first witch to poison the upstart lover who'd gotten pregnant with her husband's child. But Occultos rule society from the shadows. We don't leave clues of our existence, trails to our covens, or dead bodies of the rich, celebrated, or famous—which had been my mother's crime.

Father's lover had been a Senator's daughter and fixture on the society pages. In a city where Voodoo, voudoun, and hoodoo were rampant, after the young woman's death, rumors about the supernatural had escalated out of control.

My mother's carelessness threatened to expose the tight-knit clique of influential creole witches of which my father was a member. As punishment, the Occulto High Court stripped her of her powers and

174

banished her from the community. I'd gone from being a darling of our secret society to a pariah overnight.

Although I never agreed with the court's judgment, I'd had no interest in paying the social debt for my mother's crimes.

Would I have chosen differently if Liam had stood by me?

A foolish question to ask myself tonight, because he didn't.

No, he abandoned me long before I abandoned my mother.

When I traveled west, I'd left the disappointment of him as much as I'd left my frustrations with her. The open spaces drew me, first to California, then to the Northwest. I spent some time in Seattle, but the city dripped. The small town of Spokane, nestled on the edge of a desert to the east of the Cascade Mountains charmed me. And no one here had ever tasted real Cajun cooking—my specialty.

I'd been the only Occulto in town for decades. When I'd learned Pearl and her sister were Luminas, it had been easy to frighten them off. Luminas are so often passive.

Whatever will be will be. If you love something, set it free. Blah, blah, blah. They'd kept their distance all these years. Why now, all of a sudden, was Pearl fighting back?

I tap the screen of my phone and consider the bright panel of icons arrayed on its face.

What will Liam's help cost me? Does it matter, when losing Nico will destroy me?

I pad into my bathroom suite, close the door, scroll through my contacts, and search for someone who will have his number.

"Tatiana, I never expected to hear from you again."

I never expected to make this call, either, but I need a memory spell for Ashton and Lorriene, and it will be weeks before I'll have the energy to brew one. Daphne's proven she's not up to the task. "Times do change."

"Indeed."

I arch my back and close my eyes. How much of the truth do I confess? "A Lumina attacked me tonight." Pearl has always been so meek, but tonight she initiated the fight. I'd barely opened my mouth when she cast the first flaming sphere.

175

"That's truly fascinating."

"My grandchildren witnessed the whole thing—"

"And neither have shown themselves to be Occultos?"

As the years have passed, I've grown more reclusive, only leaving Spokane for the annual Northwest Regional Assembly. I've held the post of Grand Witch for three decades, but as each year has passed, and first my son's, and now my grandchildren's powers have remained dormant, my desire to socialize with other clan members has soured. "They still have a few more years."

"Of course."

I'm grateful he doesn't mention the catastrophe that was Gregor's twenty-fifth birthday party. I invited every Occulto in the country, certain my son would come into his own before the clock struck midnight. The theme of the party had been *A Dark Fairy Tale, The Rise of the Black Prince.* I paid a high price for my arrogance. My fellow Occultos swept out of the mansion before dawn, and their humiliating titter and loud whispers still rings in my ears. I don't know if I'll be able to bear it if Lorriene and Ashton prove to have souls as well. "In the meantime, I need to have the memory of the event wiped."

"The battle drained you?"

This phone call confirms my impotence, but objective statement of fact is more forceful than longwinded excuses. "Yes."

"Poor, poor, Tati."

I cringe at his false sympathy. "Liam, I wouldn't have called if the situation wasn't dire."

"I have no doubt of that."

He knows it's much worse than I'm confessing. No one has overcome me in a direct challenge until tonight. Pearl left me passed out and unconscious. How did she do it? "I desire vengeance."

"I have no doubt of that."

I've been pacing, but now I stand in front of my full-length, three-way mirror, and what I see terrifies me. Despite Botox and laser treatments, chemical peels and surgery, I'm looking old. Pearl's face flashes in my mind's eye. I rub my jawline, and pull the skin from my cheekbones. Her face is more wrinkled than mine and yet, there was a light. It shone from her eyes like a beacon, and her aura had glowed as if she were a woman

176

half her age. Her magenta hair hadn't looked ridiculous as I'd told myself it had yesterday afternoon. It had looked like a brilliant crown. I press the back of my hand to my forehead.

Was she doing anti-aging spells? On rare occasions, I'd indulged, but the price of their affects—stealing youth from someone who shared your blood—was too high. I'd stolen life force twice from Gregor, and once each from Ashton and Lorriene. But I couldn't take any more from them. As they grew older, the theft would cause them to age even more rapidly.

Had Perfect Pearl stolen youth from her granddaughter? That would be delicious. I turned my back on the disappointing image of myself in the mirrors.

"Can you send someone?"

"Why did the Lumina attack you?"

"A personal vendetta."

"But it's strange. I haven't heard of a Lumina instigating a solo attack on an Occulto in, well, it has been a long time. Things have been rather stable since the peace treaty after the last war."

A war which had almost destroyed humanity. The plagues we'd unleashed upon the Luminas had done more to decimate the mortal population than it had our rivals. The Occultos had foolishly retreated. But I hadn't been a Grand Witch at the time.

Liam continued. "I'm not saying one-on-one attacks don't happen, but word of these things have a way getting around, and I've heard nothing. So what's really going on out there in your little hamlet, Tatiana?"

Liam's questioned poked. "That's a good question."

"Who is this Lumina?"

"It's actually a pair of them. They're sisters."

"And what is the nature of the personal vendetta?"

"One of the sisters was in love with my husband before we were married."

"Nicolas?"

"The only husband I have." Occultos are notoriously unfaithful spouses, their marriages often failing unless agreements are made. However, through the years, I'd been extremely discreet. As long as Nico grew the Bass fortune, maintained his standing as a pillar of the

177

community, and appeared as the devoted husband, father, and grandfather, I was pleased. I'd never begrudge him fulfilling baser needs elsewhere.

"Does either of these sisters have a child?"

"Pearl has a granddaughter. Why?"

"How old do you think she is?"

"A year or two younger than my son."

"Do you have a photo of her?"

"No."

"Can you get me one?"

"What does this have to do with my issue?"

"Send me a picture of the girl, and I'll make sure two witches, who will be more than capable of easing your troubles, arrive on your doorstep within an hour."

"Thank you, Liam, for not abandoning me."

"Don't thank me yet. I'll be in touch."

19. Sweet Cupcake Reunion

ICOLAS

The moment I step inside Pearl's home, my shoulders relax, and it's easier for me to breathe. Years fall away. In this moment, I begin to understand how much I've come to hate the formality that shrouds the Bass Mansion and my life with Tatiana. The home Pearl shares with her sister, nephew and granddaughter welcomes me. It's as if there's enough genuine love contained between these four walls for me, too.

Ophelia rushes into another room, leaving me alone with Pearl.

"Is she upset?" I ask.

"No, I think she just wants to give us some privacy. Are you tired, Nicolas?"

"I can't deny it has been an emotional day."

There's a commotion in the back of the house, voices.

"Glynna and her friend must be home," Pearl says. We're holding hands, and she gazes into my eyes. "Tatiana's not going to just let you go."

"She doesn't have a choice."

"When was the last time you had some of her étouffée?"

It seems like such a strange question, but stranger still, I can't

179

remember. "I honestly can't tell you."

"Don't be surprised if she tempts you with a plateful."

"I'm confused."

"Do you remember what happened at the hospital, Nicolas?"

"Are you talking about the exchange of fireballs?"

She lowers her eyes. "You do remember."

"I'm not supposed to?"

Pearl leads me by the hand to a sofa. She pulls me down to sit next to her and sighs. "I've decided I'm going to tell you the truth."

"I'd appreciate that."

"Even though I'm not supposed to. Please, listen to everything I have to say, and then think about everything that has happened for the past forty years before you decide whether or not you can believe what I'm going to tell you."

"Pearl, do I need to know what you're going to tell me to spend the rest of my life with you? Because I'm not sure I care about anything else."

"Maybe not."

Ophelia brings in a tray. "Glynna prepared warm milk and cookies. She thought you might enjoy a snack."

"That was thoughtful of her," I say.

"Nicolas, would you excuse me for a minute?"

I nod, my mouth is already full.

When Pearl gets back, she asks me what we were talking about.

"I don't remember."

A hint of sadness ripples through her eyes and fades before she takes my hand. "Let's go upstairs."

 EARL

Nothing has prepared me for this moment of being reunited with Nicolas, and at my age. I feel like my emotions should somehow be less than they were when I was eighteen, but they're not. I'm afraid they've

180

grown stronger with time, and our lengthy separation.

He holds out his arms. "Come here."

When I reach him, he enfolds me. His embrace is strong. "I don't know how I've lived all these years without you, but I won't do it for another day," he says.

I long to tell him the truth about Tatiana's spell, and how she came between us. I don't want there to be any secrets between us, but Ophelia argued vehemently against my confession in the kitchen. There is nothing to gain by violating the secrecy that shields us all. Perhaps she's right. I gaze into Nicolas' eyes. He seems so serene and untroubled, despite the chaos that still whirls around us.

He pulls me to my bed. I don't resist. He takes my face in his hands. "I'm going to marry you, Pearl, once and for all."

Tears of joy crowd my eyes.

"I've missed you so much. I need you so much," he whispers.

It's hard to believe this isn't a dream, a fantasy I've concocted from years of desire and heartache.

When he kisses me, it's like we never parted. It's like all the years he spent married to Tati, and raising his children and grandchildren, and all the years I spent living with Ophelia, raising Glynna and Leif, exist on some other planet, out of time. They're real, but they're no longer part of a gulf, separating me from the man I love.

"Tonight, I'm the luckiest man in the world," he says. "I'm never going to let you go again."

I let the wonder of his promises in, and don't allow myself to think about tomorrow or the next day.

We have tonight.

20. A Cupcake Premonition

LYNNA

I'm standing outside, between our house and the greenhouse, in the middle of the night, with my arms spread wide, absorbing moonlight. Brewing potions and concocting spells drains my energy, unlike baking, which recharges me.

I'm definitely going to spend the day at Frosting & Beans tomorrow.

As I swirl in circles, the currents of air I create pull away strands of regret.

How did a day that started with so much promise turn out so wrong?

The light in Nana's bedroom catches my attention, and I stop spinning. It's hard to believe she's up there with Ashton's grandfather. It's also hard to believe she wanted to tell him that we're all Luminas. When Ophelia vetoed her, for once, I had to agree.

The window to my room is dark, a good sign. Kristeen is crashed in my bed. Fingers crossed that my forgetfulness spell will wipe from her mind all traces of the fight between Ophelia and Nana, and Tatiana. I spin back to gaze at the light in Nana's bedroom. If the spell works correctly, they'll remember the events before the fight began, and after it was over, but the time in between will be lost.

183

I wish I could make a forgetfulness potion for Ashton.

As long as I live, I don't think I'll ever forget how he looked at me when his grandmother crumpled. It wasn't hate. It was hurt. Like a puppy who'd been kicked by a loving owner.

Archi flutters down to land in the grass beside me. "Where's Leif?"

He cranes his head toward the driveway.

"He still hasn't come home, has he?"

"Hoo-Hoo."

"You hungry?"

Archi turns his head from left to right.

"Are you here to see me?"

He blinks three times in rapid succession.

Other than wishing me a goodnight, Archi doesn't usually seek me out. "I don't think I want a prophecy tonight." Leif has assured me his bird's visions are startlingly accurate.

Archi waddles closer. I crouch down. "All right. What do you want to tell me?"

When he's sure he has my undivided attention, he launches into the sky and franticly circles the yard. After he does this several times, getting closer with each lap, he breaks his flight pattern to dive-bomb me. Then he lands at my feet and stares up at me with his enormous golden eyes.

"I'm sorry, Archi, I have no idea what you're trying to tell me." I wrap my arms around myself. I don't need an interpreter to tell me it's not a particularly friendly message.

The sound of a car engine comes from the driveway. "Looks like we're both in luck, because Leif just got home." Archi lands on my shoulder and we head toward Leif's car. "Where in the heck have you been?"

"Someone had to clean up the mess at the hospital."

I hadn't even thought about the scorched walls and melted plastic chairs we'd left behind.

Leif eases out of the car. "Did you take care of Kristeen?"

"Yes, she's upstairs asleep."

He stumbles out of the driver's seat.

"Are you drunk?"

"I wish." He staggers a few steps. "Depleted."

"Sorry, I didn't think to go back and help clean up."

He waves me off. "Working alone is better, draws less attention. Hey, Archi."

"He's been trying to tell me something, but I have no idea what it is."

"You gotta message for Glynna?"

Archi leaves my shoulder and goes through the same motions he did right before my cousin showed up.

"Do you have any idea what he's saying?"

Archi lands on Leif's shoulder.

"Someone is searching for you, and they're getting very close."

"What?"

Leif is heading to the back door.

"How did you get all that from what he just did?"

"He circled around you without pause while scanning the ground, which is searching with determination. The circles spiraled into progressively smaller spheres, but he made sure you remained dead center. The searcher is getting closer, and he or she is specifically looking for you."

"What about when he nearly smashes into my head?"

"Your inner circle has been broken and the intruder is going to find you soon."

"Leif!"

"What?"

"That sounds scary."

Archi swivels his head and gives me one slow blink.

"I don't need any more bad news today!"

"Archi, was my interpretation correct?"

Archi's repeated slow blink sends a chill down my spine.

"I'm sorry, someone's coming for you, Glynna." He enters the house.

"Leif, wait!"

He doesn't come back outside. When I get inside, he's sitting in a chair with his head crashed on the kitchen table. "Sorry, I'm wiped out. I had to sit down."

I pull up a chair next to him. "What did you mean about my inner circle being broken?"

"It must be that guy, Ashton. He's the only new parameter in the equation of your life." Leif always breaks things down into computer speak.

"Don't you think all of this is really weird? I mean, here's this guy, who I've known since I was five. Then come to find out his grandmother is an Occulto, for God's sake. And if that's not enough, she stole Nana's boyfriend, before either of us was even born. It's crazy!"

"It's also dangerous." Leif drops his head in his hands.

Archi hops to the table and paces its length.

"You shouldn't see him anymore."

"That's not going to be a problem. He hasn't said a single word to me since his grandfather told him he was calling a divorce attorney. Ophelia and Nana ganging up on Tatiana also didn't help."

"Is he a warlock?"

"I don't know. I don't think so."

"But you're not sure?"

"His grandmother has a distinctly wicked vibe, but Ashton doesn't. I mean, how could I be attracted to him if he doesn't have a soul?"

"Glynna, you're half Occulto."

"What are you saying?"

"Like attracts like. You could be attracted to him because he doesn't have a soul."

"Oh, that's making me feel much better."

"I'm not telling this to upset you, but I doubt it's a coincidence that you've been lusting after him since you were five."

"Did Kristeen tell you that? She has such a big mouth!"

"It doesn't matter. What matters is Archi's warning. You're vulnerable until we can increase our protection spells around the house. But with everyone wiped out, it's going to be a few days. So you need to be really careful until we do."

Mise en place. Everything in its place. Flour, cocoa powder, baking powder, baking soda, salt, milk, fresh-brewed coffee, espresso powder, vanilla extract, butter, granulated sugar, brown sugar, and eggs. Just the sight and smell of the ingredients has a tranquilizing effect. I close my eyes. I've got this.

Even though I didn't sleep a wink last night, I hopped out of bed at the first ray of sunlight. The summer days are long in Spokane, so that was

186

just a little after 5 am. Frosting & Beans opens at six, so if I maintain my focus, I'll have a batch of fresh Mocha cupcakes with espresso cream frosting for my early bird Monday regulars. They'll be delighted, and maybe, just maybe, someone will fall in love today.

There are worse ways to recover from a broken heart.

No time for self-pity. I've always been better at coaxing along the love lives of others.

I adjust my pink apron and hum. First the dry ingredients, then the wet. I almost forget about the most horrible Sunday I've ever had in my entire life. But I can't seem to shake Ashton's heart-broken puppy-dog eyes as I blend the batter. A single tear plops into the bowl. Oh, dear. I run to the bathroom for a tissue.

I'm perched on the toilet with my head in my hands, weeping! It wasn't even a whole date! I stand up, still sniffling, and dab at my eyes.

Go bake some cupcakes, girl!

When I get back to the kitchen, I consider throwing out the batter and starting over, but it's almost 5:30.

One teardrop won't hurt anything.

By 7:00 am I'm on the phone with Leif. "When you come in this morning, bring a carton of tissues with you."

"I just restocked."

"Yeah, well," I peek over the counter. The booths are full of red-eyed customers. Strangers are sitting with strangers, sharing their most heart-breaking memories. "There's not any left."

"What happened?"

"I'll explain when you get here."

I really don't want to tell him that I cried into my cupcake batter and now, I lean over to remove the remaining five mocha cupcakes from the display case.

"Are those sold?"

"Uhmm..." I gulp. "No, but,–"

"I'll take them all." The woman waves a ten-dollar bill. I don't think I've ever seen her before. "Please," she wheedles.

"I don't think you want them."

"Oh, I do. Mocha is my to-die-for flavor."

"But–"

187

Her hand plunges across the counter, and she rips the cupcake out of my hand and crams it in her mouth. I don't have the energy to argue with someone so determined.

"You sure you want the other four?"

She pulls the almost empty tray toward her and crams another one into her mouth.

"I'll just get your change."

"Mmpha mmph.

When Leif arrives, I return to the kitchen. Most of the weepy customers have left. I told my cousin to offer the remaining ones a complimentary espresso beverage. It should help.

I scan our enormous refrigerator. We've got some fresh raspberries. They would be gorgeous with some lemon cupcakes.

Mise en place. Take two. Once I've got my ingredients in the right bowls, my mind wanders. Ashton agreed to help Nana. He wanted to help her. And look at the mess that got me into. My chance of finding the one has vanished into thin air. I sigh.

I don't think I'll use the electric mixer today. I feel like doing everything by hand. I churn the wet and dry ingredients with vigorous strokes.

Why is he taking his anger at his grandfather out on me? Maybe he doesn't have a soul. Maybe he's as bad as his grandmother, and I was just blinded by lust. My feelings for Ashton were nothing. I don't have feelings for him anymore.

I grab a wooden spoon and slam it against the tins as I fill them with batter.

I was such an idiot to think we ever had a chance.

I slam the cupcakes into the oven.

I won't ever make that mistake again.

"You all right, Glynna?"

I whirl around. "Kristeen, I didn't hear you come in. How are you feeling?" I check the clock. It's 10:15. "Why are you up so early?"

"Early, *chica*? I'm late for class."

"You never worry about being late."

That's true, but my International Law professor is *muy caliente*. I

188

savor every minute."

"I really don't want to hear about love or crushes or anything hot this morning."

"Okay." She tilts her head. "What about things that are irresistible and enticing?"

I snort. "You're hopeless."

She grins. "I just want to know when those yummy-looking things you're baking are going to be ready."

"Not for another twenty minutes. But they'll need to cool down in the freezer before I can ice them."

"Maybe I should just miss class and take my professor a little gift afterwards." She drifts toward the oven. "I bet one of those would make a more lasting impression than an apple." She winks.

The warm lemon scent *is* intoxicating.

Kristeen pushes herself up to sit on the only empty counter. "So tell me about your date."

"Nothing to tell."

"Oh, no." She wags her finger "You're not going to go all tight-lipped on me now. Spill, *chica*."

"There's nothing to tell. Everything was perfect. It was all, 'oh, Glynna, this' and 'oh, Glynna, that,' and I swear there were stars in his eyes."

"Really?" Kristeen squeals.

"When we were at the hospital, he told the lady in the lobby I was his fiancé."

"Oh my God, what did you do?"

"We thought his grandfather was dying, so I did nothing."

She shrugs. "So what next?"

"I told you. Everything just went downhill from there."

Kristeen massages her eyebrows. "It's so weird. I don't remember anything after we went to go get Nicolas and your grandmother on the 4th floor. By the way, when I left this morning, he was cooking everyone breakfast."

"You're kidding. Does he even know how to cook?"

"Bacon, eggs. Nothing was burning."

"Ashton is taking his grandmother's side."

"Did he tell you that?"

"He didn't have to. I just wish he wouldn't blame me."

"Maybe he'll get over it. You know, when the divorce is final."

"There isn't going to be a divorce."

"Uhmm, I think there is, Glynna. Nicolas has already hired some movers."

"For what?"

"He's going to have his clothes and personal stuff brought to your house."

I slam down the All-Clad bowl I'm going to use to mix the icing.

"I don't understand," Kristeen says. "You're always wanting people to fall in love, and now your grandmother's falling in love, and you don't seem happy at all."

"She's not falling in love. She's going through a phase."

At least Kristeen has the good sense not to argue with me.

A few hours later, Leif and I are at each other's throats.

"What did you put in that batch of lemon-raspberry cupcakes?" he asks. "They're delicious, but everyone who's had one is in a mood to kill, including us."

He's right. I run a mental list of all the ingredients. "I didn't add anything extra." But this time I was pissed off at Ashton the entire time I was making them. I tug on Leif's shirt and pull him into the kitchen. "My emotions are spilling over into my cupcakes. This morning I was sad, and everyone who ate one of those mocha cupcakes ended up sobbing. I'm furious that Ashton is blaming me for his grandfather's decision to divorce Tatiana. That anger got into my cupcakes too."

When we hear breaking glass, we run out of the kitchen. A man and a woman are hurtling plates at one another while other customers are forming an angry ring around them. The customers split in half, one group taking the man's side and the other group taking the woman's. A shouting match ensues. I can't stand it. I put my hand over my ears and scream.

Everyone freezes for a split second before the chaos resumes.

It takes the rest of the afternoon to calm everyone down and clean up the damage.

190

"No more baking for you today," Leif says.

How can I argue? If I were to bake a batch of cupcakes now, they'd be full of self-loathing.

"Go home and get some rest."

For the first time in my life, I leave Frosting & Beans feeling worse than when I came.

21. Cupcakes and Jam

 ATIANA

"Lorriene, darling."

She's sitting Indian-style on the floor, rifling through my old stacks of Vogue. "Yes?"

We haven't discussed last night. I've tiptoed around it, because the less she dwells on it, the easier it will be to erase from her mind. "Can you find me a picture of the girl your brother went out with yesterday? Something from Facebook, perhaps?"

"You don't have to worry about her anymore. Ashton's done with her. He saw the light last night." She breaks into nervous laughter. "What was that, anyway?"

"A very ancient craft. Sorry, darling, not everyone can learn it."

I'm seated at my vanity, trying to do something with my face and hair. I observe her reflection in the mirror. Her face is a contortion of disbelief.

"Are you telling me you went to the same school as Pearl?"

"In a manner of speaking. I'd still like a photo of that girl."

She flashes me a wary look. "Why?"

"Curiosity?"

"Does this have something to do with Grandpa?"

193

"I don't want to talk about Nico at the moment."

"Fine." She unfolds herself and stomps out of my room. A few minutes later my phone pings. Lorriene has texted me a photo of Ashton's date. I study the girl's face. There's something about her pale complexion and tumble of auburn hair that tugs at my memory, although nothing solid surfaces.

After I forward the photo to Liam, I step into the shower. By the time the helicopter lands on our lawn, I'm feeling refreshed.

I watch from behind the curtain in my bedroom window. Two young witches jump out of the cabin, their long raven hair blowing across their faces. Both wear black mini-skirts. One has on black gladiator sandals, the other is teetering in a pair of ankle booties with five-inch heels, making divots in the yard. A small white cat with multicolored stripes and black paws sits on her shoulder.

As they draw nearer to the house, I recognize the row of five dots across the back of one of their wrists. The marks symbolize a witch's faith in the four kinds of matter harnessed by spirit. They're members of the Seattle coven.

When I open the front door, I recognize Lyrika's daughter, Annke. The cat is perched on her shoulder.

I lead the girls and the well-behaved cat, Eclipse, to my study. Annke's friend is named Sybelia.

They speak and carry themselves casually, but Annke and her feline companion observe every detail of my private space as soon as we cross the threshold. Sybelia tugs on her hair as if she were a young child, but I can feel her concentrating on me without staring, gauging my energy and power.

"My mother, and the rest of the coven, miss you," Annke says.

"Do they?"

"My mother isn't very focused these days," Annke volunteers.

"No?"

"She's gotten into heroin."

Eclipse leaps from her shoulder and lands on my work table.

"It makes everything around her messy."

"I didn't realize."

"They work hard to keep her condition under wraps. In fact, that's

194

about all they do these days. It's getting rather tiresome, isn't it Sybelia?"

"Mmhmm," her friend offers a distracted murmur.

"Sybelia and I are the most talented witches in the coven. It's why Liam called us. Besides, he trusts our discretion. He didn't want word getting around that a Lumina had beaten you."

"Yet he didn't hesitate to share the information with you two," I point out.

"He wanted us to be prepared."

"I just need a memory spell for my grandchildren."

"And the destruction of the first witch who's ever beat you in a fair fight. It was fair wasn't it?" Annke asks.

"If you call two against one fair."

They look at each other with raised eyebrows. "Not exactly," Sybelia says.

"Actually, that's good news," Annke adds. "It would be demoralizing for Occultos all over the world to learn that a Lumina got the best of Tatiana Bass."

"I thought we were keeping this between us?"

"Oh, we are," Annke says as she and Sybelia exchange glances again.

"Can you tell us something about these two Luminas," Sybelia asks.

"They're sisters."

Annke begins pulling jars of spell ingredients from my shelves.

No one ever touches my things, not even the housekeeper. I forbid it. However, acting on my impulse to slap the young witch's hand away won't smooth our relations. I press my fist against my lips.

"I'll get started on the memory potion while we get up to speed," Annke says.

Sybelia slouches on the divan.

I pull up the stool from my vanity. "I have a history with one of the sisters." I give them the edited version of my engagement and marriage to Nico. "He's with her now, at her home."

"After we take care of your grandchildren, we should probably pay them a visit."

"I received a text from him before you got here. He's sending movers for his clothes and personal effects. They'll be here this afternoon."

"Sounds like we don't have any time to waste."

195

"Do you have anything around here that plays music?" Sybelia swivels her head.

"No, darling."

She digs through the enormous messenger bag she dropped on the ground when she settled on the divan. "Do you mind?" Sybelia holds up her phone and a gadget which I guess is a docking system.

"Please, whatever will help you work."

A synthesizer crackles through the room. The tiny setup gives out as much sound as floor speakers. Two sleepy-sounding girls drone over the music. "I love to create a mood when I do magic." Sybelia twirls and her mini-skirt flairs. *The Casket Girls* are my favorite right now." She dips and bends to the electronic beat before she elbows her friend. "But Annke's hooked on Hildegard Von Bingen recordings."

"Wasn't she a nun?" I ask.

"Exactly."

Annke stops what she's doing and rubs Eclipse behind the ears. He curls into a ball. "She may have been a nun, but she was very independent and creative. Her music clears my mind."

What strikes me about these two young witches is their self-possession and natural charisma. Although their outfits reek of Seventh Avenue, neither wears much makeup, and I seriously doubt their long, slim figures have been surgically altered. I can't help but think Daphne might benefit from their company. I'm beginning to regret discouraging her from attending their Fourth of July party.

"Have either of you experimented with love potions?" I ask.

Sybelia's lips flutter together in a soft laugh while an enormous grin brightens Annke's face.

"I'll take that as a yes?"

"You could say love potions are our specialty," Sybelia twirls and dips again.

"Most Occultos find them to be quite a challenge."

Annke's eyes twinkle. "We've discovered some tried-and-true methods."

"I have a young friend, she's struggling with one. Perhaps after we've taken care of the business Liam sent you to help with, you might give her some tips."

Sybelia taps her fingers to the beat of the song. "Maybe. If we have time."

I pull the glasses I refuse to wear in public from my vanity drawer and move to stand on the other side of the table. Annke has the double boiler on. It sits in a triangle of black votive candles. At the head of the triangle is a tarot card from the Cat People deck, *The Hang Man*. She's set a small metal saucer on the grill. I pick up the jars and study the ingredients. "I see your using anise to protect the mind from any damage the erasure might cause."

"Of course," Annke answers.

"Who taught you?" I ask.

"My mother. As you know, Lyrika has a natural aptitude for potions, so I guess it's in my blood. But Sybelia's only a one-sided Occulto. Her father couldn't spell his way out of a room with an open door, so no one's sure why she's so good. But she is."

Sybelia smiles as she reaches for the desiccated butterfly wings. She removes the lid and carefully measures two pinches into Annke's spell. "Your grandchildren aren't going to remember a thing."

ASHTON

When the two hottest chicks I've seen in a long time come strolling in the kitchen with Grandma, I choke on my coffee.

"Geez, Ashton, why don't you just spit on them," Lorriene says.

The Bass Man isn't usually such a social moron, and I can feel the reactive color rising in my cheeks. The girls are cool, and act like I didn't almost spray them with java. The whole awkward scene makes me think of Glynna, and the beer bath she gave me that night at the bonfire. Ouch. Thinking of her hurts, so I push her out of my mind, and focus on the wicked twins circling around the kitchen. They're not actually twins, but they both have chocolate eyes, long, dark hair, and matching long, slim bodies.

197

Lorriene and I have just about finished our second pot of coffee, otherwise I'd offer them a cup. We've been discussing last night, dancing around the words *witch* and *magic* because—really?

But these two chicks, one with a cat perched on her shoulder, look like they're straight out of the latest twenty-something black magic show on the WB.

"Drool much?" Lorriene won't leave me alone.

I wad up my napkin and throw it in her direction. She ducks, and it grazes off the back of the cat. He hisses. "It's okay, Eclipse, he wasn't aiming at you." The girl's voice is a sing-song as her dark liquid eyes lock onto mine. "Mind if we make another pot?" She glides across the kitchen to the coffee maker.

"Sure."

Lorriene's eyes are flashing. She doesn't appreciate real competition, which these girls are. Next to them, she looks dowdy in her over-sized ripped shirt and baggy Love Pink shorts. "Are you going to introduce your friends, Grandma?" Lorriene squirms.

"Annke, Sybelia, these are my grandchildren, Lorriene and Ashton."

"Hey, kids." The one with the leather sandals laced up to her knees has something in her hands. She waltzes across the kitchen to join her friend. Actually, she flutters her arms and leaps like there's a song playing in her head. If anyone could make me forget Cupcake Girl, I'm thinking she can.

I take a big gulp of my coffee.

Grandma pulls up a chair. "They're from Seattle. I know Annke's mother."

"What are they doing here?" Lorriene's tone is testy.

The girls make themselves at home, whispering and giggling at the kitchen counter.

"They're going to help me with your grandfather's situation."

Lorriene looks skeptical.

I'm a bit surprised myself when the pair carries over a tray of bagels—cut in half and toasted—along with several ramekins full of butter and a weird-colored jam. I wave Sybelia off. "No, thanks. I'm not really hungry."

She sets the tray in front of me and puts a hand on each of my

198

shoulders. Then she gets right up in my face and grins. "You've never had a bagel until you've had one smothered in Annke's citrus-fig preserves."

I laugh because I'm officially nervous. "Persuasive," I manage to say.

Annke sits down next to Grandma and grabs a bagel bottom. She drenches it in butter then dollops the gray-plum jam on top. "Mmm. Perfect." She nods to me and Lorriene. "You have got to try one."

My sister rolls her eyes. Grandma takes a bagel top, cuts it in half, and slathers it with preserves. "This is simply marvelous."

Okay. I follow suit. "Amazing," I admit. The butter and preserves should get married and have baby bagels.

After we finish off the bagels and their crumbs, Sybelia refreshes all our coffee cups. Grandma asks Lorriene and me what we were talking about before they joined us. My sister and I look at one another. I shrug. I honestly can't remember.

"What happened after I left the hospital last night?" Grandma asks.

My stomach sours when I remember Pap Pap asking for his phone to call Frank Langton. But I don't remember much after that. I shake my head. Obviously, Grandma already knows about Grandpa's plans. I'm glad I'm not the one who had to break it to her. Lorriene remains curiously silent.

Annke winks at Sybelia before she sweeps up all the dishes and takes them to the sink. What in the hell was that about?

"The girls and I have an errand to run," Grandma says. "We'll be back before dinner. Why don't you invite the Wardof sisters over? Ashton, call Tyler and a few of your friends, too. We'll make a party of it."

Is Grandma in denial? I figured she'd be burning things this morning, but she's all like, "We're going shopping." Grandpa's filing for divorce and she wants to hang out with our friends? Maybe she's having a mid-life crisis too, although I thought those were for people in my parents' age bracket. Maybe, despite Grandma T and Grandpa going the extra mile to preserve their minds, they're losing them anyway.

At this point, that's the only thing that makes sense.

199

22. Cupcakes and the Witches of...

GLYNNA

As soon as I hear the car doors slam, I peek out the front window. My heart approaches what I'm sure is a dangerous pace when I see two young women dressed in short black skirts heading for our walkway. At least Tatiana isn't with them, although the Cadillac's windows are black, so I can't be sure she isn't waiting inside.

Nana and Nicolas have disappeared to the greenhouse, and Ophelia left for the bakery to help Leif as soon as I returned home. Archi's warning from last night flicks through my mind. Could these be the ones the owl tried to warn me about?

The doorbell rings.

Breathe, Glynna, breathe.

If I don't open the door, will they leave?

I squint through the curtains. They have to be a pair of witches—fashionable ones who aren't from around here. A cat sits on one girl's shoulders. All they need are a couple of black steeple hats. The doorbell rings again.

"Oh, why won't you just go away," I whisper-hiss. "Don't I have enough to deal with?"

201

"Maybe we should go around back," one of them says.

No! Who knows what they'll do if they find Nana in the greenhouse with Nicolas. My gaze returns to the black Cadillac. Has Tatiana sent her minions to retrieve her errant husband? Whatever is going on, they need to leave, pronto. I yank open the door. "Can I help you?" The anger in my tone is unmistakable. The outrage from my batch of lemon-y cupcakes lingers.

"We're here to see Nicolas Bass," Cat-girl says.

"Is he expecting you?"

"No, but we won't keep him long."

Sandal-girl won't meet my gaze, she's too busy studying our house.

On the other hand, Cat-girl's eyes are piercing mine. "Do you live here?" she asks me.

"I don't see how that's any of your business."

"Touchy." Her cat leaps from her shoulder and squeezes through the partially-opened front door. Cat-girl practically knocks me down pushing her way inside to catch her devious pet.

"Hey!" I holler.

The cat tears through the house, mewing like a banshee. Sandal-girl enters the house behind me.

"You need to take your cat and leave!" I yell at both of them.

They saunter after the cat as if I'd said, "Make yourself at home." Infuriating. Then the cat runs upstairs. "There's an owl up there that eats small mammals," I fume.

"Really?" Sandal-girl says, as if I'd passed on the most fascinating snippet of gossip.

"I can't be responsible if he mistakes your kitty for an afternoon snack."

No response.

I run up the stairs after them. Leif's door is closed. I briefly entertain the thought of opening it and waking Archi up with a shout of something like, "Dinner!" but the cat is too cute and tiny for me to offer it up as a meal.

The only door open in the hall is the one to my bedroom, and the witch-girls are nowhere in sight. I race along the hardwood floors, incensed that they're invading my private domain. Cat-girl is on her

202

knees, trying to coax their cat from beneath my bed. Sandal-girl is rifling through my cosmetics.

"What in the hell are you doing?"

She swirls around. "I'm kind of a makeup fiend. Can't resist a tube of lipstick." She waves the golden tube of fire-engine red Kristeen brought for my date with Ashton. A date I have no wish to be reminded of.

"You both need to leave. Now."

"As soon as I get my cat," Cat-girl says in her slinkiest voice.

"And see Mr. Bass. You've met Tatiana, haven't you?" Sandal-girl asks. "She'll be so upset if we don't pass along her message."

"Text him."

"Oh, no, this message must be delivered in person."

Downstairs, I hear the screened door slam. My stomach sinks. Sandal-girl yanks on my hair as she whisks past me.

"Hey, what are you doing?"

I rub my scalp. It feels like she pulled a handful of hair from my head. She ignores my question as she skips down the hall. Torn between them both, I stand frozen, trying to determine which one is the most dangerous. At last Cat-girl emerges from my room with the cat cradled in her arms. "Bad kitty," she coos as she clicks by me in her pointy high-heeled booties. When we get downstairs Nana, Nicolas, and Sandal-Girl are facing off in the kitchen.

"If Tatiana has something to tell me, she needs to contact my attorney."

"But she's out front, in the car," Sandal-girl wheedles.

"Pearl, wait here while I go handle this." Nicolas follows the two girls out the front door, thunder on his face.

I grab a thick lock of Sandal-girls hair as she shimmies by.

"Ow!" She rubs her head.

I hold up the four or five stands I managed to take. "Trade you."

Her face blossoms into an irresistible smile. "No, please, keep them."

They're already out the door. I flick the long black strands of Sandal-girl's hair from my fingers. Witches or not, they're creepy-crazy and weird.

Nana and I spy on them from the front windows. The opaque black glass on the passenger's side rolls down, and I catch a glimpse of

203

Tatiana's sunglasses and platinum hair.

"She's never going to let him go," Nana says.

"She doesn't have to if he doesn't want to be with her," I remind her.

"He asked me to marry him last night."

I wheel around and grab Nana by the shoulders. "What did you say?"

"When I went to the hospital, I just wanted to apologize to him. I never dreamed all this would happen."

"He loves you, Nana."

"I hope his son and grandchildren understand."

Ashton's pained expression resurfaces. Being torn between two people I care about is not a happy feeling. "It might take them awhile," I say. "Occulto or not, Tatiana is hurt."

"Tatiana doesn't have a soul, only her pride suffers."

"Lorriene and Ashton might not see it that way." It's clear Ashton doesn't.

"Speaking of Ashton, how did your date with him go yesterday? He was so kind to help me see Nicolas."

I don't have the heart to tell her the truth. "I suppose it went as well as it could for a first date where his grandfather ended up in intensive care." And asked for a divorce so he could marry his date's grandmother.

"Glynna, what's wrong?" Nana asks.

Time to change the subject. "Those two girls, they're witches, aren't they?"

She nods. "Young Occultos."

"They were in my bedroom."

"What?" Nana's hands fly to her mouth. "Did they take anything?"

"The one who didn't have the cat pulled my hair, and she was messing with my makeup." I try to remember if she returned the lipstick to my vanity.

"Oh, dear." Nana hurries around me and out the front door.

I run after her. The girls are already inside the car, and the engine is running. The black window is sliding closed. The car pulls away from the curb as Nana bangs frantically on the Cadillac's side. It rolls right by her.

"Pearl, what's going on?" The concern in Nicolas voice is so sincere. I gulp down the lump in my throat. Whatever happens between Ashton and me, I can't begrudge Nana finding love.

204

"I'm afraid they took something of Glynna's."

"Why would they do that?"

"Voodoo? Who knows?" Nana says.

I was thinking more along the lines of DNA testing. Either way, it's upsetting given Archi's warning.

"What was it?" he asks.

"A lock of hair or something," she mumbles.

Nicolas' eyebrow quirks. "How strange."

"Very," I murmur.

Nana closes her eyes as if she's battling a confession.

Please don't tell him who I am and the danger I'm in if Tati or the Occultos discover my true identity. I have no doubt he'll share the information with Ashton, and I don't need his grandson to have another reason to hate me.

"Maybe she just liked the color of Glynna's hair and wanted a swatch for her stylist," Nana says.

Nicolas shakes his head before taking a good look at me. "It is a beautiful shade of red."

I stare at the ground, embarrassed, but grateful that my secret is safe for now.

Kristeen, Leif, and I are headed downtown to a Martini bar. I need to blow off steam the old-fashioned, non-magic way–fake IDs and booze. Kristeen has convinced me I'll love Bistangos, and Ophelia won't let me go anywhere without a bodyguard.

"How did the make-up session with your law professor go?" I ask my friend.

"It was all going fine until he blew his stack and started yelling at me for missing his class. Today was my first absence ever. He wasn't even making any sense. I just stood there with my mouth hanging open. I was so shocked."

"Before or after you gave him that lemon cupcake?" Leif asks from the back seat.

She clicks her finger against the steering wheel. "You know, now that you mention it, I think it was after."

"I wouldn't read too much into it," he says.

205

"Why?" she asks.

"Next time you go to his class, just act like nothing happened," he says.

"I thought Glynna's cupcakes made people fall in love?"

"Only if they were going to fall in love anyway. They don't work if there's no feelings there to begin with."

She falls silent, thinking. "I really thought my professor had a thing for me."

"Maybe he does. All the cupcakes Glynna baked this morning were off."

"Really?" she grins.

Hope springs eternal.

"Really," Leif says.

She cranks up the radio. *Fireball* by Pitbull blasts from the speakers. Kristeen starts her predictable bouncing in the driver's seat.

Despite the upbeat tune, my mood heads downhill.

I wish my problems were so easy to solve, but I'm not up for talking about anything going on in my life. Not today's baking fiasco, which I do need to discuss with Nana as soon as I can corner her alone. Apparently, an impossible feat, since Nicolas has moved in.

It seems my emotions spilled over into my cupcakes, and they weren't my more pleasant ones. Too many more days of sadness and/or anger-infused cupcakes, and Frosting & Beans is going to start operating in the red.

The grand romance of Nana and Nicolas is another subject I don't wish to discuss. And I definitely don't want to even think about Pearl and Leif freaking out when we discover Sandal-Girl ripped off that tube of lipstick.

The fact that I haven't heard from Ashton, and probably won't ever again, is also a touchy subject with me.

As soon as I enter Bistangos, I close my eyes. This is not happening. I swirl around and slam into Leif's shoulder. "We can't stay here."

"Why not?" Kristeen whines.

I tilt my head in the direction of the bar. My friend's gaze searches the long counter.

"At the end. Ashton is with Lorriene and the two thieves who came

206

over to our house this afternoon."

"I told you this place was popular," Kristeen says. "Everybody comes here."

"Yeah, well, I don't need to see everybody."

"Aw, Glyn, we just got here, and they have absolutely the best Martinis in town. Can't we have just one drink before we split? Besides, you need to let Ashton see what he's missing out on."

"I don't think he's going to notice me with those two hanging all over him."

And they are literally draped over him, hand-feeding him cherries and orange slices.

"You can't let them run you off, Glynna!"

"I can."

Kristeen tugs on my arm. "No, you can't."

At least she pulls me to a table in a dark corner on the opposite side of the bar.

"Don't look now, but they've spotted us," she whispers. Then she waves.

"What are you doing?"

"What? I was just trying to get the waitress' attention. I thought you wanted a drink."

Daphne and her sister Maddie emerge from the hall that leads to the restrooms. They join Ashton and his herd of girls.

My blood has just gone from a simmer to a boil "Wow. I guess two girls isn't enough for him."

"Oh, he's just mending the heart that you broke."

Ashton's lips move and his harem shimmies with laughter. This is torture. Encouraged by their adoration, Ashton's shiny white smile gleams in the dark bar. "Well, that didn't take long," I say. When Daphne inserts herself between the witches, and presses her body against Ashton's, I wish for the ability to cast some serious spell damage. A few big, nasty spots all over her face would be nice! And I could turn him into a hideous, scaly, green Ogre! "Shrek" could be his wing man.

If. Only.

But my hyper-active imagination hasn't lessened my feelings of doom. I sigh, and seethe, until I've had all I can stand. I bolt.

207

"Glynna, where are you going?" Kristeen calls.

"I need some fresh air."

The smell of rain hits me as soon as I step outside. I want a downpour. I want the whole damned city to flood. Overhead the clouds crackle and a drop of rain splatters my nose.

Two seconds later, Leif is beside me.

"Go back inside," I tell him.

"Only if you do."

"You can't leave Kristeen in there all by herself."

"And I can't leave you outside here all by herself. If you're going to make me choose, I've got to choose you, cuz."

"Why did we come here?" I fume.

"Because you wanted to get out of the house."

"Right." I did want to get out of the house. As happy as I am for Nana —she's glowing—I'm also furious with her. She ruined my relationship with Ashton, and I'm just not good at being torn between two people I care about.

"Give it another shot?" he smiles. "Maybe we can figure out a way to get your lipstick back."

"I doubt they brought it with them. Whether it's DNA or voodoo, I'm sure the lipstick is either on its way to a lab or plastered on some corncob doll with strands of my hair glued to the top of it." I don't know which would be worse. Ophelia and Leif believe they're trying to identify me as my father's daughter. Why didn't he just try to connect the normal way and send a card? My desire to meet him has dwindled to nothing. Creep. Sending his groupies and their cat to raid my home in the guise of passing messages onto Nicolas from Tatiana Bass.

"We should let them know we know they took it," he says.

"Why? What difference will it make? The damage is done. If they don't know we know they took it, maybe they'll underestimate me and assume I'm stupid."

"Look who's becoming all strategic."

I punch his arm. "It has been a rough forty-eight hours."

"Then let's do what we came here to do. Blow off some steam. Glynna, you can handle this. Those girls hanging over Ashton aren't even in your league, and I doubt he's enjoying himself."

"Did you miss the shit-eating grin plastered on his face? He's in freaking dreamland."

"Guys can be pretty cagey with their true feelings. Remember, he's been through a lot in the past forty-eight hours, too."

"Do you see me with four guys sprawled across my lap? Do you?" I stab Leif in the chest. I don't ever do that. Man, I am one pissed off witch. Thunder rolls across the sky. I wish I could crack open the ceiling of Bistangos and strike them all with lightning. A huge wind gusts Leif and I. We both stumble.

"Glynna, dial it down."

A tree branch rumbles by and I feel pride. I think of what Nana told me, that it's Tatiana's pride that's hurt, not her soul. Well, I'm half Occulto, and my pride is hurt too, damn it. Just yesterday, roses were blooming when Ashton and I walked by, rainbows were filling the sky, and cyclones of passion were spinning around us when we kissed. Tonight, he hasn't even acknowledged my presence! How dare he ignore me after crawling his fingers up my skirt yesterday! Maybe Kristeen and Leif are right. If I leave without having a single drink, he'll know he had the power to run me off, that I'm too upset to stay.

"All right, but change seats with me," I tell Leif. "I don't need to watch them like a movie."

"Not a problem."

He escorts me back into Bistangos. After my second Martini, I've actually forgotten all about Ashton and his harem. It's like a forgetfulness spell, and I'm so relieved I order a third. When Lorriene slips into the empty seat beside me, I choke on the ice I've been sucking on.

"Hi, Leif," she says. I can tell by the swoony tone in her voice, she doesn't remember the witch fight. I risk a glance at Ashton. His grandmother must have wiped their memories. I wonder if she wiped his memory of our date. I wouldn't put it past her. By the time I finish my third Martini, I've convinced myself she did, and I want to put my theory to the test.

"Ladies room," I whisper to Kristeen.

Unbelievably, Lorriene and Leif are huddled together, their two bodies forming a single-shadowed blob. I don't even want to know what's going on with them.

209

Kristeen seems blasé. "I'll go with," she pops up.

We make our way across the bar. Is it my imagination or is Ashton watching me, despite the four girls hanging all over him? Maddie is not letting her older sister's pathetic grinding get in the way of her obvious Ashton lust. How could I have ever thought he and I had a chance?

Did he just pinch that witch's butt?

A burst of thunder rattles the glasses lined up behind the bar.

Ashton and his girl's freeze. I can hear their whispered, "What was that?"

Proof of my power makes me feel delicious. Ashton is going to be so sorry he played with my heart.

Kristeen and I duck into the bathroom. "What's up with you and Leif?" I ask her.

"Huh?"

"It doesn't bug you that Lorriene Bass is practically sitting in his lap?"

"Practically? Glyn, you need to get your eyes checked. She is sitting in his lap."

"I don't get it. Yesterday morning you were swooning all over him, and today it's your law professor. Did something happen after Ashton and I left?"

"Hon, your cousin is *muy caliente*, but let's face it, we peed in the sandbox together. He's almost my brother."

"I did think it was weird when you were all over him yesterday."

Kristeen reaches up to grab my shoulders and shakes them. "Girl, we were just playing, nothing serious."

"Uh-huh. So what about this law professor?"

She gazes upward. "Now, he is someone I could get serious about, *muchacha*."

Kristeen's a player. She doesn't do relationships. "Really?"

"Oh, yeah."

"How old is he?"

"Uhmm. Thirty? Thirty-two?"

"Kind of old."

"Not old, mature. And sophisticated. He's also smart."

"I didn't know you were into smart."

"Let me let you in on a little secret. Sometimes smart is the best

210

aphrodisiac."

The bathroom door swings open. Two ugly guys in wife beaters, baggy jeans, and tattoo sleeves push their way into the room.

"*Por favor*," Kristeen screams. They do look Hispanic. "*Este es el cuarto de baño de la chica.*" She twirls her finger. "*¡Vete!*"

I'm assuming she's telling them to leave, but they aren't going anywhere. In fact, they're both staring at me and giving me the creeps. The shorter one whips out a gun and points it at me. Something clicks in my brain. He's the guy who gave me the scary vibes at Frosting & Beans Saturday afternoon. Right before Ashton and his grandfather showed up.

"*No hey problema*," he says with a thick accent. "We'll get out of here, but she's coming with us."

Kristeen screams at the top of her lungs. The other guy slams into her and knocks her onto the floor. She's on her back, flailing and jamming her high heels in the general direction of his kneecaps. He grabs her hair and punches her in the mouth with his fist! I'm in utter shock for a few seconds then I scream. I've been screaming. The guy with the gun pops me across the mouth. "*Cállete.*" He spins around me and grabs my waist in a choke hold. "Move!" The barrel of his pistol is crushing my windpipe.

He kicks the door open, and drags me deeper into the shadows, away from the main bar. I try to stomp his foot and miss. I attempt to elbow him in the ribs and he dodges. He yanks my head back. "*Hola, niña bonita*, my orders are to not hurt you, but don't try my patience."

His orders? He's heading toward a door in the very back of the bar. Something tells me if he gets me outside in an alley, I might never see Kristeen or Leif again, despite his orders not to harm me. Loud drumming sounds crash against the roof. Hail. This is going to be fun.

Something slams into us and throws me against the wall. A shot goes off. I spin around. Ashton is tangling with the badass who was trying to abduct me. He's managed to get him locked between his thighs and is pounding the guy's face in.

"Ashton!"

As soon as his fists stop flying, the guy on the floor grabs Ashton by the throat. He's going to strangle him.

Kristeen is sobbing into her cellphone.

211

I kick at the guy's ribs, but he doesn't let go. Ashton is trying to dislodge the guy's hands, but they aren't going anywhere. I hear the clatter of heels. The witchy sisters appear from the shadows. One of them bends over and yanks the short hair on my attacker's head. The other one joins her. She's got long nails that she squeezes into the side of the guy's head. She's chanting something in a low voice. Blood droplets spring from his scalp. His bellow of pain as he releases Ashton's neck makes my ears ring. Daphne and Maddie bring up the rear.

"Ashton, are you all right?" Daphne smothers Ashton with concern. My stomach heaves as much from what just happened as from watching her paw him and whisper baby talk in his ear.

Where in the hell is Leif? It's the first time in my life I've needed his protection and he's probably swallowing Lorriene's tongue.

23. Cupcake Withdrawals

 SHTON

I thank Annke and Sybelia for saving my life as the police shove the two tattoo guys into a patrol car.

"No problem, sweet thing," Sybelia says. "Tatiana would never forgive us if we let anything happen to her favorite grandson." She winks.

"Can you make sure Lorriene makes it home safely?" I ask them. I'm not worried about the Wardof sisters. They can fend for themselves.

"Oh, I don't think your sister is in any imminent danger." Annke tilts her head. I follow the direction and see Leif with his arm hanging around Lorriene's shoulder. Man that is just too weird.

"Okay, well, if he doesn't take her home."

"He will," Sybelia says.

"We should be on our way too. Eclipse will become incorrigible if he doesn't get his cream very soon. Traveling makes him cranky," Annke says.

Whatever. "I'll be home after I drop Glynna off."

"Are you sure you're all right to drive?" Sybelia steps in front of me to examine my neck. "There's some bruising."

I don't mention the throbbing on the entire right side of my torso. Glynna accidentally nailed me when she was trying to kick my/her attacker. I think she might have broken one or two of my ribs. I'll get it checked out in the morning if it doesn't feel better. "I'm fine."

"If you say so."

I maneuver around her to catch a policeman before he gets into a patrol car.

"Yes, sir?"

I'm getting the royal treatment, because as soon as they got my name, they recognized me as Nicolas Bass' grandson. "I've seen those two guys before."

"Where?"

"On Saturday, they were at the bakery where she works, with a third guy."

The policeman gets out a pad and scribbles some notes. He probes for as many details as I can remember.

When we're done, he thanks me for my help. I hurry over to Glynna. "Where's Kristeen?"

"Over there."

An older, attractive woman with dark hair is bending over a stretcher. "Is that her mom?"

"Mmm. She's going to ride with her to the hospital."

"Is she hurt that bad?"

"When that guy smashed her in the mouth he broke her jaw."

"Ouch!"

"They think she went into shock. She didn't even feel any pain until the police and her mom showed up."

"You want to follow them to the hospital?"

"I need to see Nana and Ophelia first."

"Can I drive you home?"

"What about your harem?"

"My harem?"

"Ashton, thank you for saving me, although I'm not sure why you bothered."

We're standing right beneath a street lamp and her blue eyes are piercing into me.

"I care about you, Glynna."

"When no one else is around?"

"What? No. Is that what you think?"

"I don't know what to think. Yesterday you were in high-flirt mode and we were having a perfect date."

"Did you say perfect?"

"Until your grandfather had a heart attack and everyone freaked out."

Cupcake Girl doesn't have a forgiving spirit tonight. "Glynna, this stuff with my grandfather and your grandmother is pretty messed up."

"What does that have to do with you and me?"

God, where do I even begin? "My grandmother—"

"Did your grandmother tell you she brought those two girls over to my house today, and they stole a tube of my lipstick?"

"What? No, she didn't mention that."

"I bet there's a lot of things your grandmother doesn't mention."

"What's that supposed to mean?"

"Look, Ashton, I'm sorry your grandfather is divorcing your grandmother, but I don't have anything to do with that, and it's like you're blaming me."

She's right. I am blaming her. "If I hadn't helped your grandmother visit my grandpa—"

"Oh, Ashton, do you really think it's that simple? Do you really think you could have stopped any of this from happening?"

"Yes, I do."

"Then you're stupid." Glynna pokes me in the chest, the force of her finger pushing me back a few steps.

"That wasn't nice."

"Forgive me, but I'm not in a very nice mood tonight. Something about two creepy guys assaulting my best friend and trying to abduct me has me on edge."

The rain picks up just like that, and we're both drenched.

"Come on, Glynna." I reach for her hand, but she jerks it away. "At least let me drive you home."

She casts about for anyone else to do the honors, but Leif and Lorriene are still smashed against one another, and there's really no one else available. "Fine."

I reach for her hand again, but she jams both of hers into her pockets.

"You can drive me home, but you're not going to touch me."

My Cupcake Girl has a temper, and she holds a grudge. Nevertheless, I remain chivalrous and open the door of my Firebird for her.

She doesn't even thank me.

When I get into the driver's seat, she's a silent stone. I'm starting to see the family resemblance between her and Iron Lady. I start the engine and the windshield wipers. "Man, this storm is crazy." I wipe my hands on my jeans and blow some air into my cupped fingers to de-numb them.

"Yeah, crazy," she mumbles.

Having her so close and smelling her fresh, delicious scent of strawberries and cream, with an added scent of lemon mixed in, makes me forget my grandmother's heartache. Glynna's determined silence forces me to reconsider my stance. Family is everything, but maybe I was wrong to mix-up my love life with my grandparents'. I sneak a glance at my red-headed tigress. Her eyes are glued to the road in front of us. Maybe she has a point. If her grandmother and my grandpa are meant to be, they didn't need me to bring them together. But God, this divorce is going to be a mess. And what was up with those girls stealing her lipstick? That is some weird shit.

My head throbs. I feel like I'm forgetting something, but the longer I sit next to Glynna, the more I just want to ask her out on another date.

I flip on some mood music.

"Please, don't sing to me again," she says.

Okay, Bass Man. You made a mistake. Apparently, a big one. "I didn't mean to hurt you."

"But you did."

As if my iPod has a mind of its own, *I Never Told You* by Colbie Caillat plays on. *Blue eyes, the taste of your smile...* Pitch perfect. Now, I'm gazing straight into Glynna's glassy eyes. I don't think I can handle it if she cries.

"Is there any way I can make it up to you?" I feel like such a jerk, but I miss everything about her.

"Why? Why do you want to make it up to me?" Although Glynna's voice is soft, those are loaded questions. I'm tempted to tell her the truth and spill my guts. I want her. I need her. I can't imagine my life without

216

her. But can I love her? Like really love her, and not deceive her at the same time? Right now, I'm not so sure someone like me deserves someone as good as Glynna. And the situation we're in with Pap Pap and her grandmother?

Then she voices what I'm really afraid of. "This problem of ours is only going to get worse. You're grandparents are going to get a divorce, and Nana and Nicolas are getting married."

"They're getting married?" That was kind of squeaky sounding, like Edward the first time he opens his mouth in the first *Twilight* movie.

"He's already proposed."

That's a bitter pill to swallow. "Does my grandmother know?"

"How would I know? Nicolas talked with her when she came over to the house today, but I didn't eavesdrop on their conversation."

"Wow. I wasn't expecting marriage, especially not so soon."

"Neither was I." She's pouting.

"Are you as upset with your grandmother as I am with my grandfather?"

"They're acting ridiculous." She scowls. "Like a couple of teenagers who don't give any thought as to how their decisions are affecting anyone else around them."

"I assumed you'd be happy for your grandmother."

"I'm happy she's in love. She's fucking glowing, but am I happy that she's destroying your grandparents' marriage? No. Plus–" She folds her arms across her chest. "–it's going to be terrible for business–"

"Are you talking about Frosting & Beans?"

"Yes, Ashton. When word gets out around town that Nana broke up your grandparent's marriage, even our regulars will probably stop coming in." Her rosebud lips release a long, sad exhale.

"I doubt that."

"Huh?"

"Tatiana's not that popular in Spokane. I mean she's powerful, but that's not the same thing. No one really likes her. Grandpa, on the other hand, is well-loved. The city's going to line up on his side. Besides, everyone loves a good love story spiced with a scandal. If you get out ahead of it, and spin things right, your sales could go through the roof."

Finally, she laughs, although her fingers fly to her mouth as she tries

217

to suffocate her giggles. "Is that what they teach you at Harvard?"

I pull up in front of her house. "Actually, that's exactly what they teach me at Harvard." I put the Firebird in park. "Listen, Glynna, last night everything happened so fast. It made my feelings for you seem dangerous, and threatening to my family. I just needed some time to think, but when I heard you screaming tonight at Bistangos, I didn't need any time to think."

She turns her head to meet my eyes.

"I had a great time with you yesterday. Best date ever." Whoa. That's a hard sell, Bass Man. So what! If I don't make things right with her, our relationship is going to end before it has a chance to begin, and the more I think about it, that's just sad. I do love my grandmother, but if I'm really honest, if I were Pap Pap, I might leave Grandma T for Pearl, too. Even if all I had to look forward to was the downhill slide into senility with her.

Glynna's chewing on that bottom lip.

"Can we start over?" I ask.

"It hurt seeing you tonight with those four girls hanging all over you."

Cupcake Girl doesn't pull any punches. "They're my grandmother's friends. They're just in from Seattle to help her with some stuff. It is weird they came over here and took some of your lipstick. Are you sure they did that?"

She shakes her head. "I'm not sure of anything. But that cat ran through our house and ended up hiding beneath my bed. It was just weird, finding them in my room."

"Sounds weird. But I'm not dating them or anything."

Her eyebrow arches.

"And Daphne and Maddie are Lorriene's friends more than mine."

"They weren't paying much attention to your sister tonight."

"Yeah, I noticed she's into your cousin. What's up with that?"

Glynna rolls her eyes. "I have no idea."

"So, will you let me take you out again?"

"I'm not sure it's such a great idea."

"Please, don't make the same mistake I made last night. Don't let problems that don't belong to us keep us apart." I ruffle my hair. "I know it's too early to say, but Glynna, I really like you, more than any other girl I've gone out with."

218

Her nose wrinkles with suspicion.

"What I feel for you is not going to go away easily. Someday, I'm going to tell you, Glynna Balcora, that you really mean something to me, and you won't have any doubts that it's true." I hold her hand and place it on my chest, pretty confident that I'm making inroads.

"Look, I felt really hurt tonight. I need some time for everything to settle down."

Or maybe not. She's tough. "How much time?"

When she grins, my heart grows three times in my chest. "I don't know. At least a few days. I should go. It's late. Good night, Ashton."

She jumps out of my car and is tearing up their walkway before I can even open my door and catch up with her to give her a kiss good night.

I miss those lips. I can't explain why I feel this need to be near her, to touch her, but I do! If I have to beg, I'll beg. I'll tell her I don't deserve her, that I might not be good enough for her, that every single day, her presence will be a constant reminder to me to become a better man.

I slam my steering wheel with the heel of my hand. Why didn't I say any of that when she was sitting right beside me?

I sit there for a minute, staring at the lighted windows. Pap Pap is in there somewhere. I need to talk to him about what's going on, but maybe tonight isn't the best time.

When I get home, Grandma T, Sybelia, Annke, and Eclipse are having a big pow wow. Apparently, Lorriene hasn't made it home yet.

Everyone stops talking as soon as I enter the kitchen, but I'm practiced with situations like this. It's not the first time my grandmother has clammed up when I walk in. I head to the refrigerator. Warm milk always puts me straight to sleep, and I'm feeling pretty ragged. Getting some rest tonight sounds like a good plan.

"Where have you been?" Grandma asks.

I pull the gallon of milk out of the refrigerator. "Sybelia didn't tell you?"

"I want to hear it from you."

"Glynna was pretty shaken up after the attack. I gave her a ride home. It was the gentlemanly thing to do."

I get out a pan. Grandma T takes it from me. She punches the

219

intercom. "Helene!"

"Don't wake her up. I'm perfectly capable of heating up some milk."

"You shouldn't have to."

She's in full-blown matriarch mode. I'm not going to win. I hold up my hands and join Annke and Sybelia at the table. When Helene comes in to the kitchen, I feel like a heel. She's in her robe and wiping sleep from her eyes. Grandma instructs her to heat up my milk and bring it to us in the sitting room. She motions to the rest of us to follow her down the hall. We reposition ourselves on chairs and sofas. When I slip off my shoes, Eclipse stalks over to sniff at my socks. I try to pet him, and he hisses.

"Did you speak to your grandfather?" Grandma asks.

"No, but I heard you and your friends stopped by there today."

"Is that what your girlfriend told you?"

"Yes, she mentioned it."

"What else did she tell you?"

"She's upset with everything that's happening, too."

"I doubt that."

"I know you're hurting, Grandma, but your world isn't the only one that's getting turned upside down."

"Please!"

I shrug. I'm not going to convince her of anything. "So why did you go over there today?"

"I needed to see your grandfather."

"How did it go?"

"He doesn't want to talk directly to me."

Oh, God, here come the waterworks.

"After all our years together, after having a son and two precious grandchildren together, he doesn't want to talk with me. He told me to contact him through his lawyer."

That's pretty brutal. If he's drawn that kind of line in the sand, Pap Pap must be serious about going forward with this divorce. Maybe, Glynna's right. Maybe, this isn't my battle.

Helene brings my milk, and I thank her. "Grandma, I'm sorry this is happening, but maybe you need to let him go."

Her face is a contortion of rage. "I will never let him go."

"You may not have a choice."

She stalks from the room.

"She's not ready to hear the truth yet," Annke says.

I focus on my glass of milk. Helene heated it to the perfect temperature. I'm going to be snoozing like a baby pretty soon.

"The redhead," Sybelia starts.

"What about her?"

"Has anyone ever attacked her like that before?"

"Not that I know of."

"How well do you know her?"

"Not that well. I mean we grew up together here in Spokane, but other than nursery school, we didn't really hang out."

They continue to quiz me about Glynna. Their questions are innocuous enough, but I don't volunteer that the two guys who attacked Glynna were at Frosting & Beans on Saturday. Grandma may think these two are her friends, but I'm not sure I trust them.

"So when you took her home, she didn't tell you about anyone else trying to hurt her?"

"Nope, she didn't mention a thing. Why are you so interested in her?"

They exchange looks. "Just curious," they say in unison.

"She's very pretty," Sybelia adds.

Annke nods, "Striking."

"Did you take some lipstick from her house when you went over there with Grandma today?"

They laugh. "Is that what she told you?"

All of a sudden I feel very protective of my Cupcake Girl. "I might have misunderstood. She was babbling. How long did you two say you're going to be visiting?"

"We didn't, but we'll be here for as long as Tatiana wants us to stay."

"So you're here to help my grandmother with... ?"

"You could say that we're helping her transition through this difficult period."

"How do you know her?"

"My mother and your grandmother go way back," Annke says. Her cat is curled up in her lap. "So when we got a call that she was having such a difficult time, we came as fast as we could."

"A call from whom?"

221

"Liam Gallagher."

"Who's that?"

"You don't know him?"

I hate to admit that I don't.

"Oh, he and Tatiana knew each other before your grandmother and grandfather ever met."

My gut twists.

"But you're going to have a chance to meet him yourself. He'll be arriving tomorrow."

Just. Great. I hope Grandma isn't trying to stir up some old love triangle to make Pap Pap jealous.

"Have you ever had your cards read?" Annke pulls an oversized deck from the giant messenger bag she totes around.

"What are those?"

"Tarot cards," Sybelia answers. "Let her do a reading."

"Oh, no. I don't believe in that kind of stuff."

"What kind of stuff?" Annke's eyes grow big and round.

"Psychic, witchy stuff."

"Oh, we don't believe in it, either, do we Sybelia?"

"No, we just like to play around with the pretty pictures."

Annke is shuffling the cards and holds them out to me. "Just cut the deck."

To humor her, I grab the top half of the deck between my thumb and forefinger then slide it underneath the pile that's left in her hand. An impish expression flits across her face. She looks like a Goth pixie.

"Interesting," she muses.

Sybelia scoots around to examine the cards her friend has laid out in a cross.

"*The Magician*, nice. Looks like someone might be coming into their powers in not too long after all."

"Ooh, and love, too."

My heart does a flip, even though I don't believe in this garbage.

The two exchange glances. Annke holds a finger to her lips.

"What?"

Annke swirls the cards into a single stack. "Like I said, we just like to look at the pretty pictures."

222

Whatever. First, the lipstick fetish, and then this tarot, voodoo stuff. I'm pretty sure if I stay any longer, things are just going to get weirder.

At least when I tell them I need to get some sleep, they don't protest.

24. Who's Your Cupcake?

ATIANA

For the second time, a helicopter lands on the lawn. Liam exits the cabin and waves off the pilot. Even from the distance, I can see he's fit and sharp in his custom-made suit. But why is he here? And what's his obsession with the girl?

I take one last look at myself in the mirror. Fury bubbles in my throat. The past two days have aged me twenty years. I hate that I must face Liam like this. I swallow my pride and steel myself for his judgment. I've no doubt it will be harsh. Liam has never had any patience for failure, and with Nico gone, and my heirs proving barren of witchcraft, that's what I am. The truth I've hidden from myself for over a decade splits my cocoon of denial with a single rip. A new generation of Occultos is rising, my time is fading.

"Liam," I call from the top of the stairs. Annke and Sybelia are buzzing around him. Not until I'm on the bottom step does he turn his full face to me. There's a ghastly scar running from the bottom of his right eye, in a puckered slash all the way to his jaw bone. I have to force myself not to recoil.

"Tatia." He meets me at the bottom of the stairs with a double clasp of

225

my hand and air kisses. No one but Liam has ever called me Tatia. It's both intimate and infuriating.

I lead them all into the living room. From the corner of my eye, I see him assessing every detail of our home. Regardless of the marring of his exquisite face, his eyesight seems not to have suffered. My jaw clenches. Being the object of his unrelenting scrutiny brings up unpleasant memories. Liam was my first lover, and he wasn't a kind one.

"What brings you all the way across the country, and at such short notice?" I ask once we're all settled.

"I need to confirm something for myself."

"And what might that be?"

"I'm convinced my child, the one I've been searching for, is here in Spokane."

My spine straightens with the shock of his news. How is that possible? Worse, how could I not have known? "Whatever makes you suspect that?"

Years ago, he tricked me into concocting the love potion which made Natalia—a Lumina—fall in love with him. I flinch as the painful memories are jarred from their grave. I buried them for a reason.

An intense ache swells behind my left eye. It blinks uncontrollably.

Sybelia lurches toward me. "Are you all right?"

I let her flutter around me as I sink back into the cushions. At this point, any distraction will do. She massages my temples and the twitch calms.

"Thank you, darling." I pat her hand.

After she flits away, I feel overexposed.

Liam pulls out his phone and holds up the photo I sent him yesterday. The room swims around me. How could I have missed it? Natalia's auburn curls and pale skin, Liam's crystal blue eyes and bow-shaped lips. The girl's lineage is undeniable.

"I'm sure the DNA test will confirm my paternity," he says, "but I want to see her myself as soon as possible."

The room spins around me. Add not locating Liam's heir when she lived right beneath my nose to my growing list of failures. I'm sure he is. How to recover? "DNA test?"

He waves his hand. "Just a formality. I understand she was attacked

226

last night, and your grandson saved her."

The carousel of my emotions begins to slow. Perhaps my position in the Occulto hierarchy can be salvaged. "Yes, it's true. He gave no thought to his own safety, just saved the girl at great risk to himself."

Liam slides the phone back into the breast pocket of his suit. "I'm grateful."

I'm tempted to call Ashton down to meet Liam right now, but the warlock's gratitude might be better used to gather information about his intentions. "Perhaps you can thank him yourself, later. Will you be staying in Spokane long?"

"Only until I see her."

"Does she know you're here?"

"No."

My mind is juggling the facts. Liam left me for Natalia, a Lumina, and now Nico has left me for Pearl, another Lumina, but I can't find the connection. Maybe there isn't one. Maybe this is all a nightmare, and I'm going to wake up soon. I flounder for something to hold on to. "But you've remained in touch with Natalia's family, the girl's family? You'll call them and let them know you're here. Perhaps they can help ease the shock of it all."

His eyebrows raise in admonishment. "Have you forgotten Natalia's mother and father died not long after their daughter disappeared?"

I'd been Liam's fiancé before Mother's disgrace, and I hated remembering that period in my life. "Perhaps I whipped up a little spell to forget."

Annke and Sybella are enthralled with our exchange. It irks me that he's allowed them to sit in on what should be a private conversation between the two of us. "Those weren't pleasant days, Liam." I give the girls pointed looks, but he doesn't care that I'm drowning.

"No, I suppose those aren't your favorite memories."

That's putting it mildly. I'd loved Liam—as much as an Occulto is capable of love. All right, I'd been obsessed with him. Completely besotted with him, and when he'd backed out of the wedding after Mother's exile from the coven, I'd wanted to kill him. But then he'd crawled back and begged me to help him with a love spell. I'd been so naive, hoping that by proving myself to him, his commitment to me, and our future, would be revived.

It wasn't.

And yet, I can't get things to add up in my mind. Certainly the memory spell I'd used to blot out Liam's marriage hadn't ripped that big of a hole in my psyche. "I confess I'm having a hard time putting all the pieces together. The girl in question lives with the sisters who attacked me. She's the granddaughter of the woman... the woman..." I can't finish the sentence. The woman whom Nico loves. It hits me like a cauldron of bubbling black tar. My husband loves Pearl.

My lips quiver. I cover my mouth with my hand.

"Are you all right, Tatia?" Liam scoots to the edge of his seat. Genuine concern softens his face. How touching, but not enough after all these years.

I shake my head and stand up. I need to get away from him. I need to think. I need to maintain control. I sink back down. "What exactly are you saying, Liam?"

"The women my daughter lives with aren't her blood relatives."

Pearl is short. Her granddaughter is taller than Lorriene. I try to remember the natural color of Pearl's hair. Gold? Brown? Definitely not red. Her sister's hair is dark, also not red. "Then why is she here with them? They've raised her. Did they steal her from Natalia's family?" More outrageous plays for power have occurred in the history of both covens.

"I don't think it was anything like that. When Natalia ran away, her mother and father were overwrought. Her mother suspected her daughter was pregnant and shared her suspicions with me. But Natalia left no trail, and she never contacted her parents again. I'm certain Natalia meant to hide her pregnancy from me. She never wished me to know we have a child. However, I've never stopped looking for them. And Annke discovered some intriguing information when she was doing some research for me a few weeks ago. Annke?"

"What can I say?" the young witch preens. "The history of our kind intrigues me. And with my mother in her current condition, I've been given free rein to the archives. When Liam called me about an interesting article he'd come across in New York, I recalled a record of Lumina births in the Northwest. I'd come across it several years ago, and found it quite intriguing. I suppose that's why I've never forgotten about it. There was a single witch present at all the most difficult births, a talented midwife. The last birth she attended coincided perfectly with the timeline of Natalia's disappearance. I found that curious."

"Indeed," I say.

"I did some more digging after Liam called for my help, but there were no records of where this midwife had gone. It's like she disappeared into thin air, which made me even more curious. After I couldn't find anything else in the archives, Sybelia got creative with her scrying. Everything kept pointing back to Spokane, although I admit, we were skeptical. Nevertheless, by the time you called Liam, we'd already planned a trip. We just came a few days early."

Liam gestures Annke to silence. "So when you called, Tatia, I realized we could help each other once more."

My cheeks split into what I hope resembles a smile.

"I trust the girls have been useful," he continues.

"Of course. The memory spell they brewed for my grandchildren was impeccable—"

"Memory spell?" Ashton asks

How long has he been listening?

Liam doesn't miss a beat. He rises elegantly and strides toward my grandson. Ashton's eyes widen. Liam's scar is hard to look at. The warlock holds out his hand until Ashton offers his, then Liam squeezes my grandson's palm until their eyes lock. When Ashton is stunned, Liam flicks his fingers and performs an incantation. Ashton blinks. Liam keeps hold of my grandson's hand and introduces himself as an old acquaintance of mine. "So you're the young man who played the hero and saved the beautiful girl last night?"

Ashton rubs his jaw. He's unable to meet Liam's gaze. "Yeah, that would be me."

"The world could use a few more brave souls like you."

My grandson looks a bit puzzled by Liam's effusive compliment. Thankfully, the doorbell chimes and ends the strange moment. Ashton answers the door himself.

Daphne. She throws her arms around my grandson. "Good morning, handsome."

229

I suspect we all notice that he doesn't return her enthusiastic embrace.

"Daphne, darling," I call to her, "there are some people here I'd like you to meet."

After more introductions, I encourage Annke and Sybelia to take Daphne up to my study while Ashton excuses himself. When I'm sure we're alone, I tell Liam, "Annke and Sybelia promised to help the poor girl with a love spell." I chew on a thumbnail. My grandson's engagement to Liam's daughter could prove more advantageous to me than his engagement to Daphne. I'll have to sort this out later.

"Where were we?" I ask Liam.

"As soon as the lab confirms the DNA, I want to relocate my daughter to New York City."

"You're prepared to turn her life upside down, just like that?"

"I'm not going to tell her who I am yet."

"No?"

He sits next to me on the couch and takes my hand in his. "That's where you come in, Tatia."

His hands are cool and smooth. I remember what they felt like when they were more demanding. "Whatever I can do, Liam. You know I've never been able to deny you anything." My words are calculated. Fortune has dropped the opportunity to break him right in my lap.

"Whoever tried to abduct my daughter last night must know her true identity. With her unique powers, she's worth millions on the global weapons market."

"How intriguing." I wonder if his insight into her value has anything to do with the horrid gash on his face. Whoever stitched it up was a Frankenstein.

"I've got to leave for South America tonight. Then I'm headed to Africa, and after that, a few countries in the Eastern Bloc. These are delicate business negotiations I've had in the works for months. They can't be canceled. When I travel internationally, I can't provide the kind of security my daughter will need once her identity is widely known. And it will be, once I claim her. I need you, and perhaps your grandson, to watch over her until I return."

"Of course, Liam. It would be a great honor to serve you in this way."

His relief is palpable. That he so obviously cares for her makes me like the girl even less.

"Good morning, Grandma." Lorriene trots in. "Who is this?"

"An old, dear friend, darling."

Before she sees his scar, my granddaughter is as taken with Liam as I was when I was her age. But when he turns his head, her expression freezes.

I tilt my head. "Scoot. Liam and I need to finish catching up."

She skitters from the room.

"Did Annke mention the tarot reading she did for your grandson last night?" Liam asks.

"Not a word."

"*The Magician* came up as the querent."

I hardly know how to respond. *The Magician* is the most powerful wizard in the tarot deck, and the querent is the subject of the reading. Perhaps my world isn't falling down around me, after all. Perhaps it's just rearranging itself.

Liam pats my knee. "I wouldn't give up on either of them, yet."

"I never intended to."

ASHTON

"Ashton!"

I inwardly groan as Daphne clicks across the kitchen floor in her high-heeled sandals. Why didn't I make my escape when I had the chance? Apparently, I'm not just moving slow this morning, I'm also thinking slow. Glynna's less-than-enthusiastic response to the spilling of my heart last night has sapped my energy.

Daphne's white eyelet sundress is snug around her waist and hips. The chick never puts the seduction routine to rest, but after last night I have to take some responsibility for her hopefulness. I was pretty flirty until Glynna got attacked.

231

When Daphne flashes me what I'm sure she believes is an irresistible smile, I flinch. She doesn't seem to notice as she makes a beeline for the coffee pot.

"Can you believe I haven't had any coffee yet?"

She's quite the sparkling conversationalist. Her parents are definitely getting their money's worth from that Ivy League school. I drain the last sip of my second cup. Time for me to hustle out of here.

Once the machine starts humming and gurgling, I hear the *click-click* of her heels coming in my direction. Her nails graze my shoulders before she digs in for a massage. Too slow again. She's going to prove hard to outmaneuver this morning when the only destination I've had in mind for the past twenty minutes is my bedroom. I'm not dressed to leave the house.

"How's the big hero doing today?"

Her voice is sticky-sweet. "Where are Annke and Sybelia?" Maybe I can pawn her off on them.

"With your grandmother. They'll be down in a minute."

Thank God. Maybe I can fend her off until they get here, although I do have to admit the tension in my shoulders is giving way beneath her ministrations. When the coffee pot falls quiet, she gives my shoulders a final squeeze.

"How do you like yours?" she asks.

"Oh, no, I'm good."

She slides a fresh cup of black coffee in my direction.

A sucker for the thick, dark aroma, I remain planted in my seat.

"You sure?" She prepares her own cup and sits down next to me.

When she lays her hand across my arm, I have to force myself not to jerk away, but her face is so pleading, I feel sorry for her.

No need to be mean. Glynna's not going to want to see me for at least a few days. What's another cup of coffee gonna hurt? I offer her a half-smile and take a sip. Anticipation gives her eyes an intense glow. I've never noticed they're blue before. Not a clear blue like my Cupcake Girl's, but a smoky blue.

"Do you like it?"

It's fantastic. It's the best cup of coffee I've ever had. I feel a haze cloaking my mind. It relaxes me, but little by little, the memory of the

232

clearest blue eyes in my world begin to fade. "Yeah." After I take a few more sips, I notice her nose job is looking better. Although her jaw is narrow, she has these apple cheeks that are cute.

"Let me get you another cup," she offers.

I've already drained the one she just poured. "Sure." I'm not gonna turn down a cuppa joe that delicious.

She slides the next cup toward me and sips daintily at hers.

"Man, what did you slip in this?" I ask. I'm truly impressed.

"I'll never tell." When she giggles, I smile right along with her. If she made me coffee this good every morning, maybe being married to her wouldn't be such a bad thing. I blink.

She reaches for my arm again, but this time I don't cringe. Her fingers trail my forearm. When her gaze meets mine, she looks so happy. Radiant. I can't figure out why I've always been so mean to her. Maybe it's just because we've known each other so long, and she's almost like family.

"Did you meet Liam?" she asks.

"Yeah."

"What did you think of him?"

"I doubt it's a coincidence, him showing up the day after my grandpa moves out of the house."

"Oh, I don't think he means your grandfather any ill."

"No?"

"We all know this has been a shock for Tatiana. I think it's good she's letting her walls down, letting her old friends provide some emotional support. In the end, the more people your grandmother has to lean on, the easier it will be for you and Lorriene, and your parents."

She's probably right.

"Liam wants to go by Frosting & Beans later."

That doesn't sound good. "What?"

"You know he's from the East Coast, right?"

No, I haven't a clue where he's from, but nice to know. I nod.

"Well, it seems Frosting & Beans got written up in some obscure gourmet magazine, and he wants to test its merits for himself. Apparently, he's a real epicurean."

"I'm surprised cupcakes are his thing."

233

"Oh, why?"

I shrug. His V-taper was impossible to overlook in that fitted suit. "He just looks fit."

"Not as fit as you." Daphne lightly pinches my bicep.

I have to admit her assurance calms down my inner alpha.

"So who else is going on this field trip to Perry Street?"

She holds up her fingers and starts counting. Her hands are about half the size of mine, and her fingers are so short. I don't know why I've never noticed how cute it is when she gestures with them. "Annke, Sybelia, me, your sister, your grandmother, Liam, and Eclipse."

"The cat?"

"Annke won't go anywhere without him."

With Grandpa out of the picture, maybe it won't hurt if I tag along, to keep an eye on my grandmother. I'm still not sure I like her hanging with this Liam guy. Although I can't put my finger on it, there's something dark about him. "I'm in."

Daphne squeals her delight and it's infectious.

I have to press my hands flat on the table to stop myself from jumping up and wrapping my arms around her.

25. The Unexpected Cupcake Visitor

CYNNA

When I get to her house, Kristeen's mother lets me know in a firm voice that my friend is resting. She's clearly not pleased that her daughter's jaw was broken in my company. It will be useless to defend myself. I'm pretty sure the last thing she wants to hear is me whining about how it wasn't my fault, because it sort of is.

I hold up the bag I brought from home. "Leif's special blend of coffee and homemade croissants." At least if she'll accept my gift, it will lift her spirits. She hesitates before saying thank you and inviting me in.

"I know Krissy loves your cousin's coffee. She'll appreciate you bringing her some."

I follow her to my friend's bedroom, which is military neat. Although Kristeen's emotions are messy and often out-of-control, she has the mind of an engineer. The only thing not completely ramrod straight is her body, curled up in a fetal position on the bed. I hate to wake her up, but the coffee's going to get cold, and who wants to drink cold coffee?

"*Mi niña,*" her mother whispers. "*Su amiga le trajo su cafe favorito.*"

Kristeen groans. "*Dejame dormir, Mama.*"

Her mother indicates for me to hand her one of the lattes, which I do.

235

She waves it beneath her daughter's nose. Kristeen's eyes pop open. "Mama! Why din-chou tell me it waszh Glyn?" She shoves herself to sitting and takes the cup.

I gasp.

The lower right side of her face is one enormous bruise. She waves me quiet, but when she tries to take a sip of her latte, she exclaims, "*¡Ay! Me duele la boca.*"

Even though they're speaking in Spanish, it's not too hard to follow their conversation. Hanging around Kristeen most of my life, I'm practically bilingual.

"Let me go get you a straw." Her mother hurries from the room.

I set the croissants and two other coffees down on the nightstand. "Hey, I'm so sorry you got beaten up on my account."

She grins and winces. "Izh going to make great shtory. ¡Ay!" She waves her hand, indicating intense pain. "Ton of shympathy from Professhor Vargoszh." She reaches around, pulls her phone from a drawer in the nightstand, and hands it to me.

I scan the screen. Professor Vargas' apology is somewhat effusive. More an email than a text. "Wow, I'm surprised."

"Shounds like he felt bad? *¡Ay! ¡Ay! ¡Ay!*"

My insides curdle. I don't even have a bruise. "God, I'm so sorry about your mouth."

When her mother comes back in, I notice Kristeen slips her phone beneath the covers. My guess is her mother wouldn't be thrilled to know her daughter's getting flowery personal texts from her college professor. Although Mrs. Sanchez never rides her daughter the way Ophelia rides me, her sensibilities are pretty old school. Kristeen's motto has always been: What she doesn't know, won't upset her.

"Mmm." Kristeen leans back against the pillows her mother has propped up for her and sighs.

I hand Mrs. Sanchez a latte, which I'm happy to see she doesn't refuse. Then I pass around the bag of croissants. After we're all set, Mrs. Sanchez thanks me again for stopping by. "I'll leave you two alone now."

I pull Kristeen's desk chair over to her bed.

"How bad is it?" I ask.

"Oral surgeon shaid it's not worst he'szh ever seen. Should heal fine."

"I'm surprised they didn't keep you over night."

"No pinszh. Just wires. You? Thoszhe guys tried to kidnap you! Ashton szhaved you! Did lovebirdsh kish and makeup?"

"Not exactly."

Her face falls and her eyebrows arch.

"I was still upset about him ignoring me while all those girls were falling all over him."

She nods. "Weird."

"Thank you."

"He exshplain?"

"Yes, but it was pretty lame. He asked me out again, though."

Her eyebrows lift into half-circles. "Yeah?"

"I told him I need to think about it."

"Whoo!" She shakes her hand in the air in that Latina way. "Make shim work for it!"

"I just don't know if I can trust him. He flashes so hot and cold."

She pats my hand. "Might be worth another chanczhe."

"I don't know. Everything has gotten so complicated. I'm not sure it's such a great idea to try and add a relationship with Ashton to the mix."

"Throw caution to wind. Waitsh too long..." She walks her fingers across her comforter.

"But I really don't know what I want, and I really don't know if I can trust him."

She wags her finger. "You want him, shnag him."

"I need to think about it."

"No shthinking!" She slams her hand against her heart and shakes her head. "Shfeel!"

"Kristeen, Nicolas has moved in with us."

"Ooh, ish hot."

"I guarantee you it's not hot. It's confusing. He's doing everything to fast track his divorce, including purchasing two airplane tickets to Guam."

"Him and Nana?"

"Yes! And it's making my head spin just trying to keep up with them."

"For Guam thing to worksh, Tatiana mush shign papersh. Will she?"

"Nicolas' lawyer has convinced him that he can convince her it's in her

237

and her son's and grandchildren's best interest if she doesn't fight him."

"Well, Nicolas ish forshun maker, not Tatish."

"I think he plans on being very generous with her settlement if she doesn't fight him."

She nods, but looks deep in thought.

I'm determined to get my cupcake mojo back, and have settled on a recipe for a batch of Ginger-Orange Decadence. Ophelia and Leif are handling the counters along with the twins, who usually help out on Saturdays. It's a gorgeous Inland Northwest summer day, not too hot yet, and Perry Street is packed. For whatever reason, my prediction about the Bass divorce being headline news hasn't come true. Most Spokane residents are blissfully unaware of the sordid love triangle that has broken up Ashton's happy home. And mine.

I like Nicolas. He's a wonderful man, and he obviously cares deeply for Nana. But it has been hard to wrap my head around the new addition to our family, and with no advance warning. However, I'm more worried the love birds might get their own place after the wedding. In my wildest daydreams I never imagined Nana getting married before me! I shake my head.

This is really going to happen, Glynna. Better get used to it.

I study my jar of herbs. My special somethings from our greenhouse. I'm not sure why I forgot them last time I baked. Okay, I know exactly why I forgot them. Ashton had dumped me, and it hurt so much that I wasn't thinking straight. Dumped me? Was there ever even an us to end? I've been such a fool to believe that happily ever-afters happen in real life. Argh, those romance novels are full of lies.

And last night, even though I tried to push Ashton's irresistible boyish face from my mind, he kept haunting me. It was impossible to eliminate those treacherous memories of his kisses from my thoughts. His lips pressed against mine. Ashton's warm, powerful, make-me-feel-all-gooey-on-the-inside lips. Those traitors should have a warning label.

Touching my lips, I sigh. So pathetic.

I add a pinch of dried ginger to the cupcake batter. Before I close the jar, I indulge myself with a big whiff. A tiny shiver of pleasure courses through me. Nana and I grow the ginger, grate it, and dry it ourselves. I

238

still need to corner her and ask if she knows why my strongest emotions infused my batter and spilled over into our customers when I didn't use our herbs. But she and Nicolas are attached at the hip.

Until I can talk with her, I'm going to pay attention to what I'm doing, and not allow myself to get careless just because I'm obsessing about the younger Mr. Bass.

A half hour later I've got three batches of cupcakes baking. The most delectable aroma of fresh ginger and oranges has filled the kitchen. I'm curious if it has reached the store yet, so I wash my hands and check the clock on the wall. I have a few minutes before the first batch is done.

I push on the swinging door and when I see who's standing at the counter, I almost fall flat on my face. My pulse is racing. My eyes are blinking. What is Tatiana Bass doing in Frosting & Beans? And Ashton is standing right beside her—with his arm around Daphne Wardof's waspish waist. I blink. No, they haven't disappeared. They're still there. I watch as my own nightmare comes to life! They're laughing and flirting with one another. He's tapping the end of her Pinochio nose with his finger.

Why did I ever let him into my heart? How could I ever believe he could love and treasure me? I have to remember, there's a good chance he's an Occulto. Soulless. It all makes sense now. Love has no place in his world. He can never be that guy for me.

I close my eyes, but my poor, gullible heart won't let me lie. I fell for him. He swept into my life like a tornado, twisting and uprooting emotions I've never experienced before.

I open my eyes. Daphne is giggling and Ashton has that grin—my grin —plastered on his face. The image cuts deep. He's an ache I'll never cure, no matter how determined I am, because in spite of everything, right now, my traitorous heart still wants him.

I've got to get out of here before I lose my sanity. I spin around to return to the refuge of my kitchen when I hear, "Miss! Miss! Could you please help me?"

I steel my insides before turning back around. My gaze scans the shop. Although Leif is making coffee, and Ophelia has taken on Tatiana, neither of the twins are waiting on a customer. Why is this man shouting for my help?

"Yes?"

The older man would be handsome if it weren't for the puckered scar slicing his cheek. But now I can't hand him off to one of the girls. He'll think I'm grossed out by his facial disfiguration. I am, so it's hard to look him in the eye. He whips a piece of paper from the breast pocket of his very expensive suit and hands it to me. The page is glossy, something ripped out of a magazine. I'm startled that it's an epicurean review of Frosting & Beans.

"I understand you're the Cupcake Girl." From the corner of my eye, I see Ashton's head swivel in my direction. He has the nerve to wave at me and grin, but he doesn't remove his hand from Daphne's waist.

I'm tempted to turn him into a big, slimy, ugly, green, wart-covered toad. If only I could! My blood is boiling. *Breathe, Glynna, breathe.* I count silently. *Uno, dos, tres.* I pretend I don't see Ashton. But he is still looking at me. I imagine him as that ugly, warty toad! I put all my energy into it, but when I look back in his direction, he's still a beautiful, smug, nitwit! It seems like the whole world revolves around the sun that is Ashton Bass. He's well aware of it, and clearly plays it to his advantage. It's truly disgusting to watch.

I'm pulled from my revulsion when Scarface points to the article. There's a fuzzy picture of me behind the counter. Although my facial features are blurred, my red hair is unmistakable.

"We each have a specialty at Frosting & Beans," I murmur. "Mine is cupcakes."

Scarface fans his hand beneath his nose as if he's coaxing invisible aromas into his olfactory glands. "Orange-ginger?"

I break into a grin. "Why, yes."

"My palette is quite precise."

I hand him back the article.

"Please keep it," he says. "Perhaps you can have it framed and display it here. It's rare for a bakery to receive such an enthusiastic write-up in *Gusto.*"

It would be nice to read the whole thing later, so I don't argue with him. "Thank you."

"When will those just-baked cupcakes be ready?"

"They'll need to cool down before I ice them."

"Of course." He's staring at my face so intently, I wonder if I've got batter on my cheeks. I self-consciously run my fingers down both sides of my face, but they don't find anything gooey or sticky.

"I'm sorry, I don't mean to make you nervous," the man says. "You just remind me of a woman I used to know."

What am I supposed to say to that? He's taking a walk down memory lane while Ashton Bass is groping Daphne Wardof right in front of me. Maybe, I should turn her into something with ugly, slimy, huge tentacles. "Oh," is all I can mutter. My insides are going berserk.

At the same time Daphne is melting against Ashton's side, he and his posse are watching me and this man interact. Do they know him?

Daphne catches my eye and winks! I want to punch her in the face. Or maybe I want to punch Ashton again. Turning them both into heinous repellant creatures seems like a fantastic idea after all. Do octopuses wink?

Menacing black clouds appear outside the window. Customers start piling into the shop. I rivet my attention on the man in front of me before I lose all control. "Would you like something else while you wait for the cupcakes? An espresso, or perhaps a cup of coffee?"

"A double would be wonderful."

Double-crosser! I almost shout my thoughts out loud. I glance at Ashton. "Double," I holler to Leif.

He nods, letting me know he registered the order.

I indicate the seats are filling fast. "You might want to get a seat before they're all taken."

"I'm fine standing," he insists. "How old are you?"

"I beg your pardon?"

"It's just that you must be about nineteen?"

"Yes." This is getting so weird.

"I thought so."

Is he trying to pick me up?

"I'm from New York," he volunteers.

"Here on business?" I'm scrambling to get this conversation back to normal.

"A mix of business and pleasure."

"Mmhmm." I don't ask any more questions, because I don't want to

241

encourage him.

"I'm thinking about investing in a chain of bakeries in the city."

"They have some of the best schools there, as well as some of the best pastry chefs."

"It would be so much more exciting to introduce an unknown talent." Whatever.

"Have you ever thought of leaving Spokane?" he asks.

"Excuse me?"

"You're buried here. I mean this is a nice shop, you've done wonders with the space, and I can see you're doing well, but you could have so much more."

"Are you offering me a job?"

"Glynna!" Ophelia's harsh shout interrupts.

I hold up a finger to the man. "Excuse me." I ask, "What is it, Auntie?"

"Go home, now," she whispers.

"Huh?"

"It's dangerous for you to help that man." She grabs my elbow, pinching my skin as her nails dig in. She guides me toward the double doors that lead into the kitchen. "He's an Occulto."

My heart jacks up another notch. "Are you sure?"

"What if he's the one responsible for your attempted kidnapping last night?" She's frantic. "Please, leave. Let Leif and I take care of them."

"Take care of them?" That sounds ominous.

"Sell them coffee and cupcakes." She flits her hands. "I don't like the way he was focusing on you."

My timer dings. Out of habit, I put on my oven mitts, take the cupcake tins from the oven, and line them up in our walk-in freezer. I'm not sure I want to leave.

Ophelia is wringing her hands.

"Auntie, what are you not telling me?"

When I finish emptying the ovens, I face her. "Do you know something about what happened last night that you're not telling me?"

"No. The unique powers granted by your bloodline make you a target. But now I'm afraid the Occultos have discovered your identity. I told Pearl we shouldn't have let you go out with that boy."

242

"What does Ashton have to do with this? He saved me last night."

"I don't understand everything that's going on, but there is more than one Occulto in the front of the shop, and we can't risk anything else happening right now."

I can't argue that point. A scary feeling gathers in my belly. "Is Ashton an Occulto?"

Ophelia grabs my shoulders. "I don't know."

"But he could be?"

"He's Tatiana's grandson, of course he could be. What did that man want with you?"

"You're sure he's an Occulto?"

"Yes, and I have a very bad feeling about him."

"He offered me a job in New York."

Ophelia's face bleaches. "Glynna, you have to leave. Now."

"Do you know who he is?"

She covers her mouth with her hand and closes her eyes.

"Ophelia?"

"We can't have this conversation here, now. Please, Glynna, don't argue with me. Go home and wait. When I get there, we'll have a long talk with Pearl."

"If we can pry her away from Nicolas," I mutter.

I slip out the back entrance and head down the alley, because if I see Daphne and Ashton again my head is going to explode.

26. A Cupcake Sees Through...

LYNNA

Nana's sitting alone at the kitchen table when I get home. "Where's Romeo?" I hope he's not just in the bathroom or something.

She gives me her *Now, Glynna* look. "Nicolas had to go in to the office."

My shoulders sag with relief. I can't help it. "Ophelia sent me home." I look out the window. Black clouds cover the sky, and a steady rain is falling. The entire way home, I couldn't erase the image of Ashton and Daphne, side by side, in my shop. "You wouldn't believe what happened at Frosting & Beans."

"Sit down and tell me."

"How much time do we have until Nicolas gets back?"

"A few hours."

"Okay." All the questions I've wanted to ask her for the past few days pile up in my mind. Where to begin? "I'm really happy for you, Nana, that you've found love, but I don't understand. You're breaking up a marriage, a family. Do you feel guilty, at all?"

"Glynna, Nicolas' entire life with Tatiana has been a lie."

Isn't that what every man who abandons his wife and family says?

245

"At least once a week, for the past forty years, Tatiana made Nicolas a special dish, shrimp étouffée. Have you ever had creole cooking?"

"I had some gumbo once."

"It's very spicy. So spicy, it covered the bitter taste of the spell which she administered once a week to keep Nicolas involved with her."

I try to absorb what she's telling me. "He never loved her?"

Nana shakes her head. "Glynna, we were in love. He'd bought me an engagement ring, and made reservations for dinner at the Davenport Hotel. He was going to propose to me. I didn't realize that Tatiana had been working on him for several months. It took that long for her to override his feelings for me, they were that strong. But in the past few months, she grew complacent. They skipped some meals. He had one of your cupcakes at the office of one of his clients on the Friday before he came into Frosting & Beans. Your magic was enough to weaken her spell. The second cupcake he had on Sunday broke it entirely. When his love for me re-awakened, the shock and sorrow of what we lost almost killed him."

"Does he know he's been under a spell for the past forty years? Did you tell him?"

"Oh, Glynna, I want to, but he hasn't asked. Ophelia's convinced me it's best not to burden him with the news that Tatiana and I are witches." She takes my hands in hers. "But I want to thank you for giving me back the only man I've ever loved."

My eyes are watering.

"Don't cry, Glynna. It's a miracle."

I wipe at my eyes. "It's tragic and romantic all at the same time. Your lives would have been so different if... if... "

Would she even be my Nana if she'd married Nicolas Bass all those years ago? "Do you think Tatiana sent those people to kidnap me? Does she want to hurt me?"

"I'm sure Tatiana had no idea who you are. At least not until yesterday."

"How can you be sure?"

"Glynna, your father has been searching for you. It would have served Tatiana to deliver you to him."

"So you don't think she did it?"

246

She shakes her head. "Tatiana and your father used to be lovers."

"Oh my God, please don't tell me Ashton and I are related."

"No, no, but, Glynna, darling, your father arrived in town yesterday. We believe he's found you."

"My father? How do you know?"

"I was told this morning."

"Who told you?"

"After those girls took your lipstick yesterday, I was very worried. I have a Lumina contact who's kept abreast of your father's location—"

"You've known where he is my entire life and never told me?"

"No, Glynna, because until you were attacked last night, I had no reason to know or care where your father was. As long as he left you in peace."

Loose ends tie themselves together. An explosion of recognition breaks through my awareness. I get up and pace. "He came to the bakery today."

"He did?"

"Oh, he didn't tell me he was my father, but he asked me how old I was." I tell her the rest of the conversation. "Why didn't he tell me who he was?"

"Maybe he wants to be sure."

"Sure of what?"

Outside, the rain amps into a thunderstorm.

Nana stands up and reaches for my hand. "Come upstairs with me, Glynna."

"Why?"

"I need to show you something."

"I'm so mad about all the lies everyone has told me my entire life. I feel like I can't trust anyone. And today... today Ashton..." I can't even say it.

"What happened with Ashton today, honey?"

I start crying uncontrollably.

"Glynna, what did that boy do to you?"

"He was... he came in with... he was there the same time my father was there. God, do you really think that man is my father?"

"It's highly likely. But what about Ashton?"

"He was there, with his arm wrapped around Daphne Wardof's waist, flirting with her, right in front of me. It was like he hadn't even asked me out last night, like we'd never been on a date."

Nana reaches up to wrap her arms around me.

"He was so cold and it just hurt so much." I sigh.

I'm just another Juliet who's fallen for a guy she'll never have. I hate that I'm not already over him, that I'm incapable of just walking away and forgetting him.

Moments later, we're sitting on Nana's bed, holding hands, staring into the mirror over her dresser. My face is splotchy and my eyelids are swollen, but I feel better for crying. Although the rain has steadied back down to a drizzle, I fear Spokane will never see clear skies again.

"I have a talent for seeing the past," Nana says.

"I don't understand."

"I prefer not to use my gift too often, because the past is treacherous. People get trapped in the past and lose themselves and their lives."

"But I don't care about my past, Nana. It's my present spiraling out of control."

"I know, dear. However, sometimes, the past can be helpful. Sometimes, there things buried in the past which can aid in sorting out our current problems."

"I still don't understand."

She shushes me then waves her hand. My mouth drops as her mirror clouds. After a few seconds, an image comes into focus.

A young woman with long, red hair and pale skin. She looks a lot like me.

My heart opens and breaks at the same time. I go to the mirror and press my fingers against it. Even though it looks like I could reach out and touch the woman, all I can feel is the smooth surface of glass.

My entire body aches for this woman. I long to know her, be with her, hear any words she might say.

Nana is beside me, her hand on my shoulder. "She can't hear you, or feel you, she'll never know you're watching her, but you need her now. You need to know how much Natalia loved you, and how much she wanted you to be safe from your father and his people."

I trace her cheek in the mirror. "She's a Lumina."

"Can you see her light?"

"I can. She's so beautiful." Looking at her like this frees some part of my spirit that's been locked away. "Natalia." When I whisper her name a butterfly of joy wings its way into my heart. "Thank you, Nana. Thank you for giving me this today. She's always been such a ghost, and now... it's like she's always been with me. I just didn't realize it until now."

My mother's alone, sitting in a chair, gazing out a window. Her hands are settled on her belly. Another woman enters and my mother calls out to her. "Pearl, come feel her. She hasn't stopped kicking for the past hour."

My hands fly to my mouth.

A much younger Nana approaches my mother. "How are you feeling today, Natalia?" Pearl pushes several sweaty strands of my mother's hair from her cheeks. "First, I'm cold, my hands and feet are blocks of ice, and then I'm hot, my entire body possessed by fever. As you can see, I'm perspiring as if I was wandering in the desert. It can't be good for the baby, can it? To experience such extremes. Is there some herb you can give me to manage my temperature? I worry I'm doing her damage."

"It's the two forces battling within you. The Occulto craves cold and the Lumina fights back with heat."

"Will her entire life be like this, a constant push-pull between dark and light?"

"Her path will be her own, and I doubt it will be easy. But she'll have your light, Natalia. Whatever challenges she must face, she'll have your love and your light. It will save her in the end."

My mother presses Pearl's hand against her face. "I hope you're right, Pearl. I hope my decision to carry her to term and give birth was the right one."

Pearl crouches beside my mother. "You love her?"

"With all my heart and soul."

"The choices we make out of love are always the right ones."

"Even when I hate her father?"

"His deceit is his own."

"But she'll bear the repercussions of his crime against me, and I so fear she'll always feel alone, caught between two worlds, never fully part of either one."

249

"Don't underestimate her."

The mirror clouds, as my mother and Pearl fade from view. I feel like my heart is being ripped out when another image comes into focus.

My mother is lying on a bed of tangled sheets, screaming. Pearl is dabbing her forehead with a rag. "Breath, Natalia, breathe."

A frisson of memory shudders through me. How many times have I calmed myself with those same words: *Breath, Glynna, breathe.*

My mother bellows again. "She's coming. She won't wait."

Nana runs for more cloths and a large tin bowl of steaming water. I press my knuckles hard against my teeth as I watch my mother give birth to me.

The mirror fogs and another image appears.

My tiny body is lying in my mother's arms. She's holding me to her chest. My mother's pale skin is bone white.

"What's wrong with her?" I whisper.

"I'm dying, aren't I, Pearl?"

I can't see Nana in the mirror, I only hear her voice.

"The birth drained your life force. Nothing I've done has replenished it."

"Promise me you'll take care of my little girl, Pearl. Promise me you'll never let her father find her. Promise me that she'll never, never be tempted by the Occulto power within her."

A sick feeling crawls up my spine.

"Trust in your love for her and your light. Trust in her light. She's half Lumina."

My mother shakes her head. "I'm afraid I've done the wrong thing by bringing her into the world."

Nana's hands reach for the younger me. "Natalia, your child could never be a mistake."

"Glynna. I'm naming her Glynna." As my mother's voice fades, my heart aches with longing.

The mirror fogs as white smoke swirls and curls across its surface. A few seconds later we're back in today and I'm standing next to Pearl, and we're gazing at each other in the mirror.

Nana takes me back downstairs and makes me tea. She pushes something

250

across the table. It's an antique hair comb. The design is six porcelain flowers, with the largest bloom a pale pink rose.

"It was your mother's," Nana says. "She wanted you to have it on your twenty-first birthday, but I think you need it now. Use it like a talisman. Wear it whenever you need white magic to protect yourself, and the ones you love, from the black magic, which is also in your blood."

I'm shocked quiet.

Nana and Ophelia weren't kidding when they tried to explain my bloodlines.

I'm the only Lumina and Occulto who's ever been born.

"Nana, I have to ask you about something."

"What, dear?"

"Yesterday, when I was at Frosting & Beans, some really strange things happened."

She gives me an encouraging look.

I plunge ahead. "After everything that happened at the hospital, I was feeling out of sorts. I thought some baking would be just the thing to get me centered, and help me calm down and sort through my emotions. I was so sad when Ashton pulled away after..." I glance around the kitchen. It's so hard for me to admit that I care for him, especially after seeing him with Daphne.

"Glynna?"

"He was so sweet and romantic on our date, Nana." I tell her about the magic that followed us when we were together: the roses, the rainbow, the mini-tornadoes. "But then, when he realized his grandfather wanted a divorce, he just shut down. He didn't say another word to me the rest of the night, and I didn't hear from him the next day."

"He was shocked and hurt," Nana says. "No one wants to hear that their family isn't as strong or happy as they'd hoped."

"I understand that now. But when I was at the bakery, I felt so sad, and it left me distracted. I forgot to add any of our herbs from our greenhouse to the first batches of cupcakes I made. How could I forget that? I always add a pinch of something."

Nana makes an effort to conceal her concern, but she's not very successful.

"Everyone who ate one of those cupcakes ended up in as deep an

251

emotional funk as I was. Customers were sobbing at the tables. It took me selling another batch before I caught on to what was happening." I tell her about the angry-lemon cupcakes. "Why did I completely forget to add our herbs, and why did my emotions infuse the cupcakes?"

Nana runs her hand along her forehead. What I've confessed troubles her. "Glynna, your powers are growing stronger every day. Your affectionate feelings for Ashton affected the natural world around you. But it seems your Occulto powers are asserting themselves too. As I told you, Occultos long to destroy, annihilate, and harm." She waves her hand in the air. "Nothingness, in all its forms, pleases them. But the surest way to plunge the world into darkness is to destroy love. I've always encouraged you to add our herbs to your cupcakes because we've created such a strong environment of shared love in our greenhouse. The love of one is powerful, but the love of two is even more powerful, and if three or more can join in a genuinely loving way, the Lumina magic is increased exponentially. I've always thought of the herbs as both a shield for your Occulto powers, and an amplification of your Lumina powers. It seems my instincts were accurate."

"It's almost like some part of me made me forget about them. Like some part of me wished to spread my heartache and suffering to others. And I succeeded."

"Glynna, don't judge yourself too harshly. Take the experience and use it to guide your choices."

"But what if I forget again? Baking has always been my refuge, the place I go where nothing bothers me and everything is right. *Mise en place.*"

Nana smiles. "That hasn't changed. It will never change. But it seems that falling in love has increased and altered your powers."

"I'm not in love with Ashton. I hate him!"

"But you do have strong feelings for him, stronger than for any other young man."

"Not anymore."

"Glynna, I'm afraid that denying you're hurting, and pretending it doesn't matter, will feed your Occulto side."

"That sucks."

She lets out a little laugh. "Love is the most wonderful thing in the

252

world. It is the root of all joy and happiness, all peace and harmony. But thwarted love is equally powerful. It twists and distorts. I think it is even more dangerous for you than the rest of us."

"Then what am I going to do? Because Ashton has fallen in love with Daphne Wardof, not me."

"That's hard to believe."

"Seeing is believing. And after seeing them together at Frosting & Beans; can you believe he had the nerve to flaunt their relationship in my shop?"

The sound of breaking glass bursts from the kitchen window.

Both Nana and I are trembling as we tiptoe over to examine the destruction.

My heart batters my chest. "Did I do that?"

"Like I said, your powers are getting much stronger, and it's happening very quickly."

"What am I going to do?"

"Until we come up with a better course of action, I suggest baking. Every day. We also need to reinstate our morning ritual in the greenhouse."

I throw my arms around her. "I'm so happy for you and Nicolas, but I miss you so much! I hardly ever see you anymore."

"I didn't realize you were having such a difficult time."

I agree with Nana about baking every day. "But what if I forget the herbs again?"

"For now, why don't you stick with your tried and true recipes? Nothing new."

"All right." Although experimenting with new recipes is one of my favorite parts of baking, I hand write all my best recipes in my cookbook. Included in each of them is the herb that most compliments the cupcake's flavor. It will be hard to forget to add the herb when it's on the ingredient list. "I guess I'll be baking a lot this summer!"

Maybe we'll expand the business. Open new locations. That might be what it takes for me to get over Ashton and Daphne.

27. Uh-Oh, Cupcake! You've Been Miss-Spelled!

 TATIANA

Donald pulls up in front of a converted cottage on South Hill. The street is empty. Nico isn't here.

My chauffeur comes around and helps me from the car. I straighten my black Akris peplum dress before he graciously escorts me to the plain cement path bisecting a summer-faded lawn. A worn hose, attached to a rotary sprinkler, snakes from the side of the house. This was not what I was expecting from Spokane's premier divorce attorney.

"Would you like me to walk you to the door?" Donald asks.

"No, but keep the car running. I won't be long."

A fresh coat of paint brightens the cottage's exterior, but the flowerbeds are a patchwork of dried dirt and dead plants. A single gold geranium blooms amongst leaves scarred by the recent high temperatures. The paint on the rectangular sign hanging from the eaves of the front porch is cracked. It reads: Frank Langton, Attorney at Law.

When I push on the front door, it swings open. It takes a moment for

255

my eyes to adjust to the interior's dim light. I've entered a reception area with polished wood paneling.

A perky young blonde jumps up, and circles around her massive desk. "Tatiana Bass?"

I nod.

"Please, right this way." She extends her arm. "Frank is expecting you."

No doubt.

She ushers me into a second room. It's enormous, more than half the cottage's square footage.

A balding, obese man sits behind another massive desk. Intently scratching on a yellow legal pad, he doesn't notice us.

"Frank," the girl says.

When he sees me, he stands up with his hands steepled on either side of his notepad. Frank Langton is shorter than I am in my heels. His shirt is wrinkled, the collar is open, and his enormous girth spills over the top of his belt. "Tatiana Bass, a pleasure."

I keep my hand's clasped. The receptionist exits after I decline her offer for refreshment.

Mr. Langton gestures to one of the leather chairs positioned in front of his desk. "Please, sit."

"I'm here because Nico personally requested my presence. I was under the impression he would be here, but since he isn't, I don't intend to stay."

"Tatiana—"

"Mrs. Bass."

"Of course. Please, sit. Nicolas requested you come, without your attorney, to provide me an opportunity to offer you an exceptional settlement."

I make no effort to mask my intense distaste for Nico's messenger. "If it is so exceptional, I'd like my attorney present."

"Mrs. Bass. Please, hear me out."

The troll is standing right in front of me. He smells of roast beef and perspiration. I turn to leave.

"Mrs. Bass, I've been advised by your husband that I may only make this offer once. If you leave now, it will be forever off the table. And yes,

256

the next time we meet, you will need to bring your attorney."

Volts of anger course through me. Coming here was a mistake.

"A contentious divorce will irrevocably scar your family. Your residence will be sold, and neither you nor your husband will be able to maintain the standard of living to which you've grown accustomed."

Rage rattles my bones. Pearl. She caused this. "Are you threatening me?"

"Oh, no, ma'am. Simply stating facts." He gestures again to one of the chairs. "Please, just hear me out. Nicolas cares for you, and your son, and his grandchildren."

And yet here I am. "If he cared for us, he wouldn't be leaving us."

"Mrs. Bass, I can only speak to his considerable generosity. Please, sit."

Ever since Annke and Sybelia left, I've been dabbling with potions and experimenting on Helene. Nothing has worked. The unthinkable hovers on the outskirts of my mind. Pearl and her sisters have drained my powers. Not for a day or a week, but forever.

I face down Frank Langton. Impotence, bankruptcy; whatever harm I can dream up, the power to inflict my will upon him is gone. It might never return.

"Please, Mrs. Bass."

I'm a Grand Witch. I will recover my power. "Fine."

He backs away and rests his ample buttocks against the corner of his desk and makes his speech, hands gesturing.

The offer: The title of our mansion will be transferred to me, free and clear. I will enjoy unlimited use of the Gulfstream, along with my son, his wife, and their children. Nico will establish generous trust funds for me, Gregor and Alise, Ashton and Lorriene.

The condition: I am not to contest the divorce. I'm advised to have an attorney review the divorce contract, for my peace of mind only.

The time limit: If Frank has not received the signed divorce contract within twenty-four hours, Nico will fight me for everything. Our family will be torn apart. Our wealth will be divided by our attorneys.

One hope refuses to die. Ashton's or Lorriene's dormant power will awaken. I must keep them close. If Nico hires a private investigator, random and meaningless sexual encounters I've indulged in for the past

257

forty years will come to light. For the sake of my son and my grandchildren, I can't let that happen.

Beneath his charm and likability, Nico has a will of steel. He doesn't make threats. He believes in letting things go or handling them.

He's handling me.

 SHTON

Daphne and I are at Anthony's with a perfect table overlooking Spokane Falls. It's our two-month anniversary, and I have to admit, dating a chick who's crazy about me pumps me up.

"So, Mr. Hot and Handsome, how was your day?"

"It started off great." I smirk. For the past two months, she's brewed me a fresh pot of her awesome coffee every single morning, and delivered it to me in bed, with whatever added perks I'm up for. Pun definitely intended.

She's scooted her chair around the table so she's practically sitting on top of me. I've gotten used to her tentacles, and come to appreciate the envious glances of all males present. Who wouldn't want this perfectly manufactured Barbie doll at their beck and call to fulfill their every whim and command? I might even miss her when I go back to Harvard at the end of the month.

"What are you thinking about?" she asks.

"How much I've enjoyed your undivided attention for the past two months."

"Oh, Ashton, I live to make you happy."

"I'm starting to believe you."

"Oh, please, tell me what I need to do to convince you?"

I'm wondering how far I should push this submission thing she's got going. It's almost like she craves humiliation at my hands, like it makes her even hotter for me. She's bringing out a dark side I never knew I had. My sexual fantasies are becoming more about dominating her than any

258

shared pleasure. It's like she's my plaything, and I just want to use her.

Daphne rubs against me, her pebbly nipples making it clear I haven't crossed any lines of no return with her yet. But how far should I push things? Do I even want to push them?

"What about a sex video?" I high five myself in my mind. That was bold. Just straight up ask for what you want, Bass Man.

She showers me with approval. "Ooh, that sounds super sexy." She actually gets up out of her chair and wiggles into my lap. "Just thinking about it is making me so turned on." She's running her fingers through my hair and grinding my manhood with her hips. "Tonight?" she murmurs. "So we can always remember our two-month anniversary."

"Posting it on the internet would really turn me on," I whisper into her ear.

"Ooh, on one of those anonymous porn sites?"

"Yeah, babe. If you did that, how could I doubt your commitment?"

"My place or yours?" Her breath is hot in my ear.

"Mine."

Since my grandparents' marriage has fallen apart, Lorriene and I receive even less supervision. No one cares that Daphne's practically moved into my bedroom. I guess her parents are so eager to pawn her off on me, they don't care that she rarely comes home, either.

The next morning, I follow Daphne down to the kitchen. I'm in my boxers, and she's got on the shirt I wore last night, with two buttons buttoned. The sex video thing didn't do as much for me as I'd hoped, but it certainly wasn't due to any lack of enthusiasm on Daphne's part. She uploaded the damned video herself.

It sickened me, her willingness to pimp herself out like that. That's why I'm headed down to the kitchen with her this morning. Right now, I don't want to be anywhere near a bed while she's around. Not that that will cool her down, but there's a reason *Location Location Location* is the real estate maxim. I'm hoping having our morning coffee in the kitchen will make it easier for me to extricate myself from her tentacles for the day.

My grandmother and Lorriene are having breakfast together. But their presence doesn't faze Daphne. She waltzes in and winks at Lorriene.

259

"Good morning, Tatiana." Her glee is clear in her voice.

Grandma raises an eyebrow. Apparently, her attention can't be pulled from whatever riveting story she's reading in *The Spokesman-Review*. However, when I pull out a chair, Grandam *tut-tuts*.

"The Bass men do not come to the table shirtless."

I'm not about to argue, and am thrilled to have a chance to return to my bedroom sans Daphne. I pull out a collarless T-shirt and a pair of long shorts, and check my phone out of habit. There's about twenty text messages from my guy friends. They're all back-slapping me for my performance with Daphne last night. How do they know?

I glance around for Daphne's purse. It's sitting next to the dress she dropped quicker than I could snap my fingers. Not that she'd wait for me to snap my fingers. I don't have to dig around to find her phone, it's sitting on top. She's got a ton of texts too. I scroll through the list, not believing what I'm seeing. She sent the video links to all my friends. No message, but still. My stomach wheezes. Why would a chick do that?

Oh. Right. Parlaying a sex tape into reality whoredom is probably part of Daphne's strategic life plan. Just. Great. Grandma T is going to be all over me if she ever finds out.

They always find out.

I drop the skank's phone back into her purse and gather up her clothes. I definitely need some distance from Miss Wannabe Porn Star today.

When I get back to the kitchen, the coffee is already brewed. I hand Daphne her things. "Oh, sweetie." She lightly pinches my cheek. "You didn't have to bother bringing those down. But, thank you."

I give her a fake close-mouthed smile.

"Plans today, big bro?" Lorriene asks.

"Golf with Tyler."

Daphne's eyes light up. "Ooh, I'm sure you boys have lots to catch up on."

"Yeah." I gulp down my coffee. The strange thing is, with each sip, I feel my hardness with Daphne softening, and my disgust with her sexual wantonness transforming into something like sympathy. By the time I finish my second cup, I decide that I'm too much of a Puritan. These days, women are all about sexual empowerment. Hell, Daphne's just

260

embracing her sensuality, and she's elated that I'm her partner. The Bass Man did make a pretty awesome headliner in the video. Why not just soak up the pleasure for all it's worth? So what if she's a little masochistic? Maybe I should hit the links with some of the guys today. Their texts made it clear they're all impressed with my latest score.

"Need me to make another pot before I leave?" Daphne asks.

Weird, now I almost don't want her to go. "Sure, babe."

After she gets the coffee started, she gathers her things I'd unceremoniously dumped on the table, and tugs me into the living room. Even though all the windows are open, and there's a couple of landscapers in view, she unbuttons her shirt and hands it to me, leaving her standing there stark naked in all her plasticized-Playboy glory. She gets on her tiptoes and presses her chest against mine. Then she takes hold of my mouth with her lips and my crotch with her hands. God, those guys are seeing her salacious behavior and it's making me hot.

"You sure you have to leave right now?" I whimper.

"Oh, baby, I'm so sorry, I do." Her voice is sweet and syrupy. I squeeze her to me and my hands drift down to her ass. When I press her to me she moans.

"I want you to take care of me before you go."

"Ooh, so demanding," she purrs. "I love this side of you."

I can almost feel the black shadow inside me unfurling. "Right here, right now, with the landscapers watching, I want you to take care of me."

"Oh, baby, whatever you need. I promised Maddie we'd go shopping, and I'm already late, but she'll understand when I tell her I was taking care of my baby."

"That's right, Daphne. You take care of my needs first and make sure everyone knows that's the way things are between us."

She whimpers her pleasure at my taking control. I place both my palms flat on the top of her head and push her down. Right before I explode in her mouth, I wink at Raphe and Marcus, the gardeners.

"God, you are so awesome," I tell her as she's pulling on her dress and wiping off lips. She flashes me her porcelain veneers. "Not as awesome as you." And then she's wiggling her ass out the front door.

"Ashton!" Grandma's voice smashes through my sexual haze.

"You called, Grandma?"

261

"We haven't talked in a while. Why don't you sit down and fill me in on what's going on in your life?"

Grandma's different since she signed the divorce papers. Although the hush-hush agreement she made with Grandpa allows her to keep the house and we'll all receive trust funds, the whole thing was sad, and anti-climactic.

We're still adjusting to our new routines.

My dad spends more time with Grandma when she isn't in Seattle, visiting her old friend, Lyrika. Lorriene and I fight less. Mom suffers the most now that Grandma monopolizes the Gulfstream's schedule.

The biggest change: No one mentions Pap Pap when Grandma is in the room.

"You've been seeing an awful lot of Daphne, lately," Grandma says, pulling me from my thoughts.

"Yeah, she's really into me." I don't appreciate Lorriene's snort. "Hey, I thought you'd be thrilled. You've been trying to get me to hook-up with Daphne for years." I punch my sister's arm.

"Do not hit your sister."

"Whatever."

"Just because your grandfather no longer lives under this roof doesn't mean you can get fresh with me, young man."

"Sorry."

She tips her head, indicating she accepts my apology.

"Have you spoken to that redhead recently?"

"Glynna Balcora?"

"Yes, her. Weren't you dating her at the beginning of the summer?"

"I'd hardly call it dating. We went out on one date and—" I pause. "She's not my type."

"Are you sure about that?"

"Huh?" The way I remember it, Grandma was furious I even wanted to take Glynna out. "I thought you'd be thrilled Daphne Wardof and I are together. I thought you wanted us by your side, as a couple, for that closing ceremony thing at Pig Out in the Park?" POP is the annual food orgy in Riverfront Square Park at the end of every summer. Grandma always makes a civic appearance. "I thought that with everything going on, it was even more important you don't attend alone this year."

"It's only that Liam's been calling me, dear."

"The guy with the scar?"

Grandma flutters her eyes. "He's an old, dear friend who can't help it that someone did such a terrible job of suturing what was obviously a horrible wound."

"Yeah, how did he manage to get someone to slice open his face?"

"It would be rude to ask him, and he hasn't volunteered. Nevertheless, he has an interest in Glynna."

Something in me snaps. A protective instinct surfaces from the ever-darkening swampy soup of my emotions. "What does he want with Glynna?"

"He's only concerned with her safety. He was very grateful when you saved her that night at Bistangos."

"Does he even know her? Other than that time that he went to Frosting & Beans?"

"No, he doesn't know her. But he knows her family."

"Pearl and that aunt of hers?"

"They aren't her family," she says.

"Not following."

"Those people adopted her."

"Get out of here," Lorriene pipes up. "And Liam knows her real family?"

Grandma nods.

"Does Glynna know?" I ask.

"No, I don't think she's aware of the truth of her origins, but Liam wishes to enlighten her as soon as he returns to the States. Until then, he doesn't want anything to happen to her. I was hoping you could spend some time with her, make sure she's all right, so I could put Liam's mind at ease while he's out of the country."

"I don't think Daphne's going to understand if I take Glynna out, even if it's just for lunch." My little nymphomaniac's territorial.

"Maybe we could drop by Frosting & Beans," Lorriene blurts out.

"Oh, yeah, that's a great idea. Glynna's going to be so happy to see me." Why do my insides tremble at the mere thought of facing Cupcake Girl? It's like I'm afraid of her or something. "You just want to drool over her hot cousin and his tattoos." I lash out at Lorriene, because she's

263

not being any help here.

My sister gives me the stink-eye.

Grandma ignores my jibe. "I like that idea. Why don't you go today and report back to me?"

Just. Great. Marching orders from Grandma T. I guess the Bass Man won't be soaking up the envy of all his friends today. And damn, if that didn't sound like a great way to spend the afternoon.

I pour myself another cup of coffee.

28. Sweet Cupcake Revenge

CYNNA

"Thank you, Mrs. Alcorn. I'm so glad to hear you love the raspberry-mint-crème cupcakes."

I reposition my mother's comb in my hair. Funny how just touching something that once belonged to her makes it seem like she's close by, or that she's never been far away. I inventory the bakery cases. It has been a good day, but if I want to provide the after-work crowd some variety, I'm going to have to whip up a few dozen more batches. Sticking with the old favorites has been good for business, but I've been researching new recipes online. Sometimes I just want to make something different. Although following Nana's advice has assured no more cupcake disasters. Despite the fact that my mangled heart hasn't healed.

I fidget with the porcelain rose in my mother's comb.

The after-lunch rush has just cleared out, and it would be an ideal time for me to slip back into the kitchen. The bell over the front door chimes.

Why is Lorriene Bass here? She gives me a short wave.

No, no, no. That is not her brother right behind her. When he sees me, he waves, too.

I squash my urge to flip him off, and offer him a cool glare instead.

265

Ass-hat Bass, don't expect anything else from me.

He saunters up to the counter. My counter. The one I'm standing at. Not the one Leif is standing at.

I don't offer to help him.

He flashes me that fake Ashton Bass grin. The one that leaves all the girls—including me and Daphne Wardof—fighting for the Ass-man crumbs. When I don't respond, he shrugs and starts inspecting the cupcakes in the display case.

"Would you like a tray of them smashed in your face?" I ask.

"Glynna, I just stopped by to—"

"Where's your blowup doll?"

His eyebrows rise as he takes a step back. "Temper, much?"

"Just go to hell."

"Wow, is that the kind of service you provide all your customers?"

"You're not a customer. You've never bought a single item from Frosting & Beans. So why don't you just leave?"

"Glynna, I just—Lorriene asked me to come down here with her."

I don't think I've ever felt so angry in my life. I lean across the counter. "Right. You don't eat cupcakes, or pie, or cookies, or anything else we sell here, *because you're so vain, you probably think this song is about you.*" Then I go, "*La-la-la-la-la.*" I try to sing it in tune to the Carly Simon song, but it doesn't quite have the effect I'm going for. Okay. Maybe that was a little much.

Ashton's giving me the strangest look.

I tell myself I don't care, but even I know that's a lie.

He's just standing there, retrenching my heart.

It hurts so bad all over again. "Leif can help you." I swirl around and head for the kitchen.

He runs around the counter and grabs my arm.

I don't know what to say. What's worse is that the feel of his fingers on my skin is wonderful.

Across the shop, the lid of one of the music box curios we sell pops open and starts tinkling *You Light Up My Life.*

He probably can't hear it. But he drops my arm and walks across the shop. He stares at the music and then back at me.

I shake my head and duck into the kitchen. I get out my iPad and swish

266

my finger across the screen. Time for a new cupcake recipe. I'm scrolling through all the ones I've got bookmarked. Mojito cupcakes. Yes. I start prepping my ingredients.

"Glyn?" He's standing in my kitchen. How dare he enter my sanctuary?

The pots and pans hanging from the overhead rack rattle.

Ashton pretends not to notice. For some reason that makes me angrier.

"Why didn't you ever call me again?" I ask him.

"The last time we talked, you didn't sound very interested."

"I told you I needed some time. The very next day you showed up here with Daphne!"

My wooden spoons, upright in a decorative canister, *click-clack* in a frenzied dance.

Ashton doesn't even blink. "Yeah, that was weird," he says.

Is he talking about my outraged spoons or his bringing his girlfriend-of-the-month to Frosting & Beans?

"Weird? *Weird?* It was cruel!"

A Pyrex measuring cups explodes. I jump, but again, Ashton acts as though nothing has happened.

"Glynna, I never meant to hurt you." He rubs his jaw. "You seem to be having a rough day."

"Try a rough life."

"I get it."

"You do?"

"Well, I mean, life is hard."

"Oh, thanks for the platitude."

"Sure," he says.

That was not the response I expected. I take a closer look at him. His deep blue eyes are cloudy. I wave my hand in front of his face. He doesn't register the movement. "Ashton?"

"Yeah, what?"

"You just seem kind of out of it."

"Well, you know, it's summer and all. Just trying to reserve my brain power for school in the fall."

Something is not right with him. "So how is Daphne?"

267

"Huh?"

"Your girlfriend, Daphne?"

"Uhmm, she's not really my girlfriend. She's more my sister's friend, and I just hang out with them." His eyes are wandering around the kitchen as he talks. But he doesn't comment on the shards of broken glass, or anything else.

"So why didn't she come with you today?"

"What?" His face turns beet red.

"Why didn't she come with you today?"

He folds his arms across his chest. "Shopping. She went shopping with Maddie."

"So you're going to see her tonight?"

"Yeah, yeah, we'll probably hook up later."

A pot flies from the overhead rack and barely misses his head. He doesn't even duck.

"You need to get out of my kitchen."

"Listen, Glynna, I'm sorry if you misunderstood my intentions, but if you ever need anything—"

"I won't call you."

"Listen, I care about you—"

He is abusing those words. "Get out."

The cookware above jangles threateningly until he's gone.

Pig Out in the Park is in one week. Six days of non-stop eating and music in Riverfront Park. It's our most lucrative out-of-store event every year, and it requires the most meticulous planning and baking schedule. I haven't told Nana yet, but this year, I'm going to include five new unique cupcake flavors: Caramel Corn cupcakes, Root Beer Float cupcakes, Cotton Candy cupcakes, Chocolate Cherry Coke cupcakes, and Margarita cupcakes.

I roll up my sleeves and start collecting ingredients. *Mise en place.* My first attempt at the Caramel Corn cupcakes is a melt-in-your mouth gooey mess. I predict they'll be a hit. The Root Beer float cupcakes take more than one try to perfect.

My phone *ping*s. It's a text from Kristeen.

Girl, R U still at F&B.

268

Testing new recipes.
Jimmy has a friend, go out w/us 2morrow night.

Jimmy is Professor Vargas. It seems Kristeen's broken jaw broke down all his emotional resistance to becoming inappropriately involved with one of his students. Fortunately, the semester is almost over and Kristeen isn't going to be filing any sexual harassment charges with the university.

I don't date.

OMG, girl, snap out of it.
I am snapping out of it, I'm baking.
At this hour?
What time is it?
11:45.
Nite is young, 3 more recipes to test.
Fine, I'm coming to help.
Text me from the alley.

I haven't seen my BFF for a while, and I'm jazzed she wants to come by. She can be my taste tester. Now, where was I?

By the time Kristeen texts me again, I've got the first batch of Cotton Candy cupcakes in the oven.

When I open the back door, she throws her arms around me. "I'm so worried about you." When I lead her into the kitchen, she makes an exaggerated search of the premises. "Where's the cot? I mean since you never leave anymore. Geez, I thought you were bad before, now I can't even drag you out of here. At least you used to go home and read romance novels. Now, it's just cupcakes, cupcakes, and more cupcakes. Don't you ever get sick of it, G?"

"No need to go home. I don't read romance novels anymore."

We both burst into laughter. It breaks the ice.

Kristeen comes over and works on my shoulders. As she undoes the knots, it makes me want to cry. "Wow, you've got it bad, huh?"

I shrug. "He came here a couple weeks ago."

"Girl, and you didn't tell me?"

"He was an asshole, but he was also a weird asshole."

"What do you mean weird?"

"It's like he wasn't fully present."

269

"Like he was tired or something?"

"No, it was more than that."

"You think he's sick? Like with a life-threatening illness?"

"I think—" I'm dying to confide that Ashton is under an Occulto spell —which is worse than a life-threatening illness—but I hold my tongue. After Kristeen got her jaw busted, I realize Ophelia is right. Sharing too much information with my best friend will place her in harm's way, and I won't take that risk. But keeping secrets from her sucks.

"What? What? Don't be holding out on me."

"I think, no it sounds ridiculous."

"*Chica!*"

"It's like someone's put a spell on him."

"Oh my od! You think it was one of those witchy girls who was with him at Bistangos?"

"You don't think I'm crazy for thinking someone put a spell on him?"

"Girl, my mother has told me some stories that you don't want to hear about some wicked brujas in the old country." She makes the Catholic cross gesture. "I believe in possession, voodoo, all that hocus-pocus stuff. It's real, *chica.*" She elbows me. "Aren't your lovey-dovey cupcakes brimming with woo-woo mystic juju?" She flicks her fingers at me.

I laugh, but don't disagree with her. Ophelia never told me I had to deny anything if Kristeen guessed the truth. "I'm thinking about doing an experiment at POP."

"Please, spill."

"Ashton is supposed to attend with his grandmother. I think it's on the last day, a closing ceremony thing. I'm going to offer him one of my cupcakes."

Kristeen's face falls. "That's it, Glyn? You've been pining over this guy all summer, and that's all you've got?"

"You said yourself my cupcakes have woo-woo mystic juju."

She pats me on the arm. "You're right. And if you're willing to make an effort, at least that means you haven't given up on life beyond these pale pink walls."

The oven-timer dings.

"Speaking of pale pink." I pull out my pink clouds of cotton candy

270

cupcakes.

"These are amazing," Kristeen says. "Maybe getting Ashton to eat one of your cupcakes isn't such an awful idea. If I wasn't so into Jimmy right now, I might fall in love with you. These are yummy."

I grin from ear-to-ear. When she told me she was coming to hang out with me, I was overjoyed. It looks like that happiness made it into my cupcakes. Now, I've got a decision to make. Do I offer Ashton a cupcake that I bake while letting my feelings for him run wild, or do I offer him a cupcake I bake using one of my tried-and-true recipes and Nana's herbs?

The last day of POP is hot, hot, hot. The young kids, and even some of the older ones, are drenching themselves in the fountains. If I didn't have to help out in the Frosting & Beans booth, I'd be tempted to join them. The water looks refreshing.

I keep looking at my watch and scanning the crowds for Ashton. I've got a few special Chocolate Cherry Coke cupcakes tucked away beneath the counter just for him. Chocolate Cherry Coke is old-fashioned, jukebox, diner style, like his Firebird.

The closing ceremony is at four o'clock. I don't want to wait that long. The music drifting from the main stage is bluesy. The singer's voice is smooth and sinuous, floating over the crowd like caramel. My hips are swaying because it's hard to keep still.

Nana arrives with Nicolas. They're leaving for Guam in a week. After Tatiana agreed not to contest the divorce, trusts and other legal work had to be finalized before the lovebirds take off. They're going to get married as soon as they get back. They don't want to wait. It's so romantic.

Nicolas gives me a big hug. I'm getting used to having him around. He's at the office a lot, but he's always home in time for dinner. I can tell Nana is so happy, and I can't help but be glad for her. Now, if I can just get my love life straightened out.

Oh, there he is.

My heart sinks.

Do I even want to go through with this?

Nana registers my emotional chaos and follows my gaze through the crowds. "Nicolas, there's Ashton." And Tatiana!

What is Nana doing?

271

"I'll be right back." She wanders off, leaving me and Nicolas staring awkwardly at one another.

"How's business been?" he asks.

"Very good. I think it's going to be our best year here."

He nods approvingly.

"Grandpa, hi."

Pearl is pulling a tense Ashton through the crowds.

Nicolas leans in for a bear hug. It's clear he adores his grandson. I search for Tatiana and Daphne. Tatiana is surveying the podium, from which she'll address the crowd. But I don't see Daphne anywhere.

"Hi, Glynna," Ashton says.

I'm not sure he'd have said anything if his grandfather wasn't standing right next to me, but I don't have a lot of time to pout. I whip out one of the special cupcakes I've made just for him. "It's a new flavor. Would you like to be the first one to try it? Chocolate Cherry Coke."

"Excuse me." Daphne arrives out of nowhere and inserts herself between me and Ashton. She grabs the cupcake from my hand and throws it to the ground. I'm surprised she doesn't jump up and down on it. "We don't eat carbs."

"Hey, Daphne, simmer down," Ashton coaxes.

"What are you doing over here? At her booth?" she squeaks.

"I came to say hello to my grandfather."

Daphne's face turns three shades of red. "Oh." She whirls around. "Mr. Bass, I didn't see you. How are you?"

"I'm sorry, I forget your name young lady?"

"Daphne." She shimmies and shakes her obviously fake breasts in his face. "Daphne Wardof."

"Hmm," is about all he says.

"It's so nice to see you again, Mr. Bass, but Ashton and I need to be going." It's clear Daphne wears the panties in the family.

"I'll catch up with you in a minute." Ashton shocks us all with his minor resistance. "I want to spend a few minutes with my grandpa."

She stamps her foot. I can only hope it's now covered in mashed cupcake. "Ashton?"

"Go on, Daphne, I'll be right over."

"Oh, I don't mind waiting right here while you visit with your

272

grandfather."

Thunder cracks the sky and everyone ducks as black clouds roll in out of nowhere. "Oh, my hair!" Daphne squeals. She grabs Ashton's hand again, but he won't let her drag him away.

Instead, he urges her to go find cover. "I'll find you."

"But I don't want us to get separated," she whines.

I unleash more of my anger. Rain pelts us all. The crowd's reaction is mixed. Half welcome the unexpected relief from the heat, half run for cover. Daphne runs off, but it's too late. Her hair extensions are already soaked and obvious.

I reach for another cupcake and hand it to Ashton. "I have another one."

"I don't usually eat stuff like this," he confirms his diet-Nazi rejection of my cupcake.

Nicolas comes to the rescue. He takes the cupcake from his grandson's hand and takes a big bite. "You've got to at least taste it. It's fabulous."

Ashton relents. His eyes twinkle when the flavor hits his tongue. "Man, these are amazing."

I can't help but smile as he looks deep into my eyes. Nana takes Nicolas' hand and pulls him away, leaving me and Ashton facing each other alone. I hold my breath while Ashton finishes the cupcake. Kristeen was with me when I baked them. She had music blaring as usual, lots of sultry, sexy tunes, as she teased me about my sizzling hot tamales. While we waited for the cupcakes to cool, and I whipped up the icing, she filled the time with raunchy stories about lust and love, making me blush.

I'm thrilled when Ashton finishes the cupcake, wads up the paper cup, and tosses it into a nearby trashcan.

"You have another one of those?" he asks.

"I do."

"I guess one more little cupcake won't hurt the grill." He slides his hand across his abdomen.

"Probably not." I hand him the third cupcake.

This time, while he's eating it, he starts making moaning sounds, and I can feel my cheeks turning pink. When he's done, he tosses the wrapper

273

in the trash and then leans across the counter of our booth. He gets right up in my face and says, "Wanna do me?"

My mouth drops open. I close it. It falls open again. I pray I've heard him wrong.

The live band is on break and *Bang Bang* by Jessie J is busting from the speakers.

"What?" I finally manage.

"You have the longest, creamiest legs on the planet, and I would so love to have them locked around my neck while I'm pounding away."

I slap him on the face. "Don't you ever talk to me that way again, Ashton Bass!"

He rubs his cheek and grins. "Oh, you're a feisty one, aren't you? I can dig it." He reaches up and squeezes my breast.

I jerk out of his grasp.

But he's hanging on.

People are staring.

"Would you let me go?"

Heavy gusts sweep through the park. People are dispersing, seeking cover. Random pieces of paper and decorations are airborne and dangerous. An aluminum lawn chair flies by. I need to calm down before the weather gets worse!

Breathe, Glynna, breathe.

My hand flies to my hair, but nothing is there. There were so many things to remember this morning, and we were in such a rush, I forgot my mother's hair comb. Never again! I promise myself.

Ashton is unrelenting. "Aw, Glyn, you're so hot. I just want to lick you all the way from your toes up to—"

I flatten my hand over his filthy mouth. "Stop talking!"

A flash of lightning sends everyone who's been enjoying the rain running for cover, scattering.

But not Ashton. He's determined to get into my pants. "Please, Glynna, don't make me beg." He sticks his mouth in my ear. "I bet you taste so sweet."

Although I'd much rather punch him again, I shove him away. My fist clenches and unclenches. "Go on." I wave my hands.

He doesn't realize how lucky he is the wall of the booth is between us.

It's the only thing protecting his manhood from my knee.

"I'm sure your grandmother is looking for you." I cross my hands over my chest. Salty tears are mixing with the rain coming down.

"Huh?" He looks from left to right.

I spot Daphne huddled beneath an awning. "Daphne's over there." Go screw her.

"God, I hate to leave you without getting another sample."

What a disaster. I baked lust, not love, into my cupcakes. I try to remember what happened to the rest of the batch. "Sorry, no more samples today."

He takes one step back at time, but he's still facing me. "No worries, darling, but I'll be thinking about you—" He holds up his two index fingers like pistols. "Next time I do my girlfriend."

I don't know if I have ever been more revolted.

29. Hello, Cupcake

 ATIANA

I shift in the rickety chair in Seattle Works Coffeehouse. It's on Pike Street, a short distance from the market and Hotel 1000 where I always stay when I come to the city. They allow Annke to bring Eclipse inside, so here we are. Myself, Annke, and her mother Lyrika.

"Where's Sybelia today?" I ask.

Annke stares out the window. "We haven't shared our little project with her."

I'm surprised. "No?"

"She worships Liam." Lyrika's daughter runs her fingers down a strand of her long, black hair. Eclipse is a contented ball of fur in her lap. "If she knew we were trying to steal his daughter's powers, she would tell him."

"I see."

Lyrika sways her head to the music. Annke wasn't exaggerating about her mother's heroin addiction. She's high at the moment.

My old friend sees demons, entities birthed deep in her psyche. They only become manifest through careful cultivation. From what Lyrika shared of her experiences with me years ago, the ability to see those

277

demons is a burden. She's getting crushed under the weight of it. Her arms are skeletal, and huge hollows ring her eyes. Regardless, every man who's entered the coffee shop has given her a double-take. Lyrika is hauntingly alluring, a tempting black bird with broken wings.

"So," I say, "Sybelia sent the hair to the lab for a DNA test."

"Which they confirmed," Annke says.

"What does she think you did with the lipstick?" I ask.

"I told her I lost it. She's very angry with my carelessness." Annke giggles. "Sybelia comes off as all hippie and free-spirited, but she's the most ambitious witch I've ever met. She wasn't pleased that I misplaced such a valuable object." She glances at her mother. "But she'll forgive me, eventually. She always does."

When we're finished with our coffee, we hail a cab to drive us out to Lyrika's home, and the Seattle coven's headquarters, in Washington Park.

We stand around the altar, barefoot in black satin robes. A bright red pool of melted lipstick lies in the center of a pentagram. The engagement ring Nico gave me so many years ago rests in the pentagram's upper triangle. A pair of Lyrika's earrings is in the pentagram's lower left triangle. Annke has placed a leather wrist thong in the lower right triangle. Candles are in the two remaining spaces. We join hands and recite the incantation to steal the Lumina-Occulto's power.

Take hostage the white
Extinguish the light
Drain our enemy's power
Witness the darkness flower.

It's my first effort at black magic since my visit to Frank Langston. I've not confessed to Lyrika or her daughter my fear that the Luminas drained my power, and that I worry it can no longer be replenished. Rather, I concentrate on the void of blackness within, as though my potency remains infinite.

Soon, a frisson of energy sparks my palms. Reactively, I squeeze Lyrika's and Annke's hands harder. The faint current spirals past my wrists, and up my forearms. It continues to climb. When it pulses at the base of my skull, I focus my mind's eye on Liam's daughter.

A shield of deafening innocence surrounds her. But the white shroud cannot cloak the dark potential that smolders deep within her.

I boil with envy, craving her power. Stretching my mind, I slice into the cosmic vein of her spiritual blood. I imagine it pouring from her and crossing the ether. The vacuum of my emptiness sucks with its gaping need.

GLYNNA

I'm curled beneath soft, warm blankets. My eyes open to comforting golden light beneath a white domed ceiling. I'm cocooned in a huge egg shell. Something taps above me. Now it's a pecking sound, traveling down the side of my container all around me. I throw the covers off, but there's no floor to stand on. I press my fingers against the white shell. They vibrate with the rhythm of the *rat-a-tat-tat*.

I keep looking around, wondering where I am, and how I got here.

A cracking sound draws my attention. Thin lines crawl from a small hole. A beak, as slim as a straight pin, chips at the opening. I think of syringes, and my stomach hollows. I grab a pillow and shove it against the breach. When the needle sticks my hand, all the way through the padded barrier, I yelp. Three drops of blood drop from my palm onto the silky white blanket tangled around my legs. The sight sets off alarms in my head. My mouth is dry.

I scoot away from the hole, now as big as a fist. The pin is gone. Several black tendrils snake through the gap in its place. This is a nightmare.

Breathe, Glynna, breathe.

The tendrils coil through the air. I'm ducking and shifting and scrambling to avoid them, but it's like they sense me. It's like they smell my blood. One lassoes my forearm. Microscopic razors erupt from its surface and cut into my skin. More blood spills onto the pile of snowy blankets. Something bigger is coming for me. Something that wants to

279

eat me alive.

Rage blots out my terror. My entire body shakes with anger. How dare they attack me?

The darkness hatching in the pit of my stomach throbs with power. It can destroy what is coming for me. I need to set it free. How do I do that, when all my life, I've kept it caged up?

The force inside me is roiling and boiling. I'm going to explode. Blacken the white blankets, crack my protective shell, and see what is coming for me. A single question stops me. Do I want to live outside the light?

I bow my head.

I do not.

My answer ignites a ring of flames around me.

When I startle awake, my mind's eye settles on my father's scarred face. Even if I honor my mother's wish, and never see him again, his Occulto blood will always run through my veins. Could he help me balance my dark and light? I don't have the will to defy my mother and Nana to ask him.

ATIANA

The young witch's essence pours into me—filling my belly, filling my mouth—then it turns to flame.

I gasp and choke as the spiritual fire consumes me.

Beside me, Annke struggles to breathe as well.

Lyrika drops to the floor in convulsions.

The circle is broken.

Our attempts to revive Annke's mother are met with a stubborn unconsciousness. Her eyes remained closed and her breathing shallow as her head lolls from side to side.

"The heroin has sapped her endurance," Annke says. "We won't get any more help from her tonight." She checks the pentagram. "There's only a dot of lipstick left. Not enough for us to try again, anyway."

After we get Lyrika to bed, Annke wants to discuss what happened.

We're in the loft, facing a wall of windows. Although all the lights are off, the glow of Annke's laptop illuminates her face. She rolls the gold tube, now empty of lipstick, in her tapered fingers, as she researches what might have possibly gone wrong with our spell.

Unwilling to accept responsibility for our defeat, I sit beside her, stubbornly silent. Maybe other forces were at play. Maybe Annke will find another answer.

She clicks furiously at the keyboard, pauses, and then clicks furiously at the keyboard again. I strain to hear what she's mumbling, but it's impossible. I shuffle my diamond engagement ring from one hand to the other as if it were a slinky.

Nico and Pearl are in Guam; I'll be a divorcee soon.

Finally, Annke slams the top of her computer down, leaving us in total blackness. "The lipstick must have been contaminated. Maybe she let a friend borrow it. But that's the only solid explanation I can come up with."

Stealing Glynna Balcora's power will devastate Pearl as much as it will Liam. I won't give up. "Next time we'll be more careful with the object we take," I say.

"Next time? She won't let either of us within a mile of her house again."

"But she'll let my grandson in."

Annke nods and smiles.

GLYNNA

I'm driving west on I-90. Kristeen is in the passenger seat of my Nissan Versa. We're on our way to pick up Nana and Nicolas at the airport. The Bass divorce is final. My grandmother and Ashton's grandfather will be getting married in a few weeks. The whole thing is so surreal. I should be

281

excited that Nana is coming home, but I'm not. I'm afraid she's going to move out after the wedding.

I feel drained, tired, worn down. The overcast skies don't help. Neither do my nightmares about a clan of vampires who crave my blood.

"Your grandma is so lucky, *chica*," Kristeen's wistful tone catches me off guard. "Once she marries Nicolas Bass, she's not going to want for anything. Her life is going to be smooth sailing. Do you think she's going to keep working at the bakery?"

Her question needles my own apprehensions about the changes occurring in our lives. Is she going to move out? Is she going to abandon our greenhouse, and Frosting & Beans? "I want her to keep working there."

"She might not have time."

"Why not? Nicolas is a workaholic. That leaves Nana plenty of time to do the things we've always enjoyed doing together." I fidget with my mother's comb. I wear it every day now. I have a growing sympathy for my mother; she fell in love with an Occulto and obviously had sex with him.

"Where are you, Glyn?"

"I never told you exactly what happened last week at the park." My BFF has fallen hard too, for Professor Jimmy Vargas. We've hardly texted since they crossed the line between student and teacher. I sigh. Love is blooming all around me, but not in me.

"No, you haven't. Spill it. And I want all the details."

I tell her about the whole miserable afternoon.

"Oh my God!" she squeals. "I had no idea he had such a nasty side." Her enthusiasm is so not what I was expecting.

"Don't you think it's disgusting?"

"That your long, creamy legs make him so hot? That he can't keep his hands off you? My, my, my, Glyn! What did you do to him on that date?"

"We just kissed. But he was so rude at POP! Anyone could hear what he was saying, and see what he was doing."

"Oh, Glyn, sometimes guys are just, you know, raw. The flowers, the romantic dinners, the jewelry!" She flashes a gold bangle on her wrist.

I grab her arm. "Did Jimmy give you that?"

"Uh-huh. He says he's going to give me one every year we're together,

282

until I have them all the way up my arm."

"He must really be into you."

"My mom's having him over for dinner Friday night."

"Things are happening really fast between you two."

"*Chica*, when you find the right one, you know."

I sink down in my seat. "I thought Ashton was the right one."

"Maybe he is."

"I don't even know how you can say that."

"Look, it sounds like you two have a real problem communicating. You know you have to talk through these misunderstandings. You can't just pull away and shut down. How is anything going to get resolved that way? Plus, how do you know what is really going on if you never ask him?"

"Excuse me, isn't it a two-way street? He's not trying to talk to me."

"Didn't you say no the last time he asked you out?"

"So?"

"Then at Pig Out in the Park, when he was revealing his sexual desire, you slapped him."

"Uhmm, yeah, after he grabbed my *boob*."

Kristeen cracks up. "Oh, my sweet, innocent Glynna, you can hardly even spit out the word. *¡Ay!* " She has tears running down her cheek because she's laughing so hard. "Why didn't you just knee him in the groin while you were at it?"

"Believe me, I would have, if I'd been standing on the other side of my booth."

"And you think that would have made your heart stop hurting?"

"What are you saying?"

"Love isn't just flowers and romance and happily ever afters. There's also a dark and powerful side to love. But if you want the real thing, you have to eat the whole enchilada." Her face breaks into an evil grin.

"You are as bad as he is!"

"Oh, Glynna, I can't wait until you embrace your hot pink tamales!"

"Don't hold your breath."

I'm with Nana in the greenhouse. We're harvesting herbs while the mimosas burst into intermittent song. "What's up with the flowers today? Usually, they blare like a radio or stay quiet. It's like they can't make up their minds."

"Hmm," Nana says.

"Hmm? That's all you have to say?"

"Maybe we need to have a talk, Glynna, dear."

"About what?"

She pulls me over to our well-worn sofa beneath the canopy of lace. "Glynna, I told you Tatiana put a spell on Nicolas."

"Yes."

"But I didn't really tell you how easily I gave into her, and how much I regret that. Looking back, I was so heartbroken, I hardly put up a fight."

Nana and Nicolas are getting married in two days. "Does this have something to do with the wedding?"

"Not my wedding, Glynna, dear."

I'm not sure what she means, since her wedding is the only one on our calendar.

"Glynna, has it ever occurred to you that the girl Ashton dated over the summer put a spell on him?"

"You think Daphne Wardof is a witch?" It aggravates me that she'd give her that much credit. I tell Nana about the last time Ashton came to Frosting & Beans. "I believe he was under a spell, but I thought it was Tatiana's, or one of those other witches. You remember? The ones who took my lipstick and hair."

"Maybe," she concedes. "Although, what do they have to gain by causing Ashton to fall in love with another girl?"

She has a point.

"Ophelia and I have talked several times about the day your father came to the bakery."

"We don't know for sure that man is my father." However, despite my mother's desire that I never have a relationship with him, I admit, I've been curious. What would it be like to have a dad? Someone who cares about me and wants what's best for me. Could an Occulto want what's best for his child? Sometimes I wonder if he'll ever follow up on that proposition of opening a bakery in New York City.

Nana tilts her head, but doesn't argue. "That day in the bakery, Ophelia felt overwhelmed by Occulto energy. She's certain Tatiana and

284

Liam weren't the only black witches in the shop."

"Ashton and Lorriene could be Occultos."

"They could, but so could that young lady."

I squirm, recalling the spell my Chocolate Cherry Coke cupcake put on Ashton. I haven't told Nana about it. It's too embarrassing.

"Glynna, dear, I don't want you to lose the years with your beloved that I lost with mine."

"Nana, Ashton is hardly my beloved. We went on one date, and that got interrupted."

"Because of unfinished business between Nicolas and me."

I can't argue with that.

"Your cupcake broke Tatiana's spell. What could it hurt to see if your cupcake could break the Wardof girl's spell?"

What if it already has? No. I'm pretty sure the Chocolate Cherry Coke lust-filled-fiasco-in-the-park cupcake left Ashton's deeper feelings dormant. "Nana, I know you want me to be happy, and I appreciate that. But Ashton isn't even in Spokane anymore, so it's not like we can date. He went back to Harvard." I wonder how far Boston is from New York City. Move to New York City to cultivate a relationship with your Occulto father, while pursuing a relationship with your Occulto boyfriend? Something tells me that whatever light exists inside me would be snuffed in that scenario.

"Ashton is coming for the wedding," she says.

A rush of irrepressible happiness swirls through me. "He is?"

"Yes. So please, Glynna, take advantage of this opportunity to discover the truth in his heart and yours."

I'm certainly not up for any more improvised-emotional-cupcake inspiration, but would it really kill me to test Nana's theory with one of my tried-and-true-sure-to-fall-in-love, or break-an-evil-witch's-spell cupcakes?

Later that evening, I'm standing between our kitchen and dining room, my hands full of plates.

"Don't rush off," Nana says.

She, Nicolas, Ophelia, and Leif are sitting around the dining room table.

285

"Have a piece of pie first," Nicolas says.

Why can't I say *no* to that man! I return to the table, dragging my feet. Nicolas smiles. His blue eyes sparkle.

Nana cuts her pumpkin pie into sixths and hands each of us a slice. As everyone else dives in, I hold my fork midair. If Ashton were here, that lonely piece of pie left in the tin would be his.

Tears gather in the corner of my eyes. I don't want Kristeen or Nana to be right. I don't want Ashton to be *the one*.

Ophelia offers to help me bake the cupcakes for the wedding. She's feeling kindly disposed toward Nana.

I glare at the guilty culprit, her half-eaten piece of pie. "Sure," I mumble.

Leif's cellphone vibrates. When he checks the screen, his entire face lights up.

"Who is it?" I ask.

Leif tilts his head toward Nicolas. He and Nana are gazing so deeply into each other's eyes, the rest of us no longer exist.

Lorriene? I mouth.

He nods, and whispers, "Did you know they have French roots?"

"Ashton never mentioned it," I whisper back.

"She's crazy about my croissants."

Isn't everyone? "Awesome." I set my fork down, hoping no one will notice I haven't touched my pie.

"Glynna, dear, try it," Nana says.

When did she exit the love vortex? She nods encouragingly.

Fine. Just. One. Bite.

The creamy filling explodes in my mouth. "Oh my God! Nana, this is the best pumpkin pie you've ever made."

She flutters her eyelashes at Nicolas. They're so cute!

I can't resist another bite. And another. I want to lick my plate.

Nicolas insists on clearing the table. However, he doesn't stop Ophelia or Leif from joining him in the kitchen. I hear the water running in the sink and the dishes clinking. They're laughing and having a good time.

Nana shifts into the chair beside mine. She takes my hand. "Have you considered what we discussed about giving Ashton another chance?"

286

Right now, if she asked me to pluck every single one of Archi's feathers off, I'd ask Leif to help me find the poor owl. There's more resistance to opening my heart. I eye the last piece of pie greedily.

Nana pushes it to me. While I marvel over each amazing bite, she continues to make a case on behalf of her fiancé's grandson. "Glynna, if you two are meant to be together, please, don't let anyone or anything come between you."

"He's really good looking," I agree.

Her eyes twinkle. "He's almost as handsome as his grandfather was when he was that age."

The thought of seeing Ashton in two days is making me giddy. I take two more bites of pie and burst out with, "And his kisses take my breath away!" One last bite. "Mmm. Have you ever heard him sing? It's so sexy!"

Nana pats my hand. "Just say *hello* to him at the wedding."

30. Just You... Me... And My Cupcake

CYNNA

Ophelia and I are loading up the Frosting & Beans catering van. We made the wedding cake for Nana's wedding cake together. Can you believe, Ophelia and me working in harmony, and not fighting one another? Things really are changing in my life. Even though Auntie hasn't confessed, I think she's as nervous as I am about what's going to happen after the wedding.

Last night, at the rehearsal dinner, Nicolas talked about buying his dear Pearl her own home. Again, I'm super happy for her, but not so happy for me. Our home isn't going to be the same if she moves out.

My aunt and I also baked twelve dozen cupcakes to match the wedding cake, and I have to say they're lovely. When the van's loaded, I slip into the ladies room for a quick makeup check.

I love my gauzy dress with its overlay of lace. It's a little short, but it's romantic. I adjust my mother's comb in my hair. The dress matches one of the three roses in the comb, the pale pink one. I wonder if my mother

289

and father were married.

Can someone who doesn't have a soul enter a church?

I'm nervous. What if Ashton brings Daphne? I hope he doesn't. I look at my eyes in the mirror.

You are not over him.

The ceremony is beautiful. Nana colored her hair a rich brown, which looks spectacular with her cream-colored cocktail dress. Nicolas looks striking in a dark tailored suit. They glow as they exchange vows.

I'm seated on the bride's side with Ophelia, Leif, and all of Nana's friends. Ashton is sitting across the aisle, on the groom's side, with Lorriene.

No Daphne! Gregor and his wife are also no shows, but Nicolas only has eyes for Pearl.

I wonder what it would be like to be so in love, and then be separated for over forty years. I sneak a peek across the aisle and heat suffuses my cheeks.

Ashton is looking at me!

My heart goes *pitter-patter* in my chest.

Don't get your hopes up.

But they are up.

I sneak another peek. Ashton looks dashing today. The suit he's wearing emphasizes his muscular body. And that line of sun-kissed forearm, visible when his sleeve rises? Remembering how he carried me, so effortlessly, I internally swoon. And his blue eyes, the ones staring at me every time I look at him, are hypnotic. My mind wanders to the only time Nana and Ophelia whisked Leif and me off to a tropical getaway to the Philippines. Ashton's eyes are so clear, like the waters of El Nido. I could swim in them forever.

Breathe, Glynna, breathe.

I smile. I'm not going to panic. The whole wedding is completely transforming my vibe from dark and cloudy to sunshine and rainbows. All I can think of are romantic, dreamy things. For a blissful moment, my hurt and anger melt away. Maybe this is why people love weddings.

I sneak another peek at Ashton and sigh. If looks were illegal, he would be number one on the most wanted list!

290

My eyes misbehave. Without my permission, after a quick scan of the wedding guests, they land on him again. He is still staring at me.

A knot of need? Want? Something tightens my gut. It makes me feel like I'm the one who's being spelled. I will myself to look away, but my eyes insist on betraying me. They're powerless to resist the magnetic pull of his eyes. Our eyes lock and I slip into one of those *the world is standing still* moments. Except the Calla Lily buds, on the arch above Nana and Nicolas, are bursting into full bloom. I drop my head into my hands, praying none of the other wedding guests notice.

Even though I use my sternest internal voice, I just can't stop my head from turning to see if he's still looking at me.

When our gaze meets again, I think: *You want a stare down contest? Fine. Bring it on!* So I stare and become drunk on the irritatingly, magnificent sight named Ashton Bass. I can't help but notice every detail about him. His brown hair is neatly tucked behind his ears. That chiseled jawline covered in sexy scruff makes my hands itch to touch it again. Memories of us at the lake surface in my mind. And what about that kiss?

I can't deny kissing Ashton made my body go into a wild outburst of feelings that almost made me lose my mind. I'm pretty sure if I were to let my fingers touch his skin, they'd get burned.

Quietly laughing at myself, I close my eyes and give my head a little shake. When I open my eyes, Ashton's eyes are twinkling. I scowl. God, I should hate him. My body does not. Oh, here comes the blush fest, making its grand entrance. I look away to concentrate on Nana and Nicolas completing their vows.

"You may now kiss the bride."

I may have lost the stare down, but Ashton Bass, you just wait.

I enter the ballroom at the Davenport Hotel and retreat.

I walk in small tight circles, my heart a knot in my chest. I return to the door and open it again, just a crack. Wedding guests are swaying to the Nat King Cole song Ashton serenaded me with on our one and only date. I let the door close again and walk away.

God of Cupcakes! My eyes sting, but I will not cry. Not on Nana's wedding day. I walk out to the front of the hotel and force myself to smile at the valet. I step a few feet away. *Breathe, Glynna breathe.* When I feel calmer, I go back into the hotel and head straight for the bathroom.

I blot my face with a damp cloth and pat it dry. When I reposition my mother's hair comb, I freeze. My mother never knew love. Nana almost lost hers forever. What if Ashton is *the one* for me? Am I just going to let him go?

I fiddle with the chiffon fabric of my dress. I look fantastic. So why am I hiding in the bathroom and being all weepy? *Breathe, Glynna, breathe.* You've got this.

I hold my head high when I return to the ballroom. At least, when I open the door that stupid, romantic, sexy, flirtatious song isn't playing anymore. I glance at the dance floor. Nana and Nicolas are locked in each other's arms. Beautiful strings of color radiate from their love. Strings of happiness and strings of joy, they swirl out in an expanding spiral, touching everyone. Kristeen and her professor, Lorriene and Leif.

A single tear of joy rolls down my face. I immediately wipe it away, because I will not cry. I cannot cry.

I need a distraction. ASAP. I run to the table where the hotel attendants are surrounding the wedding cake with the dozens of cupcakes I baked.

"Dance with me, Glynna." Am I daydreaming, or is that baritone voice right behind me? It sounds so real. So close. And then that clean, citrusy, masculine scent, so uniquely Ashton, makes me whirl around.

The boy who turned my whole life completely upside down is standing in front of me. I grip, squeeze, squash the cupcake I'm holding. Icing oozes through my fingers. A perfectly pink and fluffy treat has been destroyed by my furious hands. I imagine smashing another one into Ashton's annoyingly-too-perfect face!

I clench my hands. All of my swoony, forgiving, romantic, hopeful emotions have deserted me. In fact, I'd love to take the top tier of Nana's wedding cake and dump it on the top of Ashton's head. But no! I will not make a scene on Nana's special day.

I reach for a stack of napkins and accidentally grab about twenty-five of them.

Ashton pushes my handful of napkins away. He takes my other hand, the one coated in icing and lifts it to his mouth. Then he gazes at me with his tropical vacation eyes and sucks. Now, he is licking my fingers and

292

palms.

I stumble and have to reach for the edge of the table to steady myself while he removes every last speck of icing from my hand.

Eeeew. That sticky-saliva residue remains, but he ate my cupcake!

"Please, dance with me, Glynna." His voice is raspy.

My resistance crumbles. Did he really push me to the brink of insanity in June? Why was I mad at him in July? Did he really hurt me in August? It's impossible to recall why I'm supposed to dislike him.

What if I say 'no', and just let him go forever? What if he walks away, and I never see him again? Is that really what I want? Yes. No. Two Glynnas fight within me.

Meanwhile, he's waiting. As if he senses the opening, he leads me to the dance floor. His fingers are warm. When he slides his arm around my waist and pulls me to him, I place my hands on his chest, and our surroundings blur. In this moment, there is only me, Ashton, and the music.

His breathing becomes uneven. I can feel the rapid beat of his heart beneath my fingers. Our hearts are in a race. He sways his hips to the music, leading me in one slow step after another.

Ellie Goulding serenades us with *How Long Will I Love You?*

I lose myself against his chest, and his familiar scent makes me think of home, and being safe. No Luminas. No Occultos. Just me and Ashton.

We stay close and silent, letting our bodies handle all the communication. When the music fades, he tries to whisper in my ear.

"No." I press my face into his shirt. Tears are on the brink of falling. "Don't say anything." My voice is scratchy.

Ashton tightens his hold and kisses my hair. "I've tried everything to forget you, Glynna, and all the crazy things that happen when we're together."

I thought he didn't notice.

"Listen." He cups my face in his hands. "I don't know if I deserve you." He lets out a shaky breath. "But I need to tell you, whatever it takes to be with you, I'll figure it out, and I'll do it. As soon as I saw you today, a dark haze lifted. All I can see is you, Glynna. It's always been you. Only. You."

He tilts my chin and forces me to meet his gaze. No words escape my

293

lips.

"Do you understand what I'm saying?"

I tear myself from his arms before he can say more. A hurricane of emotions roars inside me. Love and hate. Desire and rage. Forgiveness and guilt. I run.

"Glynna! Wait!"

I hear him behind me. The world blurs as hot tears pour down my face. My neck is wet with them. They're spilling onto my dress. I race outside. The wedding guests have disappeared. I stop, gasping for air. I'm standing alone in a courtyard. The sweet scent of roses, tulips, and gardenias scent the dusk.

Ashton grips my shoulders and spins me around to face him. The courtyard is full of shadows, but the light spilling from the ballroom windows illuminates his face, creating a halo of light around his head.

I struggle to loosen his grip, but he pulls me closer. I try to turn away, but he holds my face, forcing me to look at him.

"I want you so bad." Frustration colors his voice. "Glynna, I don't know how to explain it, but every waking hour, you're in my head. I can't even stop dreaming about you. Do you understand? You make me feel things I can't even describe, and it's scary and amazing."

I open my mouth and nothing comes out.

He grins. Maybe he interprets that as progress. Maybe it is.

"I miss you, Glynna. Everything about you, but especially that scrumptious, delectable cupcake scent that follows you everywhere." He laughs.

I hear Kristeen laughing, too. I swivel my head, but she's not there. Her laughter only rings in my mind. *You have to eat the whole enchilada, Glyn.* I can feel myself heating up. Something is happening in my chest, and my stomach, and it's spreading!

"Glynna, I know I messed up this summer, and I'm sorry I hurt you. I'm sorry I couldn't stand up and be man enough to admit it."

Is he ever going to shut up and kiss me?

I take in my once gallant white knight, who looks so miserable and defeated. His disheveled hair is so adorable. I press my finger against his lips. "Enough, already."

"Let me finish," he says.

I shake my head.

He quirks his brows and his white teeth gleam. Then his lips are against mine and his hands are wild in my hair, and my hot pink tamales sizzle.

He breaks away. "Does this mean you forgive me?"

I grin. "I don't know."

Ashton laughs. He scoops me up in his arms and twirls me around.

Flowers burst out around us.

I throw my head back and look up at the sky.

The stars twinkle and shine brightly.

Tonight, I want to forget about Luminas, Occultos, and everything that's ever filled me with fear or anger. Tonight, I want to be in love with Ashton Bass, even if neither of us can say the words.

And the constellations above are the only witness to the silent exchange of our hearts.

Thank You

We appreciate you spending your valuable time reading *Cupcakes & Kisses*. If you'd like to share the story with other readers, please tell a friend, or post a review on any book-ish site.

We'd also like to invite you to sign up for Heidi's newsletter: http://eepurl.com/wWKUj so you can be one of the first to hear about the release of *Cupcakes & Chaos*.

Sincerely,
Heidi Garrett & Billie Limpin

Acknowledgments

I was introduced to Billie Limpin through a mutual friend on Goodreads. Her bubbly warmth and sincere good cheer struck me from our first interaction. As we stayed in touch, I continued to appreciate her humor and vivaciousness. Check out any book review on Billie's Pink Reviews, and you'll know what I mean. Several months after we met, Billie graciously offered to interview me for a blog tour. Before it was all said and done, she had me literally red-faced and rolling on the floor, laughing. Often, I'm serious, but Billie has a special way to access my lighter side. Everything about that interview exchange with her was fun. And I found myself giving it a lot of thought.

Billie is a huge romance reader. I began to wonder if we could collaborate on a paranormal romance. Finally, I floated the idea to her, and was thrilled when she agreed to collaborate with me. Since, I'd never collaborated on a book, I didn't know exactly what I'd signed us up for. But Billie's patience, kindness, and grasp of romance got us through. The result: A book that I dare say is special. It wouldn't be special without Billie. And so I thank her for writing with me, and making this first book in the *The Magic Cupcake* series, a book that I dearly love.

Sincerely,
Heidi Garrett

My reply? Squeeeeeeeeeeeeee!!!!! YES! YES! YES!

For an avid reader like myself, being offered to co-write (a book!) was like, getting my "Willy Wonka's Golden Ticket"! (Okay, I exaggerate! Teehee!) Yes, I can still remember when Heidi asked me to be her co-

299

author (December 22, 2013 to be exact! Hah!), I was on CLOUD 9! Thank you, Heidi, for everything. I could never experience all of these (the how-to's and not-to's), if not for your unwavering guidance (and patience! Haha!) all throughout our writing process. I am learning and having fun at the same time! How cool is that?!

Thank you, Mommy, for reading me fairytales every night. I've always cherished those stories about gallantry, true love, and most of all, believing "happily ever afters" do happen! You once asked me why I never grew tired of listening to same stories over and over again. I'd say, it's because I love hearing your voice, and you are the best storyteller, and I love you very much!

For my siblings, Jang, Yan, and Tom: I know you aren't big readers (more like, Teletubbies?! Hee-hee!), but when you told me, you'll read the book as long as if it's from me, it was the sweetest! Thank you!

Big Hugs and kisses to my ever-loving, always-been-there-for-me fiancé, Junar. Thank you for sticking with me during those not–so-good-days when I'm tired and cranky, when I'm overly dramatic (and a little crazy?!) When I said, "I need space", you still did not give up? (Why? Because I might mean, "I need more space... for more books?! Haha!) You are the best, and I love you! (... and YES! I will marry you!)

My reading life wouldn't be fun, exciting (and crazzzzy) without my adorable fellow bibliobelles and buddy reading bff's: Jona, Nevah, and Noi, YOU girls rule! Thank you for feeding my book addiction (darn one-click button, right?!); for encouraging me to "unleash" my fangirling prowess; and telling me it's totally normal to drool over a book boyfriend every now and then?! Hah! Let's group hug!!!!

Oooh! Of course, how could I ever forget my Haizzzt girls: Rachmi and Melly! Thank you for "peer pressuring" me into reading "those books" which turned out to be REALLY haizzzt-worthy books!!! You know how those books encouraged me to daydream more, and eventually feel very inspired to write! Pink kisses to you, girls!

Last but not the least, to the Almighty Creator, for having made everything possible.

With a grateful heart, my thanks I bring,
Billie Limpin

About the Authors

Heidi Garrett is the author of the *Daughter of Light* fantasy trilogy about a young half-faerie, half-mortal searching for her place in the Whole.

She's also the author of *Once Upon a Time Today*, a collection of modern fairy tale retellings for adults who have already left home.

Heidi was born in Texas, and attempted to reside in as many cities in that state as possible. She made it to Houston, Lubbock, Austin, and El Paso. After spending a decade in southern California, she now lives in Eastern Washington state with her husband, their two cats, her laptop, and her Kindle. Being from the South, she often contemplates the magic of snow.

You can find Heidi on her blog, Facebook, Goodreads, and Twitter

Billie Limpin lives in the Philippines where the sun always shines and people always smile!

A hopeless romantic inside and out. When she's not swooning over a book boyfriend (which she often does!), you will probably catch her daydreaming (over a fictional character!). A reader by heart, and now a writer for the first time, she is thrilled to put her daydreams into written words.

You can find Billie on her blog, Facebook, Goodreads, and Twitter.